JUNE WRIGHT
Reservation for Murder

JUNE WRIGHT (1919–2012) made a splash with her 1948 debut, *Murder in the Telephone Exchange*, whose sales that year in her native Australia outstripped even those of the reigning queen of crime, Agatha Christie. Wright went on to publish five more mysteries over the next two decades while at the same time raising six children. When she died in 2012 at the age of 92, her books had been largely forgotten, but recent championing of her work by Stephen Knight, Lucy Sussex, and Derham Groves, combined with reissues of her novels by Dark Passage Books, has restored Wright to her proper place in the pantheon of crime writers.

DR. DERHAM GROVES is a Senior Fellow in the Faculty of Architecture, Building and Planning at the University of Melbourne. In 2008 he curated the exhibition *Murderous Melbourne*, which helped to rekindle interest in June Wright's work.

June Wright with Derham Groves, 2008

Reservation for Murder

MOTHER PAUL INVESTIGATES

JUNE WRIGHT

INTRODUCTION BY
DERHAM GROVES

DARK PASSAGE

TO

MY MOTHER

A Dark Passage book
Published by Verse Chorus Press
Portland, Oregon
www. versechorus.com

Cover design and Dark Passage logo by Mike Reddy
Interior design and layout by Steve Connell/Transgraphic

Country of manufacture as stated on the last page of this book

Library of Congress Cataloging-in-Publication Data

Names: Wright, June, 1919-2012, author. | Groves, Derham, writer of introduction.
Title: Reservation for murder : Mother Paul investigates / June Wright ; introduction by Derham Groves.
Description: First American edition. | Portland, Oregon : Verse Chorus Press, [2020] | "A Dark Passage book"--Title page verso. | Summary: "June Wright had already published three popular mysteries by the time she created her most memorable detective, the Reverend Mother Mary St Paul of the Cross. The kindly Mother Paul may seem vague and otherwordly, but little escapes her attention-she has a shrewd grasp of everything that's going on beneath the surface. In this, the first of three Mother Paul novels (originally published in 1958), she is in charge of a residential hostel for young women who work in offices and shops in Melbourne. A tense atmosphere pervades the house-many of the residents have received unpleasant anonymous letters, and there is much speculation as to their author. When Mary Allen finds a stranger stabbed in the garden, who dies after uttering a mysterious name, and a few days later one of the residents is found drowned, an apparent suicide, the tension reaches fever pitch. Is there a connection between these two deaths? Or between them and the letters? The police investigation, abetted by the resourceful Mary Allen, proceeds in fits and starts, but meanwhile Mother Paul pursues her own enquiries"-- Provided by publisher.
Identifiers: LCCN 2020035245 (print) | LCCN 2020035246 (ebook) | ISBN 9781891241406 (trade paperback) | ISBN 9781891241635 (ebook)
Subjects: GSAFD: Mystery fiction.
Classification: LCC PR9619.3.W727 R47 2020 (print) | LCC PR9619.3.W727 (ebook) | DDC 823/.914--dc23
LC record available at https://lccn.loc.gov/2020035245
LC ebook record available at https://lccn.loc.gov/2020035246

Contents

INTRODUCTION 7

RESERVATION FOR MURDER 19

MOTHER PAUL INVESTIGATES 235

Introduction

Some of the twenty-five young women living at Kilcomoden, a Catholic-run hostel for 'business girls' in suburban Melbourne, have received anonymous poison-pen letters. Everyone assumes that they were written by one of the hostel's mischievous paying guests, who are a particularly catty lot, but no one is quite so sure after Mary Allen finds a stranger stabbed to death in Kilcomoden's front garden one Saturday evening. 'Jess' is the man's mysterious dying word to her. Mary informs the imperturbable nun in charge of the hostel, Mother Mary St. Paul of the Cross—Mother Paul for short—before they call the police. Murder is too big for nice old Sergeant Wheeler to investigate, so handsome young Detective Inspector O'Mara from Russell Street CIB takes over. However, things go from bad to worse when two more hostel residents are found dead. To solve the case, O'Mara needs some inside help from Mother Paul and from Mary.

That's enough of *Reservation for Murder* (1958) by June Wright to give you the general idea. The poison-pen letters are a nod to June Wright's favourite crime novel, *Gaudy Night* (1935) by Dorothy L. Sayers, '"the best mystery I've ever read,"' she told the author of 'Murder on the Brain' (1952) in the *Sun*. Mary Allen is nothing like Sayers's ultra-sophisticated heroine, Harriet Vane, though. Nor is her boyfriend, 'a slightly balding young man named Cyril,' as dashing and handsome as Harriet's beau, Lord Peter Wimsey, the aristocratic amateur sleuth. In her own words, Mary is 'an unenterprising, but adequate, secretary to an even more unenterprising firm of solicitors.' She has been living at Kilcomoden for eight years, and even though she is still 'just on the right side of thirty,' there is a hint that if she isn't careful, then she will be 'left on the shelf,' to use the common parlance of the 1950s. At the end of the book, it appears that Mary is about to ditch poor Cyril for Detective Inspector O'Mara—'"I know I don't have experience of such matters,"' Mother Paul tells her, '"but I could not help observing something odd about you and

Mr. O'Mara"'—although personally I would have advised Mary to steer clear of someone who uses her as bait and puts her life in danger.

June always denied that her leading ladies were based on her, but all you have to do is scratch the surface. She married Stewart Wright in 1941, and by the time *Reservation for Murder* was published, they had six children. Most people were amazed that June was able to be a good mother as well as a successful writer. She received little help and no encouragement from Stewart, who wanted her to stop writing. Unsurprisingly their marriage was not a particularly happy one, according to their eldest child, Patrick. Most revealingly, Stewart was an accountant, just like Cyril in *Reservation for Murder*. So, when Mary is talking about Cyril, was June talking about Stewart? I believe that she was. Mary says: 'Cyril's compliments are of a negative kind. He tells me if my colour isn't as good as usual or that he prefers my hair done the other way.' Another time she says: 'Cyril, although a serious eater, liked his food interlarded with polite conversation. I had once spent a three-course meal listening to his interpretation of the Companies Act.' June Wright's unhappiness at this time may also explain why Mary is not as feisty as Maggie Byrnes, the heroine-narrator in her first book, *Murder in the Telephone Exchange* (1948). Ten years and five children later, maybe married life was getting June down.

On a more positive note, June Wright and Mary Allen both enjoyed reading detective stories. As June told the author of 'She Never Wastes a Minute!' (1948) in the *Advocate*, a weekly newspaper published by the Catholic Archdiocese of Melbourne, she decided to write *Murder in the Telephone Exchange* after 'she managed to read her way right through the stock of [crime novels at] the local library, and then found herself short of reading matter.' Her favourite authors were Margery Allingham, Agatha Christie, Mignon G. Eberhart, Paul McGuire,[1] and Dorothy L. Sayers. In *Reservation for Murder*, Mary finishes reading a detective story just before she discovers the man's body in the garden. We learn neither its title nor its author, although

---

1 Paul McGuire was an Australian diplomat and author who wrote ten novels, including one crime novel, *A Funeral in Eden* (1938). June sent him a fan letter and a copy of *Murder in the Telephone Exchange* in 1948. 'That was very charming of you,' McGuire replied. 'I am delighted to know that someone with such pleasant notions has joined the company of authors.'

my guess, obviously, would be Sayers's *Gaudy Night*.

Another thing June and Mary had in common was a love of golf. Mary often plays nine holes with one of her best friends at the hostel, a gung-ho, mannish-looking callisthenics instructor named Clare Parker, who 'moved through various educational establishments correcting round shoulders, slack abdomens and concave chests.' She reminds me a bit of Chloe Crawley, the games instructress played by Joyce Grenfell in the English comedy film, *The Belles of St. Trinian's* (1954). 'The golf-links lay on the other side of the river just across the park,' says Mary. 'We crossed the footbridge in silence, Clare striding ahead and pulling her ridiculous little cart. She had dozens of clubs, some with silly woollen socks protecting them. She wore a leather mitten on her left hand and kept her tees in the band of her hat.' Interestingly, Mary uses her game of golf with Clare to nut out the crime in her head. I'm sure that June Wright did exactly the same thing herself on the golf course. '"You know golf is a wonderful panacea and if problems begin to get out of perspective, a day in the open air soon restores them to their proper place,"' June told 'Veronica' in 1961 in the *Advocate*.

The star of *Reservation for Murder*, however, is undoubtedly the 'rectress' (which was how June Wright spelled 'rectoress') of Kilcomoden, Mother Mary St. Paul of the Cross. Her 'face was as soft and unlined as a baby's, with bright, shrewd eyes that were nevertheless also serene,' says Mary, and 'she spoke in her soft rapid voice.' Since this was before the changes introduced by the Second Vatican Council (1962–65), Mother Paul wears an old-fashioned black habit, so 'you never saw or heard her feet—just a gentle rattle of the wooden rosary beads hanging from her leather girdle, and the swish and sway of her voluminous skirts.'

Mother Paul can be as oblique and unfathomable as Father Brown, the Catholic priest-detective created by the English writer G.K. Chesterton, although June told Lucy Sussex in 1996 that she had never read any of his detective stories. She can also be as nosy and scheming as Miss Marple, the amateur village sleuth created by Agatha Christie. However, as much of Mother Paul's detective work is based on her deep understanding of human nature and, therefore, takes place in her mind, we often only hear about it after the event, which is not exactly playing fair with the reader. Nevertheless, I agree with 'J.C.,' the author of 'June Wright Does it Again' (1961) in the *Advocate*, who concluded: 'Mother Paul is indeed a most attractive personality, worthy to rank with the great sleuths of fiction . . . We shall be very disappointed if we do not meet her again.' Indeed, I am surprised that Mother Paul has never had her own TV series.

Reservation for Murder was not Mother Paul's debut; she had already featured in a short story by June called 'Mother Paul Investigates,'[2] which appeared in the March 1954 edition of the Catholic monthly *Caritas*, published by the Brothers of St. John of God. After suffering a severe bout of pneumonia, Mother Paul (she does not use her long moniker in this story) recuperates in a private hospital. One of the night nurses, Sister Joan Brown, is a former school pupil of Mother Paul, and describes her as 'a serene and scholarly nun' who possesses 'a unique ability in guiding rebellious young wills through the tiresome years of adolescence.' After making 'a miraculously fast recovery,' Mother Paul befriends many of her fellow patients, including Mrs. Porter, a wealthy childless widow receiving treatment for diabetes, as well as some of the doctors and nurses. 'Within forty-eight hours she knew more about the staff than I had learned in two years,' says Joan, amazed. When Sister Brown discovers that Mrs. Porter has been strangled with her dressing-gown chord while in bed, the first person she tells is Mother Paul. It does not take long for the nun to figure out who the culprit is—once again, more a result of her knowledge of people than her sleuthing skills.

June Wright got the idea for Mother Paul after reading an interview with the Australian crime fiction writer, Arthur Upfield, who claimed that much of his success was due to having an unusual detective, the biracial Aboriginal Australian Detective Inspector Napoleon Bonaparte. As nuns had been influential in June's life, teaching her at school and caring for her after the births of her six children, she created Mother Paul from an amalgam of nuns who had left an impression on her. One of these nuns was a Sister of Charity, Sr. Mary Dorothea Devine, who was the head of the maternity ward at St.

---

2 'Mother Paul Investigates' is reprinted as an appendix to this book.

Possible real-life models for the fictional Mother Paul: (*left*) Sister Mary Dorothea Devine; (*right*) Sister Mary St. Paul Donovan, popularly known as Mother Paul (*standing on the right*). Courtesy the Sisters of Charity Archives.

Vincent's Hospital in Melbourne when June's twins, Anthony and Nicholas, were born there in 1946. My personal copy of *Reservation for Murder* originally belonged to the St. Vincent's Hospital Library, so maybe Sr. Dorothea even read it! June may also have modelled Mother Paul on another Sister of Charity, Sr. Mary St. Paul Donovan, a much-loved teacher in Melbourne, who was known as Mother Paul.

'"First, I hit on an unusual setting and then I try to think up a plot,"' June told the author of 'Housewife's Recipe for Murder' (1959) in the *Age*. In *Reservation for Murder*, events unfold at Kilcomoden, a young women's hostel comprising a 'lovely old mansion, set in a truly delightful garden [...] picturesquely situated on the banks of the river, five miles from the heart of the beautiful capital city of Melbourne.' In better days it had belonged to a wealthy Melbourne draper, who owned 'the first Rolls Royce in the country.' Somehow his wicked elderly daughter, Mrs. Carron-Toyne, nicknamed 'Mrs. Castor Oil' by the girls at Kilcomoden, and her henpecked companion, Miss Mabel Jones, more affectionately nicknamed 'Jonesy,' manage to live there in a separate wing of the building. While a female hostel was, as early publicity for the book said, 'the fresh and original setting for this intriguing murder mystery,' they were quite common in Melbourne

11

Exterior and interior views of Frank Tate House ca. 1991, courtesy Monash University Archives (image nos. 3554 and 3555)

during the 1950s. According to the author of 'Presbyterian Hostels for Young Rural Folk' (1954) in the *Age*, there were: 'Chalmers Hall, in Parliament Place, East Melbourne, where there are 90 girls from the country; Regent House, Regent Street, Elsternwick, where there are nearly 40 business girls with Matron D. Patterson [in charge]; and Abbotsford Hall, Princess Street, Kew, which cares for 30 girls. Though there is not the desperate need for girls' hostels that there was a few years ago, accommodation will always be required by girls starting a business career in the city [i.e. studying to become or working as typists and secretaries], or students at the University [of Melbourne] or [domestic science schools like] the Emily McPherson College.' The aim of these hostels was to provide cheap, clean and safe accommodation for young women from the country, in particular, while they were studying or working in Melbourne for the first time, separated from their families and friends in rural Victoria.

'"I love young people and, from my front window, I used to watch the girls coming to and from the hostel,"' June Wright told the author of 'Hostel Story Now' (1958), an unnamed newspaper clipping in her scrapbook. "I guess my imagination started to work, and that was the beginning of the book,"' she said. What was the model for Kilcomoden? When June wrote *Reservation for Murder* she lived in Denbigh Road, Armadale, just around the corner from Frank Tate House, a young women's hostel for female student teachers from the country who were studying at the University of Melbourne. Previously, it had been called 'Noorilim' (1879) and belonged to the wealthy Melbourne pastoralist and politician, William Winter-Irving (1840–1901). Since Frank Tate House was so close to June's home, she probably visited the hostel and perhaps even spoke to some of the girls living there, because it is quite similar to Kilcomoden in several respects.

Dorothy Bennett lived at Frank Tate House around the time that June Wright wrote this novel. 'There were strict rules for us young girls from the country in terms of curfews,' Ms. Bennett recalled in 2009. 'During the week we had to be inside by 10.30 pm, and at the weekend by midnight. You were permitted to ask your male friends inside to the common room downstairs, but no further. Girls who flouted these rules were dealt with severely, having privileges withdrawn and sometimes being asked to leave. Very occasionally, you would hear of something shocking happening, such as someone climbing in a window, being locked out after curfew.' Kilcomoden has similar sorts of rules. On the Saturday night of the murder in the garden, for example, it is Mary Allen's turn to record the times when the young women returned from their dates on a list by the door. As a result of these restrictions, some of the residents think that Kilcomoden is like a boarding school. While waiting for the young women to come home on Saturday evening, Mary hears Kilcomoden's resident music student, Christine Farrow, playing Chopin on the piano. 'I stopped at the common room door to listen [...],' she says. 'The girl really was good—almost a concert platform performer. Anyone who played like that could be excused from standoffishness.' Intriguingly, Ms. Bennett recalled doing the same thing at Frank Tate House. One of the common rooms there 'also acted as a practice room for music students,' she said. 'A friend of mine, a pianist, would practice in there for hours—I loved to sit and listen to her.'

The natural and convincing banter between young women, in particular, is an engaging feature of all of June Wright's books. But what sets *Reservation for Murder* apart is the unabashed nastiness of the young women living at Kilcomoden. Indeed, reviewing the book in the *Guardian*, the crime fiction writer Francis Iles described them 'as fine a concatenation of cats as I have ever met.' Mary Allen is just as guilty as everyone else. After a spat with Lorraine Lawrence over when she got home on the night of the murder, Mary walks to her room 'thinking nastily of all the blondes [she] had known to fade into insignificance before their thirties.' Ouch! Thank goodness social media didn't exist during the 1950s. Perhaps it was the incredible bitchiness of the young women that qualified *Reservation for Murder* for the pulp magazine series, Black Tulip Thriller Romances. It seems that June knew nothing about this abridged version of her novel, however. 'It was never mentioned!' said her son, Patrick. *Black Tulip Thriller Romances No. 23. Reservation for Murder* (1970) is as scarce as hen's teeth, and I found my rather battered copy purely by chance.

June's accounts of everyday life in Melbourne are also very authentic. While she was most at ease in white, middle-class, conservative, comfortable, Catholic Melbourne, in *Reservation for Murder* she also describes 'a flat, raw housing estate,' typical of those which had sprung up around Melbourne after the Second World War to house returned servicemen and their growing families. In search of information about one of the victims, Mary and her other close friend at Kilcomoden besides Clare Parker, the wisecracking and pragmatic Fenella King, venture into the outer suburbs to speak to Mrs. Herbert Baker, formerly Rhoda Jamieson. "'Can you imagine anything more deadly, Mary?'" asks Fenella. "Born, bred and married all in the one place—and what a place! I bet she never ventures further than town and then only for the summer sales, and her husband potters in the garden all the week-end." When she sees the few depressed-looking shrubs struggling for life in the Baker garden, and the sun-burnt couch lawn, she adds: "Or tinkers with the radio wearing a waistcoat and no collar."' Mrs. Baker has two children, 'a dirty-faced child anchored on one spreading hip,' and 'a fat baby [...] dressed in an elaborately smocked silk frock.' Mary and Fenella awkwardly quiz the young mother while sitting in her small, untidy, lounge room, 'bulging with a genoa velvet suite.' This is a glimpse of the future if Mary and Fenella are not very careful. It could easily have been June's lot, too, if her writing had not saved her.

Detective Inspector O'Mara is helped by a mysterious American (FBI?) agent named Joe. But as he does not do very much, why did June Wright include him in *Reservation for Murder*? Australians were so besotted by American popular culture during the 1950s that the

(*Left*) the original 1958 edition of *Reservation for Murder*; (*right*) the 1970 paperback reissue.

Australian architect Robin Boyd even invented the term 'Austerica' to characterize it: 'Austerica thrives in the matted fringe of the entertainment business, as in the fake American accents on the radio and television, the crew-cuts in the Australian magazine illustrations laboriously plagiarised from American journals, and all the muddled Americana of the clothing fashion world,' he wrote in his highly critical book, *The Australian Ugliness* (1960). 'Advertisements of all kinds, displays, window dressing—all of the visual trivia of modern Australia—is dominated by the Austerican outlook, for Austerica's credo is that everything desirable, exciting, luxurious and enviable in the twentieth century is American.'

I believe that the presence of Joe in *Reservation for Murder* was intended to highlight this love affair with America. To bring all of the suspects together at Kilcomoden, Mary Allen organises a barbecue and a square dance, two of the most popular American-inspired fads in Australia at the time. While Joe arrives suitably dressed in 'tight Texan jeans, high-heeled boots and a shirt of unparalleled brilliance,' Mary fears that some of the girls' Australian boyfriends may 'require a lot of coaxing to don a plaid shirt.' But she need not have worried, because 'even Cyril was doggedly enjoying himself as though, having suffered the indignity of being draped about in [Mary's] red silk scarf, he was determined to go the whole hog. Fenella had dragged him into her set where he was painstakingly applying his systematic mind to the caller's chant.'

In *Reservation for Murder*, places are often highly symbolic. For example, the Melbourne teahouse, the Green Lounge, represents the unsophisticated Mary, who calls in there for a cuppa every afternoon on her way back from the bank. 'The place was usually empty at that hour, but the tea was always scalding hot, the biscuits [i.e. cookies not scones] fresh, and there were back numbers of glossy American magazines to glance through at better leisure,' she says. When Mary meets Detective Inspector Steve O'Mara and Joe there for a briefing, Joe tells her that, '"In America, I believe tea is served as a pot of hot water with a muslin bag of leaves attached, which you immerse." "No wonder Americans mostly drink coffee,"' she replies, nonplussed. In Melbourne during the 1950s, there were many genteel tea houses like the Green Lounge, such as the Hopetoun Tea Rooms in the elegant Block Arcade, which was established in 1893 and is still going strong.

On the other hand, the Ming Restaurant, a Chinese eatery probably in Little Bourke Street, since it was 'quite near to [police] headquarters' in Russell Street, symbolises the sophisticated O'Mara. When he meets Mary there for a briefing, the smell of 'bowls of succulent, steaming soup' make her 'feel ravenously hungry. "Does it affront your conservative palate?" O'Mara asks presently. "No—delicious!"' answers Mary. '"What is it made from?" "It is as well not to inquire too closely into ingredients," he replies gravely. "Curiosity has ruined many a tasty dish."' O'Mara and Mary's Chinese meal at the Ming Restaurant was about as exotic as it got in Melbourne during the 1950s, when most people ate rice not with meat and vegetables as the main course, but with raspberry jam and milk as a dessert.

Even though *Reservation for Murder* was June Wright's fourth published novel, it had been a bumpy road. Her professional writing career began when she entered an international literary competition run by the London publisher, Hutchinson. While 'in the Judges' opinion, no novel was of sufficient merit to justify the award of a prize of £1,000'—suggesting to me that the competition was a scam—the company neverthless wanted to publish her entry, *Murder in the Telephone Exchange*. It was her first book and it was a huge success in 1948, even outselling Agatha Christie in Australia that year. Hutchinson also published June's second book, which she originally titled *Who Would Murder a Baby*, then *Murder in the Making*; it was ultimately published as *So Bad a Death* (1949). It was also very popular, being serialised nationally on radio by the Australian Broadcasting Commission and in print by *Woman's Day*. Maggie Burns is a single telephonist in the first book and a young mother in the second, having married the policeman who solved the murder. (Maggie and Mary Allen were similar in that respect, at least.)

Hutchinson rejected June's third book, *The Law Courts Mystery*, for which 'Mrs. Wright spent many hours in the Melbourne law courts (the setting for the book), absorbing atmosphere and gathering accurate detail,' the author of 'People and Parties' (1952) reported in the *Age*. June subsequently destroyed the manuscript. (How could she have done that?) But the fickle publisher accepted June's fourth book, a gothic thriller titled *The Devil's Caress* (1952) with a new leading lady, Dr. Marsh Mowbray. (Wendy Lewis wrote a play based on this novel, which debuted at the Star of the Sea Theatre in Sydney on 24 March 2018.) Then, true to form, Hutchinson rejected the fifth book that June wrote, *Hostel for Homicide*. 'My disappointment was all the greater because I was so certain of the book's appeal,' June wrote later. But as luck would have it, 'Mr. Davie from Bendigo,' a writer who knew some publishers in London and was planning a trip over there, offered to show her newest manuscript around. Ironically, at that time, Hutchinson was being reorganised, so that instead of having one overall imprint that published all their books, it would consist of several specialised imprints publishing different types of books. 'Thus, while *Hostel for Homicide* had been thrown out of Hutchinson's, it was now entering through a side door of John Long with a new title—*Reservation for Murder*,' June said, triumphantly. With the royalties she earned from this book, 'she had sliding doors put in the living room,' she told the author of 'Housewife's Recipe for Murder.'

June Wright's sixth book, 'a text-book detective story' called *Duck*

Season Death, was rejected by John Long. Fortunately, this time she kept the manuscript, which was published posthumously by Dark Passage in 2015. While it took the rejection of *Duck Season Death* for June to realise it, she had finally found the right style, the right voice and — most importantly — the right character with *Reservation for Murder,* because her seventh and eighth books, *Faculty of Murder* (1961) and *Make-Up for Murder* (1966), also featured Mother Paul, and were published by John Long without any fuss whatsoever. Dark Passage will also republish these two Mother Paul novels in 2021.

Derham Groves

RESERVATION FOR MURDER

All characters and incidents in this novel are wholly fictitious

One

I

The brochure ran:

Kilcomoden, picturesquely situated on the banks of the river, five miles from the heart of the beautiful capital city of Melbourne, provides a happy and healthy home for business girls. Conducted under the auspices of the Sisters of St. ———, this lovely old mansion [inset picture] *set in a truly delightful garden* [more pictures] *fulfils every requirement of young women seeking board, lodging and wholesome companionships for week-end recreation. For further particulars . . . etc., etc.*

One of the girls found the twenty-year-old pamphlet between the leaves of a forgotten book in the library and showed it around during the worst of our troubles, raising hollow and mocking laughter. Not that Kilcomoden was not everything the writer claimed. It was one of those fine old colonial-style houses built to weather the passing of years—but unfortunately not of domestic staff. Once the family home of a rich draper, and no doubt intended by him to be the home of his descendants, it now sheltered twenty-five business girls from shrewish landladies, malnutrition and week-end boredom.

There was no need nowadays for beguiling brochures with self-conscious pictures of girls, in short, tight-fitting clothes and too much hair, reading in the garden or playing tennis with the river shining in the background. Friends in their chilly, independent bed-sitters, or minute bohemian flatlets, might talk of their wonderful freedom from the few restrictive rules which bound our stay at Kilcomoden, but they eyed us enviously and the waiting list for admission was long.

We had been a fairly contented community until now, for, although there were occasional displays of temperament brought on by natural incompatibility, no squabble ever disturbed the hostel as a whole. For this we had to thank the wise, yet unobtrusive, rule of the rectress, and our practice was to continue about our lawful affairs until the tension dissolved, showing only a mild interest in the source of contention.

For eight years now I had been catching the eighty-twenty bus to the city (*every facility in the way of public transport is within easy walking distance of this hostel*), where I was an unenterprising, but adequate, secretary to an even more unenterprising firm of solicitors, and returning home on the five-thirty. Over the weekend I played a little diffident golf or tennis, worked in a frustrated sort of way on two crossword puzzles, and enjoyed the mild courtship of a slightly balding young man called Cyril.

I was getting along for the most part happy with my uninspired lot, when I was jolted from this pleasant, though vacuous, existence by murder!

II

It was late spring and a Saturday. I was lying on my bed waiting for the supper bell to ring when Fenella came in, bare-footed and clad only in a peach-coloured slip. She was getting ready to go out with her fiancé, and the rays of the setting sun, streaming through my window, caught the emerald on her left hand as she flourished a slip of paper under my nose.

'And what is all this about?' she demanded, between annoyance and amusement.

I closed my eyes again. 'Don't tell me—let me guess. You've had an anonymous letter?'

'Got it in one, smarty. Now I'll be clever. When did you receive yours?'

'Sorry, but my turn is yet to come. Someone told me that anonymous letters were in circulation. Where did you find it?'

'In a drawer as I was looking for stockings. By the way, you haven't a whole pair, have you, Mary? Every blinking one of mine has a ladder.'

'Dressing-table drawer on the right—and show me the latest piece of abuse. I want to become attuned.'

'It made me mad for a minute,' remarked Fenella, opening the drawer on the left and scattering my neat piles of handkerchiefs.

'Yes, it would,' I agreed, reading. 'The other drawer, wrecker. There's a pair of nylons still in their wrapper you can use.'

'You're an angel! I think I'd better take a job at a hosiery place for a while to stock up.' Fenella had been shifting positions quite a bit lately—from expediency, not through boredom like some of the girls. Just before she became engaged, she worked for a wholesale jeweller and left unashamedly once she had her emerald at a special rate. Since then, she had been employed by a Manchester warehouse, a furniture store and a china and glassware firm, her trousseau increasing with each move. At the moment she was a stenographer in an estate agent's office, but did not wear her ring to work lest an ulterior motive should be read into her intense interest in properties on the market.

She pulled a stocking on, balanced like a stork. 'Well, what do you think of Miss Poison Pen?'

'Just a silly phase. She can't get enough exercise, as Clare would say.' At the thought of the strenuous round of golf I had just finished with Clare, I added: 'So it counts us both out as suspects. Eighteen holes that stalwart made me play—and now she's gone off to play squash at her gymnasium. Anyway, she's had a letter; something un-kind about her hairy legs. She told me all about it as I was trying to putt.'

'Jolly unsportsmanlike, what!' Fenella could imitate Clare's abrupt, mannish speech rather well. 'She must have been pretty upset to forget herself so far.'

'The girl writing such scum deserves to be shot. In fact, bad show!'

My impersonation was not as good, but Fenella laughed as she went back to her own room, coming in again presently wearing tiny suede sandals and pulling a black frock over her head. It had a white organdie jabot at the neck and set off her bright hair and camellia skin admirably. 'Who do you think is writing the letters, Maria?' She had started the habit of calling me that with a long *i* like a name in a comic song. It made me feel even more of an institution at the hostel. 'I do think it's the sort of thing which should be trodden on pretty smartly. Do you think it might be Alison—or maybe Verna?'

'Not subtle enough for Verna,' I replied, giving the typewritten slip a fleeting glance. 'If it is Alison's work I suggest we forget about it. There's no surer way of putting the lid on her crazy starts. Where are you off to tonight?'

'Just a show,' replied Fenella through taut lips as she applied lipstick at my mirror. 'Care to come?'

'And play gooseberry? Don't make me feel my years.'

She gave a delicate snort. 'Anyone would think you were forty the way you talk.'

'No, just on the right side of thirty. Anyway, I have work to do — and Cyril may ring.'

Fenella darted into the next room to finish off her face and to collect the squirrel coat she had bought while working for a furrier. 'It beats me why you let that awful mutt hang round,' she said frankly, when she came back for assistance in pinning gardenias to the collar.

I smiled. 'He keeps me from thinking I'm completely on the shelf, and he's not an awful mutt. He's a very nice mutt.'

'And so are you,' Fenella retorted, 'but you could still do with a good shaking-up. I hope our poison pen writes to that effect.' She glanced at her wrist-watch and gave a squeal. 'I must tear. Tommy becomes pulverized if he has to talk to Mother Paul too long. She asks every time if it is the apostle or the doctor he is named after.' She whirled off, the scent of her flowers lingering in the room as a reminder of her vivid presence.

Then the supper bell rang and I rolled off my bed and went down to the bathroom for a wash. During the week dinner was served as the last meal of the day, but on Saturdays and Sundays you helped yourself to tea, bread-and-butter and slabs of Sister Berthe's succulent orange cake from a trolley tray in the common-room at four-thirty, while a cold collation was set out cafeteria-style in the refectory at seven. There were never many girls in on either evening, while quite a few would be away for the week-end.

Next door to the bathroom was a room where we did our laundry and ironing. The sound of acrimonious voices, raised in a did-didn't type of quarrel, seeped in as I dried my hands and tucked an escaping sports blouse into the waistband of my grey flannel skirt. Jean and Betty, I thought resignedly. Bang goes my new perm for a while!

They were known as Jeanette and Bettine to the youth-and-beauty-seeking women who haunted the expensive salon where the employees were always young and pretty, and went under the glossy pseudonyms of coiffure stylists or beauticians. Away from their work they were still inseparable, sharing each other's boy-friends, clothes and a room at Kilcomoden. Even their not infrequent rows were exclusive, providing you were careful not to show bias. If you had booked their services for a hair-do over the week-end and they weren't playing speaks, you waited diplomatically until the quarrel was over, rather than ask one without the other.

This current row seemed different from their usual ones, which were conducted in the third person in accents of haughty refinement. I put my head in the ironing-room door and said peaceably: 'Can the noise! You'll have the riot squad along.' Both girls swung round, flushed and angry. Betty had been pressing a taffeta dance frock, the colour of an American Beauty rose, but Jean was fully dressed with silver sandals showing beneath her frothy, green skirt.

'Look what she wrote!' the latter cried, thrusting a slip of paper at me. 'If I'm a man-chaser, then she's . . .' Jean always became tearful and inarticulate when she lost her temper.

Betty slammed the iron upright and put her hands on her hips. 'All right! Speak up—what am I?'

'A devastating brunette,' I put in soothingly. 'As irresistible as our honey-blonde Jeanette.'

But Jean continued to stride about the room, dashing tears away to the ruin of her mascara and Betty said, enunciating carefully: 'It may interest you to know, my dear girl, that I have had an anonymous letter, too. Furthermore, I would not dream of accusing you of writing it. If your opinion of me is so low, then this is the end. I'm asking for a separate room,' she finished rather on an anti-climax, especially as a Miss Farrow had just moved into the last vacant room.

I took the opportunity to read the letter while Jean was looking nonplussed. It was the same sort of thing as Fenella had received—unpleasant, but not really harmful.

'Is this what the fuss is about? These things are the fashion for the moment—someone's idea of fun, I suppose. The best policy is to ignore them. Don't be a silly child, Jean! Bet wouldn't write a thing like this, would you?' I winked at her on the side Jean couldn't see, and she gave up looking like a picture of outraged virtue and grinned instead. They were forced to make it up, otherwise their evening out would have been spoiled.

I pocketed the note and went back for Fenella's. I was just a little disturbed. If the anonymous letters were going to cause strife, then they were going to be more than merely annoying.

Lorraine came out of her room as I was passing. I paused and gave her her first wolf whistle for the night. She was looking stunning as usual, in a golden-brown, faille dress that matched her enormous eyes—cow's eyes, someone once said unkindly, irritated by so much studied loveliness. A sequined juliet cap hugged her blonde hair, which she always kept at shoulder length in spite of changing fashions. For a moment she stood in her doorway carefully posed, one slender foot at right angles to the other and her left arm raised negligently from the elbow. Lorraine was a salesgirl in a 'little' shop which sold high-fashion clothes at even higher prices, but her life's ambition was to be a model.

'Hullo, Glamour!' I said. 'Where's it to be tonight? And with what wealthy scion?' We were frequently being titillated with social column names.

Her lips curved into the smile she had once been caught practising in front of a mirror. 'That,' she replied sweetly, 'is my business.'

'Mine too, unfortunately. I'm probably on the door tonight, so get in at a respectable hour like a good child.'

She raised her brows superciliously. 'Not going out, dear? Too bad! You always seem to be on the door. You're getting to be quite a figure around Kilcomoden.'

That was a nasty one, so I said, surveying her anxiously: 'Talking of figures, Lorraine, isn't that the slightest bulge I can see? You must be putting on weight. Oh, please don't think it doesn't suit you. You were much too thin before.'

She closed the door behind her with a snap, but spoke with an air of nonchalant candour, 'I don't think I like you, Mary.'

'Dear,' I returned, 'your sentiments are identical with my own. Now run along, have a good time, but remember the clock, Cinderella!'

Following her downstairs and admiring the graceful way she made the descent, with head well up and fingers just trailing the banister, I asked, 'By the way, have you had an anonymous letter lately?'

She stopped so suddenly that I nearly fell on top of her. Then she plunged forward and ran down the rest of the stairs to the hall, sweeping past Mr. Sparks, who was waiting for Alison, and leaving him wavering like a wispy sapling after a strong gust of wind. Lorraine has had one too, I concluded.

Mr. Sparks was a meek-looking little man, like a figure in a cartoon about henpecked husbands. He was always ill at ease in the ultra-feminine atmosphere of the hostel, and even now had his hat on, ready to duck out of the door the moment Alison appeared. What with clutching his satchel, his neat pigskin gloves which he usually wore over his small, white hands, and the bulky umbrella without which he never moved at the faintest hint of a cloud in the sky, he became quite tangled up in trying to remove it as I greeted him overwarmly. I always felt rather sorry for him. Alison, we all agreed, treated him abominably.

I picked up one of his gloves. 'Alison keeping you waiting as usual, Mr. Sparks? I'll buzz her room and give her the hurry-up.' There was a bell system under the stairs which the rich draper had installed to prevent his house guests from keeping him from his dinner.

'Thank you. Miss—er—, thank you. So kind! Perhaps I was a little early. I like to be a bit before time, just to be on the safe side. I wouldn't like Alison to think I had slipped her up.'

I usually told him my name each time we met, but he still called me Miss—er—, and the nuns Sister—um—. He regarded me so unhappily while I gave Alison a long ring that I felt constrained to stay until she appeared, in order to explain he had nothing to do with it. I wondered yet again what incredible impulse had caused Mr. Sparks to forsake his happy bachelorhood, when marriage had entailed taking on a ready-made daughter as difficult and volatile as Alison. Although her mother had been dead for several years now, he doggedly did his duty by his stepdaughter—or at least what he considered must be his duty.

In the middle of a painful conversation revolving around the weather, I saw Alison peeping over the stairhead. 'Hurry up, there!'

I called. 'Papa's rarin' to go. What excitement have you planned to-night, Mr. Sparks?'

In trying to greet Alison, who promptly withdrew her head, and answering my question, he became verbally tangled this time. 'Good evening, chicken!' He frequently tried to propitiate her with this re-volting pet name. 'So glad to—er—I thought perhaps the pictures—that is, if Alison cares to go. Then a nice little supper somewhere. She'll be home in good time, Miss—er—. I know how strict—that is, not strict but so sensible.'

'I'll probably be the one to let her in, so don't worry too much,' I said soothingly.

'I'm not going,' said Alison. She was standing half-way up the stairs, her hands behind her back and her body thrust forward defi-antly, but her voice did not carry conviction.

You never knew if Alison meant what she said. She always seemed to lack decision, and liked to be coaxed and persuaded into a line of action. That sort of behaviour became tedious after a while and, added to other irresponsible habits, led to her being left out of the hostel af-fairs and friendships. When that happened she would assert herself to our attention by scenes of hysterical aberration. Her business career was astounding in its variety. Since taking a sketchy secretarial course two years before, she had had eleven jobs—that is, if you counted the one she stayed in for precisely thirty-seven minutes and left because the accountant clicked his fingers at her.

'I don't want to go out,' she repeated, while Mr. Sparks stared at her helplessly.

'Rubbish!' I said briskly. 'You're all dressed and ready.'

She started to unbutton the jacket of her beautifully tailored suit. Alison loved clothes and was always buying new outfits as she tired quickly of this or that. Most of the bills went to her hapless stepfather. 'I changed my mind coming down the stairs.'

'Well, just change it again, and don't be silly. You look very charm-ing in that coat, so don't take it off.'

'Do I, Mary?' She ran down and stood very close to me, her round, childish eyes alight with pleasure at the passing compliment. 'Do you really mean that? And my hat? No, you don't like it. I can tell by your face. I'll run up and get another. I bought the loveliest thing at that place where Lorraine works. They're sending the bill to you,' she added over her shoulder to Mr. Sparks, who had been making soothing murmurs of approbation concerning the feather curvette she wore on her fair, wispy hair.

I pushed Alison towards him gently. 'You look fine the way you are. Now *en avant*, and don't forget to say thank you to the nice gentleman when he brings you home.'

'All right. I'll go then. I would like a fur coat. Fenella King has one. I must look at some next week. There'll be plenty of time, as I'm going to chuck my job. The head typist is a beast!'

I gave Mr. Sparks a look of amused sympathy as I pushed his unbegotten brat into his conservative sedan. He whispered to me before he went round to the driver's seat, which held a cushion so that he could see out the windscreen. 'Thank you, Miss—er—, thank you. I find Alison is sometimes—well—er—'

'Exactly! I suggest a good spanking.' But he looked quite shocked at the idea.

III

The refectory was in the basement of Kilcomoden, but, because of the steep slope on which the house was built, high windows set on the east wall brought daylight in from ground level. On the west side a heavy door was shut on the cobwebby labyrinth of wine cellars, relics of the original owner's grandiose ideas. They were now used as storerooms for disused furniture that Sister Emerentiana was always talking about giving to the St. Vincent de Paul Society. There was also an old service lift, connecting the basement with the ground floor. It was built into the wall between the stairs and the servery window which opened into the kitchen, Sister Berthe's domain.

On a table beneath the servery, plates of cold meat, salad and bread-and-butter were set out, flanked by steaming jugs of tea and coffee. A rack of trays stood nearby. I took one down and joined Miss Jones, who was picking over the meat to find the leaner pieces before setting a tray to carry upstairs to Mrs. Carron-Toyle.

Miss Jones was an incredible survival of an inglorious past known as a companion. Her employer was the rich draper's sole surviving child, a cantankerous and vulgar old tyrant who had inveigled herself into the hostel when not even her alleged wealth made her tolerable to her relatives. Miss Jones was a thin, straggly woman with a long, drooping pink nose perpetually twisted in a nervous sniff, for she suffered from a chronic head cold and a doormat type of humility. Her Christian name was Mabel, and although she had often invited us to make use of it, no one could bring herself to do so. We compromised on 'Jonesy', and pulled her leg unmercifully in an endeavour to make her assert herself with Mrs. Carron-Toyle, whom we all loathed.

'Not on the loose tonight?' I asked, spearing a slab of corned beef and piling salad on top. 'You ought to complain to your union.'

She always laughed extravagantly, even at the feeblest joke. 'Yes, there should be a union for us poor companion-secretaries.' The comforting double-handled title made it sound as though there were hundreds in her unfortunate livelihood. 'I did hope to get away this evening. There is a film down at the local theatre that I badly want to see, but poor Mrs. Carron-Toyle isn't feeling quite herself, and so I thought perhaps I shouldn't leave her.'

I surveyed the heaped tray. 'Her appetite seems fair enough. You just trundle that up to the old girl, and then shoot through to see your flick.'

She poured a cup of tea and added three teaspoons of sugar. 'Oh no, I couldn't do that. She asked me specially to stay home. She feels she might have an attack tonight. I would never forgive myself if that happened while I was out enjoying myself.'

I took the jug out of her hand. 'No, you mustn't miss a chance of being in at the death.'

She looked distressed. 'You know I didn't mean it like that, Mary.'

'Well, I would, if I were in your shoes,' I replied frankly. 'Your Christian forbearance with that unpleasant old woman has me beaten.'

She regarded me earnestly. 'You don't understand poor Mrs. Carron-Toyle. She doesn't mean half the things she says. Why, I just don't take any notice of some of the funny old remarks she passes,' she said bravely.

'It's a pity you don't ignore her faked heart attacks at the same time,' I returned. Several years, doctors and companion-secretary-slaves had passed since Mrs. Carron-Toyle had, as she had expressed it, thrown herself on the nuns' charity and begged for a quiet corner of her childhood's home in which to await the imminent approach of the Grim Reaper. She had remained firmly entrenched ever since in a neat set of rooms in a wing off the ground floor, with Miss Jones to bully and her latest hypochondriac specialist in constant sycophantic attendance.

I carried my tray over to the scattering of girls eating supper, and sat down next to our latest recruit, a dark, pale, silent girl called Christine Farrow. She had Verna on the other side and did not look too happy about it. I guessed Verna was at her inimitable probing game.

'We don't often have students here,' Verna was saying, her sharp, sallow face alert. 'Most of us go to work. Aren't you lucky to be studying music! I suppose your people live in the country, do they? It must be marvellous not to have to earn your own living. You would need quite a big allowance, I suppose?'

She worked on the suggestion technique in her hobby of knowing more about others than anyone else, and even if this failed she still pretended to know more than there was to know. She had a routine job in some Government office and seldom went out over the weekend, preferring to slide about the hostel looking secretive, or breaking into conversations as though she knew what was under discussion and something more besides.

'Surely you won't be so crude as to ask the amount!' I interrupted, pulling the pepper and salt nearer by means of a fork.

One of Verna's more annoying accomplishments was never losing her temper. Even jibes and insults went over her head. She kept on smiling in her sly, know-all fashion and made some innocuous remark containing a double edge. 'Hullo, Mary! You look tired. Clare plays a good game, doesn't she? You have to be frightfully good to beat her at golf.'

I shook my head. 'It didn't hurt, Verna. I'm not that serious about the game. Try again!'

'Oh, I didn't mean that you can't take a beating like a sport,' she said, with a little protesting snigger. 'Mary's so quick on the defensive,' she added to the girl between us. 'The older single girls get the more aggressive they become, don't you think so, Christine?'

The girl got up, and began packing her half-eaten meal on a tray. Her loose hair, which she wore parted in the centre, swung over her cheeks as she said in a tense little voice, 'The name is Miss Farrow, if you don't mind.' She walked over to the servery, left her tray, and went out of the room without a backward glance.

I looked at Verna. 'Well, that was one straight to the jaw, wasn't it? You really shouldn't try to be too familiar, Verna.'

'She's funny, isn't she?' she remarked, quite unruffled by the rebuff. 'Not a bit friendly. I wonder if she has had an anonymous letter and that makes her quiet.'

'You're not responsible for that poison-pen nonsense, are you?'

It was just the sort of accusation that Verna delighted in pervertedly. 'Now, why should you pick on poor little me?'

'Because poor little you could quite easily have written them.'

She put her head on one side as she folded her table napkin into a neat roll. 'But consider closely, Mary! Have you seen any of them? You have? But not yet received one of your own, I take it. How very odd—but that is by the way. Do you think they are in my style?'

'No, they're not,' I admitted grudgingly, 'but the general idea could be your notion of fun.'

'So I may or may not be the culprit,' she said, unperturbed by my poor opinion. 'I won't say yes or no. But I'll tell you this, Mary—if it is not I who is writing the anonymous letters, then you should have a pretty good idea of the culprit.'

'Who?' I asked quickly.

She shook her head, smiling. 'Ah, that would be telling! Besides, it doesn't do to go round accusing people without proof, does it?' That was one of her double edges.

'Look, Verna, I apologize if I've been rude, but if you know who is responsible, please speak out.'

She got up from her chair, her eyes veiled. 'You sound quite worried. Is it because you may be accused?'

'I don't believe you know anything,' I declared, after giving her a searching look. 'Go away, and stop trying to be mysterious. The notes aren't as important as all that.'

She glanced down at me over her shoulder. 'Don't you think so?' she asked softly. 'Let's wait and see.'

I allowed her the Parthian shot and went on with my supper. The big old house was quiet when I went back upstairs. The Saturday night rush to get out was over, and Sister Emerentiana was rustling along passages and poking into rooms to check on unnecessary lights. As a result, the whole place was in half-dark, and the desultory readers and knitters in the common-room needed just that discouragement to make them decide on an early night for a change. She switched off the hall light, and I allowed her enough time to reach the nuns' quarters, which were situated away from the main building in what were once the rich draper's magnificent stables, before nipping back to put it on again. I wasn't going to walk across that chilly hall in the dark every time the doorbell or telephone rang.

Unlike the common-room, which was originally a reception-room, the library had retained its identity. It was a beautifully proportioned, high-ceilinged room overlooking the shrub-lined driveway, which swept round from the street gates to the front entrance facing the river. Tall french windows, opening on to a terrace, took up most of one wall, but the remainder were covered with bookshelves, now happily devoid of their first burdens, which had been obscure calf-bound tomes ordered by the crate for the purpose of ostentatious culture. The present tenants of the shelves were usable items that a good library should possess, catering for all tastes and moods of the moment. Whenever any of us suffered from common-room claustrophobia, we took ourselves off to the library to travel through realms of gold or gore in one of the deep leather armchairs.

Lately I had been spending most of my time there, though not through a desire to shun my companions. The reason was that I had been slipped into the position of an amanuensis. For some time now the rectress had been working on a life of the foundress of the Order. There were those who maintained that she had commenced the monumental work in her far-off postulant days, and that it had become retroactive like one of Mr. Juggins's ventures. When I took my place behind the typewriter set on a table in one corner of the room, I found a pile of notes on the guild system of the Middle Ages. What the Noble Order of Bread Makers had to do with the saint I did not know, but I dutifully set about deciphering Mother Paul's note-making handwriting.

Presently she came gliding into the room with her inimitable carriage, as though the floor was sliding her along. You never saw or heard her feet—just a gentle rattle of the wooden rosary beads hanging from her leather girdle, and the swish and sway of her voluminous skirts. She looked exactly the same as when I first met her eight years ago; face soft and unlined as a baby's, eyes bright and shrewd, yet serene. She spoke in her soft, rapid voice. 'Mary dear, so patient! You should be out somewhere enjoying yourself. And I write so badly when I'm in a hurry. Why aren't you out, dear? That nice steady young man. But you know how it is with notes—ideas always come at the most inopportune moments.'

'Why bread?' Sometimes I tried to catch Mother Paul by being as apparently irrelevant as she was, but she never stumbled.

'Even saints must eat, Mary. It will give a more accurate picture of the times. Unless she was one of the ascetic kind. But I don't think so. Such a practical woman even with all her holiness. Perhaps a subsection on asceticism? I know the very person who can help me there. A Dominican. His life's interest is asceticism in the mystics.'

'You don't think it will be getting away from your original subject?' I ventured, visualizing a flood of even more incomprehensible notes.

She had been moving about the room while speaking, shutting windows, picking out books and replacing them in other positions, gathering up fallen petals from the huge bowl of Sister Felician's iceland poppies on the mantelpiece. Hers was not a fidgety restlessness, but a motion as continuous and soothing as the lapping of the river at the foot of Kilcomoden's garden. But she stopped still suddenly, her bright eyes serious.

'The atmosphere—Sister Emerentiana says it's all wrong.'

I protested. 'The atmosphere's wonderful! It—uh—pulsates with vigour and accuracy.'

She shook her head gravely. 'No, Mary. The suspicion and the petty tiffs. It must stop.'

I gaped at her. She frequently succeeded in catching me.

'I presume these silly anonymous letters are the cause. Who is the naughty child, do you know, Mary?'

It was inevitable that Mother Paul should be aware of the

poison-pen writer right from the beginning. She had some uncanny sense when anything threatened the harmony of Kilcomoden, for all that she gave Sister Em the credit.

'I haven't any idea,' I replied, putting a hand in the pocket of my cardigan, 'but here are a couple of samples.'

She read them through distastefully. 'How tiresome! Have you not had one, dear?'

I shook my head and asked, 'Does that render me instantly suspect?'

'Don't be foolish! And they seem quite pointless, too. I wonder why.' She gazed thoughtfully at the etching of the Pantheon over my head for several minutes.

I inserted a sheet in the typewriter and rolled it down. 'I wouldn't worry overmuch. It's just a phase someone is going through. Do you want these notes typed, or shall I continue with "Background to Childhood"?'

'Goodness, you are far advanced. I was thinking perhaps I should have done some further research into the parents' lives. What do you think?'

'No,' I said definitely.

Her eyes twinkled. 'Dear Mary! That's what I meant—so patient. You should be out somewhere enjoying yourself,' she repeated.

'I'm quite content. My nice steady young man may ring.'

'Bishop, Confessor and Doctor of the Church,' Mother Paul murmured automatically, for it was thus that she remembered names. 'I must go. I promised Miss Jones to visit Mrs. Carron-Toyle.'

I glanced up. 'Did Miss Jones go out after all? I was advising her at supper to cut loose.'

'Such a good soul,' remarked Mother Paul, as she floated over to the door, 'but I really can't see her inheriting the earth.'

Soon after she left, Cyril's call came. As I crossed the hall to the telephone I could hear someone—Miss Farrow, I presumed—at the common-room piano. It was not much of an instrument, having been strummed on for a generation now, but her exquisite playing of a Chopin nocturne was conducive to romance—even one as staid as mine. Cyril and I had an exciting conversation about each other's health, and finished up by making an even more exciting date to take a walk the following afternoon—rather late, because he had brought some figures from the office to work on over the week-end.

I stopped at the common-room door to listen to the rest of the nocturne. The girl really was good—almost a concert platform performer. Anyone who played like that could be excused from standoffishness. I pushed open the door on the last bitter sweet notes, prepared to risk a snub in return for a few words of appreciation, and was surprised to find the room in darkness.

'Here!' I said, and switched on the light. 'I'm a touch typist too, but I do like to see where I'm going.'

She swung round at once. Although the switch I had pressed lighted only the lamp near the door and her face was in the shadows, I thought I saw tears on her cheeks.

'You frightened me,' she exclaimed, with a nervous laugh.

'You delighted me,' I rejoined. 'What heavenly magic have you in your fingers to make that old box sound like a Steinway Grand?'

She rippled a treble scale. 'Do you think I'm good?'

It seemed rather an odd question to ask because her tone was not smug, but dispassionate.

'I would say very good, but then I am not an expert. What do your teachers say?'

'Yes, they say I have great talent,' she agreed, almost listlessly.

'Please go on,' I said. 'And would you mind if I left this door open? I'm all tied up with an erudite account of a saint's childhood, and Chopin is very soothing. Er—do I turn off the light again?'

She jumped up, closing the piano-lid with a bang. 'Don't try to be funny at my expense! And I don't play to please other people.'

'I wasn't trying to be funny,' I replied mildly. 'I'm a great respecter of other people's idiosyncrasies—like playing in the dark. It's a good deal easier to get along with your fellow-man that way.'

She stopped half-way across the room. 'I loathe people who give advice.'

I eyed her stormy face speculatively. 'You seem to have a general hate about everything, Miss Farrow.'

'All I want is to be left alone.'

'I'll spread that good news around,' I returned cheerfully.

She gave me a fierce look, then brushed past and ran upstairs.

I told Clare about the encounter with Christine Farrow when she came in at ten—the first of the Saturday-night prodigals.

'Regular exercise is what she needs,' she declared briskly, hitching one foot on to the rung of a chair and leaning her forearm on her bent knee. She had several mannish habits as well as diction. 'I know these so-called artists. They start cultivating a temperament at school—should be squashed then. In my schools I make a practice of giving 'em double P.T. at the first sign.'

Clare was a callisthenics instructor. She moved through various educational establishments correcting round shoulders, slack abdomens and concave chests. With Clare nearby, you would not dare sprawl with your spine twisted comfortably anyhow—she automatically gave you a thump between the shoulder-blades.

I straightened up and kept my elbows in as I held my fingers over the typewriter keyboard. 'How did the squash go?'

'Wizard! Played four sets, got a wonderful sweat up, showered off and came home. I'll sleep like a top tonight. How about some tennis tomorrow, old thing? We'll organize the pianist into playing.'

'I wish you luck. She's a prickly customer.'

'She probably had one of those damn letters and it upset her. Mine made me see red for a while, too. It took a brisk walk to work off the nasty taste.'

She lowered her foot and ran her square, strong hands over her hair, which was cut in the nearest approach to an Eton crop I had seen outside of magazine pictures of the 'twenties. 'Heigh-ho, I'm for bunky-do! Any chance of scrounging some cocoa?'

I typed a letter absently with my forefinger. 'There's some in my room—the cupboard near the window. Who is it, do you know, Clare?'

She turned back from the door, loosening the tartan tie she wore with her shirt-style blouse. 'The A.L.'s? Some silly ass. Alison, I bet.'

'She hasn't had one. We would have heard about it.'

'So what!'

'Well,' I said thoughtfully, and typed another letter, 'if I wanted to remain anonymous I would send one to myself, to put people off the scent.'

Clare shook her head and dragged off the jacket of her heather-mix suit. 'Not Alison—she's not smart enough. Besides, she probably doesn't want to remain anonymous. You know how that girl thrives on scenes.'

'I wish she would stop. Grapevine news has reached the nuns.'

Clare undid the top button of her blouse and eased her neck. 'Bad show!' she said seriously. 'Someone had better have a word with young Alison.'

'You!' I said promptly.

She grinned, her even, white teeth making her plain face look almost attractive. 'You just got in first there. I dunno, though, Maria. They say tact is not my long suit.'

'It's getting beyond the tactful stage, and I think Alison—that is supposing she is our poison pen—has a respect for you,' I said artfully.

'Ratty little devil! These letters seem right up her alley. Okay, I'll bawl her out tomorrow.' She raised her hand in a vague salute. 'Good night, old girl!'

I worked on the saint's childhood until the pictures crowd came in, when I put it aside in favour of a detective story. I was tired and the close work was inducing very unsaint-like reactions. Then Fenella came in, her eyes radiant and her lipstick smudged. She stayed talking for a while and presently went off upstairs, humming a gay little tune.

Alison followed soon afterwards, scrupulously delivered to the door by a relieved-looking Mr. Sparks. He had not driven up for fear of disturbing the house, and Alison was making quite a fuss about the walk up the drive.

'That's over for another week,' I told him, and spared him the rest of Alison's scene by the simple procedure of shutting the door in his face. 'Good night, Alison,' I added hastily, using the same technique for my own sake. She was capable of switching her victim without changing the tone of her tantrum when frustrated.

'Mary!' she called, her high, childish voice echoing in the tiled hall.

I turned unwillingly. 'What? And don't talk so loudly. You'll wake everyone up.'

'Come back here,' she said imperiously. 'If you don't, I'll scream and shout.'

I took a step forward, then paused. 'What do you want?'

'No, right near,' she beckoned. 'I mean it. I will scream.'
I went closer. Well!'

A little smile of triumph flickered on her mouth. 'I just wanted to see if I could make you come to me—and I did, didn't I, Mary?'

There were times when I wondered whether Alison's streak of irresponsibility was not a streak of something more serious. This was one of them. Her eyes were bright and her cheeks flushed as she repeated in a whisper, 'I made you come, Mary.'

'Yes, you made me,' I agreed grimly. 'Is that all now?'

She reached out her hand and took hold of a button of my cardigan. 'You sound cross, Mary. You don't like me. Why don't you like me?'

'I like you all right when you behave yourself.'

Her eyes opened wide. 'But I always do. I want to be friends with you, Mary.'

I pulled the button away. 'That's fine! Only count me out of your more intimate circle. I'm getting up in years, and I like a quiet life. Now go to bed like a good girl.'

'I don't want to go to bed yet. I'm not tired. Can I come into the library with you?'

I sighed. 'No! And if you start pulling any silly threats about screaming, I'll forget my kindly nature and slap you hard where you should have been slapped more often as a child.' Being tired, I spoke with more vehemence than my wont, but it had a good effect. Alison blinked nervously and then turned up the stairs.

'Good night, Mary,' she said in a meek voice, but I stalked back to the library without replying.

I had just finished the detective story when the crunching of gravel outside the windows and gay heedless voices sent me back wearily to the front door. Jean and Betty tumbled in giggling, their early differences forgotten. They rushed madly into the library to wave through the glass at their departing escorts, and would have stayed indefinitely had I not pushed them off to bed.

There now remained only Lorraine Lawrence to check in, according to the list Sister Emerentiana had left on the table. I ran haphazard strokes through her neat writing and marked a few slap-dash times in the 'arrived home' column, wondering irritably just what Sister Em got out of her lists and appreciations and inventories anyway. She put in more paper work than a quartermaster, which was the nickname she had earned among the girls. Proposed visits from the bishop, the Provincial or even persons like health inspectors entailed vast folios of procedures, reports and itemized data.

I picked out another book at random, and sat down in an armchair to wait for Lorraine. The house was so quiet that the ponderous ticking of the grandfather clock in the hall was audible even though the library door was closed, while the mulga wood clock on the mantelpiece and my own wrist-watch combined to make an irritating irregular pattern of monotonous sound.

The book was one that could hold the attention at midday but not well after midnight. Twice it fell into my lap as my head slumped forward, and I cursed Lorraine mildly. I knew how it would be—she would come in still looking fresh and soignée after her night's fun, while I would be owl-eyed with a jaw stiff from yawns.

I dozed off for a short time, then woke sharply thinking of Mabel Jones. She had not yet arrived home. The thought kept me alert for a minute or two. Any problem, however small, was worth mulling over just to allay the boredom of the last hours. Then I remembered the door at the side of the house which led into Mrs. Carron-Toyle's apartment, and began a further fret and fume against the butterfly keeping me from my bed.

I compared my watch with the opposition on the mantelpiece and then pulled myself up and went out to inspect the grandfather clock, aggrieved though not surprised to find that they all pointed to the same time. It was getting to be too much of a good thing. I pottered around the library, replacing books and covering the typewriter, preparing a savage and eloquent homily for Lorraine, which I knew I would not be bothered using when the time came.

'It may interest you to know, my dear girl, that I have had a particularly strenuous day and I am not prepared to—' I broke off my peevish mutterings and looked towards the long velvet curtains shrouding the windows, imagining I heard some sort of far-off sound. My ears pricked at the gentle hum of a car being carefully driven in low gear. I opened one of the windows and slipped out on to the terrace, intending to walk up the drive to meet Lorraine.

Dratted little gadabout, I thought, shivering in the clear chill night. I'll pin her ears back.

But although I walked as far as the impressive iron gates, which bore some baroque coat of arms that the rich draper had manufactured from his imagination, there was no sign of her.

I must have imagined things too, I thought, preparing to turn back. I was trying to recall precisely what had caused my impression that someone had stopped at the gates when a whispering groan came from the shrubbery behind me.

Executing a neat about-turn in fright, I quavered, 'Is that you, Lorraine?' But the only reply was another sickening moan. Then there was a long silence, while I worked up courage to crawl into the thicket.

'Lorraine! Where are you?' She must be ill or drunk, I thought—perhaps a bit of both. Those parties she goes to—she's stepping out a bit too high lately.

I stumbled against something soft, and knelt down in the earth, feeling with my hands and saying her name. But it was not Lorraine. It wasn't even a woman. Suddenly the body I was feeling gave a horrible convulsive twitch, and there came the choking sound of someone trying to breathe. A whisper of a name struggled through the slowly closing throat.

'Jess!' said the strange man as he died.

Two

I

I found difficulty later in giving the police a coherent account of the next half-hour. The first thing I remembered was finding myself back in the library, panting and gulping like a hunted animal. That was when I saw the sticky mess on my hands, and was hard put not to start yelling my head off. Next I was in the ground floor bathroom scrubbing at my hands until they were clean and cold and pink. I must have come to a bit in the bathroom, for it was then that the temptation occurred to forget the awful thing I had found at the gates. I even worked out how I would go straight up to bed, close my mind to the nightmare scene just past, and let someone else have the doubtful honour of finding the body.

I would like to say that innate honesty and a desire to spare others the shock I had received prevented this course of inaction, instead of the unpleasant dark streaks on my blouse and skirt which would be difficult to explain away to the close community in which I lived.

I snatched at other doleful straws. Perhaps the man had been the victim of a hit-run driver, and had crawled in from the street. I could have sworn I had heard a car. Or maybe one of Sister Berthe's derelicts—she had a regular clientele of unsavoury-looking individuals who came to the kitchen door begging for food—with some horrible illness.

But drunken reckless drivers do not usually frequent quiet *cul-de-sacs*, and as for being a sick hobo—I shuddered, recalling the inexplicable loss of blood.

I was three-fourths aware by this time—trying to plan a constructive move and wondering with half-hysterical humour if Sister Em had anything like the present situation in her procedures—'Bodies—what to do in event of finding'. I wavered between doctors and policemen, and then decided to get in touch with the rectress first. As she was in charge of Kilcomoden, she was also in charge of what dead bodies should litter its garden.

There was an inter-house phone near the bell system under the stairs, which had been installed when the original owner had moved with the times from a carriage and pair to the first Rolls-Royce in the country. I rang Mother Paul's special call signal and presently a sleepy voice answered absently, '*Et cum spiritu tuo*,' which was the reply to the conventual equivalent of 'rise and shine'.

'It's Mary Allen,' I said in a rush. The sooner an explanation was out, the sooner the desire to giggle meaninglessly like a lunatic would pass. 'I'm very sorry to disturb you, but something has happened that you should know about. There's a—a dead man in our grounds.'

There was a long pause. Then Mother Paul said, quite placidly: 'Oh dear! How very dreadful! You're quite sure, Mary?'

'He's in the shrubbery near the gates,' I enlarged. 'He died just as I found him. There was an awful lot of — of blood.'

My voice wobbled a little, and Mother Paul said swiftly: 'I'll come over to the house right away. That nice policeman, Mary—the one who came last year. Ring him at once. And get Bartholomew—so much better to have a man around.' She rang off, never one to waste words in times of crisis.

I sent a fleeting glance up the dark stairs as I sped to the telephone in the hall, marvelling, yet thankful, that everyone should remain so peacefully oblivious to the crazy situation below. 'That nice policeman' was the night sergeant at the local station who had been called in to deal with a burglar scare eighteen months ago. My fingers were shaking as I dialled the number. I told him briefly that Mother rectress wanted him to come as an accident had happened. Then I turned to the second part of her instructions.

Bartholomew was the gardener and odd job man at Kilcomoden. He occupied a bungalow near the kitchen garden on the opposite side of the house from the driveway—a circumstance in which I felt a craven relief when I let myself out by the front door. But a light, still showing from his room, made me wonder if he would be up to playing the strong man of the party. Bartholomew had a sly and surreptitious liking for the bottle, which the nuns probably knew about, but overlooked. Not that he ever became hilarious or sodden; drink merely deepened his natural moroseness and contrariness, and made him more difficult to handle.

I heard him mumbling to himself inside and felt further doubts. 'Bartholomew!' I called, knocking on the door.

The mumbling ceased at once. There was a pause, then the scrape of a chair and his heavy plodding steps. The door was opened a crack and he peered out, flashing a torch. 'Who is it?'

'Oh, good!' I said briskly. 'You're still up and dressed. Some man has met with a fatal accident at our gates. The police are coming and Mother Paul wants you to be there to lend a hand if necessary.'

He stared at me sourly, as though he wanted to refuse just out of principle. 'Can't a man have his rest in peace?' he grumbled. 'All right, I'll come.'

Mother Paul was waiting at the front door. She was wearing a black cloak over her habit, such as the nuns wore on the rare occasions they left the hostel, and also carried a flashlight. How she had managed to don the complicated robes in such a short time I do not know, for it is not as though nuns can cut corners over dressing.

'What's been going on, anyhow?' Bartholomew growled, just to let her know that he was not being wholeheartedly cooperative in spite of his presence.

Mother Paul placed a light hand on my arm. 'Poor Miss Allen found a dead man. An unpleasant experience for you, dear. Do you feel all right?'

'A bit shaken.'

'So glad it was you—always so sensible. Is the house quiet?'

'Not a sound!'

'It couldn't have happened at a better time,' Mother Paul remarked ingenuously. I laughed, but with a high uncertain note which made me think that I had better not laugh again for a while. The hand on my arm had grown firmer. 'Yes, we must all keep very calm.'

Bartholomew interposed grimly, 'I warns you if any females get hysterics I won't be answerable.'

'We won't,' she promised. 'Now we'll go along the drive to meet Mr. Wheeler. You did ring him, Mary?'

'He is coming at once.'

Mother Paul walked close beside me. 'Naturally we must not

begin to surmise about this dreadful business, but there are one or two odd features one can't help considering. Who is the poor creature and why must he choose our garden to die in?'

'Perhaps he had no option,' I replied unguardedly.

She sighed. 'Yes, I'm afraid that might be the case. Was it the shots, dear?'

'Shots?' I queried, puzzled. 'I didn't hear any shooting.'

'Then what was it that brought you down to the gates?'

I suddenly remembered Lorraine. If Mother Paul knew she was still out, there would be a terrific hullabaloo. We had enough to cope with already without sending a search-party out for Lorraine. 'A walk,' I said. 'I wanted a breath of air before going to bed. I wonder where Mr. Wheeler can be!'

Pat on his cue, the sergeant came meandering through the gates on his bicycle. His lamp lighted up our group. He dismounted ponderously, pushed his machine against a handy tree, took off his trouser clips, flexed his arms and then faced us. 'Now then!' he said indulgently. 'What's the trouble? Ah, good evening, Mother Mary St. Paul of the Cross—perhaps I should say good morning. One of your young ladies called me about an accident.'

'Yes, that's right, Sergeant—only it's wrong. Such a shocking thing! We think a man has been murdered. Mary dear, could you bring yourself to show Mr. Wheeler where he is?'

Sergeant Wheeler suddenly lost his pontifical manner and made a gulping sound in his throat. I don't think he expected anything worse than a somnolent drunk to eject from the grounds. Murder, as he was to tell us many times later, was not quite his cup of tea. When I said, 'He's right behind you,' he gave a well-defined jump. He pulled off his bicycle lamp and pushed gingerly into the bushes.

'I hope it is still there,' Mother Paul whispered anxiously. 'In books, you know—sometimes the bodies are removed in the interval between discovery and alarm. We would look so foolish.'

For my part I would have preferred agonies of embarrassment, and said so. 'This ain't books,' endorsed Bartholomew grimly, as the policeman's lamp lit up a momentary sickening view of staring, glassy eyes and slack mouth. The light travelled down to the dead man's hands, blood-stained and pathetic from their desperate attempt to staunch the mortal wound in his abdomen.

The sergeant picked his way back carefully to the gravel drive, and for a while seemed incapable of saying anything. 'We'll have to call in Homicide,' he announced, after some ponderous thinking. 'This sort of thing is not quite my cup of tea. Mother Mary St. Paul of the Cross, I would like to use your telephone.' She agreed readily, and he turned to Bartholomew. 'I want you to stay right here and keep an eye on things until I come back. And keep an eye on my bike too,' he added, heavily jocular. 'I had one pinched only last week.'

II

We congregated in stiff, unnatural attitudes in the library to await the arrival of Homicide detectives. Although it was Wheeler's second visit inside the hostel, even his official status did not seem to sustain him. He stood anchored uneasily in the middle of the room, fiddling with his cap as though he were shaping it on a potter's wheel. When Mother Paul took it away and invited him to sit down, he stared unhappily at his boots and appeared unable to meet her gaze. I felt sure he was remembering some stalwart nun of his parish schooldays who had drummed and prayed the Ten Commandments into his little bullet head.

Fortunately this state of affairs did not last long. We could hear cars arriving at the gates. Mother Paul flitted over to the windows and drew back the curtains.

'We'll have half the house downstairs to know what's going on. Mary dear, will you help me? So much quieter if they come in this way.'

I went over and raised one of the french windows. Sergeant Wheeler snatched up his cap thankfully. 'I'll just step outside and tell them, Mother Mary St. Paul of the Cross.'

The rectress whispered: 'Such a mouthful, poor man. You must drop him a hint, Mary. It makes me nervous.'

'I think the boot is on the other foot,' I said with a weary smile. I was feeling too tired to be complicated by tact.

Her eyes twinkled. 'Some of those early Irish nuns were very formidable,' she said, with her uncanny perspicacity.

The name of the detective Sergeant Wheeler brought back with him was O'Mara; a comparatively young man, very quietly spoken and courteous. Unlike the sergeant he seemed wholly at ease, as though his job had taken him into queerer places than convents, and he had developed an indifference to environment, high or low.

'This must be a great shock to you,' he said with an effortless sincerity, dropping his hat casually on the table. 'You must be very tired so I shall try not to keep you long.'

He gave a slight bow as he passed Mother Paul, then calmly seated himself at my desk, pushing aside the typewriter to make room for his notebook. More notes, I thought, but the small imp of humour danced briefly in my tired mind and I hoped the detective meant what he said.

After writing a few words, he raised his head and gave me a pleasant smile. 'Miss Mary Allen—have I the name correctly? Will you please tell me how you came to find the dead man? Just quite simply—in your own words.' What he meant was don't clutter up the evidence with extraneous matter, but he was too polite to say so. It seemed to justify my keeping Lorraine Lawrence's name out of my walk up the drive.

He heard me out in attentive silence, then made a few queries. 'You say it was just after one-thirty when you went for your stroll. How is it you are able to give the time so closely?'

'I had been waiting up to let the girls in,' I explained. 'You find the last hour rather tedious when you're a sitter. You keep glancing at the clock wondering how much longer.'

'Then I take it the last girl had just arrived home?'

'Yes!' I tried to answer without hesitation.

'I see you have a list here of those girls who were out this evening. There is one name you haven't crossed out yet—Lorraine Lawrence.'

'Oh!' I started up with a laugh, which sounded like a silly giggle capable of deceiving no one. 'Didn't I mark Lorraine off?' I took Sister Em's list out of his hand and ran a line through her name.

'You haven't put the time she came in,' he pointed out gently. I thought unkind things about Sister Em and, under the wretched man's gaze, wrote one-fifteen, hoping it would protect me from further questioning. There was a good chance that Lorraine had come in during the interval in which I had been calling Bartholomew.

'Did Miss Lawrence mention seeing anyone as she came in the gates?'

I was starting to regret protecting Lorraine. 'Not a word,' I said firmly. 'She went straight upstairs without speaking.'

'Well, I won't ask for her to be awakened now,' he remarked in a genial tone, that I did not like at all. 'To get back to your own movements—you were still observing the time even though your responsibility had ended with Miss Lawrence's arrival. After waiting for an interval of about twenty minutes you decided to go for a stroll.'

Tired and keyed up, I snapped: 'I wasn't waiting. I was tidying up in here. And, furthermore, if I'd known I was going to stumble into a corpse I most certainly wouldn't have taken that stroll. If I'd had any sense I would have done what I thought of doing—go to bed and let someone else do the finding in the morning.'

'Poor Sister Felician!' Mother Paul interjected. 'I'm so glad you didn't, Mary.'

Sergeant Wheeler looked rather shocked at my outburst, but O'Mara gave me another friendly smile. 'During that twenty minutes, Miss Allen, did you hear any sort of cry?'

'No cry, but I did hear a car somewhere—not near our gates though. It seemed to be in the main street.'

He made a note of it. 'Just one last question, Miss Allen. The name the man spoke as he died—are you quite certain it was Jess?'

'I'm certain that is what it sounded like.'

'Do you know anyone by that name?'

When I shook my head, he turned to Mother Paul. 'We've never had anyone by that name here to my knowledge,' she said promptly. She had been sitting miraculously still and quiet during my interrogation, but I could guess how her quick, darting mind had been absorbing and working on every word.

'Have you any idea who this man might be?' O'Mara asked her. 'Have there been any suspicious-looking characters loitering around your hostel?'

Sergeant Wheeler broke in apologetically. 'Quite a ring of down-and-outs come to the Sisters for meals, sir. I've warned them to send them away but—er—well, they just won't. No offence meant, Mother Mary St. Paul of the Cross.'

She gave him a winning smile, and when O'Mara asked if the dead man was one of these, replied: 'I'm afraid I can't help you there. Sister Berthe, who is in charge of the kitchen, sees these unfortunates and passes out food. Very naughty of her, I know, after what the sergeant said. I make a point of not seeing her do it. I do hope you won't want the poor soul to view the body—a most unpleasant sight.'

'There will be photographs,' he reassured her. 'You were not in the house when Miss Allen gave the alarm, I understand?'

'The nuns' cells are in a separate building. I was asleep when Mary called me on the house phone. Such a calm, sensible girl—she always does the right thing.' She beamed at me fondly, and I wriggled uncomfortably as O'Mara glanced quizzically in my direction. 'I told her to get Mr. Wheeler who was so kind to us last year.'

The sergeant's blush waxed as mine waned. 'An attempted burglary, sir,' he explained. 'A window was forced and a lot of mess made, but nothing taken.'

O'Mara made another note. 'I would like your report on that in the morning. You have it on file?'

'Oh yes, sir,' said Wheeler, shocked. 'Three pages.'

'Only three pages?' Mother Paul repeated incredulously. 'Sister Emerentiana took an inventory of the contents of the house. We all had to double-check it, do you recall, Mary? The only thing missing was my visiting cloak, but I'm sure the burglar wouldn't have wanted that so I dare say I mislaid it somewhere.'

Without a change of expression, O'Mara asked, 'You then joined Miss Allen?'

'No, she wasn't here when I arrived. But there is nothing odd in that. I had told her to rouse Bartholomew.'

'The handyman the Sisters employ,' Wheeler said. 'You met him at the gates, sir.'

'He didn't take much rousing,' I put in. 'He was up and dressed, but he still had his moan about being disturbed.'

'Well, you really can't blame him, dear,' Mother Paul said fairly. 'I must admit having felt a little put-out when you called me. We're not used to this sort of thing, Mr. O'Mara.'

'I'm sure you're not,' he replied gravely. 'However, I'm convinced that facts will come to light to indicate this—er—unfortunate incident is in no way connected with your establishment.'

'Good gracious, I hope not,' she returned placidly. 'I can't think of any reason why the poor man should have been murdered in our grounds.'

O'Mara rose and slipped his notebook into his pocket. 'I'm leaving a man on duty until the morning. My team will have done some preliminary work by now, but we will be back again when it is light. There may be some information as to the man's identity by then, but I would be grateful if you could arrange for those girls who were out last night to remain in until I see them.' He took out the list which he had pocketed coolly. 'Perhaps I'd better give you a copy of the names.'

Mother Paul shook her head. 'Sister Emerentiana will have one already,' she declared simply. 'She usually does lists in duplicate.'

'One last matter—I need not impress upon you the seriousness of this happening. The success of a murder investigation relies for the most part on immediate clues and the advantage to which they are used. For this reason I want both you and Miss Allen to be as discreet as possible and to refrain from telling anything but the bare facts. The name "Jess", for example, must not be mentioned to anyone, until we find out more about her identity.'

'Mary is the most discreet girl I know,' Mother Paul assured him earnestly, and he seemed to regard this remark as a promise to comply with his orders.

He went out by the window, followed by Sergeant Wheeler. Together Mother Paul and I shut and secured it, pulling the long curtains across. We remained there, silent and still, until the sound came of the cars being driven away. Then the rectress said on a sigh: 'I do hope that nice young man is right about its having nothing to do with us. However, we are not going to talk any more now. And we'll think tomorrow how to tell everyone about this shocking business. Let me out through the front door, Mary, and then go straight to bed.'

I saw her leave the house, then wearily climbed the stairs. But before seeking my own room, I went along to Lorraine Lawrence's door and opened it a crack. An unmistakable but extraordinary sound of snoring made me think that Lorraine was putting up a ludicrous pretence at sleeping. I pressed her bedroom switch, but the bright light did not cause her to stir. She was dead to the world, sprawled inelegantly on her back, with her mouth gaping and puffing like a landed fish's. Her discarded clothes lay scattered between the door and the bed, and—most remarkable of all—her face still retained its stale make-up.

III

Sister Emerentiana was the first to learn of the sensational overnight events. Going down to breakfast a few uneasy hours later, I found Mother Paul waiting to draw me aside. But she barely had time to inquire how I had slept when Sister Em rustled towards us, concern in her face. 'Mother Rectress, do you know there are a whole lot of men in our garden? They are trampling Sister Felician's seedlings.'

'Oh dear, have they arrived already? They are detectives, Sister.'

'Detectives?' Sister Em repeated, in a stunned way.

Mother Paul nodded. 'From Homicide—that is what Mr. Wheeler said, wasn't it, Mary? Such a classical word—Latin derivatives.'

'Sergeant Wheeler has been here? Surely not another burglary.'

'*Homo*—man, *cida*—slayer of,' Mother Paul derived in detached tones, while Sister Em turned pale and clutched at a chair.

'What has happened? Please tell me at once.'

'Mary dear, you're so good at facts. Tell Sister about last night.' I think Mother Paul was giving me a chance to rehearse my story.

Sister Emerentiana listened, shaking her head in dismay, but presently the habitual gleam of determination was back in her eye. 'What about the girls? Do they know of this dreadful murder?'

'Not yet, Sister.'

'Perhaps I had better go down to the refectory now and make an announcement,' Mother Paul said vaguely.

'No,' said Sister Em definitely. 'The less announcing the better. Mary can circulate quietly and tell them. Keep to the plain facts and there will be less chance of any fuss. We don't want hysterics on our hands.'

There was a sympathetic twinkle in the rectress's eye as I promised unenthusiastically to do my best.

The breakfast bell had sounded some time ago, but I went down the stairs slowly, trying to think of some way in which to break the news guaranteed not to incite hysteria.

'Stop blocking the gangway, Mary,' Fenella said, from behind. 'Are you going down or coming up?'

'Going down—unfortunately.'

She slid an arm through mine. 'No likee breakfast? I heard you wandering around at some ungodly hour. What's up?'

I hesitated for a moment, then said, 'Without wishing to put you off your own breakfast, I found a dead man at our gates last night.'

'How ghastly! No wonder you feel under the weather. Of all places to die! Most inconsiderate of him.'

'Very,' I agreed. 'But unfortunately he did not have time to pick and choose. All very messy, Fen, but the fact is he was murdered.'

'What!' Fenella promptly sat down on the stairs.

'For goodness' sake don't screech!' I begged. 'Sister Em said I was to break the news quietly. You're forbidden to have hysterics.'

'Tell me all at once—or I will have hysterics. Don't you drum your heels or something? Consider me about to drum.'

It was a relief to talk to her for a moment. She was always so gay and insouciant. But even so, I chose my words carefully, mindful of O'Mara's warning on discretion, and concentrated on the lighter side of the wretched affair. 'I woke Mother Paul up and she said how dreadful, get Bartholomew and Sergeant Wheeler. You remember him, don't you? That big blushing copper who came last year at the time of the burglary scare.'

Fenella nodded. 'He wore boots that squeaked when he tried to tip-toe. Mother Paul wanted me to ask him to walk naturally.'

'She wants me to drop a hint about his calling her Mother Mary St. Paul of the Cross. There were several moments like that last night.'

Fenella screwed up her eyes. 'What I missed! Who was the man and how was he murdered?'

'A knife in the guts,' I replied, with vulgar succinctness. 'At least, that is what we presume. I don't think they have found the actual weapon yet, nor do they know who the man is. The detective in charge of the case is coming back this morning, so we may learn more then. The place is already overrun with policemen. Sister Em thought she was seeing things.'

'Mary!' Fenella jumped up excitedly. 'I wonder if it is the man who asked us the time. Tommy said it was fishy. He was waiting, outside the gates, and when we came out he sort of edged up, as if he wanted to speak to us about something more important than the time.'

'Could have been someone's boy-friend. Quite a few went out last night. Which reminds me—Mr. O'Mara wants to interview you all. Keep your story of a mysterious stranger for him.'

'I'll see if I can't improve upon it—sinister scars and furtive manners. This is going to be fun!'

'Glad you think so,' I said hollowly. 'I'm sorry to be so unenterprising, but I would rather people weren't murdered on our doorstep. I think you had better go easy on the improvisations, Fen. O'Mara is not the type to appreciate your sense of humour.'

'What's he like?'

'Quite at ease, unimpressionable and most polite—rather nice in fact.'

'He sounds a pill,' Fenella voted unreasonably. 'Come on, Maria! Let's tell the others. Would you like a fanfare?'

'Definitely no! Sister Em said I was to circulate quietly.'

'It sounds a frightfully difficult thing to do before breakfast. How does one circulate quietly?'

'She didn't demonstrate. But maybe it's an idea to eat first. All right, open the door. Dying, we salute you, Caesar!'

I walked into the refectory, trying to live up to my uninteresting reputation of being calm and sensible. Two or three faces turned our way, but there was not the staring avid battery I half expected.

'Clare is pulling faces fraught with hidden meaning,' observed Fenella, joining me at the servery. 'Does she know about the you know what?'

'Not unless she has been eavesdropping,' I replied, selecting a slice of toast and pouring a cup of black coffee.

'My dear, don't mention the word! She would instantly demand a dawn meeting. Tell me—are you dieting or suffering from a homicidal hangover?'

'Work it out for yourself, and please don't choose the sausages if you plan to eat alongside.' I turned away, knocking against Verna Bassett who had come up behind us unobserved.

'Excuse me, girls—I just want another cuppa.' She smiled in her Uriah Heep fashion, sliding her gaze over the paucity of food on my tray. 'Aren't you feeling well this morning, Mary? Perhaps last night was too much for you. I always think—'

'What do you mean?' I asked sharply.

Her smirk grew even more obsequious, but her eyes were alert. 'How you do pounce on one. Not that you do as a rule, but then I thought you looked strange as soon as you came in.'

I looked her over for a moment. 'Come and sit with me while I have breakfast,' I said abruptly.

Verna squirmed—you would really think she deliberately imitated Uriah. 'Thank you, Mary. It's not often anyone asks me to sit with them. But are you sure? Clare would like you to join her and Christine.'

'You never miss a trick,' Fenella remarked admiringly. 'And so early in the day too. The rest of us may be jaundice-eyed, but little Verna knows everything that happens.'

She seemed delighted by this dubious compliment. 'Oh, not everything, Fenella. You do exaggerate so. But I have always been an onlooker, and it is such fun to put two and two together. Let's go over to Clare's table, and Mary can tell us all about it.'

'What do you mean by it?' I asked carefully.

She lowered her eyelids, still smiling. 'Why, whatever happens to be on your mind, of course.'

Clare saw us approaching and pushed used plates aside untidily. For all her tailored appearance and decisive ways, she was messy about domestic arrangements. We were always pitching in, as she called it, to help straighten her room before one of Sister Em's tours of inspection, or emptying a bath or turning off a light she had forgotten. An egg-cup of thick institutional china rolled off the table on to Christine Farrow's lap, and then to the floor as she made no attempt to catch it.

'There you are—your reflexes want tuning up,' Clare told her reprovingly.

Miss Farrow muttered something inaudible and ducked under the table. Clare turned the corner of her mouth towards me. 'About last night, old girl!'

I choked over my first sip of coffee. I was becoming allergic to those two words. Clare gave me a hearty thump between the shoulder-blades, and glanced at Christine, who was taking a longer time than necessary to find the egg-cup. 'All right now, Maria? You look a bit seedy—thought so when you came in. Don't let it get you down.'

'I won't,' I said. 'But how did you know? Who told you?'

'Who told me?' she queried, puzzled. 'Why, you did, old thing.'

I closed my eyes and thought back rapidly. 'No, I didn't,' I retorted, opening them. 'Unless I walked and talked in my sleep.'

Clare regarded me anxiously, and stopped talking like a parodied gangster. 'You're sure you're okay, Mary?'

'I always think the older you get the more you should look after yourself,' Verna chimed in. 'Health is such a precious thing. But Mary has some excuse for looking poorly this morning, haven't you, Mary?'

Clare turned on her. 'I could give you fifty yards on fitness,' she said severely, 'and I'm older than Mary. Just look at those shoulders of yours, and that spotty chin. You're as pimply as a schoolgirl—and not one of my girls either.'

'Oh, I know I look dreadful,' Verna said. 'I really must get round to a diet and exercise. But then, why should I bother? No one notices little me.'

'Mary!' Fenella said in clear tones. 'Did you think sausages would make you feel ill? I see Miss Farrow is leaving, and I don't blame you, my dear. But please defer judgement on Kilcomoden for a little while longer. You will find some purple patches.'

'Don't go yet,' Clare said, putting one of her square hands on the girl's slim, supple wrist. 'You don't want to let these chumps worry you. They're good kids, actually. Mary—' she turned her profile and winked significantly.

Miss Farrow was flying her usual storm signals at the interference. 'Let her go, Clare. She was in all last night, so it won't matter if she's not here.'

Relaxing her hold, Clare gave me another puzzled glance, while Verna leaned forward eagerly. Christine Farrow moved away and then paused abruptly, looking down at me for a moment with a tense little frown between her dark brows.

'Git while the gittin's good,' Fenella advised cheerfully, and she moved off slowly.

Clare said: 'Mary, you sound quite queer. What doesn't matter because the girl was in last night?' She glanced at Fenella and then back.

'Look here, what's wrong with you two? You're both behaving like cuckoos this morning.'

'The floor's all yours, Mary,' Fenella said. 'Go into circulation.'

'Presently,' I replied, and addressed Clare. 'You tell me what you were talking about first.'

She shook her head in a dumbfounded way. 'Maybe I'm the one who's bats. Last night—'

'Clare, please don't use those two words again or I'll have hysterics.'

Fenella broke in gleefully, 'Don't forget Sister Em says hysterics are taboo.'

Clare began to get cross. 'Look, Mary, didn't we agree last—well, yesterday evening, dash you!—to take the Farrow girl in hand? I was well on the way to getting her to agree to some tennis this morning—in fact, it only wanted you to back me up to clinch the matter, when you started all this rot and she shied off.'

'I'm so sorry,' I said soothingly. 'I forgot about our chat. I'm afraid we'll have to shelve the problem of Miss Farrow for the time being. We are going to be rather occupied with the police.'

'Police?' Clare muttered, incredulously.

'Custodians of the law,' Fenella explained obligingly.

'Perhaps we'd better quit the facetiousness, Fen,' I said quietly. 'All right, Verna! Here it is! Last night I found a murdered man in the shrubbery near the gates.'

There was a moment's silence. Verna's gaze was lowered, and as she often wore that thin, secretive smile, her expression did not convey much. Clare, however, had turned pale under her tanned skin. She was badly shocked, and tried to relieve her feelings by blurting out tritely, 'Bad show, what!'

Fenella winced with me. 'Grim!' she agreed. 'Mary says the police are crawling around like flies outside, looking for clues, and anyone who was out last night has to be interviewed by a stuffed-shirt detective from Russell Street.'

'You're making that up,' Clare said uneasily. 'It's got nothing to do with us. The idea is too ridiculous.'

'No, she's right,' I said. 'Mr. O'Mara requested Mother Paul to keep the girls at home until he saw them this morning.'

'O'Mara? Is he the detective type? What's he like?'

'Quiet and pleasant. There is no need to feel nervous.'

Clare snorted. 'I'm not scared.'

Verna leaned over and touched my arm. 'But why our grounds, I wonder? And who is he?'

I gave her the censored story, but it seemed to satisfy her. She leaned back again, nodding and smiling complacently.

'You look like a cat licking its chops,' Fenella observed, eyeing her critically.

Verna got up from the table. 'I've just had such a funny little thought.'

'Okay, let's have it,' Fenella sighed. Verna's thoughts were either barbed or trite, but never funny.

'Our poison pen! Perhaps she knows something about the murder.'

'That's a thought you can forget about,' I said swiftly. 'Clare's right when she says this has nothing to do with Kilcomoden, but the less gossip and speculation the better. Do you understand, Verna?'

'Oh, I quite agree with you, Mary. You know how I loathe people who gossip. But,' she continued, unmoved by the derisive sounds from Clare and Fenella, 'it is odd, isn't it—having two nasty things happening in our midst. One can't help feeling there might be a connection.'

'Well, this one can!' Clare said trenchantly. 'Those letters are only damn silly nonsense, but murder is quite another dish of spaghetti. So cut along, and don't try to make mischief.' She waited until Verna was out of earshot, then added: 'That should fix her. She's a real trouble-maker, that girl. If she took up some sport now—'

'Perhaps she is going to ask the police to play hopscotch with her now,' Fenella suggested. 'I can't think of any other reason why she should make such a bee-line upstairs.'

Clare surged up. 'Why, the little—'

'Leave her,' I said, stacking cup, saucer and plate together. 'She won't get far. Sorry about the tennis, Clare—after all your good work too.'

'That's okay, old girl. Quite understandable under the circs. Regarding that other little matter we discussed last night, that Verna just brought up—someone had a shot at the Cunningham kid before me. I guess we'd better leave things be. She is already in one of her moods.'

'Drat the girl!' I said irritably. 'And she'll be one for the interview queue. Fen, be an angel and grab as many as you know went out, while I handle Alison.'

Fenella snatched the carafe from the table. 'I'll arm myself in case of hysterics. Come on, Clare! You're used to managing girls in bulk.'

I walked across the room to where Alison sat alone, ostentatiously reading a book as she picked sparingly at her breakfast—a sure sign that she was in her nobody-loves-me mood. Her emotions ran in a sort of cycle, and this aura of pathetic loneliness with which she now surrounded herself was usually a prelude to feverish self-assertion, when she was liable to the most outrageous behaviour.

'Hullo!' I said, perching on the edge of the table and tweaking the book away. 'Detective story, eh? Any good?'

She folded her hands in her lap and stared blankly over my shoulder without speaking.

I rippled through the pages. 'Funny the vicarious thrill you can get out of this sort of thing.'

'I don't know what that word means,' she said coldly, and held out her hand. 'My book, please.'

I put it into her hand and then kept drawing it away before her fingers had time to close on it. 'I have often wondered how we would react if we had to face such startling events in real life.'

She made a sudden grab at the book, which I eluded. 'Damn you, give it to me!' she cried, half-laughing in her exasperation.

'How would you react, Alison?'

'I'm not interested. All I want is to be left alone. I hate this place and everyone in it.'

'You mean you wouldn't be interested even if a murder took place right in our midst? Well, perhaps not in our midst—that would be rather forcing your interest. Say somewhere in the garden.'

'I wish you wouldn't tease,' she said fretfully. 'You're only trying to be nasty.'

'No, indeed—kind, but firm.'

'Kind! Who's kind to me in this place? I get so miserable sometimes I feel like throwing myself in the river—truly I do.'

'I wouldn't do that if I were you. You might get wet.'

She bit her lips together like an angry child. 'You're just being horrible. And look at those girls staring at me. I know what they're thinking—there's accusation and dislike in every eye,' she declared dramatically.

I glanced over my shoulder. Clare and Fenella had done their work well, and groups of girls were gathered together, whispering excitedly.

'Sorry to disappoint you, Alison,' I said meekly, 'but I'm afraid they are staring at me.'

'That's only because you're talking to a pariah,' she replied, determined to maintain her role of unwanted loneliness. The effect was rather spoiled by Jean and Betty joining us. You can't be an outcast when you have three people with you, pulling you willy-nilly into the conversation.

'Alison! Has Mary been telling you? Isn't it too thrilling!' They were arm in arm, inseparable friends again.

'Glad to see you two are buddies once more,' I greeted them.

'Mary, you really are the most amazing person! To think that you walked into the refectory and callously ate your brekky without so much as breathing a word. Don't you think she is amazing, Ali?'

'They mean dull, not amazing,' I explained.

The pariah was waging a losing battle with curiosity. There was something thrilling in the air, and Alison throve on excitement. It was only when her life followed a prosaic routine that she became difficult. She stood up, shedding the pathetic aloofness. Her eyes sparkled and her cheeks became flushed. She was now one of the girls, shrill and hyperbolical. 'What's thrilling? Mary, you're frightfully mean not saying anything. What has happened? Quick, quick—tell me!'

'My dear—a murder! A lovely gory murder! And all the most gorgeous looking detectives looking for clues in the garden. We're off to try our luck.'

'No, no—wait for me!' Alison cried, hopping from one foot to the other like a child before a Christmas tree. 'Tell me more. Who's been murdered?'

'Here, steady!' I said, gripping her arm.

She tried to struggle free. 'Let me go! I want to go with Jean and Bet. Let me go, blast you!'

Fenella dashed up, brandishing the carafe. 'Cold water treatment needed?'

'Not imminently, but stick around. Here, pull yourself together, Alison.'

'I want to go with the girls,' she repeated, on a high note. 'If you don't let me go, I'll scream and scream.'

'Ha! A sure sign of hysterics,' said Fenella, with the air of one making a profound diagnosis. 'Scream away, old thing. I've always wanted to chuck water over someone.'

'Dry up, Fen. Listen, Alison—you don't want to go with those two hen-wits. I know more about the murder than they do.'

'I don't believe you,' she choked furiously. 'You're just trying to keep me out of things. How can you know more?'

'She found the body!' Fenella announced, in sepulchral tones. Alison stopped struggling and turned dilated eyes towards me.

'Yes, truly,' I nodded. 'Come on now, relax. I'll tell you all about it.'

IV

Lorraine Lawrence had not come down to breakfast. I went in search of her, entering unceremoniously into her room where she was seated in front of the mirror, anxiously surveying her face from every angle. She was dressed in a pencil-slim grey skirt and a high-necked black jumper. Her fair hair was tied back in a pony tail—a style that did not suit her when she had no make-up on. I think I startled her, for although she glanced away carelessly, her attitude became tense.

'Do come in,' she said. 'I couldn't have heard the knock.'

I shut the door, leaned against it and talked to her reflection. 'You sound sweeter than ever this morning. Good party?'

She ducked her head, rummaging in a drawer. 'Marvellous! Stephanie always has the most fascinating guests.'

Stephanie was the proprietress of the shop where Lorraine was employed. She had a top-floor flat in the city somewhere. Lorraine regularly assisted at the parties she gave.

'A pretty rum lot from what I've heard,' I remarked, watching her work foundation cream into her smooth, young cheeks.

She smiled pityingly and made a gesture. 'Of course you can only judge from this type of environment. You have rather a narrow outlook, Mary. I wish I could get away from here. I feel so—so caged in. Stephanie often wonders how I stand it.'

'Why don't you leave then?'

'Oh, I shall soon—when my people come back from overseas.' Lorraine told some good stories about her unknown parents, even though they did not quite match up in accuracy. 'Ah, yes, your people—the wealthy pastoralists who are making a luxury world tour.'

She gazed at her reflection dreamily. 'Of course, they may send for me any minute now. When Mummy was in Paris, she was invited to all the best dress shows. I could model over there any time I wanted.'

'I'll get up a collection among the girls to send you to Paris,' I promised. 'By the way, what time did you come in last night?'

The dreamy look vanished. She shot me a frightened glance. 'Oh— one-ish! I found the door open so I didn't bother to disturb you.'

'I've marked you down on Sister Em's list as one-fifteen. Do you think you could keep that time in your pretty empty head? One-fifteen!'

She picked up a bottle of polish remover and began to get rid of last night's crimson varnish. 'Why are you so concerned that I should remember the time?'

'Because I all but got myself into a frightful mess over you last night. Now this is your story for the police. You came through the gates and along the drive without seeing or hearing anyone. I let you in and you went straight upstairs to bed.'

Lorraine swung round and stared wide-eyed. 'The police? I'm not telling any story to the police. I don't want to see them.'

'Don't get shrill! And mind that stuff. You're dripping it on the floor.'

She hunched herself in a most un-model like attitude, with her hands grasped together on her knees. 'I feel sick. They can't see you when you're sick, can they? Mary, you've got to stop them.'

'Here, calm down,' I said, puzzled. 'There's no need to get the wind up. They would never suspect you of being involved in anything so ghastly.'

She looked up at me with pathetic eagerness. 'You're sure? You're not just saying that?'

'Certain sure,' I answered, without thinking. 'They would see in a minute that you wouldn't have the guts to knife anyone.'

She mouthed at me blankly, but the fear that had been in her eyes a moment ago faded. I suddenly realized that we had been at cross purposes. She didn't know anything about the murder. How could she when she had not yet left her room? While I hesitated, she snatched at the initiative. 'Yes, I heard there had been some accident,' she said coolly. 'So that is why the police are here. What happened?'

'No accident—murder!' But she took it calmly along with the rest of my story, that I was now capable of chanting in my sleep. 'Mr. O'Mara will probably check on your movements fairly closely. Just stick to the story I gave you. You didn't see or hear anyone, and you didn't pause to chat with me when I let you in. Have you got it?'

She turned back to the mirror, plying her lipstick. 'I suppose you think I should be grateful for your protection?'

'Not at all. I was mainly considering my own peace of mind. The less complications the police find at Kilcomoden the sooner they will depart. But if O'Mara sees you looking furtive as you did a minute ago, he'll keep sniffing around to find out why. An anonymous letter writer in the house I can stand—just, but I draw a line at murder suspects.'

She bristled. 'Are you suggesting I wrote those notes?'

I smiled faintly and opened the door. 'No, I don't think it is you. You would have made certain of my receiving one.'

She stood up and posed nonchalantly, one hand on the dressing-table, the other at her slim waist. 'I don't dislike you, dear, if that is what you mean. Actually, I feel terribly sorry for you.'

'Nice of you, Lorraine,' I returned meekly, as I left, 'but don't break your heart.' I went along the corridor, thinking nastily of all the blondes I had known to fade into insignificance before their thirties.

The door of my own bedroom opened and Christine Farrow appeared on the threshold.

'Lost your bearings?' I inquired politely.

A little flush crept up under her pale skin, and she swung the two dark curtains of her loose hair forward to hide it.

'I wanted to speak to you,' she muttered. 'I—I wasn't prying, if that's what you think.'

I laughed and pushed her back into the room. 'Sorry, but I was feeling foul-tempered for the moment.'

She stood in the centre of my lambswool rug with her hands clasped behind her back, struggling to unbend. I moved her gently aside so as to strip the bed. She was the sort of person who always stood in doorways you wanted to go through or in front of drawers that you wanted to open.

'Well, come on,' I urged, heaving the mattress over with a grunt. 'What did you want to say?'

'It's—it's about last night,' she began hesitantly.

I held the sheet between my hands for a moment. 'Oh yes, last night. What about last night?' Here was someone else who had not been present at the breakfast murder session.

The struggle was terrific. I could imagine her as a leggy, black-browed child standing rebelliously before a fond, chiding parent, dying to give in but not knowing how to without losing face. 'I want to—to apologize,' she announced stiffly, without looking in the least apologetic. 'I was very rude to you.'

I flapped the sheet out briskly and tucked it in. 'Is that all? I mean—were you rude? Oh yes, I remember now—in the common-room.' I dragged at the blankets I had thrown over a chair, and nudged Christine's foot off one corner where they trailed on the floor. 'Forget it—you didn't worry me. I thought you were going to ask about the murder. Would you mind tucking in the other side for me?'

'What did you say?' she asked, startled.

'Tuck in the other side. It will save my having to trot round and back all the time. I'll come and lend a hand with your bed then, if you like.'

'You're being deliberately provoking,' she declared fiercely. 'You know what I mean.'

'Sorry,' I said again. 'I'm just a little tired of repeating the same story. Some strange man was knifed at our gates late last night, but it's no use asking me anything because that is all I know. Pass over the spread like a good girl—it's hanging on the other chair.'

She handed it over automatically. 'But you must know something,' she burst out. 'You can't just leave me in the dark like that. You're keeping something from me on purpose.'

'Why should I do that? The murder has nothing to do with us here at Kilcomoden. It just so happened that the killer met up with his victim at our gates. Bad luck for us, but there it is!'

'Worse luck for the poor bloke,' Fenella said, as she came in on the end of the sentence. 'Maria, the quartermaster is in a froth. She wants you to help draw up some list or other before the cops arrive. You'd better make tracks.'

Christine Farrow muttered something inaudible and left the room. Fenella jerked her head. 'What's eating her? She looks even more like death warmed up this morning.'

I ran a swift comb through my hair, dabbed on some make-up and found a clean handkerchief. 'She doesn't like strange men being murdered either. How are things downstairs?'

'Oh, my dear!' Fenella threw out expressive hands. 'Verna is sliding around like a hungry snake. Clare went out for one of her brisk tramps "to take the nasty taste", etc. She's frightfully indignant because the police sent her back indoors. The same thing happened to Jean and Betty. Verna stayed the distance longer, having a more unobtrusive technique. Alison, of course, is trying to make capital out of the situation. She would just love to be suspected of murder. Then to cap all, Mabel Jones keeps popping along with futile messages from Mrs. Carron-Toyle. The old hag is dying to know what the commotion is about. Poor Jonesy has been trying to gather titbits with which to placate her, but each time she gets sent back for more.'

We went downstairs. In a babble of talk, girls were wandering around the hall and in and out of the common-room, while Sister Em, a note block in her hand, was vainly attempting to organize them into staying put, so as to weed out those whom O'Mara wanted to see. She gave me a sharply reproachful glance as though I had lapsed badly, and told me that Mother Rectress was in the library.

'Have the police arrived yet?'

'Any minute now—and I'm not nearly ready. Just glance through this list, will you please, Mary? Have I all the names, and in their correct order? It is most difficult—if only the girls would co-operate. I've never known such a thoughtless lot of girls.'

'Don't worry about them,' I said soothingly. 'Mr. O'Mara

wouldn't expect you to go to all this trouble. Fen, herd them all into the common-room and keep them amused.'

She made a face and went off unwillingly as Sister Em made further sheep-dog runs in an endeavour to corral them.

I went into the library. Mabel Jones was there, talking to Mother Paul. 'So you will come, won't you, Mother Rectress? She is most anxious to have a clear-cut account of this distressing affair. Those are her exact words—a clear-cut account!'

Mother Paul directed a fond smile at me, cast a brief yet longing glance at her bulky manuscript near the typewriter, and then said in her disarming way: 'I'm not very good at being clear-cut about anything, I'm afraid. Vague outlines are more in my line—as Mary here will vouch.'

I knew what was coming and also gazed fondly at my littered table. How good it would be to sit down there and muddle and moan my way through Mother Paul's incomprehensible footnotes and appendices. 'Mary dear, Mrs. Carron-Toyle—do you think you could—'

'Mr. O'Mara will be here any minute now,' I interrupted firmly. 'Tell Mrs. Carron-Toyle that it is quite impossible for anyone to come at the moment.'

Miss Jones looked flustered. 'Oh dear! What shall I say? She will be so upset. You must know, dear Mother Rectress, this dreadful murder almost brought on a heart attack.'

'In that case,' I intervened, 'it would be better if she were left alone. Tell her that in view of her poor health, Mother Paul is most anxious for her to remain undisturbed. You don't mind, Mother Paul?'

'Very tactful, dear,' she nodded. 'And I will try to visit her as soon as the police have finished in the house,' she added, and Miss Jones brightened a little.

I followed Jonesy to the door and said in a low voice: 'I was a bit anxious about you last night, not knowing whether you had come in or not. You don't often use the side door.'

She gave a nervous titter. 'I didn't want to disturb you as it was so late.'

'Was it a good show?' I asked, watching her fidget with the buttons of the shapeless mauve cardigan she wore over a rayon dress, printed with red and purple grapes.

'Yes—that is—well, actually I left half-way through. I was concerned about Mrs. Carron-Toyle, you know. She was feeling so bad that she had me call Dr. Yorke.'

'If you left half-way through the programme you couldn't have been very late,' I pointed out.

There was a pause, then she said breathlessly: 'I must go back to Mrs. Carron-Toyle now. She'll be wondering where I am.'

I put a hand on her bony arm and felt it twitch. 'Does she know when you came in?'

Her eyes blinked rapidly. 'No, she was asleep. She was snoring.'

'Okay, Jonesy,' I said quietly. 'You came home at half-time. You couldn't raise me so you used Mrs. Carron-Toyle's private entrance. The police want to see those who were out last night, but they will be primarily concerned with the ones who were late.'

She stared at me for a moment without speaking, then turned and hurried off.

Mother Paul, who had been poking through her manuscript during the conversation, looked up. 'Poor creature! Such a disagreeable position to be in. But I really think Mrs. Carron-Toyle wanted to be rid of her last night. So odd of her, don't you think, dear?'

I was trying to think of a suitable way to phrase 'not so odd, when her fancy-pants medico was coming', when Sister Em bustled in to arrange the room in such a way as she considered necessary for the police to conduct their inquiry.

'Now, Mother Rectress, you will sit here—rather away from the table, with Mary a little behind you.' We sat down, while Sister Em regarded us with the air of a stage manager.

'But, Sister, what about yourself?'

'I shall be much too busy to sit down. Now stay just so, and I'll go out into the hall so as to be ready to let the police in at once.' She gave one last glance around to ensure everything was in order and rustled out.

Mother Paul broke the unnatural stillness by saying apprehensively, 'Oh dear, I hope nothing goes amiss after all Sister's good organization.'

With farce-like timing, O'Mara, followed by Sergeant Wheeler, appeared on the terrace outside the window. 'Good morning,' the

Homicide detective said, entering the room. After glancing from Mother Paul to me and back again, he seemed to become aware of something wrong. 'I'm sorry if we startled you. I thought if we came in this way we would cause less disturbance.'

'Most considerate of you,' Mother Paul rejoined, but cast a dismayed look in the direction of the door, as though she could see through it to where Sister Em was pacing patiently in the hall, and occasionally going to the common-room to shush the chattering girls.

'I have some good news for you,' O'Mara announced. He was looking as carefully groomed as he had on the first visit, but faint, tired lines in his face showed that he had been up all night. Sergeant Wheeler, being on night duty, was merely working overtime. 'We are satisfied that this killing has nothing to do with your establishment. We have identified the man and hope shortly to make an arrest.'

I felt an enormous surge of relief but Mother Paul said, 'Oh!' in a blank sort of fashion, as though she experienced a sense of anticlimax.

'He was one of those habitual petty criminals, who start off as hoodlums and are in and out of gaol most of their fives,' the detective enlarged, as though he owed her something more.

'He must have been more than petty to get himself murdered,' Mother Paul remarked. 'Though, to be sure, it is a dreadful way to earn distinction.'

O'Mara did not speak for a moment, and I wished Mother Paul wouldn't try to hit nails on the head. Then he said, 'Our theory is that Braddock—or Bradley, as he was sometimes known—was a victim of some gang feud.'

'I suppose they were after him, and the poor creature tried to take shelter in our grounds,' Mother Paul said compassionately, and turned to me. 'What a pity, Mary, that he didn't come to the house. You could have hidden him.' I gaped at her, horrified at the thought.

'She probably would have been murdered, too,' O'Mara observed dryly.

'Then you won't want to see any of the girls—or Sister Berthe?' Mother Paul was making brave efforts to salvage something from the wrecked organization.

'No, it won't be necessary to worry them. Some of my men will be about for a further time. We are making a routine search for the murder weapon—an unusually long-bladed knife like a bayonet is suggested by our pathologist. If the killer took it away with him, which I think is most probable, then we won't have to impose upon you again.'

Mother Paul said warmly, as though to make up for her first lack of appreciation: 'Well, this is good news indeed. How clever of you to solve the case so quickly. Burglary is bad enough, but murder is—what was it you said, Mr. Wheeler? Something mild and understating.'

'Another cup of tea,' he mumbled obediently, instead of pretending not to hear her.

'Ah, yes, your burglary,' O'Mara said easily. 'I glanced through Wheeler's report. An entry was forced but nothing taken, is that correct? Under those circumstances there is no way in which we can tie up the two incidents. Unless,' he added, even more genially, 'you can suggest what the burglar was after?'

Three

I

We all went back to work on Monday, flat and exhausted after the excitement of the week-end. The garden at Kilcomoden was swept clear of detectives, still unsuccessful in the search for the murder weapon, and Sister Felician, who was very old and very Irish, was once more pottering around with a gardening fork. She had gone into hiding the previous day, for in her ancient clouded mind the word 'police' was synonymous with 'Black and Tans'.

The only ones left in the house were Mrs. Carron-Toyle, her unfortunate companion, and Alison Cunningham, who was enjoying one of her out-of-work spells. We were all rather glad to get away from Alison, who had behaved in an intense sort of way all Sunday, as though to make up for the flat outcome of the murder inquiry. As Clare observed, 'One of these days that silly kid will play-act herself round the bend.'

II

It was my custom to drop into the Green Lounge tea-room early afternoon on my way back from the bank. The place was usually empty at that hour, but the tea was always scalding hot, the biscuits fresh, and there were back numbers of glossy American magazines to glance through at better leisure.

Today, however, there was another customer near my favourite corner table. He lowered a copy of the *Saturday Evening Post* to receive his tray from the waitress, waited until the girl had taken my order, and then said quietly across the intervening space, 'Good afternoon, Miss Allen.'

I stopped goggling with an effort. 'Well, this is quite a coincidence,' I said feebly.

'Yes, isn't it,' O'Mara agreed. He got up and calmly moved his tray to my table. 'Do you mind?' he asked, sitting down in the opposite chair.

'Not at all,' I replied, but with an edge to my politeness. 'Please have your tea. I'm sure you are in a hurry.'

'No, I'll wait,' he said, impervious to the hint. He reached across to my magazine, which lay open at a high-powered article on the penitentiary system in the States. 'You find this interesting reading?'

'I've hardly had the chance to find out,' I retorted.

'There are many conflicting ideas about the right approach to the problems of incarceration and rehabilitation of criminal lawbreakers. Social workers present the theory—ah, here is your tea now?' He tossed the magazine casually on to the adjoining table, and said to the waitress, 'Just the one check, please.'

I started to protest, but he glanced at me with such an air of surprise that the protest sounded ungracious. There is a no more frustrating barrier than that of extreme courtesy. I decided to try the O'Mara method. 'Shall I pour out for both? Or have you a special system?'

'Thank you.' He pushed his cup and saucer nearer, and the phoney conversation along. 'In America, I believe tea is served as a pot of hot water with a muslin bag of leaves attached, which you immerse.'

'No wonder Americans mostly drink coffee. Do you take sugar?'

'After you. Do you come to this place often, Miss Allen?'

'Every day. But I don't remember seeing you here before. In fact,' I added reflectively, stirring my tea, 'I consider your being here today is rather strange.'

'Strange? How is that?' he asked, raising his brows slightly.

'I should have thought you would be out combing the underworld for your killer.'

'It is not the best time of day for combing,' he said gravely, but with a lurking twinkle, 'but just to set your mind at rest, we have three raids planned for tonight.'

'Aren't you a little unwise telling me that?' I asked, turning the dish of biscuits around. 'A careless word of mine might spoil your show.'

'An unlikely contingency. Your Mother Rectress seems to think a great deal of your discretion and good sense. Would you care for one of my scones?'

'No, thank you. You consider Mother Paul's judgement can be relied upon?'

'She impressed me as a remarkably shrewd woman.'

'Funny!' I remarked. 'Most people think she is vague and naive, whereas she sees and understands things that go on under the surface better than anyone. If she were here now, for instance . . .' I stopped, eyeing him narrowly. I had once told Mother Paul of my afternoon tea haunt.

'Do go on,' he encouraged, with a smile.

'She does not need to be here. She told you where to find me, and knows exactly what your motive is in arranging this meeting.'

'Do you know my motive, Miss Allen?'

'No, but I can guess your being here is no coincidence. Seeing under surfaces is not one of my accomplishments.'

'Then I am glad it is you and not your rectress. Over-acute people can sometimes be an embarrassment to the police. Will you have some more tea?'

I shook my head. 'I must go back to the office now.' I found my gloves and began to draw them on slowly, waiting for the detective to say more. When he did not speak, I pushed my chair back and rose. 'Well, thanks for the tea.'

'Just one moment, Miss Allen!' He got up too, frowning at his hat which he swung round on one finger. The light from the window was full on his face. He looked very tired. 'Murder very often has repercussions,' he said quietly. 'If you should even feel—shall we say—not quite happy about matters at your hostel, will you let me know?'

I was suddenly aware that my heart was beating faster. 'Very well,' I replied calmly, 'but that too is an unlikely contingency.'

He took a card from his pocket, leaned over the table and wrote on the back of it. 'My extension number at Russell Street. Will you keep it?'

I took the card reluctantly and put it into my bag. 'Nothing is likely to happen,' I repeated. 'The murder has nothing to do with us. You said so yourself.'

'Good-bye, Miss Allen.'

'Good-bye,' I echoed automatically.

I walked slowly back to the office, curbing an impulse to go home to see if all were well. But as the afternoon wore on, the impulse became a frantic desire. I considered telephoning Kilcomoden and then wondered at once what I could say. If Mother Paul answered she would immediately guess my reason had something to do with O'Mara. I was certain that he had obtained my direction from her, and I wanted to free myself from his ambiguous warnings before coping with Mother Paul's gently persistent inquiries. Even if someone else answered, the fact that I had called would reach her ears in some way. I was fully in agreement with O'Mara's statement that over-acute people can be embarrassing.

I thrust the telephone away only to draw it back again as a cunning idea came into my mind. Supposing I rang, but did not speak. If anything had happened at Kilcomoden—anything really serious, which of course was quite ridiculous—some sort of emotion would be reflected in the voice of the person who answered.

I dialled the number swiftly, and prepared to wait. At that hour there would be no one near the telephone. I could visualize its ringing to the placid emptiness of the hall. But after only two vibrations, the receiver was lifted. I had a second or two to register this as being unusual, then a faint voice said 'Hello.' I cleared my throat, hoping to encourage the voice nearer for I could not recognize it, let alone judge anything from the tone. It was not Mother Paul, who always answered with a lilting 'Yes?'—or Sister Emerentiana who briskly recited the number.

Then the voice spoke again, this time high and clear. 'Yes, this is Miss Cunningham. I'll have that fitting at the time you suggested.'

I put the receiver down gently, and rubbed the palm of my hand dry, a wide grin relaxing my tensed jaw. So much for O'Mara and his repercussions! There was no finer barometer to trouble than Alison. She wouldn't be confirming a booking with her long-suffering dressmaker when she could be revelling in emotional disturbances. I turned to my littered desk with a lighter heart, and for the next hour my concentration showed some improvement.

It was when I realized that accumulation of work would keep me overtime that my mercurial anxiety mounted again, and I longed for the moment when I would be seated in the refectory at Kilcomoden, listening to the dinner-table bicker and banter and knowing that all was well. I felt resentment towards O'Mara for planting the seeds of doubt. It was impossible not to think of many things about which I was not quite happy. Although he had declared at first that the murder of the criminal, Braddock, had nothing to do with us, there must be some connection between either the killer or the dead man with a member of Kilcomoden. It could be that he still suspected that the name Braddock had whispered belonged to one of us.

I thought back hard through the frightening confusion of those moments of discovery, whispering the name feebly as the dying man had breathed it. But there was no mistaking the soft consonant and the sibilant ending. It could be no other name but Jess. Who was she—the mysterious woman called Jess?

III

Dinner was half-way over by the time I reached the refectory. There was a tacit rule that everyone stayed in on Monday nights, and I was relieved to see that it was unbroken that night. Moreover, there was the customary flat and slightly surly Monday atmosphere which was reassuring in its mundaneness.

I greeted those nearby lightheartedly, and attacked the shepherd's pie with gusto.

'As though you've just come in from the fields,' Fenella observed. 'What makes you so revoltingly hearty?'

'Sheer joy of living,' I returned blithely. 'Normal living. I never before realized the value of uneventfulness. Bread, please, Jeanie! I like your new hair-do.'

'You said last week it made me look like a golliwog,' Jean stated without rancour.

'Well, I like it tonight. You look piquante. How did everyone get on today? Happy in their work?'

Betty Martin leaned across. 'Mary, breathe!'

'Onions in the pie! It tastes well tonight, don't you think? I wonder why we don't have it more often.'

With superciliously raised brows, Lorraine drawled: 'What plebeian tastes you have, Mary. Personally, I couldn't touch a morsel. It made me feel quite ill. But I suppose it all depends on what you have been brought up.'

'You, of course, were weaned on caviar and champagne,' Fenella remarked.

'Well, it's a break to see some jolly faces for a change,' Clare's boisterous tones broke in. She had been over to the servery to collect puddings, and held four compotes of stewed fruit in her big, capable hands.

'Mary is being a little ray of sunshine,' Jean said. 'She rejoices in the dullness of life.'

'Same here,' Clare agreed, setting the plates down in her slapdash way so that some apple juice spilled on the cloth. 'Any more alarms and excursions round here, and I look for new digs.'

'There won't be,' I said, and spoke more seriously than I had intended. They glanced at me immediately. I threw the ball back to Clare to take their attention. 'You don't think it likely, do you?'

She sat down and ran a hand over her crisp hair in her habitual gesture when perplexed. 'Shucks, I dunno! But sometimes murders have—what do you call it—'

'Repercussions,' someone suggested helpfully.

My heart gave a nasty jump at the familiar word. 'Rubbish!' I said lightly. 'What do you know about murders?'

'Nothing, I suppose, but. . .' she pushed her plate aside and leaned her elbows on the table. 'Well, take a suicide, for example. Mind you, I'm only going on what I read in newspapers. Someone gets the bright idea and jumps off Sydney Harbour bridge. Then a whole lot of other fools follow suit. Wouldn't you say they were definite repercussions of the first suicide?'

A small silence met this grim theory. Fenella broke it by saying plaintively: 'I won't feel safe until all knives are locked away. Betty dear, are you brandishing yours at me or are you merely going to butter your bread?'

'Clare is only trying to impress us, Fenella,' Lorraine said. 'These school-marms are all the same.'

'You're quite impressionable enough as you are, my good child,' Clare told her severely. 'You think you are sophisticated and full of the know-how, but you are really just a silly little girl. And now call me a jealous, dried-up old maid!'

Lorraine, who had been about to say something like that, compressed her lovely mouth into a hard, angry line. She sprang up ungracefully, but Fenella pulled her back. 'Relax, gorgeous! You don't look nearly so stunning when you become emotional. Where's our ray of sunshine? Mary, pull us out of this scene before Lorraine disintegrates before our eyes.'

'If I were Lorraine I'd tear you to bits and throw the scraps into the rubbish bin,' I declared, giving her a sympathetic smile. She came in for more than her share of verbal ragging.

Her brown eyes were still blazing, but she had recovered some of her poise. 'So kind of you to champion me, Mary,' she said sweetly, 'but please do not bother. I'm quite capable of looking after myself.'

'You're not,' Clare stated in her downright fashion. 'And that reminds me—you may think that Mrs. Garland you are always talking about is just too marvellous, but take my advice and don't get too intimate.'

'Garland?' Betty repeated. 'So that's who she was. She asked me if I knew you, Lorraine. I did her hair today—a henna rinse. A real red-hot momma from her conversation!'

Lorraine had stiffened, but she still held her ground. 'What do you know about Stephanie, Clare? Don't tell me you've been to the salon to buy clothes! Stephanie must have shrieked laughing at the sight of you.'

'You wouldn't catch me going near her fancy shop or any other like it. No, I happened to meet that pansy son of hers at the gym. He comes in for massage or some such nonsense. Now there's a shrieker for you!'

'Rupert is charming,' Lorraine said defiantly. 'He has the most exquisite taste and designs a lot of our fashions.'

'He ought to wear 'em,' Clare returned rudely.

'Mary!' Fenella said imploringly, as she patted Lorraine's slim, clenched hand soothingly.

'Well, I wasn't so good last time,' I answered, with a grin. 'But here's another pint of oil! Who likes parlour games? I know a beauty. It's called Second Names.'

'Never heard of it.' Jean shook her head.

'Of course you haven't. I've just made it up—and dedicated it to

Lorraine because her name is almost too euphonic to be real.' I encountered a glance of startled hatred from her and added hastily: 'No dedication after all. Now, here are the rules! We all know each other's first names, but second names are sometimes shrouded in deepest mystery. Why? Because they are frequently expediential and being so—'

'They are what?' Jean asked, cupping an ear.

Betty illustrated neatly. 'I've got a ghastly second name. There was a rich old aunt my parents wanted to please. But all she left me when she died was a pair of ugly vases and—Euphrasia!'

'I don't believe it,' Fenella said incredulously. 'My poor girl!'

'You shouldn't have told us,' I rebuked. 'It spoils the game.'

'Sorry! Does it mean I'm disqualified? I've got a third name almost as bad.'

'Evangeline, Tabitha, Augusta,' Fenella rattled off with relish. 'You're a bright girl,' I told her. 'Fen has the idea. We'll start with Clare. But first we'll divide the game into two parts. If your second name is a fancy one, then we'll have to ask for a clue—say the first letter. A plain one—then it's a free for all. Righto, Clare! Plain or fancy?'

Well into the spirit of things, Clare gave the question some deliberation. She was a parlour games enthusiast, and on wet week-ends had us crawling around picking up peanuts with knives or eating suspended apples with our hands tied behind our backs. 'I wouldn't say it was a fancy name exactly, yet it is a bit different. It starts with a J.'

'With wh-what?' I stammered, unable to believe my ears.

'J,' Fenella repeated, giving me a brief, puzzled glance. 'Is it Josephine, Clare?'

Clare shook her head, grinning. 'Nope! Okay, Bet's turn next.'

'Joanna?'

'Judith? Come on, Lorraine!'

'Jabberwocky,' Lorraine drawled, trying to be clever.

Clare roared with laughter and slapped her thigh. 'You'll never guess it in a month of Sundays. What about you, Maria?'

I pretended to think. 'Jess—or should one say Jessica?' I asked, and held my breath.

'No, you're all miles out, and I don't blame you. It doesn't sound a bit like me—Joy! Can you beat it!' She gave a little jump in her chair and rubbed her hands together. 'Who's next? What about Lorraine?'

Lorraine got up, this time with one of her even, flowing movements. 'Please don't think I'm trying to break up this fascinating game Mary so cleverly invented,' she said, with wonderful disdain, 'but I am expecting an important phone call.'

'Anastasia, Walburga, Selina,' Fenella recited. 'Gladys, Bertha—golly! I nearly said my own then.'

Lorraine gave a tinkling laugh. 'Very amusing, Fenella! I really can't understand how such childish games can entertain you. As a matter of fact, I haven't got any other name.' And she turned and walked swiftly out of the room.

'I'd like to have that girl under me for a few weeks,' Clare remarked. 'She wants the nonsense knocked out of her. Sorry about that, Mary!'

'Heavens, I don't mind!' I replied.

'It's quite a good game too,' Clare insisted, her eye roving. 'Look, Verna's coming over. She can join in.'

'Clare, it really doesn't matter.'

Betty said thoughtfully: 'It's funny what you said, Mary. I wonder if that is what scared her off. She gave you quite a look. It has occurred to me before this.'

'What has?' Jean demanded.

'Her name—Lorraine Lawrence. It is rather unreal, don't you think?'

'Like a film star who was born Sarah Jenkins,' Fenella nodded. 'Let's ask Verna. She would know if anyone would.'

'Now what makes you say that?' Verna smiled, as she slid quietly into a chair. 'You make me sound as if I were one of those horrid snooping persons I despise.'

'Which, of course, you are not. We were talking about Lorraine, which I'm sure you overheard. Is that really her name or is it Jessie Jones or something less glamorous?'

Fenella always was needle-sharp, I thought to myself, hoping the others had been deceived.

'Why ask me?' Verna said. 'Why not ask Lorraine?'

'Don't quibble. Do you know or not?'

She glanced swiftly around and seeing us all agog, smiled complacently. 'If poor Lorraine wants to have secrets, I think it would be frightfully wrong of me to divulge them. Don't you agree, Mary?'

'If you consider they are important, yes,' I replied.

Verna was sharp too. She leaned over and touched my hand with a cold, clinging forefinger. 'You seem quite interested in the possibility of Lorraine being a pseudonym. So unlike you, Mary. You never worry about other people's affairs as a rule, do you?'

I moved my hand away. 'We are only idly curious about the matter,' I said indifferently.

'We were playing a game that Mary made up,' Jean explained. 'She calls it Second Names.'

'Mary made up a game!' Verna repeated, with noticeable incredulity. 'She is behaving strangely tonight. I wonder what has happened to our staid, reserved Mary?'

'For Pete's sake!' Fenella broke in, with swift impatience. 'You are always trying to put significance into unimportant matters, Verna. It's a terribly boring habit. Have you finished your meal, Maria? Let's beat it!'

Clare scraped back her chair. 'It's a wizard game, old girl!' she assured me, thrusting her table-napkin untidily into its ring. She was still concerned about the slurs cast on my inventive powers. 'Tell you what—we'll get all the kids playing it the next time they get fidgety. Just as a matter of curiosity—what gave you the bright idea?'

I was spared the necessity of answering this one by the door of the refectory being flung open. 'Hullo! What's up with Jonesy?'

Mrs. Carron-Toyle's companion tottered on the threshold, clinging to the door-knob as though for support. Tears were flowing unchecked down her cheeks. For one who preferred to creep about unobtrusively, effacing herself against walls to allow others to pass, her abrupt appearance was decidedly dramatic. It held us all immobile for a moment, so that those who were preparing to rise from their chairs were caught in odd attitudes, like Pompeians engulfed by volcanic ash.

'Who did it?' Mabel Jones demanded, in a high, shaking voice. 'Which one of you is responsible?'

Clare was the first to rouse herself. 'Now take it easy, Jonesy!' she said briskly. 'What's the trouble? Who did what? Here, sit down for a jiffy. You're all of a tremble.'

Miss Jones allowed herself to be guided to a chair. We all gathered round silently. "Oh, it's dreadful—dreadful!' she whimpered, searching for a handkerchief. The weeping had loosened her chronic cold. 'You shouldn't have done it. I'm the one who suffers.'

I found a clean handkerchief and pushed my way through the crowd. 'What has happened?' I asked in an undertone, bending over her. 'Quickly, tell me!'

She accepted the handkerchief gratefully, burrowing her face in it. 'Oh, it's hard—it's hard!' she moaned, rocking to and fro.

I clenched my teeth. 'I'll shake you in a minute, Jonesy.'

Two startled, watery eyes appeared. 'I will,' I threatened.

'I've never heard you speak so—so roughly before,' she whispered, gazing at me fearfully. 'You didn't write it, did you, Mary?'

'Write what? Oh, lord! Don't tell me you're making all this fuss over an anonymous letter. Buck up, you're not the only person who has received one.'

Miss Jones gulped and sniffed. 'Not me!' she wailed. 'It's Mrs. Carron-Toyle.'

A ripple of gleeful satisfaction went through our group. She sat up and blew her long, drooping nose. 'It's all very well for you to laugh, but poor Mrs. Carron-Toyle is most upset. She almost had one of her turns.'

'When did she find it?' Clare asked, making a music-hall gesture of wiping the grin off her face.

'Just as she commenced her dinner. The note was wrapped up in her table-napkin, so one of you must have put it there because her tray has been on the servery-table over there since lunch. I told her that, but she seems to think I wrote it.' At the thought Miss Jones fell into my handkerchief once more.

'Here, cheer up,' Clare said, patting her heartily on the shoulder. 'Of course you didn't write it. You're not capable of a dirty, underhand game like writing anonymous letters.'

Jonesy looked up at her like a grateful spaniel. She was rather in awe of Clare. 'Oh, Miss Parker, do you know who did?'

'No, I don't—but I'm going to make a damn good effort to find out.' Her jaw jutted as she swept a grim look around the faces, which became correspondingly serious. The girls had been waiting for such a lead.

'The shot about the hairy legs must still rankle,' Fenella whispered, her chin on my shoulder.

'Now look here, you girls!' Clare began in a hearty, man-to-man fashion. 'This business has been going on long enough. Maybe it was fun while it lasted—though it didn't click with my particular sense of humour—but now the party's over and it's got to stop. I'm warning whoever is responsible for these despicable letters that I intend to hound you down and see that justice is meted out. You've been giving us a rough ride—okay, now it's our turn. What do you say, girls?'

A wave of angry approval sounded among those who had suffered from the poison pen. I grew even more troubled. Fenella summed up the situation neatly by muttering, 'Just like a lynching party!'

Clare held up a hand. 'Just a moment! Before we start on anything drastic, I suggest we offer the culprit one last chance to own up and apologize. Fair enough?'

'I don't know whether Mrs. Carron-Toyle will be satisfied,' Miss Jones objected timidly. 'She is really most upset. It's her health, you know, that makes her temper so uncertain.'

Clare glanced down at her impatiently, and then at me standing alongside. 'Mary, you cut along and see Mrs. Cee-Tee. She'll listen to you. Cool her down and explain how we're going to nip this thing in the bud. We must not allow it to get too big.'

'Don't you think that is just what you are doing?' I ventured quietly, while a subdued but angry buzz went on as the girls discussed the lead Clare had given.

She stared at me blankly. 'I don't follow, old girl! What do you mean?'

'Everyone is simmering now. They weren't like that before. I don't like it. It—it's dangerous.'

'Rot!' she replied trenchantly. 'Look, Maria, what did you feel like when you got a letter? Didn't you immediately want to get your hands on the person who wrote it?'

'I haven't had a letter,' I replied.

She gave me an odd look, recovered herself quickly and then patted me on the back. 'You leave this to me, old thing. I bet you I'll have the game sewn up within twenty-four hours. Go and amuse the old lady with that super game you thought up. That wouldn't worry anyone.'

IV

In the original design of Kilcomoden, the two wings jutting north and south from the main building had been planned as a conservatory and a ballroom respectively. The chapel now stood on the site of the former, while the ballroom had been subdivided into several rooms now occupied by Mrs. Carron-Toyle and Miss Jones. To reach these there was a passage going off almost opposite the library.

Much to everyone's relief, the widow rarely entered the main house, but her continual presence was felt through Miss Jones, one of whose unpleasant duties was that of liaison officer. The only times we saw Mrs. Carron-Toyle, except on those occasions when Mother Paul coaxed one of us into paying a visit as an act of charity more for Jonesy's sake than the old lady's, was during her daily airing around the grounds. Rugged in an ancient sable coat with a magenta scarf about her dyed head, she sat like a raddled old actress while her companion guided her wheel-chair up and down the paths.

The door of the apartment was ajar, probably as Miss Jones had left it in her agitated dash to the refectory. I could see Mrs. Carron-Toyle standing unsupported at the sideboard, pouring herself a glass of port. She gulped it down, smacked her lips appreciatively and then proceeded to replenish the glass. I coughed discreetly, but she did not turn.

'Well, come on in, you fool!' she said in her throaty voice. 'What the hell do you mean by clearing off like that? I pay you to be my companion, don't I?'

Then she turned and saw me standing in the doorway. The wine-glass was pushed swiftly behind another row of medicine bottles, and a podgy hand was clapped to her ample bosom. 'Have you no consideration for a poor sick woman?' she asked faintly, tottering to a chair. 'You should know better than to startle someone in my condition of health. Quickly, a glass of wine. It will help ward off the attack.'

I poked among the sugar pills and coloured water for the port. She took it with a shaking hand, tossed it off and then handed the glass back as though I were a waiter. 'Ha! I feel my strength returning. Leave it on the table and find the bottle. I may be compelled to have some more presently. Bring me over that footstool—and that cushion on the sofa for my back. No, not the red one—the orange one. I want my handbag too. It is probably hanging on the door-knob. But if it is not there, find it just the same.'

Mrs. Carron-Toyle followed my movements with an expression of pleased triumph. She belonged to an age when it was fashionable to be rude to waiters and shop-girls. The pleasure of being overbearing to someone other than Jonesy did not often come her way now.

'This looks the genuine article,' I remarked, inspecting the dusty bottle.

'It should be. My sainted papa laid it down the year I was born. I brought that bottle up this afternoon.'

'You mean some is still in the cellars here?'

'Never you mind what I mean,' she replied craftily, taking her lorgnettes from her bulging crocodile-skin bag. After subjecting me to a long, critical gaze as though I were a prize animal, she asked: 'What are you doing here, anyway? It's not often any of you gals deign to visit a poor old woman. Did Jones ask you to come—the silly, frightened sheep?'

'Miss Jones is very distressed because she thinks you blame her for an anonymous letter,' I said gently.

'Of course I blamed her,' retorted Mrs. Carron-Toyle. 'She sat there asking for it—wriggling and blushing and being apologetic. What's more, she probably did write it. Only someone who was at home today could have wrapped it up with my table-napkin.'

'Is that where you found it? Would you mind letting me have the note? You are not the only victim. There is a meeting on downstairs at this moment to discuss the problem of these letters. Altogether too much fuss is being made,' I hinted, lest she should consider making an even bigger issue of the matter.

She fumbled in her bag again, then tossed a crumpled piece of paper on the table. 'I suppose you can have it. Now go and tell Jones to come back. It's time for my medicine. And take my dinner-tray with you. Murders and anonymous letters—what next, I wonder!'

I did not go back to the refectory. The service-lift was standing open on the ground floor, so I slid Mrs. Carron-Toyle's tray in and pulled the rope to send it down to the kitchen. A clatter of footsteps sounded on the refectory stairs, and Alison Cunningham stumbled into the hall. She shot past me, sobbing hysterically.

'Alison!' I dashed after her and caught her arm just as she reached the stairs.

'Let me go, damn you!' she cried, tugging away furiously.

'Calm down like a good girl,' I said soothingly. 'What's the trouble?'

She continued to struggle, but it was an easy matter to hold her childish weight. 'They're after me. Please let me go, Mary! I can't stand much more.'

'Don't be foolish! No one is after you.'

'Yes, they are!' she insisted shrilly. 'You heard what Clare said—'

'Oh, damn Clare!' I exclaimed, losing patience. This outburst was evidently the outcome of her stupid meeting. 'Look, Alison, stop your row and listen to me. If you're the one who has been writing these silly letters—'

'I won't listen,' she cried, clapping her hands over her ears. 'You can't make me. When I'm gone they'll be sorry. Everyone has always hated me here. Even you are against me.'

It was impossible to reason with her while this crazy storm was on. She fled upstairs sobbing, and I turned wearily towards the sanctuary of the library.

The silence of the room was like a balm. The echoes of Mrs. Carron-Toyle's strident tones and Alison's shrill voice faded as, with a sigh of relaxation, I took my place at the typewriter. A fresh pile of notes lay across the manuscript of the Foundress's life. They were scribbled on all manner of scraps of paper, including a hostel grocery bill and the back of a holy picture. I touch-typed a few lines, and then glanced automatically at the result as I turned a page. An exclamation of annoyance escaped me for what I had just typed was out of alignment with last night's work. I ripped out the sheet and was preparing to insert a fresh one, when an unpleasant thought, such as I had hoped to leave behind on entering the library, came to my mind.

Someone had used the typewriter that day! My work had been taken out and then reinserted. Only a stroke of luck would have made the alignment correct—and as a further proof the duplicate sheet had slipped. I thrust my hand into my pocket and brought out Mrs. Carron-Toyle's anonymous letter. A careful comparison of both scripts left me in no doubt that my machine had been used by the poison pen.

Surely, I thought, I would have detected the similarity before if the library typewriter had been used for the other notes. Mother Paul had confiscated them, so I was sitting back racking my memory of them when, most opportunely, Fenella strolled in. Her hands and eyes were raised heavenwards.

'I take it the meeting was not a success,' I said, with a smile.

'Poor Clare did her best, but it became quite unruly—not to say out of hand. Everyone ended up seething with indignation against everyone else, and then to cap all, Alison sprang one of her scenes. There was practically a riot.'

I nodded. 'I ran into some of the backwash. You're a bright, observant girl, Fen! Come over here for a minute. This is Mrs. Carron-Toyle's anonymous letter. What think you?'

She read it appreciatively. '"You are a common deceitful old hag." Golly, was she wild?'

'Not as bad as I anticipated. Jonesy evidently bore the first brunt. Does anything else strike you?'

'Rather! Is it a plant? You surely would not be so unsubtle as to use this typewriter.'

'Wonderful girl!' I applauded. 'Go a little further. Have you recognized the typing in any other note?'

Fenella thought for a moment, and then shook her head.

'Neither have I.' I turned in my chair and faced her. 'Fen, someone used this machine today to write that note. Then it was folded up with Mrs. Carron-Toyle's table-napkin. Whoever it was must have had both time and solitude. Someone who was in the house while the others were all at business.'

There was a pause, then Fenella said lightly: 'Looks like Alison will have to think of a new stunt to amuse herself with. Now it only remains for the cops to catch their killer and we can all settle down to a quiet life again.'

She stretched herself on a yawn and relaxed into a chair, only to turn her head sharply as the door opened. 'Ah! the convener! Come on in, Clare. Mary has solved the case of the anonymous letters for us.'

Clare entered, looking rather sheepish. 'Have you, Maria? That's goodo. I'm afraid I made a bit of a mess of things in the refectory. Who is it?'

'Suspect number one—Alison,' Fenella announced in bored tones.

'I didn't say so, Fen,' I said uncomfortably. 'It's just that certain circumstances seem to indicate that Alison may be connected with the letters.'

Fenella, who had closed her eyes, opened them to say censoriously: 'Mary, it's high time you quit that law shop. You are becoming pedantic—not to say prosy.'

'Sorry, but Alison is so beastly highly strung that I hesitate to accuse her outright.'

'Highly strung!' Clare gave a contemptuous snort. 'Just another name for lack of discipline. What that girl needs is firm treatment. Come on, Mary! What are the certain circs?'

'The letters could have been written and planted by anyone. Nearly all of us at Kilcomoden have access to typewriters at our places of business. But this latest note—Mrs. Carron-Toyle's—was typed on this machine.'

'Was it, by Jove!' Clare said. 'How did you spot that?'

I told her about the change of alignment and gave her a sheet of Mother Paul's manuscript to compare with the letter. 'Those two facts and the fairly intricate placing of the note indicate that it was done today between the time when Mrs. Carron-Toyle's lunch tray went back to the refectory and we all came home from work.'

'Was Alison here then? I know she's chucked her job, but she may have gone into town or something.'

Remembering the phone call I had put through I said, without explaining my certainty, 'I'm afraid she was here.'

'That's opportunity,' Clare remarked thoughtfully. 'What about motive?'

I shrugged. 'Does there have to be a motive for such things as anonymous letter-writing?'

'I bet psychiatrists have a whacking long explanation,' Fenella observed.

Clare, who included psychiatry in her large index of things to be despised, squared her shoulders and stuck out her jaw once more. 'I'm going up to have a word with young Alison.'

'Oh, leave the child alone,' Fenella said, putting out a slim leg to bar her passage. 'We'll have her throwing herself out a window if we're not careful.'

'Yes, let's forget about it,' I agreed.

'That's all very well for you,' Clare grunted. 'You didn't get one of the beastly letters.'

'Neither did you, Maria.' Fenella turned to me mockingly. 'And you seem very anxious to pin the blame on poor Alison.'

'You horrid piece!' I grinned at her.

'I don't think that insinuation at all funny,' Clare said stiffly. 'I would no more consider Mary capable of stooping to such rotten tricks than—well, than poor old Jonesy. Bad show. Fen!'

'Thanks, Clare!' I acknowledged. 'You've raised an interesting point. Did Alison receive a letter?'

'I don't think she did,' Fenella said slowly. 'I'm sure she would have made a scene about it if she had.'

Without trying to be humorous, Clare said, 'I must say I find it difficult to disentangle the causes of Alison's outbursts, but I can't remember an anonymous letter being one of them—which rather explodes your theory of poison pens always sending one to themselves, Mary.'

'The best poison pens,' I corrected. 'That's the odd feature about this business. Unpleasant though they are, the letters could have been a darned sight worse. For example, if Verna had written them, she would have made some startling disclosure or accusation. Instead of writing to Fen, "You are a carrot-topped show-off" or whatever it was, she would have put, "Does your fiancé know you dined with another man last—"' I broke off as Clare cleared her throat warningly, and Fenella rose to her feet.

There was a soft jingle of rosary beads and Mother Paul came sailing into the room. 'Such a lot of talk and scampering about!' she said, giving us her soft, flickering smile. 'So unusual for a Monday evening. Everyone so glum as a rule. Mary dear, those notes—did you see them?'

'Notes?' I repeated, before realizing she was referring to the 'Life'. 'I put them aside to attend to later.'

'We'll go now,' Fenella murmured, edging away. Mother Paul had a habit of passing out work to anyone who happened to be in the library.

'Dear me, who left those books lying around so untidily? Fenella and Clare, do put them away. It must have been the Farrow child. She is not yet accustomed to our ways. Mary, tell her tactfully about replacing books on shelves. We mustn't upset her—she is certain to be temperamental.'

The word was an anathema to Clare. 'That is no excuse for breaking rules—or sullenness.'

'Not sullen, dear,' Mother Paul contradicted gently. 'Unhappy. All those scales this afternoon—enough to make anyone weep all over the piano.'

Fenella, her pointed chin resting on the pile of books she held, glanced across at me inquiringly. 'I thought Miss Farrow went to the Con. today.'

'She came home about lunchtime quite done up too, poor child. She doesn't seem strong. Mary, ask Sister Berthe about more milk puddings. We must build her up. Then perhaps she will tell me—' She broke off and looked up at the chandelier. 'Sister Emerentiana says the electricity bill is exorbitant. Perhaps if we were to take out some of the lamps—Clare, you're so tall—'

But Clare had had enough of odd jobs. 'Fenella and I were just leaving,' she said hastily, 'and Mary doesn't need the centre lights on.'

'Well, remember to turn them off as you go out like a good girl. Good night, my dears.'

V

I sat half-turned in my chair, watching Mother Paul as she glided over to the mantelpiece to wind the mulga wood clock. She fumbled for her own small watch in some mysterious pocket under the starched wimple, and then opening the glass door adjusted the minute hand a delicate fraction.

'You seem put-out, Mary,' she said, moving the mantelpiece

87

ornaments about with her forefinger. 'Like Sister when you girls don't do things to time. Any reason why the Farrow child should not come in here?'

'She has messed up a cut-and-dried theory of mine,' I answered ruefully, and told her about Mrs. Carron-Toyle's anonymous letter and our suspicions of Alison. 'Miss Farrow is the most prickly person of my acquaintance. She appears to regard everyone with dislike, but somehow the role of a poison pen doesn't quite suit her. It must be Alison.'

'Poor child!' the rectress murmured charitably. 'Such an unfortunate upbringing. That long-suffering little man was telling me. Her mother adored her. So detrimental to the character—much better to be like the birds.'

'You mean Alison wasn't pushed out of the nest? She is certainly extraordinarily immature for her age. Then you do think she is our anonymous letter-writer?'

'If there is no reason to these notes—yes, she could be. They seem so silly.'

'What reason could there be? Beyond wishing to make a sensation or to cause annoyance?'

'I'm sure I can't say, dear,' she replied on a sigh, adding reluctantly: 'Perhaps I should have a little talk with Alison.'

'Yes, but not now—she was rather upset by the protest meeting Clare misguidedly staged after dinner. Talk to her tomorrow.'

Mother Paul brightened and said hopefully: 'She may realize by then how foolish she has been, and the affair will blow over. Such a relief!'

I was silent. Knowing Alison I was not so sure, nor did Mother Paul sound at all convinced. She caught my eye and began to twinkle. 'That atmosphere of Sister's has penetrated the library,' she declared plaintively.

I laughed and swung round to the typewriter. 'Let us transport ourselves back into the Middle Ages at once.'

The Foundress's Life, however, proved only a temporary anodyne. We worked together until the chapel bell cut across Mother Paul's dictation. She rose at once and bade me good night.

'I'll go on for a while,' I told her.

'Don't overtire yourself, dear.' She floated out, only to pop her head back again. 'It was Green, wasn't it, Mary? That place where you have your tea every afternoon?'

Some time must have passed before I could rouse myself. It was quite late and the house was silent. I tidied the papers on the table, and, covering the typewriter, went slowly upstairs. Only one or two doors showed a pencil line of light. I put my head into Fenella's room to say good night and found her asleep, her bright hair brushing the shoulder of her blue satin bed-jacket and her fingers still caught in the leaves of a novel. She stirred, but did not awaken, when I took it away and gently removed one of the pillows.

The other light came from Alison Cunningham's room. I eyed it speculatively for several moments, wondering to what I would expose myself were I to knock. Then, with a mighty yawn I opened my own door and prepared for bed.

I passed a restless night, laying equal blame on the unusual worries of the day and the shepherd's pie. In between dozes I tried to decide whether it was a sleeping tablet or an indigestion powder I needed. In that confused state between uneasy sleep and full consciousness, sounds seemed to contract the hours to a short period of time. There was someone tip-toeing along the passage every few minutes. Then Bartholomew's scrofulous mongrel barked for what sounded to my resentful ears like hours. It was only just quiet when Sister Berthe's rooster started his egotistical prelude to the dawn twittering of the birds, and the first faint, grey light reminded me of a busy day ahead at the office.

I sighed and groaned, immensely sorry for myself as I thought of my peacefully sleeping companions. Their untroubled slumber, in the face of what seemed now the hideous clamour of the predawn period, was so infuriating that I got out of bed and stamped noisily about the room in a search for aspirin. My sense of grievance became acute when I discovered my water-jug empty, which meant a trip to the nearest bathroom.

Leaving my door ajar, I padded down the passage. Coming back, carefully carrying my jug, I was at once gratified and childishly disappointed by another light-rimmed door manifesting that I was not the only sufferer from insomnia. I was half-way into my room when I realized the door was Alison's. Her light had been burning when I had come up to bed, and now—several hours later—it was still burning.

I was suddenly wide awake, the silly frustrated ill-temper of semiconsciousness gone. Putting the jug down, I swiftly crossed the passage to the opposite room. Alison had probably dropped off to sleep like Fenella, but—

The room was empty and the bed had not been slept in.

Four

I

For a long time I stared stupidly at the empty bed with its flowered chintz counterpane folded neatly over the footrail. The rest of the room was just as tidy—almost impersonally so. It was as though Alison had gone—for good, and the room was waiting for another girl to invest it with another personality.

Then I caught sight of the note lying on the bed. If it had been propped on the dressing-table, I would have seen it at once. But it lay open in the middle of the bed, its colour blending with the cream-tinted blankets. I crossed the floor slowly, fearfully, wondering what new trouble Alison was bringing on us all.

It was a single sheet of unfolded paper. I bent over the bed without touching it, and read Alison's sprawling childish handwriting.

I know you all think it is me. I can't stand this place any longer. Good-bye for ever! Life is not worth living.

I tried to think clearly, exasperation mixing with my confusion of mind. Where was Alison? What had she done? Those footsteps I had heard during the night—had they been hers? What time had it been? What time was it now? I was too late. No, she was only trying to frighten us—to make us sorry for her, as she had so many times before. She would not—she could not do what that note of hers implied. It was all a trick to draw attention to herself—like the anonymous letters. The letters—last night I had never seen her so overwrought. Even careless, care-free Fenella had believed in her distress—'Leave the child alone, or we'll have her throwing herself out a window.'

Without thinking, I made a dive at Alison's window. With the slope of the ground on which the house was built and the excessively high ceilings of the floor below, there was. a drop of about thirty feet.

Was thirty feet enough to—to—but the window was not only closed, but locked. I twisted my hands together, biting my lip as I paced the floor. Then I pulled up short, as into my mind coldly and clearly came Alison's own words, 'Sometimes I feel like throwing myself into the river.'

'Oh, you silly, mad child!' I groaned aloud. Death from misadventure—while of unsound mind. It wasn't too late to stop her. I must hurry. It mustn't be too late!

'I wouldn't do that if I were you—you might get wet!' Wet! She couldn't even swim. She wouldn't have a chance even in that narrow stream that flowed so sluggishly at the foot of the garden. But they could do things with people who had been in the water—artificial respiration and there was an iron lung—or was that only for paralysis cases?

'Oh, I'm so stupid,' I muttered. 'Think, you fool! Hurry!'

I must go down to the river. Perhaps she's there still wandering around and hoping someone will catch up to her. Maybe that is why she left the light on—to draw our attention. But if no one comes, she might feel obliged to go further and try to—try to . . . Supposing I can't get her out. I'm no great shakes as a swimmer. 'Miss Allen, who went to the girl's rescue, was dragged down. The bodies have not yet . . .' I cringed, feeling the cold muddy water in my mouth and clogging my nose.

Then I thought of Clare. Good old Clare, who was strong and athletic and who performed all sports so creditably. She probably had a certificate for life-saving somewhere, tucked away with her physical culture medals and other attestations of athletic prowess.

I ran out of the room, along the passage and burst into Clare's room unceremoniously. She sat bolt upright in bed at once, her shoulders square and strong under the striped pyjamas she affected.

'Oh, it's you, Mary!' she mumbled, falling back again. 'You gave me the heck of a fright. What's all the commotion about?'

'Clare, you must get up at once. Hurry! Alison has gone.'

She rubbed her nose with the back of her hand, yawning prodigiously. 'What's the dratted girl up to now? Good Heavens, Maria, it's not properly daylight! What is the time?'

'I don't know,' I said impatiently, and then caught sight of her masculine-looking watch on the bedside table. 'Nearly five. Do be quick!'

Grumbling, she rolled out of bed. 'What on earth are you doing up at this hour? Couldn't you sleep?'

I threw her dressing-gown at her. 'I went to the bathroom to get a drink, and I saw Alison's light. It was on when I came to bed. Clare—she's left a note.'

A troubled frown appeared between her thick brows. 'Run away, has she? Well, we can't do much about that now, Mary. Better wait and tell Mother Rectress.'

'We can't wait. I think she means trouble. She was talking so wildly last night. You know the way she gets. Clare—I—I want you to come down to the river with me.'

Her head jerked up and she stared at me incredulously. 'Here, take it easy, old girl? You're not suggesting—'

I nodded, unable to speak. Without taking her eyes from mine, Clare pulled on her gown and tied the cord. 'All right, old thing,' she muttered, gripping my arm hard. 'Let's go.'

Together we hurried quietly downstairs and out into the clear, cold dawn. It was becoming lighter now. I could see Clare's face drawn into grim, rigid lines, making her look plainer than ever at that unfriendly hour. She glanced at me as we hastened down the narrow winding path which led to the river, and said: 'Buck up, Mary! I wouldn't be surprised if we were up the pole about all this.' Evidently I was not looking so dewy and fresh myself.

There was a high fence at the foot of Kilcomoden's garden, which left just enough room on the other side for a foot-beaten track along the river's edge. The path on our side led to a gate which was bolted every sundown by Bartholomew. Brushing through the flowing tendrils of weeping willow trees which lined the bank, we came on it abruptly—swinging to and fro in the early morning breeze.

'Clare, it's open!'

'All right, all right, old girl! It mightn't mean a thing. Just keep your eyes peeled. Wait a jiff, and I'll give a call.' She cupped her mouth and bellowed Alison's name with the full force of her well-developed lungs.

I stepped out on to the narrow river path, looking anxiously from left to right, then across the slow, brown water to an identical path on the other bank. The long, green curtains of the willows stirred and rustled, and seemed to mock our searching eyes.

'No sign,' Clare said, after a second call. 'It's quiet, isn't it?' She shivered and then brought herself up taut. 'We'd better keep moving. Take opposite directions—you go down as far as the boat-sheds, and I'll go up towards the bridge.'

'Okay,' I agreed briefly, turning to go. But she put out a hand and grasped my arm again. 'I say, Mary!' There was an odd tight note in her voice.

'Yes, what?'

She did not meet my eyes 'If—if anything has happened to—to Alison, you won't blame me, will you?'

I gazed at her blankly before I understood her reason for saying this. 'Clare, we haven't got time to talk now, but of course I wouldn't blame you.'

'Thanks, old girl,' she replied roughly. Turning, she strode away up the path.

There was no time to talk and no time to think. I ran along the narrow track, searching for some sign of Alison and calling her name again and again. The dampness of the muddy ground soon penetrated the thin leather soles of my slippers and the edge of my gown flapped clammily about my bare ankles.

Presently I came to the bend of the river which marked Kilcomoden's boundary, and where our next-door neighbour, a greasy-looking character called Molloy, conducted his pleasure boat business. There was a landing-stage with a few brightly painted canoes tethered to it, and anchored against the bank lay the launch in which the boatman conducted bay and river excursions. I had been on it once with Cyril, and we had cruised around ships lying in the Bay one hot January evening with several other couples more romantically affected by the moon shining on the sea than we were. Cyril had not liked it when Molloy, cutting off his engine, had produced a concertina on which to play syrupy love ditties with a leering eye.

I gathered my gown together and stepped out on to the landing-stage. It creaked under my weight and the river slapped gently at the rotting pylons. I peered fearfully into the brown water, where the debris of the river had been left as the current negotiated the sharp bend. There were twigs and odd pieces of paper, scraps of fruit peel and a discoloured scarf lost overboard from some canoe skylark. But of anything pertaining to Alison there was no sign.

A faint call caused me to lift my head sharply, and I saw Clare standing afar off, beckoning furiously and pointing down into the river. I stumbled to the path and ran back. She was hanging over the river when I arrived, holding on to a sapling with one hand, while in the other she held a long branch torn from a nearby tree. She was reaching out in an attempt to catch a piece of material trailing beneath the surface of the water.

'What is it? What have you found?' I recognized it even as I spoke—the hand-painted chiffon scarf that Alison sometimes tied over her head. Clare fished it out—shrivelled, dirty and pathetic. For a long moment we stared at it.

Then Clare moved. She pulled off her dressing-gown. 'I'm going in. Get help!' She took one look at the river and dived steeply, the water closing over her with barely a splash. Sick and chilled, I waited for her to appear. She came up gulping for air and then duck-dived. Her unquestioning courage made me ashamed of my trembling limbs and helpless, indecisive mind.

I turned and sped down the path towards the river gate of Kilcomoden. Movement set my brain in motion, and I could think more clearly. Get help, Clare had said. She did not say what kind of help. That she left for me to work out. There was nothing to be gained in rousing the girls and thereby creating a panic. What was needed was a boat and strong arms, rope and a boat-hook.

I shot past the gate and on towards the boat-sheds. Molloy, I knew, lived in a shack not far up from the bank. I pushed and scrambled up the steep incline, the undergrowth tearing at my face and hands. Presently I found the hut, noting with relief the wisp of smoke coming from the iron chimney-pot.

Molloy came to the door wearing greasy grey flannels and an un-buttoned pyjama jacket displaying an interesting collection of tattoos. He demanded my business in suspicious, surly tones, but eyed my appearance with his customary leer. After listening to my brief, incoherent explanation, he said grudgingly: 'All right. Hold on until I get the key.' He stepped back into the room, the door swinging wide. I had one sordid glimpse of the fly-blown interior, the table scattered with stale scraps of food and the stained blankets on the sagging, rusty bed.

He led the way down to the landing-stage without a word or a backward glance. I followed him on to the launch, and stood shivering with cold and nerves while he took his time over starting up the engine. I could see Clare still diving and surfacing, and shouted to her. She lifted an arm out of the water in reply. Then the engine of the launch chugged into life and we edged away from the bank.

'Please hurry!' I pleaded to the boatman.

'Can't do it any faster, miss,' he replied surlily. 'Engine's cold.'

A lifetime seemed to pass before we reached the place where Clare was swimming in a circle. Molloy kept the engine going to hold his boat against the current and threw laconic instructions over his shoulder as I fumbled with the anchor.

Clare pulled herself up the gunwale. Her face was ghastly. She said, between chattering teeth: 'I think I've found her. Give me a rope!'

She snatched it from me and fell back into the water. Molloy dived for the other end of the rope and made it fast against one of the built-in wooden seats. I hung over the side anxiously. Minutes seemed to pass before Clare came to the surface, her face livid as she gasped for air. She must have been near exhaustion, but she went down again.

Molloy unhooked a lifebelt and held it ready. 'Over the other side, miss. You'll have us capsizing. There's not much ballast on.' As I moved across the deck, he tossed the belt in. Then Clare's voice panted, 'Okay, pull!'

Molloy pulled and the deck sloped. I braced myself against the starboard gunwale.

'Mary!' I looked down as Clare swam feebly round the launch, supported by the lifebelt. 'Give me a hand, will you, Mary?'

I leaned over grasping her forearms, her wet, cold hands gripping mine. 'Heave!' she said, and jerked herself out of the water.

She lay sprawled on the deck for a moment, panting and trembling with her eyes closed under the wet streaks of hair. I glanced about helplessly, then noticing an old piece of canvas pulled it around her numbed body. She opened her eyes and said, 'Isn't she up yet?'

Molloy was grunting and swearing under his breath, the muscles on his arms standing out. Once or twice the rope slipped through his hands and he let out some unsavoury epithet as he wound it around a beam. 'Stay put,' he grunted, and leaned far over the side. The deck tilted again, then with agonizing slowness he began to straighten. Tears pricked my eyelids as I watched the sodden flaccid bundle being hauled over the gunwale to roll with a sickening thud on to the deck. Clare let a rough sob escape her, and buried her head in her arms.

I walked slowly across and stood looking down at the poor drowned body covered with river slime. Alison's head lolled grotesquely askew on her swollen throat, her light, feathery hair now lying in dark lank streaks over her face. I knelt down and gently wiped it with a corner of my gown and closed the staring eyes, shuddering at the touch of the cold, dead flesh. I tried to straighten the clothes. She had been wearing her favourite dress—a blue one with a full-pleated skirt cut on the cross which had swung out gracefully with every movement. The blue was now a dirty grey, its folds streaked with mud. How ridiculously upset she would have been to see it now—Alison, who made such a fetish of lovely clothes. Never again would she describe in minute detail a forthcoming adjunct to her wardrobe. Never again would she be making appointments with her pet dressmaker . . . I rose to my feet slowly and backed away, a new bewildering fear creeping into my mind.

'Mary!' Clare said harshly. 'Isn't there anything you can cover her with?'

I looked across at her dazedly, a terrible suspicion uppermost. 'Clare, she—' I began, and then pulled myself together. Molloy handed me an ancient oilskin coat and I spread it over the body with my head averted. I could not bear to look at Alison now—not with that dreadful thought in my mind. In the events that followed our tying up at the landing-stage it was still with me. Clare had collapsed completely, leaving me to deal with the situation. Molloy, too, showed a marked disinclination to have anything more to do with the affair, but I managed to extract a promise from him to stay with the body until I sent relief.

I half-dragged and half-carried Clare up to the house. Long shudders kept passing through her body which she did not seem to have the strength to control. Her face was ashen and her flesh almost as cold as Alison's had been. I managed to get her to her room and into bed, where she lay staring at the ceiling with blank, miserable eyes. I knew she was blaming herself bitterly for having hounded Alison to her death, but not even to assuage her feelings could I bring myself to share with her that thought which had come to me so suddenly on the launch.

II

I found a certain grim humour in the practised ease with which I went through the same motions as on the previous Saturday night. I roused the rectress and broke the news in two short sentences, following on with an even briefer call to Sergeant Wheeler at the local police-station. Then I went back upstairs to scramble into a few clothes before going to tell Bartholomew to take over from Molloy. Hard on Sergeant Wheeler's double-quick appearance an ambulance arrived and took Alison's body away to the morgue, everything being accomplished with a minimum of delay unlike the fumblings of our first experience—although, as Sergeant Wheeler pointed out, this other sudden death was quite a different cup of tea from the murder.

'Poor young lady,' he said with compassion, as we retired to the library for the inevitable quiz session. 'You say she was highly excitable and easily upset, Mother Mary St. Paul of the Cross? I've known it happen before with other murders. It's like an atomic explosion.' Sergeant Wheeler enjoyed a little pseudoscience. 'There is not only the big bang, but the after-effects—the radiation—can be just as dangerous. This trouble of the anonymous letters came at an unfortunate time.'

Mother Paul, who had been appalled by the tragedy, although her remarkable self-discipline had disguised any outward manifestation, said sorrowfully: 'I blame myself bitterly for not giving more care to the child. But she was rather difficult to understand. It was hard to distinguish between genuine shock and pretended emotion.'

I sat quiet and still throughout the interview, not saying a word. I wanted time to think.

Sergeant Wheeler put Alison's farewell note carefully into his pocket and got up. 'I can't tell you how sorry I am about this unfortunate affair,' he said, even redder in the face with distress. 'There will have to be an inquest of course, but don't let the prospect worry you. I'll put everything you told me about the young lady into my report. It's quite clear that she was mentally unstable. They're very sympathetic in these cases, you know. No one is likely to be blamed.'

Mother Paul shook her head. 'We will always blame ourselves. She was such a child, a silly, irresponsible child, who needed firmness and affection at the same time. She was not ready to assume adult responsibilities.'

I still said nothing.

When Sergeant Wheeler had gone, we both sat silent for a long time. Then Mother Paul roused herself and said briskly: 'We must get in touch with her stepfather. I don't know what I am going to say to the poor little man. He did try to be fond of her.'

'I think that after the first shock he will regard Alison's death as what they call a happy release,' I remarked with a weary smile. At once the thought crept in on me again, fantastically involving Mr. Sparks. I frowned it away—not yet, not yet, I must have time to think.

Mother Paul was regarding me closely. I said quickly, 'If you like, I will ring him.'

'Would you, dear? There are so many unpleasant tasks to do. I don't wish to sound frivolous, but we seem to be dealing more efficiently with this second trouble.'

I nodded. 'That is just what I thought. A few more murders and we'll be competent performers.'

There was a slight pause. Then the rectress said gently, 'But Mr. Wheeler said Alison's death was suicide, Mary.'

I stared at her blankly, searching vainly for some way in which to recover my slip.

She reached over and patted my hand. 'I won't worry you now, dear. It has been a dreadful shock. You've hardly had time to sort matters out—and neither have I.'

She opened a drawer and found the indexed notebook containing the names and addresses of the girls' nearest relatives. I took it with me to the telephone, and with a heavy heart dialled Mr. Sparks's number.

Fenella came out of one of the bathrooms swinging her sponge-bag, her bright hair damp and curly. She broke off her cheerful whistling to say, 'Didn't you go to bed last night?' Then she took another look at my face. 'What's up, Maria?'

I put a finger to my lips for there were other girls tottering with half-closed eyes in and out doors, and followed her to her room. As soon as the door was closed she turned on me, the sudden anxiety in her expressive eyes not masked by the flippancy of her words. 'Never tell me! Not another body!'

I slumped down on a chair. My knees had a nasty tendency to give way at unexpected moments. 'Alison Cunningham was drowned in the river. We found her a couple of hours ago.'

Fenella's eyes widened with horror. 'Mary!'

'Fen, do you think you could get me a glass of water? I feel a bit over at the knees—and several other places besides.'

'Poor darling!' she said swiftly. 'Here, hop on to my bed for a jiffy. I'll make you a cup of tea.'

She helped me up, then lit her little spirit stove and brought out cups and saucers. Without speaking, she began to dress in her quick, economical fashion. There was never any uncertainty about Fenella even in donning clothes. The little kettle was boiling as she finished whisking a brush over her curls, and she made the tea in silence.

'You're a dear girl,' I told her, taking the cup she held out. 'Most other women would have been exclaiming and asking questions.'

'I must admit I'm bursting with curiosity,' she said with a grin, passing the sugar. 'Can I start exclaiming now?'

I sipped the hot tea, and dunked a biscuit. 'Questions now invited. I think I must have been hungry.'

But Fenella hesitated a moment. 'When you say Alison was drowned, just what do you mean? Did she fall into the river or—or what?'

I nearly told Fenella then of my wild, unhappy suspicion, but something held me back. 'She left a note,' I said shortly, without meeting her intelligent eyes.

'Oh—suicide! Poor child! That's rather grim. Was it over the letter business?'

I nodded. 'Sergeant Wheeler has the theory that murder begets other calamities, not necessarily related.'

'Clare will be bucked to find her theory endorsed. She said

something similar last night.'

'Clare!' I exclaimed, setting down my cup and swinging my legs over the bed. 'She needs this more than I do. Can you scrounge another cup and I'll take it to her?'

Fenella's brows went up. 'She's more likely to say I told you so than faint from shock.'

I told her of the circumstances leading to the discovery of Alison. 'Clare is pretty knocked up—mentally as well as physically—so go easy on the banter, old thing! She's got some sort of distorted notion that it is all her fault.'

But Clare was up and dressed when I entered her room. She appeared to have recovered from her ordeal. 'Thanks, old girl,' she said gruffly, as I put the tea on the dressing-table. 'Sorry to have made such a complete ass of myself. What's the latest?'

I told her about Sergeant Wheeler's opinion that Alison had committed suicide while of unsound mind. 'The note clinched the matter,' I added.

Her lips tightened. She jerked her head to the door. 'What's everyone saying?'

I replied with dreary humour: 'Nothing yet. We'll tell them at breakfast. It seems to hold precedence as the time to break bad news.'

The girls took it very well, although there was little time in which to register emotion; week-day breakfast was a hasty uncommunicative sort of meal. Clare, on whom I had pushed the onus, left it until the last possible moment and then stood up, banging a teaspoon against a cup.

Jean, sitting alongside me, muttered, 'Not another meeting at this hour!'

'Just before you go, girls!' There was nothing breezily managing about Clare's manner this morning. Her voice was quieter and more subdued. It was probably for this reason that the whole room suddenly hushed into immobility. I went on toying with my breakfast, wondering what sort of fist she was going to make of the task.

'Something ghastly has happened,' she announced, after a heavy pause. 'Alison Cunningham drowned herself last night.' She did not wait for the gasp, but went swiftly out of the room.

I kept my eyes on my plate as, one by one, the girls left the refectory in shocked silence. There was nothing to show that I had any part in Clare's announcement, but when the room was nearly empty, Verna Bassett slid in alongside me. 'Poor Mary! she said, in her soft, insidious tones. 'You must be feeling awful."

'No worse than anyone else,' I answered shortly.

'So strange that you should be the one to find poor dear Alison!'

Some uncontrolled revulsion rose up inside me. Steady, I thought. 'How do you know I found Alison?' I tried to ask calmly.

Verna wagged her head knowingly. 'There's not much that passes me by. That's one of the advantages of being a solitary person. One has far more chance of observing others. You were the only girl who seemed unimpressed by Clare's news.'

I rose and packed up my breakfast things. 'I'll miss my bus if I don't hurry.'

She followed me to the serving-table. 'You seem worried though, Mary. So unlike you—such a lot of things lately seem unlike you. When anything is on your mind, it is far better to tell someone about the trouble.'

'Meaning I should confide in you, Verna?'

'Ah, you're being sarcastic, aren't you? I'm sure I don't expect you to tell poor little me anything. In fact, it may not be necessary. Perhaps I might know already. I might even know what was on poor Alison's mind that caused her to take such a drastic step.'

I glanced at her without speaking. 'Perhaps I do,' she repeated, nodding complacently.

'Anonymous letters were on her mind,' I said curtly, and moved to the door.

She slid after me. 'Such a silly reason for suicide, don't you think, Mary? I mean—the letters weren't that bad. And it wasn't as though we could actually do anything to her, even in spite of Clare's threats.'

'I don't think Alison had much reason left,' I said, as I mounted the stairs, but Verna was as unshakable as a leech and kept at my heels.

'Maybe Alison wasn't quite as crazy as everyone thought. I had one or two very interesting little chats with her.'

I did not check my step. 'Did you? What about?'

She gave a little titter. 'Aha! That's my secret. You know, Mary, I think you're quite keen to know what we talked about—for all that you pretend you're not.'

'Please, Verna,' I said. 'Don't go making capital out of this terrible affair. If you know anything that may throw more light on Alison's death, tell Mother Paul. Don't keep information to yourself to use to your own ends. This is more serious than the identity of an anonymous letter-writer.'

She did not meet my eyes, but then she never did look straight at anyone. With that thin, complacent smile that aroused the worst in most of us, she replied: 'Oh, I agree with you completely, Mary. It is most serious. But did I say I actually knew anything? You do pick me up so. Why should I know more than someone clever—like you or Clare or Fenella?'

'Because you're an observer,' I said dryly.

'Now you're making fun of me again. Perhaps one of these days I may surprise you properly.'

'I'd rather not be surprised, thanks. The honour and glory will be all yours right now if you speak out. Do you know something about Alison or are you merely being aggravating? Please, Verna, tell me!'

Her smile grew as she listened to my voice becoming louder. If only one could make her lose her temper instead of ending up in frustrated annoyance oneself. As usual, she tagged her reply on to an unimportant phrase. 'I'm sure I don't know why you should think I'm trying to be aggravating, Mary, when I merely want to offer you my sympathy. Such an unfortunate coincidence that you should be involved in two tragedies. Your poor nerves must be quite ragged.'

There was a double-edger hidden away somewhere in that speech. I was fast approaching that state when I would have gone on in-definitely making hopeless assaults against Verna's secretiveness, but Mother Paul intervened. She floated up vaguely as though she were not quite certain where she was going—a trick that had once deceived me into thinking that she contrived and curtailed by accident. 'Dear me, such lenient employers nowadays! So late and you haven't got a hat on, Verna. Run upstairs and get it. Sister doesn't like anyone leaving the hostel without head-covering. Do you know, Mary, in my young days, one wasn't considered ladylike if one left the bedroom without gloves. Six buttons too, dear!'

The latter part of this speech covered Verna's banishment from earshot. With a light hand on my arm she walked with me to the hall-stand, where I had left my own hat and gloves. There was an umbrella in it and a little Homburg hat hung on a hook.

'Poor Mr. Sparks!' Mother Paul said. 'He must have been truly devoted to her. So embarrassing, Mary! He wept all over Sister Berthe's egg and bacon. Sister Emerentiana said breakfast, although I am sure he did not want it—so uncomfortable eating with a nun looking on. Miss Jones is showing him the rhododendrons. Such a help! I was quite at a loss. Now I must go and tell Mrs. Carron-Toyle that I have borrowed her companion. That is a nice hat, dear. I don't think I've seen it before!'

'New,' I admitted, thankful that for the moment her verbal interest was in trivialities and not in what Verna had been saying. 'My others are all hopelessly out of date, I'm told.'

III

The morning dragged slowly into the afternoon, and I kept glancing at the office clock as the time for my daily trip to the bank came nearer. I made my preparations slowly, taking special care over my appearance before going out. I had it fixed in my mind that O'Mara would be waiting in the Green Lounge again, and while I dreaded the meeting, my mind was obsessed with the idea that it was inevitable. At the last minute I nearly bypassed the tea-room, and with an unpleasant going-to-the-dentist feeling forced myself to descend the dingy, badly lit stairs. But the detective was not there.

I might have turned tail and gone off without my tea, had not a sense of bravado prevailed. I sat down at my usual table, gave my order to the same waitress and defied O'Mara to come. But as time went on and I was finishing my second cup, a feeling of anticlimax began to outweigh my first relief. I considered I had been ill-used. After all his beastly warnings and getting me wrought-up and worried, he did not even have the courtesy to turn up when he must have known that I would want to see him.

The waitress came ambling up the aisle to clear my place—a sure sign that I had outstayed my money's worth.

I went back to the office trying to rid myself of the O'Mara obsession, but spent the rest of the afternoon with an ear cocked to the switchboard where the office boy answered the telephone. You cannot work even in a solicitor's office with only half a mind on the job. Consequently I was kept late at my typewriter, humiliated by the mild reproof of one of the partners. It was nearly six by the time I put on my new hat, making a face at it when I remembered just why I had worn it. I had hooked my bag over my arm and was drawing on my not-so-new suede gloves when the buzzer on the switchboard sounded through the empty office.

Dropping everything, I made a dive for the phone, ricochetting off desks and sending a wastepaper basket into a drunken spin.

'Hullo?' I said breathlessly.

'Miss Allen?' asked a man's voice, as clearly as though he were standing alongside. 'O'Mara speaking. You were wanting me?'

'Yes, I was, but—' I began. There was something odd somewhere.

'What is the trouble, Miss Allen? Can you tell me over the phone or would you prefer a meeting?'

'The first trouble is how the heck you knew I wanted you,' I declared frankly.

'Didn't you call this afternoon? I have a message here to ring you. I have only just come in.'

I wondered vaguely if my subconscious mind had pulled a fast one sometime during the afternoon, and then brushed the problem aside. 'I think I had better see you if you don't mind—and if you can spare the time. You knew we had another—more trouble at—'

'Yes, I know all about that,' he cut in. 'Where are you now?'

'At my office. I was just leaving.'

There was a pause. 'Will that tea place of yours be open?' he asked.

'I doubt it. It's only for shoppers and office workers.'

Another pause. Then, 'Do you like Chinese cooking, Miss Allen?'

'Bird's nest soup?' I asked foolishly.

'There is Australian food as well. Can you find your way to the Ming Restaurant? I'll meet you there in a quarter of an hour.' And he rang off before I had time to thank him for the royal command.

I put a call through to Kilcomoden to say I would not be coming home for dinner. You were not supposed to miss mealtimes at the eleventh hour without some very good reason, so I had the slightly mendacious excuse of working ready. A strange, eager voice answered at the hostel. I requested that my message be relayed to Sister Emerentiana, and the voice said: 'Oh? Yes, all right, then,' with the vibrancy replaced by listlessness.

I hesitated, frowning. 'Who is that speaking?'

'Christine . . .' There was an abrupt pause, then more distinctly, 'Christine Farrow.'

'Oh, hullo there, Miss Farrow,' I said brightly. 'How's the music?'

'All right,' she replied curtly. 'I'll give Sister your message.'

'Put it over well like a good girl. I don't want a lecture when I get home. Actually I'm playing hookey, but keep that to yourself. How is everyone behaving there?'

'I don't know.' I could visualize the scowl on her narrow, pale face as she listened and answered reluctantly.

'Listen,' I said, teasing her a little, 'if there's a milk pudding on tonight, you eat my share.'

The receiver was hung up in my ear with force, but I frowned at my own for a moment before replacing it slowly. Something Christine Farrow said had flicked a chord of troubled memory. I pondered for a moment, then came to the conclusion that it was not her words that bothered me, but the definite pause before giving her name. It reminded me of that ridiculous game I had invented in the refectory — my misguided attempt to find out if the woman called Jess was one of us.

I took a taxi to the Ming Restaurant, but even so O'Mara was there before me. He was sitting in one of the booths with the curtains drawn back, but stood up swiftly when I appeared, coming forward to greet me warmly.

'I'm sorry if I am late,' I said, feeling suddenly and inexplicably shy. 'I had to phone the hostel.'

'I was a bit ahead of time. This place is quite near to headquarters.' He waited until I had wriggled into the red plush seat and then drew the curtains across, disposing himself opposite. The light inside the booth was now a rosy dimness, making a pleasant, companionable atmosphere. 'I hope you don't mind, but I ordered dinner while I was waiting, so as to save delay.'

'I'm only too relieved that you did, although I hope it does not entail using chopsticks. When I dine out, it is usually at some conservative hotel where the food, in spite of being ruinously expensive, is quite ordinary.'

'Here it is just the opposite,' O'Mara said, smiling. He seemed relaxed and friendly, unlike the serious, reserved police officer of our previous meetings.

I took a piece of ginger from the glass-covered dish between us and began to nibble it, wondering why I was thinking somewhat guiltily of Cyril. 'Ah, but my usual escort would rather pay for propriety than save on bohemianism.'

The curtains parted and bowls of succulent, steaming soup were placed on the table. The smell made me feel ravenously hungry.

'Does it affront your conservative palate?' O'Mara asked presently.

'No—delicious! What is it made from?'

'It is as well not to inquire too closely into ingredients,' he replied gravely. 'Curiosity has ruined many a tasty dish.'

I glanced up sharply. There had been an underlying nuance in his tones. 'I don't think I am naturally inquisitive,' I said. 'Nor would I intentionally spoil any tasty dish.'

He did not speak, but sat turning his spoon over in the soup. There was a little frown on his face which made him look tired and turned him into a stranger again. The small, warm moments of intimacy had passed by swiftly.

'Look, Mr. O'Mara, I would much rather not be in this business,' I said nervously. 'Ordinary dinners at conservative hotels are more in my line.'

'No one regrets it more than I, Miss Allen,' he answered quietly. 'Are you ready to tell me why you wanted to see me? What is your trouble?'

I made a helpless gesture. 'I could say everything. There seem to be so many things wrong. Perhaps they were there all the time, but I didn't seem to notice them until—until after that talk with you yesterday.'

'They were there,' he said briefly, his eyes on my face.

'Were they? Are they? How do you know?'

He smiled a little. 'That is my tasty dish, Miss Allen.'

I thought for a moment, dispassionately. 'You mean you know

something about us at Kilcomoden? There is some big wrong at the hostel that we are not aware of?'

'Please don't start being curious now,' he said quickly. 'Just go on quietly with what you want to tell me. Is it about Miss Cunningham's suicide?'

'Yes, Alison. Oh, I know I'm probably well off the line. It's the most horrible thing to contemplate, but—'

'—you don't think she committed suicide,' he finished casually. 'You think she was murdered.'

I stared at him, shocked. The word was not part of my daily vocabulary. 'No, I don't. . .' I began hastily, then went on with more honesty. 'Yes, you're right. I've been smothering the suspicion for so long now that it is difficult to speak straight out.'

'You haven't mentioned your suspicions to anyone at the hostel?'

'Oh no—at least, I think Mother Paul knows I'm worried about something.'

There was a pause as the curtains were discreetly drawn aside and the next course was placed before us. 'Chicken,' the detective said, as I poked surreptitiously at the sauce-covered gobbets.

I could not resist a gibe. 'You don't mind telling me the ingredients of some tasty dishes then?'

'You would have recognized it yourself sooner or later—like the truth of your friend's death,' he added gently.

'Then you think Alison was—murdered?' I faltered.

'I would like to hear more first. What makes you suspect murder, when all the facts point to suicide? Sergeant Wheeler seemed satisfied. His report was quite definite. I read it through carefully in case of any doubtful circumstances. Miss Cunningham was an hysterical, unbalanced type of girl. There was also evidence of a persecution mania which found a not uncommon vent in the writing of anonymous letters. I understand discovery was catching up with her. Self-pity, a distorted sense of guilt and the seed planted by one violent death all combined to lead her into taking her own life.'

'Yes, it all sounds so pat,' I agreed, on a sigh.

'It could be too pat. Is that why you suspect murder?'

I put my knife and fork down and laced my fingers together. 'Oh no! Knowing Alison, she was just the sort to do such a thing—even in order to draw attention to herself. I thought it was suicide immediately. She had even talked about throwing herself in the river.'

'What made you change your mind?'

'Her dress. It was when I saw her dress. She was mad about her clothes. The one she was wearing was her favourite. She would never have worn it knowing it would become so ruined. But that is not all,' I added hastily. 'Maybe that is mere feminine intuition, but from the dress I remembered the phone call.'

'Phone call?' he queried.

'Yesterday, after I had seen you at the Green Lounge. I was so worried that I rang Kilcomoden to see if there were any—well, you called them repercussions. Alison answered and thought I was her dressmaker. She confirmed an appointment for a fitting or something.'

He surveyed me with keen, narrowed eyes. 'Go on!'

'That's all, I'm afraid,' I replied lamely. 'Is the evidence too frail? But a girl doesn't go making arrangements about important matters like dressmaker's fittings—and they were incredibly important to Alison—and then commit suicide. At least, I wouldn't,' I added defiantly.

He smiled. 'I'll remember that. This phone call to Miss Cunningham—could you repeat her exact words?'

'I'll try,' I said cautiously, and went on to describe my subterfuge while calling the hostel. He made me repeat the story twice more, then suggested my going on with my meal. He pushed his own plate aside and stared absently at the mirror on the wall. It was my profile he was gazing at, but I did not flatter myself that it was interesting him at that particular moment.

Dessert arrived, a dubious-looking dish and highly spiced. O'Mara saw me toying with it, and interrupted his meditations to recall the waiter, who presently brought along a pot of fragrant tea and a plate of rice cakes. After settling me into the change of menu, he retired once more into abstraction. The silence worried me at first. Cyril, although a serious eater, liked his food interlarded with polite conversation. I had once spent a three course meal listening to his interpretation of the Companies Act. But presently I found myself relaxing comfortably, the tension of the last three days evaporating. Having imparted my suspicions to O'Mara, I felt that my responsibilities were over and all that remained was to forget the unpleasant interlude. I was quite relieved that the meal was almost at an end—otherwise I would have been having a free dinner under false pretences.

Then O'Mara ruthlessly shattered my feeling of well-being by asking abruptly: 'This guardian of Miss Cunningham's. Do you know him?'

'He was her stepfather. Her mother was dead. I don't think she liked him much, but that is nothing to go by. She would have pulled a poor persecuted foster child act, if he'd been the right type. Instead she behaved as badly as she could to him. He is a nice ineffectual little man, the sort who practically ask to be trodden on. Alison all but wiped her shoes on him. It was a wonder that he didn't become fed-up sometimes. In fact—' I stopped short.

'Go on,' he prompted at once.

I said ruefully: 'When you say that, I usually continue with something weak. It was just an ill-timed remark I made to Mother Rectress, that Mr. Sparks might come to regard Alison's death as a happy release.'

'Having made the remark,' O'Mara said conversationally, 'you went further and wondered if it were possible that the stepfather had pushed Alison into the river?'

I had given over trying to smother thoughts. 'Yes, I did,' I admitted frankly. 'It must be the way one violent death gets you. No doubt I'll end up by being suspicious of my best friends.'

'And who are they, Miss Allen?'

'My friends? Oh, come now—you're surely not—'

'I'd very much like you to talk freely about your companions at the hostel,' he cut in, raising his voice slightly. 'Is there any one girl you are particularly intimate with?'

'Fenella, I suppose. Fenella King. Then there's Clare and Betty—Mr. O'Mara, I don't want to be in this business. I've told you all I know. Can't my part end now?'

He shook his head in genuine regret. 'Your part is only just beginning. I'll be frank with you, Miss Allen. We haven't been making much progress with our inquiries into Braddock's death. Those raids we made got us precisely nowhere—his underworld associates refuse to talk. We haven't even got a clue to the weapon which killed him.

The whole investigation has become static. I'm at the stage when I'm willing to play any hunch—which is where you come in. I could do with a calm intelligent person right in the thick of things—which is your hostel.'

'At this moment I'm feeling far from calm, and imbecilic with fear to boot,' I retorted. 'Look, I know just the person for you. She's always saying she's an observer, and that is what you want, isn't it? Her name is Verna Bassett, and she is marvellous at finding out our deepest secrets.'

The detective took a piece of ginger and eyed it reflectively. 'She can't be too well liked.'

'She isn't,' I replied, falling straight into his trap.

'Then she would be no good. I must have someone who is liked and trusted by the majority. You seem to be friendly with everyone.'

'There are one or two whom I seem to rub the wrong way,' I said hopefully. 'Lorraine and a new girl called Christine Farrow.'

'How long has the Farrow girl been at the hostel?'

'A week or so. She's a music student at the Con. Beyond that I know little about her. She keeps herself to herself, as they say.'

'And Lorraine was the girl you were covering up for the night of the murder, isn't she?'

'I wasn't covering—' I began.

'Look, Miss Allen,' he interrupted, 'I'm asking for your full co-operation. There is no place for misguided loyalties in murder investigation. I want you to be quite frank and honest with me in all matters—even if it concerns your friends.'

'You're asking a great deal. I don't like telling tales or—or spying. Honestly, I'm not the person you want.'

His face softened again and he put a steadying hand on my tensed one. 'I know it's a rotten job to ask you to do. Believe me, I wouldn't make such an outrageous demand unless it was very necessary. If you really feel you can't . . . He left the sentence incomplete and waited for my reply.

I looked down at my covered hand, suddenly thinking of the poor bleeding body at the gates of Kilcomoden and the pitiful slime-covered girl on the deck of the launch—the one a petty criminal valueless in the eyes of society, the other a foolish, soon-to-be-forgotten child. Then I lifted my head and met O'Mara's anxious gaze, saying quietly, 'I will do whatever I can.'

'Thank you, Miss Allen,' he acknowledged, giving my hand a brief pressure and settling back into role again. 'We'll go back to the beginning. When did you last see Miss Cunningham?'

'Last night after dinner,' I replied, and went on to describe the climax in the anonymous letters affair, the subsequent meeting and our reasons for supposing Alison was the culprit. 'I met Alison at the head of the refectory stairs. She was so violently upset that it was impossible to calm her. She said something about not being able to stand much more, that everyone was against her, and that she would make them sorry. All the genuine, pre-suicidal clichés.'

'You didn't see her again?'

'No. Her light was still on when I went up to bed, but I did not feel like another scene so I went straight to my room. But I heard her go out sometime during the night.'

'What time was that?'

'I don't know,' I replied wearily. 'If I had known she was going to her death I would perhaps have paid more heed. But at the time footsteps going up and down the passage were just another aid to my insomnia.'

'Up and down?' he queried.

I was startled out of my tiredness. 'That's strange,' I exclaimed involuntarily. 'Our rooms are almost opposite and the last in the bedroom passage. The footsteps went past my door, then there was an interval when I dozed off. I woke up and heard someone go past again. Alison must have returned for something.'

The detective made no comment, but after a pause nodded to me to continue. I told him about finding the note and how Clare and I had gone down to the river in search of her.

'Just one moment. Miss Allen. Your suggestion is that Alison did not commit suicide. How do you account for the note?'

'I can't,' I admitted frankly. 'I was hoping you would say it was a forgery.'

He shook his head. 'Our handwriting experts say Alison wrote it. Sergeant Wheeler obtained a sample of her writing.'

'Oh!' I slumped down in my seat. 'Well, that just about fixes things.

Unless,' I sat up straight again, 'unless Alison was only running away, which is what Clare thought at first. She didn't write precisely that she was going to drown herself. Perhaps it was a farewell note.'

O'Mara shook his head again. 'Why would she go down to the river? If she was merely leaving the hostel, she would have gone out of the gates, and perhaps even at a more rational time. She wasn't being kept at Kilcomoden by compulsion, was she?'

'Of course not,' I answered indignantly. 'There is no accounting for what Alison might or might not have done. She liked to make high drama out of everything. Supposing she was running away when she met someone at the gates—after a man being knifed there, anything can occur at our gates—who inveigled her down to the river and pushed her in. How's that?'

He smiled a little. 'Quite good, but you forgot something. She took nothing with her. You said she was very attached to her clothes. You can't use the same clue to back up one theory and dismiss it for another. If she were running away at such an inconvenient hour, surely she would have taken something—her night attire, for example.'

'You're right, I suppose,' I admitted. 'And yet—when I entered Alison's room before I saw the note, it gave me the impression that she had gone for good. She was an untidy person as a rule, but her room was as neat as though Sister Emerentiana had just prepared it for a new boarder. The bedspread was folded over the footrail and cupboards were shut. It even looked as though the dressing-table top had been dusted.'

O'Mara's expression of tolerant interest changed. 'What did you say about the bedspread?' he asked suddenly.

'It was hanging over the foot of the bed,' I repeated patiently. 'Who folded it?'

'Alison, I presume. It's one of the rules that bedspreads have to be folded before . . .' My voice trailed away as I realized what he was thinking.

'Then it would appear that whatever else she was planning, Alison expected to sleep in her bed last night. You should have noted the significance of the spread before, Miss Allen.'

'I'm sorry,' I replied meekly, 'but I warned you my talents don't lie in detection. What about the strange neatness? What significance should I have read into that?'

He paused for a moment, then asked: 'When you have time on your hands, what do you do? Supposing you were in your room and you knew you had nothing to do for a certain period of time.'

'I'd soon find something to do,' I retorted. 'I'd start by tidying— it's when you give me the cues that this detection game is not so difficult. All right! Alison filled in a period of waiting by putting things away in their right places. What next?'

'Why did she have to wait?'

'Because,' I struggled with this one, 'because I had not gone to bed. She wanted everyone to be settled for the night.'

'She had probably taken that into consideration previously. No, Miss Allen, she was waiting for the time of her appointment. She went to meet someone down at the river, where she was pushed in to drown.'

I shut my mind to the ruthless picture his words conjured up and said, trying to match his impersonal attitude: 'Her favourite dress! That should mean something. She was always at pains to select the right outfit for the certain occasion.'

He asked, even more carelessly, 'Had Alison any male friends?'

'Not many. Certainly no steady boy-friend. She was too volatile for any lasting friendship. You are thinking that she wore that dress to keep a romantic assignation?'

'That seems the obvious reason.'

I gave a fleeting glance in the mirror at my new hat. 'Sometimes a girl will choose her pet outfit to give herself moral support for an important occasion. Dutch courage, as it were.'

He smiled again. It was amazing how different it caused him to appear. 'My former chief worked in a similar way. We could tell the various stages of a case by the tie he wore. He always made his arrest in a red one.'

Instinctively I glanced at the knot below his chin—dark blue with a thin white stripe. 'This case has a little way to go yet, Miss Allen,' he said gently. 'Let us go on. Dismissing the theory of a romantic assignation on your suggestion that she wore that particular dress to lend moral courage—'

'My suggestion may be wrong,' I protested.

'And it may be right. I don't know the rules of your establishment, but I doubt if any of Miss Alison's fleeting male acquaintances would venture into Kilcomoden should they even know the position of her room, which is unlikely.'

'Why should anyone—' I began, puzzled.

'The letter, Miss Allen,' he interrupted crisply. 'The farewell note that Alison wrote. Whoever pushed her into the river must have seen that note first.'

'But—but that means that we—that one of us—'

'You're making good progress in detection,' he said grimly.

I stared at him, horrified by the implication. 'Oh, I don't believe it. I can't. I know them all so well.' I snatched at a wild hope, as I tried to free Kilcomoden from the ghastly web he was weaving. You said the folded bedspread showed that Alison expected to stay the night at the hostel. Why, then, did she leave that letter before she went out?'

'That was written and put aside before the arranging of the river meeting, when she was planning to run away. Someone knew about it and planned a death to look like suicide. After meeting Alison and pushing her in to drown, that person came back and put the letter in a prominent position. I'm sorry, Miss Allen, but it must have been someone from the hostel.'

'But why?' I asked violently. 'Why should Alison make an appointment to meet someone from the house at the river, when she could see them just as secretively in her own room?'

He shrugged. 'You said yourself there was no accounting for the girl's eccentric behaviour.'

I thought desperately back on what I had told him, and found another, stronger straw. 'The footsteps I heard—up and down and back again. There was an interval between them, but not enough to allow someone from the house to get back after meeting and drowning Alison.'

He frowned quickly. 'You're sure of that? It's not just what you'd like to believe?'

I closed my eyes for a minute, back in the restless confusion of the previous night. 'I'm positive,' I replied. When he did not try to dissuade my conviction, I added apologetically: 'I seem to be helping with one hand and hindering with the other. I'm sorry.'

'That's all right, Miss Allen,' he returned equably, sitting back. 'The case is bound to be confused at first, but we'll get there.' He shifted his gaze to the mirror once more and remarked, rather abstrusely: 'If Miss Cunningham's death is murder, it means we are getting closer to the heart of the matter. We must guard against showing our hand too soon.'

I sat silent, respecting his abstraction but bewildered by his attitude towards Alison's death. He had spoken of it as a composite part rather than a definite incident.

Presently he said briskly: 'We'll hold back the inquest on Miss Cunningham until further investigations are made. That is where you come in, Miss Allen.'

I tried to appear eager and co-operative, but evidently only succeeded in looking apprehensive, for he said kindly: 'Don't get hot and bothered. You won't have to do much. I merely want you to be my eyes and ears in Kilcomoden.'

'Oh, is that all!' I said heavily.

'I want to use the utmost discretion in this new phase of investigation. It must not be known that the police are interested in Miss Cunningham's death.'

'I'm sorry I brought the subject up,' I murmured bitterly. 'Your job,' he continued, oblivious to my remarks, 'is to bring me every scrap of information you can lay hands on. It doesn't matter whether it seems relevant or not to you, but it may be important to us. You must mingle freely with your companions and find out everything about them—where they work, whom they see and where they go for entertainment.'

'Public snooper number one! I'll get myself as disliked as Verna.'

'Most important of all—you must guard against appearing suspicious or any other outward change in your demeanour. I can rely on you for this, Miss Allen?'

'I'll do my best,' I promised unenthusiastically.

He regarded me closely, but in a detached sort of way. 'It is as well you have a placid expression.'

'Like a cow,' I agreed. 'I'll cultivate a chew if you think it will help.'

He gave a quick smile, then said seriously: 'A word of warning!

Whatever you discover, please do not act upon it independently. I'll be at that tea-room of yours every day for your report, but if anything urgent should crop up, get in touch with me at once.' He held out his hand across the table. 'I know you'll work well for us, Miss Allen.'

After shaking hands, he rose and pulled back the curtains, but showed no intention of leaving the restaurant with me.

'Good night,' I said. 'And thanks for the dinner.'

'I trust you found it tasty,' he returned gravely.

Five

I

My narksome job began while I was waiting at a city bus stop. It was now going on to eight o'clock and crowds were thronging into town for the evening shows. An incoming bus drew up on the opposite side of the street, and amongst the load it disgorged were two familiar figures. On impulse, I plunged through the traffic after them.

Arms linked, their bright, crisp frocks easily discernible, Jean and Betty made their way through the crowd. I was able to follow at a short distance, and, when they paused, took up an observation post close by. Presently two young men in merchant seamen uniform joined them, and for a while they stood laughing and talking together. After a lively discussion—evidently on how they were going to spend the evening—they split up into pairs and moved off against the main stream of pedestrians. They seemed to be heading away from the city, and as the throng became thinner, I was forced to drop back to keep from being observed.

On the bridge over the river they stopped again and leaned over the parapet. Then Jean pointed excitedly, and tugged at her companion's hand. I slunk into the shadow of a news-stand as they seemed to make a dash towards me. Then they swerved and the four of them scuttled down the steps which led to the river bank. I moved forward quickly and peered over the parapet, just in time to see them climb on board one of the boats at the landing-stage.

It was Molloy's launch. The balmy evening had brought him down to the city anchorage in search of business. He was standing alongside with his concertina in his hands, alternately squeezing a tune and calling out the attractions of his river cruise to encourage customers. He leered in recognition as the two girls stepped aboard.

I waited in the shadows until Molloy had shoved off and the launch had chugged away, leaving a creamy wake. Then, awakening to a feeling of self-loathing, I went slowly back to the bus stop. Perhaps O'Mara could make something out of two pretty, carefree girls taking a river trip with a couple of nice sailors. I could not.

II

Fenella, on door and phone patrol, let me in. 'Where have you been?' she demanded at once. 'Not with Cyril, I know. He rang up and was almost upset to learn you were out. And you weren't working either, because he had already tried your office. You've got your new hat on too. Come on, own up!'

'I thought I'd like a meal in town for a change,' I replied lamely, dodging her bright gaze. 'How is everything here?'

Fenella rolled her eyes. 'Grim! Everyone is wearing a stiff upper lip and trying to be nonchalant. Sister Em keeps popping into the common-room to count heads in case one of us should follow Alison's example. She's told me at least five times to let her know when Jean and Betty come in. No one knows where they are.'

'They've gone for a trip down the river,' I said absently.

'Oh, drat them! She will be in a stew. Why didn't you tell them they weren't to go—respect for the dead and all that?'

'I wasn't speaking to them. I just—uh—happened to see them in the distance.'

Fenella put her head on one side like an inquisitive bird. 'Coincidence! What were you doing near the river? Looking for more bodies?'

'Heaven forbid!' I said lightly, moving to the stairs. 'I must go and take off my things.'

'Where did you have your meal?'

'At—that is, I don't remember the name of the place. Some out-of-the-way chop joint—nothing very thrilling.' I paused, and said clumsily over my shoulder: 'Look, Fen! I really was working. It was hard to concentrate today. I had to stay on to correct some stuff. Cyril must have rung when I was out feeding. Don't—I mean, you won't—' I put out a hand appealingly.

'Of course not,' she answered quickly. 'What's the matter with you, Mary? Losing faith in your friends?'

I started to mount the stairs. 'No,' I said. 'No, I'll never do that!'
You handled that badly, I told myself. You will have to be more careful. Fenella is always quick to sense anything wrong. But she won't give you away—she is too good a friend. You were lucky that she was the first you had to face. It will give you more time to adapt yourself. If it had been Verna now . . .

I paused outside my bedroom, and stared at the door almost opposite—Alison's room. That same faint line of light showed on the polished floor. Someone was moving about inside, then the door opened and Mother Paul put her head out. 'I thought I heard you,' she declared happily. 'Do come in here, Mary.'

I crossed the passage. 'You know you shouldn't—' I began awkwardly.

'No need to look so concerned, dear. Nothing has been taken away. I've been doing a little of the groundwork for you—so good always doing mine—I thought it might help. Such an untidy child—Alison, not you—masses of old letters and photographs stuffed everywhere. Dolls too—can you believe it, Mary! Did you have a satisfactory evening, dear? What did he say?'

Somehow she knew I had seen O'Mara. I made some rapid calculations—not even Mother Paul's peculiar powers of penetration could help her nail a fact as certain as that.

'It was you who rang that detective today,' I said, resignation in my voice.

She nodded. 'You seemed so worried and uncertain. Far more sensible to get expert advice than to try working things out yourself. Don't you recall how involved I was becoming over somatic theology, and that good, clever Jesuit had me all straight in a trice?'

I smiled at her. 'Yes, I remember. Perhaps the cases may be considered parallel. What would you say if I told you that I am no longer uncertain and that there is nothing to worry about?'

She looked at me serenely. 'I would say that is good news, Mary.'

I knew she didn't believe me. 'Mother Paul, will you leave it at that?'

'Very well, dear, if that is what is required. But,' she added naively, 'I sometimes think the best way to keep a secret is to share it with someone else. Please don't think I am trying to pry, but there is always something so—so unrelaxed about a person with a secret burden.'

'Am I as obvious as all that?' I asked, remembering Fenella's bright, inquisitive gaze.

'Not quite, but you've been fiddling with your hat ever since you came in. And you're not a fiddler as a rule. I'm sure she would notice it at once.'

I dropped the hat on to the bed, and willed my hands to stay inactive. 'Who would?'

'The guilty person. The girl who sent poor Alison to her death.' Mother Paul looked surprised at my obtuseness.

I took a deep breath and sat down. 'Mother Paul, how much do you know?'

She took a chair opposite, folding her hands in the loose sleeves of her habit. 'Not much—yet. But one cannot help pondering on one or two odd features. I do know that Alison's death was intended. Such a wicked scheme! Those silly anonymous letters—just the sort of pointless prank the child would play.'

'I don't follow you,' I said, knitting my brows.

'But don't you see, Mary? Turn the picture upside down. Give those letters some purpose and suppose that Alison did not write them.'

'You mean'—I struggled incredulously—'you mean that someone else wrote them with the idea of forcing Alison to commit suicide?'

She nodded, and poked through the neat piles she had made of Alison's belongings. 'Ah, here they are! I found these tucked into her compendium. Flowers and fairies on her writing paper, Mary! So odd when you recall that she wrote her farewell note on a sheet from an old exercise book. Though perhaps not. I must show you something else presently.'

I took the three typewritten slips, wishing that Mother Paul would not fall into irrelevancies at crucial moments. They were short sentences of silly abuse, similar to the anonymous letters that had been circulating through the hostel. I read them carefully, and then looked up. 'But don't these rather prove that Alison was the culprit, as they are among her papers?'

The rectress shook her head. 'No mistakes,' she said simply. 'I asked her to do some typing for me only a week ago, and there was a slip in nearly every word. No concentration, you know.'

121

'Then it was not the suicide note that was planted but these,' I said thoughtfully. 'Mr. O'Mara will be interested in your theory of coerced suicide. He whipped up a plausible story that Alison went to meet someone at the river—someone from the house. But I let him down badly by insisting that the interval between Alison's leaving her room and the footsteps that went past my door was too brief to allow it to be that person. He suggested that the suicide note could have been merely a good-bye—' I broke off to say wryly, 'I seem to be sharing the secret after all.'

Mother Paul leaned forward and patted my hand. 'A very good notion, too. Do go on, dear. You'll feel much better, and I may be able to help.'

Fully conscious of my ineptitude as a private eye, I had no qualms about confiding my troubles. She listened attentively, her eyes fixed on my face, and presently commented: 'A very clever young man. I thought so that first night. Poor Mr. Wheeler was quite outshone. Of course he is at a grave disadvantage not being able to get inside Kilcomoden. So very shocking to realize that something bad is going on among us, but we must close our minds to that and give him all the help we can.'

'I shall certainly tell him of your theory concerning Alison's suicide.'

She frowned. 'I am not so sure of that now—after what you have told me about Mr. O'Mara's suggestions. Perhaps there is a particle of truth in both theories, and the correct solution is a composite. It is a matter of selecting which parts match.'

'Well, that is not our job,' I said firmly. 'All we have to do is to provide the information and let the detective do the matching.'

Mother Paul nodded wisely. 'He wouldn't like it if we did. But it is rather difficult to refrain from trying. Just like a jig-saw puzzle. Only Mr. O'Mara has an idea of the whole picture—so unfair! One piece is that poor creature who was stabbed and another is Alison. How can they possibly fit together? Where is the fragment that connects them?'

'Jess!' I said, on a wild guess.

'Ah yes—Jess!' she repeated softly. 'Who is Jess?'

There was a pause, then she turned aside from the question and handed me a yellowing sheet of blue-lined paper with a heading written in Alison's hand—'My Last Will and Testament'.

'In books they always start by looking for clues in wills,' she explained ingenuously. 'Now, if the police can only find that man whom Alison wants to inherit her estate! She put his address in too. What is it again, Mary?'

'Hollywood, California,' I replied, a quiver in my voice. 'That's in America, isn't it? We have several houses there. We sometimes correspond. No *u*'s and single *l*'s, so peculiar! Why are you trying not to smile, dear?'

'The man you want the police to check on is a film star. He was very popular a few years ago. I don't think Alison actually knew him.'

Mother Paul said apologetically: 'I'm rather out of touch with such matters. What about the other person mentioned—the one Alison wants to have her tennis racquet?'

I turned the paper to the light, examining it carefully. 'I think Alison wrote this years ago—when she was a schoolgirl. It is just a piece of nonsense. What estate had she to bequeath?'

'She had a tennis racquet.' Mother Paul gestured to where it was propped in a corner of the room.

'You think I should follow it up?' I asked, checking the address of the second legatee. 'I suppose if I can't go wild goose chasing to Hollywood, Cal., at least I can make a trip to the northern suburbs of Melbourne, Vic. I'll take the racquet to this Rhoda Jamieson and ask if she pushed Alison into the river to inherit it. I don't suppose Mr. Sparks will want the thing, anyway.'

'He told me to distribute all Chicken's things among her friends,' Mother Paul announced dispassionately. 'In memory of the happy years she spent here. He really meant it, too. So odd!'

'So odd!' I repeated, with a touch of peevishness. 'So many things are so odd—Alison's notepaper, the way Christine Farrow practises scales, Miss Jones being a companion! Kilcomoden seems to be a museum of idiosyncrasies.'

'You're tired, dear,' said the rectress soothingly. 'Otherwise you would realize that it is just those seemingly unimportant things that Mr. O'Mara wants to know.'

'He said something like that,' I admitted, 'but please don't think of anything further that is odd for the moment. I'd better go to bed and give my brain a rest.'

'No, wait!' she said swiftly. 'We haven't discussed the most important item of all.'

'What is that?' I asked, puzzled.

She put a finger to her lips, and pointed to the door. 'It is something no one must know,' she said, gliding past me softly. 'I can't tell you how imperative—' She opened the door abruptly and the listener in the passage straightened hurriedly.

'Well, Verna?' Mother Paul asked conversationally.

The girl's eyes flickered from the nun's face to mine, and back again. She did not seem to have lost the least countenance. 'I'm so sorry to interrupt, Mother Rectress, but Sister Emerentiana is looking everywhere for you.'

'Why wasn't my bell rung? Sister can't be wanting me very urgently.'

Quite composed, Verna replied: 'I'm sure I can't say. Of course, if she had known you were in Alison's room, she would have come upstairs.'

The double-edger failed as Mother Paul said softly, 'But I told Sister where I would be.' In the silence that followed, Verna passed her tongue over her narrow lips. 'You are a very foolish girl,' the nun went on with unwonted severity. 'Eavesdropping is a dangerous and stupid pastime. No one can possibly obtain the full context through a keyhole. Far better if you had come right in.' Without waiting for a reply to this crushing speech, she sailed down the passage, her rosary beads rattling indignantly.

I glanced at Verna quizzically. 'I don't understand what Mother Paul means,' she said, in her slightly whining voice. 'I was merely passing the door when I dropped my handkerchief. Eavesdroppers never hear any good of themselves, do they? But of course, you couldn't have been talking of unimportant little me.'

I put my head on one side. 'Are you odd too, Verna?'

She smiled. 'Everyone likes to think they are different, but I know I'm quite ordinary.'

'Are you? I hope so, for your own sake.' Leaving her to construe this cryptic remark into whatever she had overheard, I turned into my own room and shut the door.

I was in bed staring at the same paragraph of a novel when, some time later, Fenella knocked. 'Are you still awake, Mary?'

I dropped the book and sat bolt upright. 'Yes, what is it? Come in. Has anything gone wrong?'

She put her head into the room. 'Jean has just arrived home. Some man pounced on her as she came in the gates, and gave her the fright of her life. Do come down and convince her that she is amongst friends once more.'

I was out of bed and slipping on my robe before she had finished. 'Just like the Navy—everything at the double. Relax, Maria! It's not like you to be so jumpy. Your role is to be a tower of strength.'

'Where is Betty?'

'Oh, she's okay—got home an hour ago. Jean and her escort went back to town for supper.'

Fenella had pushed the girl into one of the wrought-iron hall chairs. She was still there, weeping noisily, with her hair all over her face and her skirt rucked up one side unheeded. She seemed in a bad way, hysteria not far off. I knelt in front of her, taking both her hands soothingly. There was a red mark on one cheek, which looked like the imprint of a slap. 'You shouldn't have hit her so hard,' I reproved Fenella.

'I didn't lay a finger on her,' she protested indignantly. 'That's the pouncer's work, not hysteria treatment. All I did was to threaten cold water or to send for you. Isn't that so, Jeanie?'

The girl tried to smile waterily, then suddenly put her head down on my shoulder. 'Oh, Mary, he—he—I was so scared! He—'

'Yes, never mind. It's all over now. Just try and calm yourself, and then you can tell us all about it.' I turned my head. 'Fen, there's a bottle in Sister Emerentiana's medicine pantry labelled—er—"Stimulant". Make up a dose a little stronger than the instructions.'

She shot me a suspicious glance, but went off obediently. I soothed and patted Jean until she came back with the drink, saying laconically, 'I don't like it drowned either.'

I put the glass into Jean's cold, shaking hand. 'Come on! Down the hatch and you'll feel fine.'

Fenella squatted down beside me. 'What a jolly little group we are! Now, Jeanette, if you're feeling perky enough—and you should be—what was the man like? He may be the lurker Tommy and I saw on Saturday evening—youngish, wearing a raincoat and a slouchy sort of hat pulled well down?'

The other girl shook her head. 'I think I know who he was,' she said hesitantly.

'Who?' we demanded together.

'Bartholomew!'

'The old devil,' Fenella said, with force. 'He must have been soaking badly. Mother Paul will have to get rid of him.'

'No, we mustn't worry Mother Paul with this,' I said. 'There is probably some explanation. Jean, tell us exactly what happened. He may have thought you were an intruder.'

'I was walking up the drive when suddenly he grabbed me from behind and twisted me around. It all happened so quickly and it was dark, but when he spoke I knew it was Bartholomew. He said something and slapped me across the face. I cried out to him to stop and he let me go at once.'

'What did he say before he hit you?'

'I can't remember exactly. Something like "I warned you this would happen".'

'And had he?' Fenella asked pertinently.

Jean glanced at her in a puzzled way. 'I don't understand—'

'Of course you don't,' I said briskly, pulling her to her feet. 'Into bed with you. I'll look in presently and tuck you up. You've had a nasty fright, but we won't mention it again. What you've got to do now is to forget all about it.'

'I intend to,' she agreed. 'Good night, Fen—Mary. Thanks for the comfort.'

We watched her cross the hall. At the stairs she turned back and said with a wan smile. 'I suppose Sister Em would say just deserts for going out tonight. Maybe she'd better not hear about it.'

'A good notion,' Fenella agreed. 'We won't mention your adventure to anyone, then she won't hear about it.'

Jean went up the stairs. At the landing she paused again. 'I don't know how you two feel,' she called softly, but with a note of puzzlement in her voice, 'but I think there's something wrong about this place.'

'Not really,' Fenella said gravely. 'Now what do you think, Mary?'

'I think there has been enough talk for the moment. Good night, Jean,' I said finally.

Left alone together, Fenella gave me a sidelong glance. 'She didn't see his face, therefore he couldn't have seen hers. She recognized his voice, but when he heard hers he let go at once. Come on, Maria. What do you really think?'

'The same as you,' I replied with a smile. 'Bartholomew mistook Jean for someone else—the person he had warned about something previously.'

'Who?'

'Yes, who?'

Fenella tilted her head. 'Provoking woman! You have some idea?'

'No-o,' I answered hesitantly, 'but there's something concerning Bartholomew that puzzled me earlier. I can't remember what it is now, but no doubt it will come back.'

'But you won't, of course, tell me when you do remember?'

'No,' I replied equably. 'I don't suppose I will.'

Fenella drew a deep breath. 'Mary, I think you're a low mean body. How dare you keep me out of the fun.'

'I'm sorry—but it's hardly fun.'

'I've got half a mind to teach you a lesson. In fact, more than half. Presently it will be a full mind.' She looked at me from under her absurdly long lashes.

'What do you mean?' I asked, but I knew that mischievous twinkle of old.

She gave a little mocking laugh and ran to the stairs. 'Just you wait and see!'

III

At breakfast, Clare muttered lugubriously in my ear: 'Glad it's you, old girl. Fenella's a brick too—volunteering like that. Frankly, I haven't got what it takes when it comes to funerals.' I raised my eyes from an unenthusiastic contemplation of a poached egg. 'Funerals?'

'Poor Alison's. It is going to be this morning. You and Fenella are to represent Kilcomoden. Here's the girl herself.'

Fenella, dressed in a neat dark suit and her sanest hat, dropped into the chair alongside. 'Good morning,' she said cheerfully. 'Sleep well, Mary? Ravelled sleeve of care all knitted up?'

I eyed her suspiciously. 'I understand we are to be co-mourners. Whose idea is that?'

'Why, Sister Em's to be sure.' She met my eyes limpidly. 'She considered you were the least likely to disgrace Kilcomoden.'

'Which is why she asked you to go with me,' I said dryly. 'I'm quite capable of wailing alone.'

'And I thought you would be glad of the companionship.'

Fenella's injured tone did not deceive me for a minute, but Clare spoke up, 'Jolly sporting of you, Fen.'

'Perhaps Mary would rather have Jean,' Fenella suggested, as though anxious to help. 'She's over there with Verna. I'll slip over and ask.'

Clare glanced across the room. 'What's the matter with you? That's Lorraine. Going blind, old thing?'

Fenella gave a foolish giggle, an imitation of Mabel Jones's. 'Well, aren't I silly? I thought for a moment it was Jean. Though she and Lorraine are rather alike, don't you think, Mary?'

I choked drinking coffee and spluttered inarticulately into my table-napkin.

'Can't say I see a resemblance.' Clare frowned, as she thumped me on the back. 'Jean's eyes are blue.'

'But if you met Jean in the dark? She is the same height and figure as Lorraine, and they are both wearing their hair the same way at the moment. I do think of all the girls here, those two are the most alike. What do you say, Mary?'

'I agree with Clare,' I replied shortly, and got up. 'I'd better go and change this dress.'

'Yes, do, dear,' Fenella said amiably. 'Definitely not a funeral frock. I'll meet you at the front door.'

'Talking of Jean,' I heard Clare say. 'What's the matter with her? Looks like she got a black eye somewhere.'

I hurried upstairs, furious and anxious at the same time. Fenella had evidently spent her waking moments going over the girls and matching one up against Jean. And she was right—blast her! Of all those at Kilcomoden, Lorraine Lawrence was the one most like her—though what connection Lorraine could have with Bartholomew any more than Jean, I could not fathom.

Lorraine and Bartholomew! I checked my step in the bedroom passage and stared unseeingly as I groped for a flickering thought. I thought back to the night of the murder when Lorraine had not come in, and Bartholomew had been up when I had called at his bungalow for help. There was something odd—odd, I repeated to myself ruefully—about Lorraine having got into the house unobserved. And something still odder about her distress the next morning when I told her about the police coming. I struggled with these two pieces of Mother Paul's jig-saw as I changed into the dark grey suit I had worn the day before, and began an aimless hunt for my hat.

Lorraine and Bartholomew! What affinity could exist between two such dissimilar persons? Or rather, what hold could that ruffianly hobo have over lovely silly Lorraine that would make him capable of assaulting her?

I poked under my bed. One handkerchief and a hair-pin, but no hat. And I'd worn the dashed thing only yesterday. Fenella had remarked on it when she had let me in. From there I had come straight upstairs and . . . With an exclamation of triumph, I scrambled up. I must have left it in Alison's room during my session with Mother Paul. She had remarked on my fiddling and I had thrown it on the bed.

I shot across the passage and opened Alison's door. 'Hullo!' I exclaimed in surprise. 'What are you doing in here?'

With a gasp Mabel Jones swung round from the dressing-table, trying awkwardly to hide an open drawer. A slow, unbecoming flush spread over her plain face. 'Oh, how you startled me! I didn't expect—I mean, I thought everyone . . .' Her voice trailed off defencelessly and she averted her head.

I shut the door behind me. 'What are you looking for, Jonesy?'

'Nothing—nothing, really! It's just that I—' She sought desperately for an explanation, while I watched her squirmings, longing to put an end to the uncomfortable scene.

'Did Mrs. Carron-Toyle send you?' I asked.

She grasped at the suggestion eagerly. 'Yes—yes, she did.

She—some handkerchiefs of hers did not come back from the laundry. I thought perhaps Alison—that they might be . . .' The explanation faded and she stared at me like a trapped animal. But there was a look of resolution behind the hunted appearance. She moistened her pinched lips and said with a kind of bravado, 'What are you doing here, anyway?'

'My hat,' I replied, picking it up from the bed. 'I left it here last night.' I went over to the dressing-table mirror and fitted it on. 'No handkerchiefs in this drawer, Jonesy,' I said lightly and closed it. 'Try the tallboy.'

She shrank away from me, but seemed to force herself to hold her ground. 'What were you doing in here last night?'

'Helping Mother Paul to tidy up,' I replied, after a slight hesitation. 'Mr. Sparks said Alison's belongings were to be divided among us.'

'Then—then, anyone can come in here?'

'I suppose so. Was there anything in particular of Alison's that you wanted?'

She came back into the middle of the room. 'There—there may be. Perhaps I'll have a look round. Don't let me keep you. I know you're going to the funeral.'

'Very well,' I replied quietly, and opened the door. There was nothing I could do to prevent Miss Jones from staying if she wished. But from the doorway I turned suddenly. 'By the way, just where were you the night that man was murdered?'

Mabel Jones stared at me blankly, then her face contorted and her chin began to wobble. To my acute embarrassment she burst into a flood of tears.

'Please,' I expostulated feebly. 'Really, Jonesy, I didn't mean—what are you crying about, anyway?'

She rocked herself to and fro, as she had done in the refectory after Mrs. Carron-Toyle's anonymous letter. 'Oh, I'm so unhappy,' she moaned. 'I know it will all come right in the end, but—that horrid, wicked girl! I'm glad she's dead. Drowning was too good for her.' She made a sudden dive for the door, and fled sobbing down the passage.

I stared after her in bewilderment. She had been talking about Alison—and in a way I had not heard or even considered before.

Usually it was 'poor Alison, round the bend of course, poor kid!' The phrase had become her panegyric. What had Alison done to Mabel Jones to cause her, of all persons, to speak ill of the dead? And why should her name be associated in Miss Jones's mind with the murder? Maybe you've got quite a deal to report to O'Mara after all, I told myself as I went downstairs.

Fenella was waiting in the hired car that was to take us to the funeral. She was reading a morning paper, and did not look up until the door had been slammed and the car had moved down the drive. Then she caught sight of the tennis racquet I had slipped in and said, raising her brows, 'Rather an incongruous touch! Alison's last wishes or are you planning a game somewhere en route?'

I gave a careful and non-committal explanation. 'I'll drop off somewhere afterwards, and try to trace this girl, Rhoda Jamieson.'

'Seems an awful lot of effort for something relatively unimportant. But,' Fenella added, with a cheerfulness that I found sinister, 'if Mother Paul says so, it's good enough for me.'

'You really need not bother to come with me, Fen,' I said weakly.

'It's no bother,' she assured me, with a bright smile.

'Now look, Fen!' I began, and stopped as I met her innocent gaze. 'Oh, never mind. Come if you want to. You may even be of some help.'

'That's much better,' she said, in normal tones.

I grinned at her reluctantly. 'Don't pry too much, old thing.'

'I'll try not to,' she promised. Then she dragged out the paper she had stuffed in the seat alongside. 'The police don't appear to be any further forrader with our murder. They've got a photograph of Braddock published today.'

I read the paragraph she indicated. 'An appeal is made to anyone who saw the above man on Saturday, October 18th, to communicate with Russell Street C.I.B.'

'Not a very impressive creature,' was Fenella's comment on the picture. 'He hardly looks worth murdering. By the way, he is not the man Tommy and I saw—you know, the one who asked us the time.'

'Tell me exactly what this loiterer of yours looked like,' I requested, in carefully casual tones.

She made a gesture. 'Descriptions are such futile things unless there are birthmarks or sinister scars or such. He was of medium height, medium build—in fact, medium all round. But I think I would know him again.' She paused and glanced sideways at me. 'Shall I let you know if I ever do?'

'It might be a good idea,' I rejoined. She seemed content to let matters stand at that, and forbore any further teasing.

Alison's funeral was a small, pitiful affair. Besides ourselves, there was only Mr. Sparks and some aged great-aunt that he had managed to dig up to lend family support. She seemed to find ghoulish pleasure in the unexpected outing, while the little man himself was unashamedly emotional. I was glad of Fenella's presence when the time came to shake his clammy little hand and to speak a few words of condolence. She got me away from the graveside and on to our task of finding Alison's beneficiary before the going became too hard.

We found Rhoda Jamieson with surprising ease. After a call to her parental home, we learned that she was now Mrs. Herbert Baker and lived not far away in a flat, raw housing estate. Fenella found this fact rather depressing. 'Can you imagine anything more deadly, Mary? Born, bred and married all in the one place—and what a place! I bet she never ventures further than town and then only for the summer sales, and her husband potters in the garden all the week-end.' When she saw the few depressed-looking shrubs struggling for life in the Baker garden, and the sun-burnt couch lawn, she added: 'Or tinkers with the radio wearing a waistcoat and no collar.'

Her spirits sank lower when we caught sight of our quarry chatting over the side fence to a neighbour, with a dirty-faced child anchored on one spreading hip. She saw us coming up the overgrown path, said something to the neighbour who stared at us with frank curiosity and made for the back door, automatically running a hand along the flapping row of diapers on the clothes-line. Fenella and I proceeded to the front door and pressed a bell which didn't ring, determined to do the thing properly.

Apron and child off, Mrs. Baker opened the door suspiciously. 'If you're selling anything—' she began.

'We're not,' I assured her, wondering if I should put my foot in the door. 'Your mother gave us your address. We are fortunate in finding you at home.'

'Oh, I never go out,' she returned, without the slightest hint of grievance. 'What with Billy and the bubbie, I don't get the time. Nor want to. How I once travelled to work in the city every day, I can't imagine. Absolutely deadly! What did Mum send you for? Do come in. The lounge is in a mess, so please excuse. I just haven't got round to it this morning.'

She squeezed us through the minute hall into a slightly larger space, bulging with a genoa velvet suite. 'There's Bubs now. Sit down while I get her. Here, Billy! You talk to the nice ladies.'

The child set up an inarticulate whine at the suggestion—inarticulate, that is, to Fenella and me, but his mother said: 'Of course they won't. You are a silly! The things children take into their minds. Aren't they funny?' she appealed to us as she dragged her skirt free of the grubby hands.

Not knowing what we wouldn't do, we merely smiled indulgently. I even ventured to touch the small head coaxingly, but it set up such a wail that I retreated hastily, wondering uneasily what fearful horror the child saw in me.

'All right,' said Mrs. Baker resignedly. 'Come with Mums then, and we'll get our little bubbie up to show the ladies.' She went out, but we could hear her admonishing him through the thin, flimsy walls.

Some time elapsed before Mrs. Baker returned. There were sundry off-stage noises of drawers being opened and taps running, along with infantile expostulations. She came in pushing the reluctant Billy before her, now scrubbed and clean in a blue ranger suit, and holding a fat baby who was dressed in an elaborately smocked silk frock. Although she had not changed her own house-dress, she had done something to her hair and there was a circular mark of powder on one cheek, indicating a hasty dab with a puff.

Fenella came out of her domestic blues. 'What a little pet! Do let me hold her. Or do you think she would cry?'

Mrs. Baker passed the infant into the amateur arms. 'She'll be all right. Takes after her Mum—placid! Now Billy here—he's like his Dad. Real nervy type is Bert—never takes to strangers. Which reminds me, I don't know your names yet.'

'Miss King,' I introduced Fenella. 'Mine is Mary Allen.'

'I see you're engaged,' Mrs. Baker said coyly to Fenella. 'Perhaps it won't be long before—well, you know what I mean.'

Fenella looked agonized as the baby hiccoughed and was sick on her crisp, white blouse. Mrs. Baker had turned to me and was asking kindly if I had any marriage plans. When I said I hadn't, she tried not to look sorry for me, but before she had time to offer the inevitable comforting reflection about Mr. Right coming along one day, I said: 'We know you must be a busy person, Mrs. Baker, so I'll come to the point at once. Were you ever at school with a girl called Alison Cunningham?'

Without having to search her memory, she said at once: 'Oh dear, was that her? I saw it in the paper and I said to Bert, I'm sure I used to know that girl. I couldn't think where for a while. Terrible, wasn't it? But I can't say I'm surprised. Whatever happened? Was she in trouble with a m—a—n?' She spelled it out with a significant glance at Billy. 'Little pitchers have long ears, you know.'

'No, nothing like that,' I said, and Mrs. Baker tried not to look disappointed this time. 'Why did you say you were not surprised?'

'Did you know Alison? She was queer, don't you think? She used to pretend all sorts of nonsense. Mind you, I didn't have that much to do with her as she was in a lower class, but for a while there she used to follow me everywhere. I think,' she added, with a little self-conscious laugh, 'she had a bit of a crush on me. You know how silly some kids are at school, but Alison always went to extremes. I suppose in a way it was my fault—her doing what she did. Of course, it was all hushed up, and I didn't hear the full details because I was away sick at the time. As a matter of fact, my being sick was part of the whole trouble.'

'What did Alison do?'

Mrs. Baker widened her eyes and lowered her voice for dramatic effect. 'She tried to take her own life. She climbed out on to the roof through the science-room window and was ready to throw herself down to the tennis-court when she was spotted. They'd found the letter she'd left sooner than she thought they would, and climbed after her and pulled her back. But here's the funny part,' she added, oblivious to the blow she had dealt my theories concerning Alison's death, 'she did it on account of me.'

'Oh? How was that?'

'Well, you see, it was ptomaine poisoning I had. You know the muck schoolgirls fill themselves with. By Jove, Billy, if I ever find you with some of the messes Mum used to eat there'll be trouble!'

'Please go on,' I urged.

'Well, as I was saying, I was quite bad. In fact, they had to call in a specialist. He told me afterwards I must have had an iron constitution. But it's had its effects. Even now I have to be careful what I eat. Take tomatoes—they're absolute poison to my poor old turn.'

'Why should Alison want to commit suicide on your account?' Fenella prompted, changing the baby to her other arm.

'They thought she did it—tried to poison me. Wasn't it a scream? So silly really—because it turned out to be tinned salmon, or so the doctor said. And believe you me, I still can't look at tinned salmon. But to cut a long story short, it seems the other girls started twitting her about my being ill. I'd got a bit tired of having Alison follow me around all the time. I couldn't even go to the la-la without her waiting outside. So I told her off properly. She became terribly upset. She was like that, you know—some little thing would go wrong and she would practically have a brainstorm. When the girls started teasing and saying she'd poisoned me out of revenge, she really thought they meant it and felt she couldn't go on. Now, wasn't she a funny girl?'

'Quite a character!' Fenella remarked. 'Now you know why Alison made a will, Mary.'

Mrs. Baker leaned forward eagerly. 'I suppose I shouldn't ask and without wishing to seem inquisitive, what made her do it this time? I promise that whatever you say won't go beyond these four walls.'

Remembering the avid neighbour and the collarless, waist-coated husband of Fenella's imagination, I very much doubted the good intentions. I held my breath for Fenella's reply, for she had given me no indication of her ideas concerning Alison's death. Scooping the baby up carefully, she put it back into Mrs. Baker's arms. 'Oh, Alison had become even queerer since you knew her. Persecution mania and what have you,' she said, with discreet vagueness. 'I think we'd better be going, Mary.'

'Oh, must you?' exclaimed our hostess, hoisting the baby to one shoulder where it stared blankly at nothing. 'Won't you even stay for a cuppa? It won't take a jiffy to make.'

I could imagine a wedding-present tea-set being produced, and a cloth that Mrs. Baker had embroidered for her 'hope-chest'. 'No, really—we must go. We're both working girls, you know. I must get to the office.'

'You poor things,' Mrs. Baker remarked, as we all squeezed through the hall once more. 'I don't know how you can bear being tied to an office day in and day out.'

'By the way,' I said, turning back and holding out the racquet, 'Miss King mentioned Alison's will. That is why we got in touch with you. She wanted this to be yours.'

Mrs. Baker took it gingerly. 'What on earth can I do with a racquet? I haven't played tennis since before Billy was on the way. Bert doesn't like me doing things without him, and he was never one for games.'

'Keep it for Billy then. Good-bye.'

'Good-bye,' she echoed, still regarding Alison's bequest dazedly. Then as we were nearly at the gate, she called: 'Do come again now that you've found the way. Perhaps when you get married, Miss King, you might like to live round here. There are some awfully nice houses for sale.'

Fenella shuddered, and said sotto voce: 'I would rather have one room in Fitzroy. At least that would stop one from becoming wholly vegetable. Mary, how grim!'

'Yes,' I replied, thinking of what Mrs. Baker had told us, and wondering what O'Mara would say when he learned of Alison's previous attempt at suicide.

Fenella stepped out briskly, as though eager to forget the ordinariness of domestic bliss. 'Now we know why Alison made a will,' she repeated. 'She must have had treasured memories of her schoolgirl crush not to redraft a fresh one before her second, and this time successful, suicide bid. Perhaps you might have got the racquet, Mary.'

I halted my step so suddenly that Fenella sailed ahead a few paces before pulling up. She grinned back at me mischievously. 'Aha! I've given you to think, have I? Didn't it strike you at once? If Alison made a will before her first suicide, why didn't she make a new one this time? You can't tell me she even remembered Rhoda Jamieson's face, and as for that passé film actor—well, you know the number of crazes she's had since we knew her.'

I wandered along slowly without speaking. Perhaps I was still right about Alison's death, and that lack of a fresh will was another point in the score that all added up to murder.

'Thanks, Fen,' I said humbly. 'I knew you would be of help.'

IV

We parted in town; Fenella going off to her job evidently satisfied that she had punished me enough for my reticence. I put a call through to my office from a public pay-station, and after explaining about the funeral was allowed the rest of the day off. Solicitors usually take a solemn, leisurely view of death. I decided to go back to Kilcomoden to report the morning's doings to Mother Paul, but by some extraordinary chance she was not in. I went through the empty hostel, arriving in the kitchen as the last place to search and learned from Sister Berthe that both the rectress and Sister Em had gone out on an errand early that morning, and had not been sighted since.

Christine Farrow was eating a solitary lunch in the refectory. I took some bread and cheese and a glass of milk, and went over to join her. There were other lines of snooping to be pursued.

'Do you mind?' I asked, pulling out a chair.

'I suppose not,' she muttered ungraciously. 'I've just finished, anyway.'

'No, please don't go. I would like to talk with you.'

She scowled, but there was a guarded look in her dark eyes. 'What do you want to talk about?'

'The subject that should interest you most.'

'What subject? What do you mean?'

I glanced up from my task of making a sandwich and said mildly: 'You are the subject. What else? Did you think I wanted to talk about the person you were expecting—or perhaps hoping—would ring you last night?' This was a shot in the dark, but it paid off dividends.

'How do you know that? Who told you?' she demanded fiercely.

'No one—and I didn't know until now,' I replied honestly. She shot me such a justifiably furious glance that I asked hastily, 'How's the music?'

'You asked me that last night,' she snapped.

'So I did! Sorry! Uh—are you eating Sister Berthe's milk puddings?'

'I think you're . . .' she began, and half rose. But I doubted if she really intended to walk out just then.

'Again apologies. Honestly, Miss Farrow, it's like trying to walk a tight-rope conversing with you. I'm trying so hard to be conciliatory,' I added pathetically, 'but all I seem to do is to put my foot in it.'

'I don't want—'

'I know, I know,' I interrupted. 'You don't want anyone to be friendly. All you want is to be left alone—that is, except by one person. By the way, is Farrow your right name?'

'What—of course it is.'

'I'm trying to guess again,' I explained apologetically. 'Christine pause Farrow. Why the pause? You haven't another name tacked on to the Christine, have you? Christine Jessica Farrow—is that it?'

'I don't know what you're talking about.'

'Neither do I,' I said with a sigh. 'Let's be friends, Christine.'

'You sound like Verna Bassett,' she said, with a sneer. 'What are you trying to pry out of me?'

'We don't like anyone being unhappy or worried at Kilcomoden. If any one girl is in trouble, we all rally around and try to help.'

'Now you sound like that hearty Parker woman.' Christine was quite adept at sneering when she came out of her sulks. 'Was Alison Cunningham an object of your solicitude?'

I winced at the shot. 'Alison was a difficult person to understand—and to help.'

'Like I am? Is that a warning? I can assure you that I won't be found in the river.'

'Flippant words, but I'll take them seriously. If ever I do find you in the river, I'll know you didn't get there of your own free will.'

Her eyes widened and stared into mine. I returned her gaze steadily. Perhaps I was wrong to drop such a broad hint, but I knew whatever else was at fault with Christine Farrow, she was not likely to gossip over the thought I had just implanted in her mind. 'Unfortunately in Alison's case I treated her remark about throwing herself in the river without seriousness. Did she ever say anything like that to you?'

'I barely knew her,' she replied curtly.

'But you were with her in the library on the afternoon before she died.'

'I was in the library, but as far as I know Miss Cunningham did not come in. As a matter of fact—'

'Yes?' I encouraged, and was surprised to see a small, rueful smile touch the wide, drooping mouth.

'I went in there to escape from her. She was waiting for a phone call, and her incessant chatter nearly drove me mad. She was in and out the common-room as I was practising.'

'What was she chattering about?'

'I wasn't interested, so I didn't listen closely. Something about some new clothes she was planning to get and . . . Oh yes, a car. She said she was going to buy a car.'

'Alison didn't have the money to buy a bicycle, let alone a car. Was she talking sensibly or merely pipe-dreaming?'

'I don't know,' Christine said slowly, 'but she reminded me of myself before a music exam—excited, yet sort of scared. Then she seemed to lose her spirits and said something like "If I don't succeed, it will mean the end." '

'For someone who didn't listen closely, you are very observant,' I told her approvingly. 'Is there anything more you remember as a disinterested listener?'

'She spoke about the girls. She told me to beware of Verna Bassett, never to tell her even the smallest matter if I wanted to keep my affairs private.'

'Poor Verna!'

'And she said,' Miss Farrow went on maliciously, 'that you weren't such a bad old stick sometimes, and that Miss Parker—'

'Nice of you to tell me,' I interrupted. 'Did the character resumés follow on the bit about something being the end?'

'I can't remember. I told you—she was in and out all the time, waiting for this phone call.'

'She was merely throwing off impressions as something came into her mind, then?'

'Yes, I should say so.'

'Did she make any remark about the murder?'

'No-o,' replied Miss Farrow hesitantly, 'but she did say something about the police. She asked me if the police rewarded people for important information and if I knew how much it would be. I replied that it probably depended on the information, and that I had once seen a £500 reward offered for a murder information in a police-station. She said, how paltry, and that she wasn't interested in murder anyway.'

I sat silent, digesting and memorizing all this information and strongly regretting not having had a talk with Christine Farrow earlier.

Presently the girl rose quietly from the table. She spoke in an oddly softened tone. 'I did not know the poor girl, but—but if I should remember anything more she talked about that afternoon I will tell you at once.'

I looked up at her. I would appreciate it if you would. I know I can rely on your—discretion?'

She nodded and slipped away. I finished off my lunch, pondering for a while on the psychological effect of another's troubles on one's own. The system put milk puddings and any of Clare's energetic remedies in the shade.

I hung about Kilcomoden for a while, hoping that the rectress would return. But as time wore on and it came nearer to my appointment with O'Mara, I gave up and went into town. He was not in the Green Lounge when I arrived, and I was further disconcerted by the presence of another customer. After ordering tea, I opened a magazine, hoping the strange man would leave before the detective arrived.

'Do you mind if I sit with you?' asked a voice with a strong American accent. I lowered the *Saturday Evening Post* in annoyed surprise. He was a man about forty, dressed in a light-coloured gaberdine suit and a bow tie. His grin was engagingly boyish, but his eyes under their deceptive brightness were hard and shrewd.

'I'm very sorry,' I said coldly. 'I'm expecting someone.' But he was already moving his tray to my table and seating himself opposite. 'If I promise to push off as soon as your date comes, will that be okay?'

'Is this your first visit to Australia?' I asked, deciding to shake him off by being pleasantly dull.

'You wouldn't be wanting to know too much, would you?'

'I'm not in the least interested,' I replied indignantly. 'I only wish you would go away.'

He grinned again. 'Don't be mad at me, Mary!'

'How do you know my name?' I gasped, for it was recognizable even though he pronounced it Marry.

'I'm sorry if I'm late,' interrupted a quiet, even voice behind me. O'Mara's hand touched my shoulder for a fleeting moment, then he nodded a greeting at my American pick-up and drew up another chair. 'I see you've introduced yourselves, so we need not waste time. What have you got for us, Miss Allen?'

I said faintly to the American, 'Are you—I mean, I suppose you're a detective too.'

His eyes twinkled. 'You suppose wrongly, Mary. Steve is the only copper here.'

'Then who are you?' I asked, after a dubious glance at O'Mara.

'Oh, I'm just a guy called Joe.'

After that I did not press for his identity or the reason for his presence on our conference, for I recognized a brush-off even if he did not. 'Well, I don't know if what I have will be of any use, but . . .' And I gave an exact account of my actions and findings since the previous evening when I had followed Jean and Betty to the river ferry. Both men listened intently, O'Mara in silence and Joe occasionally murmuring uhuh.

'That's all,' I said at last, after winding up with Christine Farrow's recollections of Alison's conversation.

There was a pause, then O'Mara asked, 'You still do not believe that Alison committed suicide?'

'Yes,' I replied defiantly. 'Do you?'

He evaded the issue. 'If the girl was murdered, we will find it very difficult to prove in the face of the mass of evidence that points to suicide. The anonymous letters in her room, the farewell note, the previous suicide bid—they are stronger facts than the letter-perfect typing and the fact that she did not make a fresh will.'

I cast an appealing look at Joe, but he shook his head. 'Not my angle, Mary. Just you and Steve go on thrashing it out.'

'There is only one thing that can tip the scales in favour of your beliefs,' O'Mara said. 'The identity of the anonymous letter writer. If Alison was pushed or coerced into the river, someone wanted her out of the way—why?'

We were on to our old game of cues and answers. 'Because she knew something dangerous,' I replied promptly, 'and was about to try her hand at blackmail. She had ideas of making money—hence her talk about buying a car.'

'What did she know?'

'Well, nothing about your murder. She told Christine she was not interested in it. Perhaps,' I added slyly, 'she knew something about your tasty dish.'

He glanced at me inquiringly for a moment, then, quite unruffled, replied, 'There is a good chance that she did.'

I had a flash of inspiration and turned on Joe. 'Is that your angle, then? You're interested in Mr. O'Mara's tasty dish.'

'Maybe,' he admitted. 'Depends what is in it.'

'I can tell you some of the ingredients—a criminal type stabbed at the gates of an innocuous hostel for business girls, an apparent suicide, and a woman called Jess. There are other minor ingredients, small but necessary to the full flavour. The only things lacking are the recipe, which I think you two gentlemen can guess at, and the chef who concocts the dish who is as yet unknown to you, but is the person in whom you are chiefly interested.'

A silence greeted my summing-up. 'I'm sorry if I spoke out of turn,' I said apologetically, 'but this working in the dark and wondering what everything means is a bit nerve-racking.'

'You're doing a marvellous job,' said O'Mara swiftly. 'Be patient and keep up the good work.'

'I'm still not enjoying it,' I assured him. 'I'll be very relieved when I see that red tie.'

The American cocked an eyebrow and said uhuh in quizzical tones. 'Have you any idea what Mabel Jones was looking for in Alison's room?' O'Mara asked, at his most expressionless, as though the red tie anecdote was a lapse from discretion best to be forgotten.

'None at all, I'm afraid,' I replied, equally distant. 'Mrs. Carron-Toyle may have sent her there to snoop, but I don't think so. She leapt too readily at my suggestion that that was the reason. Perhaps Jonesy was the person Alison was thinking of blackmailing, though it seems hardly likely. A paid companion wouldn't be a financial proposition, especially as Alison considered £500 a paltry amount.'

There was a swift, almost imperceptible, exchange of glances between the two men. 'How long has Miss Jones been with Mrs. Carron-Toyle?'

'A little more than a year. She's stuck it longer than any of her predecessors. But honestly, if you knew Miss Jones, you wouldn't suspect her of—of anything criminal. She's a helpless, timid sort of person. Mrs. Carron-Toyle treats her abominably.'

From Jonesy the conversation turned to her employer, and I told them all I knew. O'Mara interrupted once to say, 'She is not wholly confined to her rooms, then?'

'We all consider that Mrs. Carron-Toyle's poor health is just sham, but even so she never leaves her apartment except when Miss Jones wheels her.'

'And when she goes down to the cellars after her special port,' the detective added.

'Yes, that must be so,' I agreed, surprised. 'It's odd that no one has ever seen her. The only way to the cellars is through the refectory.'

Again there was that swift glance, as though the two men were comparing notes. Then O'Mara said casually. 'By the way, we have traced the murdered man's movements a little further. He was seen on a river ferry during the afternoon. A neighbour of yours recognized the newspaper photograph and came forward.'

'Molloy? Was it his boat?'

He nodded. 'Braddock was one of his passengers on a river and port cruise. He disembarked at a city landing-stage about five with most of the passengers. Molloy took the others farther up the river. There was a group of girls from the hostel, so I understand.'

'Yes, I remember a few went for a trip that afternoon. There will be a bit of excitement over your photograph tonight.'

'Find out if anyone recalls Braddock and whether he spoke to any of the passengers.'

'I'll try,' I promised, gathering up my bag and gloves and making a move to rise. 'Is there anything else you think I should do?'

'Yes, follow up this connection you consider exists between the odd-job man at Kilcomoden and Lorraine Lawrence. I'm curious to know why he should want to attack her.'

'That is Fenella's theory,' I reminded him. 'She thought Lorraine was nearest in appearance to Jean.'

'Hold it a minute!' the American said abruptly, as I was getting up to leave. I looked at him with apprehension, wondering what else I was going to be coerced into doing. 'I would like to give the place a once over,' he said across the table to O'Mara. 'Care to be in on it?'

'What do you mean?' I asked, with a hollow feeling of foreboding as the detective nodded agreement.

Joe said soothingly: 'We want to get into your place sometime — say when everyone is asleep — and do a prowl. What time do you girls go to bed?'

'Everyone should be quiet about midnight — that's counting the girls who may go out for the evening,' I replied hesitantly. 'But you can't —'

'That's fine! Now where's the best place to get in?'

'The library window,' O'Mara suggested. 'Could you arrange to leave it unlocked, Miss Allen?'

'But you can't possibly —' I began in expostulation. 'Look, I'll ask Mother Paul if you can come sometime during the day.'

The American shook his head. 'No good — we mustn't be seen.'

I threw a helpless glance at O'Mara, but he seemed quite unmoved by the clandestine plan. 'Let Joe handle this,' he advised quietly. 'You can trust him.'

'Sure you can trust me, Mary. Now all you've got to do is to leave that window undone tonight, pile into bed and forget all about us.'

'I wouldn't sleep a wink! If you're going to break into Kilcomoden, I would much sooner be around to lend some semblance of lawfulness. I very often work late in the library, so my being up won't be considered unusual. What time do you propose — er — calling?'

Between them, they calmly fixed a time, and I withdrew, strongly regretting my malleable nature.

Six

I

The salon of Stephanie et Cie, where Lorraine Lawrence was employed, was tucked away in an exclusive high-rental arcade. I approached it diffidently at first, having heard that it was frequented only by expensive females who did not know the meaning of budgeting. Then the knowledge of my capacity as a secret investigator stimulated a mad, childish streak, and I rehearsed a swift, crazy role. If Lorraine could be the daughter of a wealthy grazier, so could I. I was down in town on a shopping spree—helping Daddy spend his wool cheque. My new cherished suit was no longer my best outfit, but a little country *tailleur* in which I had made the trip.

There was a dress show in progress when I swung nonchalantly over the peerless threshold, and the salon was packed with synthetic-looking women and a scattering of men with pouches under their eyes and paunches under their waistcoats. The crowd and the cigarette smoke and the parakeet babble gave me time to sight not only Lorraine and her employer, but a beautiful young man in a pale grey suit with a lavender satin cravat under his dimpled chin whom I guessed was Rupert Garland—Clare's object of derision. He was floating around after the models describing the clothes they displayed in a choir-boy voice, and calling the clients 'darling' when they addressed him.

Then the old-faced woman with the incredibly youthful figure and henna-lacquered hair, whom I took to be Stephanie, saw me. She gave a swift assessing up-and-down look and spoke to a still unconscious Lorraine.

Slim and lovely in black with her semi-business, semi-social smile pinned on, Lorraine was moving through the crowd ready to greet another customer when she suddenly realized who it was. The smile went out like a fused light and she had to force herself forward. 'What are you doing here?' she demanded, in a fierce whisper.

Borrowing a touch of Fenella's brashness, I went right into my role. 'I say, are you Stephanie? Bobo Cavendish told me I simply must come to you. In fact, she absolutely insisted. She always buys her things here. Acksherly'—I had heard one of the expensive ladies pronounce the word that way—'I usually shop in Sydney—do you know Clauderine's over there?—but Daddy wanted to see his wool broker here, so he flew our plane down this morning. I warned the sweet that I hadn't a rag to my back, and that Bobo had told me of the most marvellous place—I say, you do know Lady Cavendish, don't you? I haven't come to the wrong shop? How frightfully funny if I've got the names mixed.'

Poor Lorraine could only stand and gape, but Stephanie was alongside in a flash. She knew that no one so ordinarily dressed would have the nerve to enter her salon unless their poor taste was backed up by a substantial bank balance. 'I am Stephanie!' she announced, revealing an elegant set of dentures in a glittering smile. 'I heard you mention dear Lady Cavendish. Of course we know her well here. Have you come to see some of our pretties? I warn you they're quite wickedly expensive. Now what would you like to see?' She ran her hard, wrinkle-set eyes over me expertly. 'A little sports frock to start with—h'm? Lorraine dear, ask Rupert to bring out our Country Life collection—something very exclusive that we keep for our special clients, Miss—er . . .'

'Douglas-Smythe,' I said firmly, going in big. I had always longed for a double-barrelled name in my teens.'

'Miss Douglas-Smythe! Ah yes, I know your name well.' I was fortunate that Stephanie was as grand a liar as myself. She chattered through the social cream of two states, while by dint of repeating their names a syllable later I gave the impression that I was palsy-walsy with the best. We got on famously as the parade continued and the 'little blacks for those after-six dates' were translated into luscious evening gowns which would probably cost three months of my salary. I was careful not to enthuse over the show, and when a model swayed to a standstill at Stephanie's bidding, treated a *lamé* house-coat—'for those leisured intimate hours'—to a careless flip of my fingers.

Now and then I caught Lorraine glancing across the room with angry, worried eyes. I knew somehow she would manage that the exclusive Country Life collection would not be brought on to be treated to the mockery of my impersonation. Her attitude towards Stephanie impressed me as being sycophantic, as the older woman cooed endearments with her orders, while some of the customers treated her as just another pretty thing that dear, clever Stephanie had created for display. I listened in on some of the exclamatory conversation of the mildly debauched-looking group nearby.

'My dear! Stephanie's parties! So delightfully wild—and her adorable flat, just the right setting.'

'If you ask me,' broke in a sour voice, which probably belonged to a poor relation brought along for a sartorial feast, 'they sound too wild. You'll find yourself being raided by the police if you're not careful.'

'But how thrilling! I would simply adore . . .'

I switched over to the male section. 'Such delectable bait! Stephanie's such a smart bitch. I felt like a donkey with a carrot in front of my nose. Take my advice and give it away, old boy. Stephanie will never let you touch her. She keeps her locked up in a convent when she's not on display. Really, old boy, I'm not joking. The girl told me herself that she lives at some Popish hostel. What about trying your luck with Stephanie? They say she's still hot stuff. Or Rupert, if your fancy runs that way. Ha, ha!'

Golly, I thought. I seem to have wandered into Sodom or Gomorrah.

Then Lorraine sidled up quickly. 'Will you please go away!'

'I'm trying to learn how to be broad-minded,' I whispered back earnestly. 'The things that go on in this big, wide world!'

She bent a furious look, then moved off hastily as Stephanie called: 'Lorraine, my angel! Here a minute!'

I waited until their attention was fully occupied by a tightly corseted woman who was enamoured of a strapless bouffant gown of pink tulle, which might have suited her if she had been twenty years younger and many pounds lighter, then made a discreet exit.

II

The rectress and Sister Emerentiana were in the hall, home from their errand, when I got back. They were clad in their visiting cloaks and had big black cotton umbrellas hooked over their arms. I thought

Sister Em looked rather tired and cross, but Mother Paul seemed as imperturbable as ever.

'Mary, how nice to see you! Aren't you early, dear?'

'I took the day off.'

'Such a good notion. We did too, didn't we, Sister? We went to the Public Library. There were several references I wanted to check and Sister kindly chaperoned me. Full of old men reading newspapers—there all day, some of them. Imagine having nothing to do but read news, which of course cannot be accurately called news now.'

'I can't imagine,' Sister Em said, in what sounded like something of a snap. 'There is always plenty for me to do here.'

'You work too zealously,' Mother Paul told her tenderly. 'I'm so glad I insisted on your coming. The change has done you good, I'm sure.'

I tried to picture Sister Em enjoying watching Mother Paul pottering happily from one book to another, taking endless notes and whispering to the librarian to go up steps for her. She probably spent the time feverishly thinking of all the tasks she could have been accomplishing at Kilcomoden.

I said: 'You know I am always ready to do your reference work, Mother Paul. Please don't put yourself to the tiring trip into town.'

'I do know, dear. So obliging always. But they were slightly different references this time—a very tedious work, but not unrewarding. I didn't think you would care for it—though perhaps that is not so. However—so much more satisfactory to follow up one's own ideas oneself. Yes, Sister, of course you may go now.'

The quartermaster shot away in a whirl of skirts, as though she had a whole day's work to get through in half an hour. She probably considered she had.

'Not for the "Life", dear,' the rectress prattled on. 'The murder. I sat down with all the old men. That nice polite detective knows, of course—he said he was in and out of gaol—but I wanted to make sure.'

'Sure of what?' I asked, struggling with her train of thought.

'The man who was murdered—Braddock. He was the one who broke into Kilcomoden last year. You couldn't imagine the number of newspapers I went through. He was sentenced to fifteen months gaol for some misdemeanour or other. That's why he didn't make another attempt here. They get something off for good behaviour, don't they? You ask Mr. O'Mara if Braddock did not come out of gaol on the very day he was murdered.'

I gaped at her, but she went on triumphantly. 'That's why he wasn't worried about Braddock's being one of Sister Berthe poor, hungry men. But the odd feature is this; the last place Braddock visited before he got—I think the word is nabbed, dear—was Kilcomoden and then as soon as he came out of prison the first thing he did was to come back here. Why?'

I shrugged helplessly. 'I don't know. You tell me.'

She regarded me reproachfully. 'It's just a matter of applying one's mind to the question. There was something that he particularly wanted at Kilcomoden—something of such value that he had to be put out of the way lest he should keep on making attempts to get it. For if it was here for a whole year while Braddock was in gaol, the murderer must want it to stay.'

'What on earth can it be?' I asked. 'A cache of jewels left by the gang years ago before Kilcomoden became a hostel?'

She considered the frivolous suggestion seriously as she peeled off her gloves. 'No, nothing like that,' she decided, as she pulled out each finger, folded the gloves into a neat ball and slipped them down the fold of the umbrella. 'Now I'll know where they'll be next time. Such a hunt I had this morning!'

Privately I thought the idea similar to tying a knot in a handkerchief and then a string around a finger to remind one of the reason for the knot.

'No gang,' Mother Paul said pensively. 'Nothing so simple. Someone would have been arrested by now. Mr. O'Mara thought so at first, of course. That is why he said it had nothing to do with us.'

She went over to the hall-stand with its silly unnecessary bits of brass that Sister Em panted over daily, and absently hung the umbrella up. 'I want to hear all about your day, Mary. In the library after dinner.' And she left me abruptly, her voluminous cloak billowing out as she turned.

I thought of one thing that she would not hear—and that was the proposal of her nice polite detective and his bow-tied American buddy to break into Kilcomoden. However lenient and tolerant she might be, she could not, as rectress, sanction such a plan.

Lorraine sought me out as I hoped and guessed she would. She was in a magnificent fury, very different from the eager sycophant of the dress salon who was compelled to restrain her indignation for fear my imposture should be discovered.

'How dare you make such a fool of me! Coming in like that and pretending to be a client.'

I was changing out of my suit into a skirt and jumper. The dinner bell was due to ring any minute. 'We all like to pretend to be something more than we are occasionally,' I told her soothingly. 'Childish, but such fun and so good for the ego. I thought the one about Daddy and his wool pretty good.'

Her lovely golden eyes flickered, but she went on, probably hoping that her angry eloquence would overwhelm any awkward questions that might be coming. I let her have her head. 'Spying on me, that's what you were doing,' she stormed.

'I admit it,' I said cheerfully. 'Also spying on your desiccated-looking employer and Rupert. Clare may be rude but oh goodness! Rupert!'

'What's Stephanie got to do with you?' she asked quickly.

'Nothing, thank heaven! And the sooner you have nothing to do with her the better.'

'What do you know about Stephanie?' she asked sullenly. 'Just because she is someone far removed from your narrow bigoted world, you and Clare—well, why should I have nothing to do with her? Not that I am interested in your opinion, but just give me one reason.'

I sought for one vainly, feeling like an anxious parent who knows that her child's companions are unsuitable but is unable to put her finger on the crux of the unsuitability. Lorraine watched me with a smile of triumph curving her lovely young lips.

'I heard a line of talk among your customers that was most unsavoury,' I said, knowing that I sounded prudish and unconvincing.

Triumph changed to a patronizing pity. 'My poor prim Mary! Just as I've always said. You're not used to that social strata and the way they talk. Really, you looked so out of place this afternoon I nearly died laughing.'

'I thought you were more upset than amused—and frightened.'

She looked away. 'Well, naturally I was worried in case Stephanie found you out.'

'Nothing else?' I regarded her with my head on one side.

She gave a little tinkling laugh. 'What else could there be?'

I turned to the mirror and began to brush my hair. 'I heard some mention of the parties Stephanie gives—the ones you are always attending, Lorraine.'

'What of it? She likes me to be there to help with the entertaining.'

'Someone—she sounded like another simple-minded prude—suggested that one day the police might raid one of those parties.'

'How—how ridiculous! You surely did not take any notice of that.'

'Just enough to remember how allergic you are to the police.'

'Allergic—what do you mean?'

'A great deal!' I turned and scrutinized her closely. She seemed to have lost some of her surface assurance. 'You weren't too keen to be interviewed by the police after the murder. Why?'

'I didn't know anything about the murder,' she rejoined, backing against the door as I came forward, brush in hand.

'Exactly!' I tapped her on the shoulder. 'You'd been to a party at Mrs. Garland's flat, came home with all the appearances of having had what is known as a good time, and the next morning when I mentioned the police you looked ready to faint.'

'I knew there had been some sort of accident and that was why the police had come.'

'You didn't know about the murder, but you knew there had been an accident,' I repeated. 'Just how did you know that anything had happened?'

Lorraine fumbled for the door-handle, her eyes wide like those of a frightened child. 'Where were you when Braddock died?' I asked sternly. 'What time did you come home that night?'

'Let me go,' she whispered as I gripped her slim, delicate wrists easily with one hand. 'I didn't see anyone. I swear I didn't. I don't know anything about the murder.'

'And how did you get into the house without my seeing you? How did you overhear my telling Bartholomew about an accident?'

Her eyes moved to and fro, dodging mine. 'I—I—'

'You were in his room, weren't you? When Mother Paul sent me to get him, you were there. When we went off to meet Sergeant Wheeler, you slipped into the house.' I paused and took a deep breath before the final question. 'Lorraine, who is Bartholomew? What hold has he over you?'

She wrenched herself free and tugged the door open. 'I'll never forgive you. You'll pay for this.' Weeping furiously, she rushed along the passage to her own room.

III

The talk at dinner that night centred mainly on the photograph of the murdered man and the news release that Molloy had identified him as one of his launch passengers. Our murder swung into focus once more and Alison was forgotten in the excitement of several girls claiming instant recognition of Braddock. Fenella called it 'photo-suggestion', and I was inclined to agree with her when I heard Betty say, 'As soon as I saw him, I felt something was queer. He looked just the type to get murdered'—as though she rubbed shoulders daily with criminals and knew all about them.

'Excuse me, you said at the time that he must be a bus conductor by the way he pushed through,' Jean said dampingly.

'And when he spoke,' Betty went on with a shudder, ignoring the interruption—they were evidently hovering near one of their periodical rows—'he sounded so sinister.'

Jean gave a disparaging laugh. 'Rot! All he wanted to know was when Molloy was going to play his concertina.'

Fenella broke in soothingly as Betty's eyes began to flash: 'Anyone who mentions that agonizing instrument is certain to sound sinister. Do go on, Bet!'

She tossed her head and threw a glance of triumph at her friend, who sat inspecting her nails with an air of superior boredom. 'Then he asked Molloy if there were any overseas ships in port worth seeing. I guessed why, of course.'

'All done by guesswork,' Jean murmured.

'He was planning to stow away on one, and escape from the gang who were after him,' she announced loudly, and Jean laughed outright.

Clare came up to the table with a laden tray. 'What's the joke? I could do with some laughs.' She was late home as it had been her evening for 'Health and Beauty for Busy Business Folk', after-work classes that she conducted to correct 'that typist slouch and clerk curvature'. She tucked her napkin into the collar of her blouse, powdered her plate and the table with salt and fell on the braised steak with gusto. 'Well, what's so funny?' she asked, munching at us.

'The girls were on the ferry on Saturday,' I explained. 'They recognized Braddock from his picture and the fact that he spoke to Molloy.'

'Miss Martin did the recognizing,' Jean corrected. 'Count me out, please. I like to be quite sure of my facts before committing myself. Several passengers talked to Molloy—though why anyone should choose to chat with that leery customer I can't fathom.'

'He helped us find Alison,' Clare said, as though defending him. Her mouth was twisted and she pushed her plate aside, her appetite suddenly spoiled. She had the effect of silencing us for a moment.

Verna had pussy footed up with her usual genius at spotting a discussion group. She leaned over my chair so that I could feel her breath on my cheek. 'Of course it's only a coincidence, but doesn't it seem funny that Mr. Molloy should be connected with both our tragedies!'

'There's a laugh for you, Clare,' Fenella pointed out. 'Sit down, Verna, and give us some more.'

'Oh, I didn't mean to make a joke.' Verna simpered in the skin-prickling way she had when anyone paid her special attention.

'You didn't!' Fenella opened her eyes wide. 'What did you mean then?'

'I can't explain exactly. Perhaps I shouldn't have said anything. I don't know how it is, but I always seem to be taken up the wrong way. Of course, I never had much to do with Molloy myself, but poor Alison . . She stopped and slid her eyes around the table, admiring the effect she had created. We had all stiffened involuntarily except Fenella, who said ironically: 'Behold us all agog! Do continue, Verna dear.'

She flicked a glance in her direction and smiled mirthlessly. 'My mother used to say it was awfully common to use terms of endearment haphazardly, but perhaps manners have changed since her day.'

'Oh, I'm as common as dirt, my pet,' Fenella said airily. 'So glad you didn't take it for affection.'

Verna shook her head sadly. 'I wonder why you don't like me. I do try so hard to be friendly and nice. If only I knew what I did to put your backs up so.'

'I could tell you,' Clare said bluntly, 'but I would take all night. I wish you would go away. You're giving me indigestion.'

'What about Alison?' Betty said, undiverted by the scrapping.

But Verna had risen. 'I'm spoiling Clare's dinner—and actually I've forgotten what it was I was going to say. Anyway, you're never very interested in anything I say, are you? Perhaps I may remember later. If I do, I'll tell Mary.'

'What makes you think I'll be interested?' I asked, getting up too and gathering the dirty dishes on to a tray. I was in truth keenly interested, but knowing Verna's form, I tried to hide it.

But she must have guessed, for she slid on to another subject. 'Do let me take the tray, Mary. You must be tired after your big day.'

'I can manage, thanks,' I replied shortly.

'What do you mean—big day?' demanded Jean, who had never learned to ignore Verna's nuances.

'Why, the funeral of course—poor Alison's funeral! What else could I have meant? You girls always seem to be reading something into my words.'

'Clare, I'll go and get some bicarb from the quartermaster,' Fenella offered. 'I guess we could all do with a dose.'

'Oh yes, you went to poor Alison's funeral with Mary. What was it like?'

'Fine! We enjoyed ourselves no end,' Fenella answered, piling plates to teetering point on my tray.

'I know you don't mean to be flippant, Fenella, but do you think it quite nice to refer to our poor dead friend's burial like that?'

Fenella paused, weighing a cup, containing the dregs of someone's tea, thoughtfully. Verna backed away hastily. 'Well, I must go now. I thought I would offer Lorraine a game of draughts or something of that nature to help steady her nerves.'

'What has glamour-pants got nerves about this time?' I heard Jean ask, as I carried the tray to the servery.

'If that girl,' Fenella said later, as she handed me a cup of coffee, 'keeps on with her nasty innuendoes there will be another murder.'

We were in her room where she usually made coffee after dinner on her little spirit stove. I refused milk and drank it hot and black, hoping it would keep me alert for the uncomfortable hours ahead. Fenella picked me up at once. She was always sharp about little matters.

'You remind me of Tommy when he was swotting. Are you sure you wouldn't like a wet towel round your head, too?'

I said thoughtlessly, 'All I would like is my nice comfortable bed.'

Fenella rooted in her cupboard for sugar. 'Why don't you go to bed, then?'

'I promised Mother Paul a session in the library—on the "Life",' I added, glad that her back was turned.

'Skip it. She won't mind. And you do look worn. You're losing your smooth, cultured appearance.'

'I didn't know I had one,' I said, peering in the mirror and feeling depressed by the reflection.

'Hasn't Cyril ever told you?'

'Cyril's compliments are of a negative kind. He tells me if my colour isn't as good as usual or that he prefers my hair done the other way.'

Fenella made a face. 'If you marry him, Maria, he'll probably turn out like the husband of that Rhoda woman we saw this morning.' That she was relying solely on her own imaginative creation did not prevent the comparison from sounding disparaging. She went on adding wonderfully dreary bits to the image, making me laugh. Then, in the middle of a mordant description of the hapless Mr. Baker's fixed habits like laying out his slippers at the precise angle ready to receive his toes in the morning, she broke off to say impulsively, 'I wish it would all stop, don't you, Mary?'

I felt my face going rigid and expressionless again. 'You wish what would stop?'

'Oh, don't pretend,' she said impatiently. 'You know what I mean. There's Clare with a Spartan boy face every time Alison's name crops up, and Jean and Betty bickering . . .'

I got up from her bedroom chair and drained my coffee. 'That's nothing new.'

'. . . and Verna slithering around with that I-know-something-you-don't-know look on her beastly, secretive face, and Lorraine—what's the matter with her? I saw her coming out of your room.'

I moved over to the door. 'It's a short story, but I'll make it as long as I can some other time.'

'Cagey, huh? Take care, my girl!'

'No, Fen, please!' I said wearily.

'Okay, okay! But why won't you let me help?'

'Too many cooks may spoil—a tasty dish.'

She regarded me knowingly. 'There must be some significance in that. You never talk in platitudes as a rule—not even misquoted ones.'

'I don't know how it is,' I said, in a recognizable imitation of Verna's whine, 'but you always seem to read something into whatever I say.'

Fenella grinned, and then asked seriously, 'Does she know anything, Maria?'

'I don't know. She likes to keep us guessing, I think.'

'She presumes on knowledge, and we, like flats, fall for her trap and give things away unwittingly.'

'Don't let her worry you. She has so few amusements.'

'Oh, I don't,' she said quickly. 'It's just—she could have written the anonymous letters for all your grand proof. Do you think we were wrong about Alison being the culprit?'

I was silent, not wishing to make a comment in case I should give myself away. It was inevitable that Fenella should start thinking along other lines than the ones we had all accepted on the surface. 'I'd better go,' I said, opening the door. 'Mother Paul will be waiting.'

But the rectress was not in the library. Jabbing at the keys, I remembered the ribbon needed changing. The last few pages of the Foundress's childhood promised to fade out before her adolescence if I put the tedious job off any longer. I fiddled around, fitting in a new reel, but still Mother Paul did not come. After wandering about the room aimlessly, I opened the door and went into the hall.

Mabel Jones came out of the passage leading from Mrs. Carron-Toyle's apartment. She was carrying an empty dinner-tray, the napkin crumpled in one corner. She hesitated, blushed embarrassingly, then went along to the service lift near the refectory stairs.

I went after her. 'Hullo, Jonesy! Have you seen Mother Paul anywhere?'

She kept her head ducked as she pulled the rope. 'She is with Mrs. Carron-Toyle.'

'I'd better go and rescue her then.'

'Mary!' Miss Jones picked up the napkin and folded it into its ring, near to tears with agitation. She gave a gulp and said in a rush: 'I want to apologize. I really don't know what came over me this morning — talking of a poor dead girl like that. I didn't mean anything I said. Please be so kind as to forget it. I'm so ashamed of myself.'

'Don't worry about it,' I replied, feeling uncomfortable at such self-abasement. No wonder Mrs. Carron-Toyle kept pricking at her. 'Nothing to apologize about, actually. You didn't wound my feelings.'

'But you will forget it, won't you?' she sniffed. 'I could not bear anyone to know.'

I was about to reply with soothing acquiescence when the same maliciousness that Mabel's grovellings induced in her employer caused me to change. 'What don't you want everyone to know? That you called Alison wicked or that you were looking for something in her room?'

She gave a soft moan. 'Please, Mary! You are not hard as a rule. You don't understand —'

'No, I don't,' I agreed bluntly. 'There are many things I don't follow at Kilcomoden, and you're one of them, Jonesy.'

She backed away, her watery blue eyes frightened. 'I must go. Mrs. Carron-Toyle will be wanting me.'

'No, she won't,' I said, pinning her up against the passage wall. I felt like Clare in one of her overbearing moods. I was borrowing traits from all my friends. 'Why didn't you like Alison? What did she do to you?'

'Nothing — nothing,' she whispered in gasps. 'I told you — I didn't mean anything.'

'Then why are you so anxious that no one should know? What was Alison up to?'

'I don't understand — please, Mary —'

'Come on, Jonesy! Did Alison have some hold over you? Was the silly child trying to blackmail you?'

'No—no! Really, Mary—nothing like that.' She seemed genuinely horrified at the suggestion.

'Did you ever receive a letter?'

'A letter?' she repeated, stark with apprehension.

'An anonymous letter. You know—Mrs. Carron-Toyle got one. You can't have forgotten the fuss. Alison was supposed to have written them.'

She shook her head dumbly.

'Mrs. Carron-Toyle's was wrapped in her napkin—the one you folded tonight. Do you always fold it?'

She saw what I was driving at and moaned again. 'I didn't write it. I swear I didn't. Oh, how can you treat me like this!'

'Easily,' I said ruthlessly. 'I want to know who wrote those letters.'

'Alison . . .' she began.

'Alison wasn't the culprit. Another person wrote them—someone who was in the house when we were all at work and used the library typewriter. You were here. You could have written it and slipped it in her napkin here at the service lift.'

Her face crumpled and she began to weep. 'I didn't—really I didn't. I—I can't even type.'

That was an anticlimax with a vengeance. She could have been lying, of course, but her distress seemed too genuine to be doubted. I moved aside and said inadequately: 'Sorry, Jonesy! I'm a beast to use you so badly.'

She pulled out a handkerchief and removed her misted glasses to wipe her eyes. 'What is the matter with you, Mary?' she quavered. 'You're behaving so strangely.'

'A few things on my mind. Forget it, will you?'

IV

Mrs. Carron-Toyle was speaking in the unctuous tones that she used in her dealings with the nuns. 'I only wish I could be of more help, dear Mother Rectress. My poor heart just bleeds for you in this time of terrible anguish.' She looked round sharply as Jones and I entered. 'Ah! One of your dear girls come to visit a poor sick woman.'

Mother Paul, who had been drifting about the overcrowded room touching this and that with her finger-tips, said tactlessly, 'Mary probably came to find me, didn't you, dear?'

'Jones,' snapped Mrs. Carron-Toyle, who did not like her lines spoiled, 'did you make that call? No, of course you didn't. I can tell by your doltish expression. What I pay you for I don't know.'

'I'm so sorry,' her companion said in a flustered voice. 'The phone was engaged and then Mary—I'll go back at once.'

The widow shot me a sharp glance as she pinched the bridge of her fleshy nose. 'I am feeling far from well. If Jones had had the consideration to ring my doctor at once, I wouldn't have to suffer like this. Such a devoted man and so interested in my case—he always comes at once.'

'Are you ill?' the rectress asked, in surprise. 'Why didn't you mention it before? I wouldn't have disturbed you.'

Mrs. Carron-Toyle managed a brave smile. 'I knew how anxious you were to consult me, so naturally I put aside all thought of self. But I really must ask you to retire now.'

'Oh, dear!' said Mother Paul, as we went back to the library. 'I hope I wasn't indiscreet.'

'She is no more sick than I am.'

'I didn't mean that precisely.' She played around with the switches at the door to find the table light. 'But since you mention it, it does seem rather odd the way she is always sending for the doctor.'

'Some people enjoy poor health, you know.'

'Such an impressive-looking man. That hat and satchel—just like a politician!' She moved about the room to knock up crushed cushions and straighten chairs, then floated over to the windows. I felt an insane temptation to tell her to leave them unlocked. 'No work tonight, Mary. We'll have a little chat and then off you go to bed.'

'I'm not tired,' I protested, with an involuntary glance at the curtains. 'I mean to get quite a bit of your manuscript done tonight.'

'No, I forbid you,' Mother Paul said firmly. 'Now, what happened today?'

The account of my movements took some time, even though there were several parts I deemed it expedient to omit. Bartholomew was not mentioned and Lorraine barely touched on, and as for O'Mara's American mystery man—that name was kept well out of the discussion.

'Naughty, teasing child,' Mother Paul remarked, when I told her of Fenella's dogging my footsteps. She was very interested in the visit to Mrs. Baker which had been her own idea, and seemed quite satisfied with the outcome, even though I was not.

'No, that's all right, Mary. Clever Fenella to see that point about no second will.' She nodded her head slowly. 'I'm beginning to understand now.'

'Understand what?' I asked, glassy-eyed as usual when Mother Paul could see significance where I could not.

'Why Alison was supposed to have written the anonymous letters, of course,' she replied, as though surprised at my dullness.

I sat back and let her do the theorizing, glancing anxiously at the clock and wondering if she would take long.

'Yes, it is getting late, dear. Perhaps you'd better go to bed and we'll discuss matters in the morning.'

I tried to look alert. 'No, go on, please. I'll have to go to the office in the morning. I can't give over all my time to the police.'

'Well, just as you like, but you do seem very weary.'

'I believe you're trying to fob me off,' I remarked, trying to achieve a bright smile.

'Indeed no,' she replied quickly. 'In fact, there is something I need your advice about. How many typewriters are there at your office?'

'Three, but they haven't been used for anonymous letters.'

'Don't be silly, dear. What make are they?'

'All the same—Royals.'

Mother Paul suddenly swooped across the room. 'Now, that is most interesting. Would it be possible that most offices use the one brand of machine?'

'Quite possible, I should say. Why?'

'Then whoever wrote the notes must be someone who has been moving from one job to another lately. None of the typing seems to be identical, even in the three letters we found in Alison's room.'

'We are right back where we started,' I said despairingly. 'Alison held the record for changes in jobs. All the other girls—though there's Fenella. She has had a few moves. She . . .' I stopped, shooting a swift glance at the nun. No, no—not Fen! The idea was ridiculous.

But Mother Paul was apparently pursuing her own line of thought. 'The idea being either to render the typing untraceable or to point still further to Alison. Tell me, Mary—what made you consider Alison the culprit at first?'

'Well, it was the sort of thing she would do and then the typewriter in this room had been used the day Mrs. Carron-Toyle received her note. I had broken off in the middle of a page and the alignment was different. But that theory is well up the pole now. Christine Farrow tells me Alison did not come into the library.'

'In that case we can cross Miss Farrow off the list of suspects, for I think you were intended to notice the change of alignment after identifying the typing of Mrs. Carron-Toyle's note and to blame Alison, who had presumably been alone in the house. To my mind, all the letters had been prepared some time ago and delivered in a planned sequence. When the time was ripe, the final one was sent to Mrs. Carron-Toyle who could be counted on to make a tremendous fuss— a climax at which the real writer was aiming.'

'But it was Miss Jones who made the most fuss,' I objected. 'Though I dare say if she hadn't become so distraught over the matter, Mrs. Carron-Toyle would have caused a sensation in some other way. And as for the planting of the letter, perhaps it wasn't so difficult after all. Miss Jones uses the service lift to transport the tray. The note could have been folded into the napkin while she was climbing the stairs from the refectory.'

Mother Paul beamed approval of my theory. 'We know why and how—now we must find out who. Dear me, how very interesting a detective's life must be!'

I tried to share her enthusiasm, but privately I considered it must be abominable.

With her uncanny perspicacity, Mother Paul said: 'Don't think in positive or personal terms, Mary. If we allow our feelings to enter into the matter, we are useless both to Kilcomoden and to the police.'

'I try not to, but it's hard when you remember that one of the girls—perhaps a friend—'

'Hush!' She raised one hand, regarding me with a mixture of sympathy and sadness. 'We won't talk any more now. I've kept you up long enough.'

I got up thankfully, thinking the session was over and that she would precede me to the door. I did not need the chiming clock to remind me that the time was fast approaching the hour I had guaranteed O'Mara as being safe to enter Kilcomoden. But Mother Paul picked out a book from one of the shelves and sat down under the table light. I eyed her in dismay, knowing from experience that once she got into a book, time sped by unheeded.

She turned a page and glanced at me vaguely. 'Is anything the matter, Mary?'

'No—no, of course not. I—'

'Don't fiddle with your cardigan, dear. You're pulling it out of shape.'

I clasped my betraying hands together. Soon O'Mara and his American friend would be creeping into the grounds. I had to get her out of that book and away from the house. 'I've—I've just thought of something, Mother Paul.'

She kept one delicate finger on the page as she looked up.

'About Christine Farrow. I had a long talk with her today.'

'Did you, dear? I had one yesterday. Such an odd girl, until one knows her better. She came to me wanting to know how she could join the community. People still cling to the belief that convents are places for broken hearts. Do go to bed, child!'

'She talked about Alison,' I said desperately, taking another swift glance at the clock. Perhaps the two men were even now below the terrace.

'Yes, she told me all about that too. But we won't discuss it now. You're far too tired.'

I put a hand to my reeling head. 'I'm not tired. I think I'll read for a while too.'

Mother Paul rose suddenly and snapped her book shut. 'I'm giving a bad example. I know what you are like once you get into a book. Like myself,' she added, with her disarming smile.

She swept me out of the room and along to the stairs, where she waited until I had reached the landing before turning off the hall light. 'Good night, Mary.'

'Good night, Mother Paul.' I hung over the dark banisters, listening for the front door to open and close as she let herself out. After a long wait, when it seemed safe to move, I crept down again and back to the library, wondering why I had given in to Joe's audacious suggestion without more protest. My hands were clammy and my heart had started an apprehensive thumping and I felt a strong aversion to the whole idiotic scheme.

Unlike the rectress, I knew just which switch to press. The lamp shone directly over the typewriter and I paused for a moment, trying to absorb from the familiar sight some of the daytime mundane peace I had known so often sitting at it. A slight noise came from the windows and I glanced fearfully at the long green curtains. Smothering a craven impulse to run upstairs and pretend later that I had forgotten all about the midnight tryst, I locked the library door and hastened across the room.

The two men were ready to slip in as soon as the window was raised. O'Mara looked anxious as he whispered: 'Is anything the matter? You are late.'

Both were dressed in trousers which were evidently borrowed for the occasion from the police department store, and high-necked dark sweaters. 'You look like a pair of thugs,' I told them, the outrageous informality of the escapade making me less respectful. 'I had a bit of trouble getting rid of Mother Rectress, but all is clear now. Where do you want to go? For heaven's sake be quick, for my nerves are ragged already.'

Joe patted my shoulder. 'Take it easy, Mary. What say you push off now? We'll let ourselves out.'

'And leave the place unlocked? Sister Em goes round every morning to open up. She would have a fit if she found this window unlocked—and blame me—and rightly so.' I made the two additions with increasing gloom.

He crossed the room, moving quietly in his black sneakers. 'What's out here?'

'The passage. To the left it passes the stairs and widens into the hall. The parlour opens off one side of the hall and our common-room the other.'

'To the right?'

'Telephones—a pantry where medicines and stuff are kept—a passage to Mrs. Carron-Toyle's apartment. Then the stairs down to the refectory, service lift, the small back parlour and a bathroom. That's all.'

'No back door?'

'Downstairs through the kitchen. The house is built on a slope, you know. What seems to be the basement from here opens on to the ground level towards the back.'

'What's down there?'

'Refectory, kitchen, storerooms. The last are more underground being in the front of the house. They used to be wine-cellars.'

The American nodded as though he had the floor plan clear in his head. He looked across to O'Mara. 'Ready to move, Steve?'

'Do be careful,' I quavered. I felt moderately safe with them behind the locked library door, but the idea of their prowling about the rest of the house was unnerving.

'Basement first,' I heard Joe mutter. 'I want to see the other side of that trap-door we found.'

O'Mara looked back. 'Can you whistle, Miss Allen?'

I nodded, wondering what further antics I was to be called upon to perform. 'Keep this door ajar. If you think we are likely to be disturbed, come to the head of the basement stairs and give us a warning. Okay?' He lifted his hand in a gesture of either admonishment or encouragement, and disappeared after Joe.

Seven

I

The clock on the mantelpiece struck sonorously and I gave a startled leap—for such was the state of my reflexes. Its sound, echoed by the grandfather clock in the hall, reverberated in widening waves until surely it must reach the ears of the sleeping girls above and cause them to awaken, suddenly uneasy. I was so hypersensitive to the knowledge of strangers in the house that I could not imagine everyone else remaining unaffected.

I endured another duet between the library and hall clocks and then another. Half an hour had passed since the two men had disappeared in the direction of the refectory stairs, leaving me on guard at the half-open door of the library with a dimmed light for company. Had they made their exit through the kitchen door, leaving me forgotten and compelled to descend into the darkness to lock up after them?

Suddenly the sound of soft-soled feet moving along the passage broke across my anxious boredom, causing my heart to take an unpleasant leap upwards. Quelling a cowardly pang, I slid cautiously into the dark passage. A few yards ahead was a faint reddish glow, as though the person held a torch covered by the fingers. Creeping along the wall, I approached near enough to hear heavy breathing. I did not feel so frightened now because, although a flashlight was being used, there was nothing furtive about those solid footsteps. I had also realized that they had begun beyond the library door, and there was only one place from where the person could have come—and only one person who would breathe and walk so heavily. Mrs. Carron-Toyle!

The light was flashed full strength down the stairs leading to the refectory. Was she going down for another bottle of the special port which her sainted papa had hidden there?

I stood still and tried to think. All very well O'Mara telling me to whistle a warning, but an interruption between the library and the two intruders had not been taken into account. Perhaps Mrs. Carron-Toyle's heavy steps and flashlight would be enough warning—I hoped so. Then she gave a throaty cough or two, which I silently applauded.

If you two can't hear her coming, I thought, descending carefully after her, then you deserve to get caught.

Once at the foot of the stairs, I felt my way towards the right. There was a door near the servery which opened into the kitchen. Sheltered in Sister Berthe's domain, I would be able to give a warning if the need arose. Mrs. Carron-Toyle was at the other end of the room, but there was neither sight nor sound of the men. She vanished with her light through the cellar door and I comforted myself with the reflection that, even if they were in the cellars, there was enough junk about for them to hide.

I ran my hand along the wall, feeling for the kitchen door and only encountering space. They had evidently been into the kitchen—careless of them to leave it open. Perhaps they were in there now. I ventured a low, soft whistle and then whispered, 'It's Mary!'

There was a movement in the darkness and a hand touched me on the face, closing over my mouth. Too terrified to move, I felt a rough serge sleeve scratching my skin and heard the faintest click-clack of wooden rosary beads. A nun—it was someone dressed as a nun. Sister Felician's devil who came out of the river! I never dreamed it would be Mother Paul until her voice whispered close to my ear, 'Quiet, child!' After a moment she removed her hand and led me silently to the servery window. Uneasy questions raced through my mind as we stood there together in the kitchen, which was still warm from Sister Berthe's stove.

How long had the rectress been here? Had she seen the two men? What was she doing here, when to all intents and purposes she had left the house some time earlier? What did she make about my being there, whistling and whispering through the dark?

We peered out of the servery window for some time before Mrs. Carron-Toyle emerged from the cellars, threading her way heavily through the chairs and tables as she flashed her light unheedingly around the refectory. Mother Paul drew me down behind the window and we waited until the heavy steps had died away up the stairs.

'It was Mrs. Carron-Toyle,' I murmured, with my lips close to the nun's veil.

'Yes, I know,' she returned softly. 'She guessed what I was after. I was afraid she would.'

'She comes down to get some special wine. She told me once.'

'Not this time. She wasn't carrying anything.' Mother Paul was silent for a moment, then she said, 'I'm going back to have another look.'

I caught a fold of her voluminous skirt. 'Let's look tomorrow,' I begged, still mindful of the illicit presence of my two unwelcome guests.

'Very well,' she agreed, after a pause. She began to laugh gently. 'You naughty child! You were trying to get rid of me tonight and so was I. Mary, have you any idea what we are looking for?'

I had been making some rapid calculations. She had not seen the men. She had been in the cellars and had taken flight only on Mrs. Carron-Toyle's appearance. She was presuming that I had fallen in with her theory about Braddock's secret cache, and had come on a solitary search as well.

'No idea,' I returned, grateful for the darkness that hid me from her shrewd yet candid eyes. But when she paused again, I wasn't so sure that I had deceived her.

'Let me out through the kitchen door like a good child. And Mary!'

'Yes, Mother Paul?' I asked meekly.

'You will go to bed this time, won't you?'

'I've been wanting to all evening,' I quibbled.

She slipped out into the night. I shut and bolted the door and leaned against it, trembling a little. Presently, pulling myself together, I ventured into the refectory and along the wall to the cellar door. A draught of cold, damp air swept out as I opened it.

'You can come out now,' I whispered. 'All clear!'

There was no reply. I took a step or two, keeping one hand outstretched. They were probably in one of the small storerooms which opened off the main cellar passage. 'Are you there?' I called, my teeth chattering unashamedly. The echo of my voice came back lugubriously.

I called and whistled futilely once more and then, wishing Joe and

O'Mara to perdition and myself safely in bed, gave up. I did not know where they were and cared less. They had no right to involve me in their nightmarish antics. If they were still in the house they could get themselves out somehow, and I would risk a scolding from Sister Em.

The library light shone faintly under the typewriter cover I had thrown over, but I rejoiced in it after the confusing blackness of the basement. I removed the cover in case its unusual position might be observed in the morning and arouse speculation. There was a sheet of paper in the typewriter, and though my mind was numb with fatigue and past reasoning, something struck me as odd. Then I remembered about fitting in a new ribbon before starting another page. But the words on the paper were not mine, because I had not inserted a new page.

Ripping it from the roller, I read, *Operation successful. Thanks, Mary!*

II

The row which had been simmering for several days between Jean and Betty broke into full force. Although the cause was lost in obscurity, a general mood of spoiling for a fight had involved some of the girls into taking sides. As Clare stated, frankly including herself, everyone was becoming browned-off.

Even the rectress seemed distrait and vaguer than her wont. When I suggested working on the 'Life', which we had not touched for several days, she said: 'Not just now, dear. Later on, perhaps.' Neither did she make any mention of our night adventure, for which I was uneasily thankful.

I leapt at Fenella's suggestion to have dinner in town as a change from the dissident atmosphere at the hostel. We met at a bar first for what she termed a 'quickie', and when we came out a few drops of rain were falling.

'Looks like a wet week-end! Oh dear, we'll all be at each other's throats.'

'Don't worry! Clare will be in her element organizing pencil and paper games to keep us occupied.'

We dodged either side of a group of people talking in the middle of the pavement. 'Where are we going?' I asked, as I rejoined her. We had dinner like this about once a week, and it was a point of honour with Fenella to find a different place each time—the more out of the way and cosmopolitan the better. I always ended up with a dose of antacid after dinner with Fenella.

She swung easily through the crowds, confident and slender in her green gaberdine suit and small matching hat that so enhanced her pointed, piquant face. I kept a little to the rear, following her course. People had a habit of giving ground to Fenella. She radiated attraction to both sexes. So intent was I on keeping in her steps that I did not notice the Café Restaurant until she paused.

'Do you like Chinese cooking, Mary?' she asked, just as O'Mara had.

'No, not here!' I exclaimed involuntarily. 'We can't go in here.'

'Why not? Oh, come on, don't be stuffy!' She grabbed my hand as I hung back, and pulled me through the door.

A sleek, white-coated Chinese boy came forward, and I averted my head for fear he would remember me and say something about that regular customer. Detective O'Mara from Homicide.

'This is fun,' Fenella announced, peeling off her gloves as we settled into a booth. 'I bet you've never been to a place like this before, Mary.'

'How much would you bet?' I asked, glancing anxiously at the nearby booths.

'I wouldn't fleece you, dear. Can you imagine Cyril here! Stop staring about. What do you expect to see—opium smokers?'

I pulled the curtain across and settled back while she pored over the menu, finally selecting a weird array of dishes while I stuck prosaically to tomato soup and a sole.

'Leave the curtain back,' she said coaxingly, as the first course arrived. 'I want to see who comes in.'

'Well, I don't.'

'What's the matter with you, Mary? This is all perfectly respectable. Look at that man coming in now. The only daring thing about him is his bow tie. Polka dots—must be a Yank.'

I choked over the soup and dived into my table napkin, but of course Joe saw me at once. He came up while Fenella was thumping me on the back. 'Well, this is a surprise! It's swell to see you again, Mary.'

'She's a little indisposed,' explained Fenella, after dividing a bright, speculative glance between us. 'Have a drink of water, Maria, and introduce your friend.'

Joe edged his way into the seat next to her. 'You a friend of Mary's? Glad to know you. I'm Joe.'

'Glad to know you too, Joe. Funny that Mary hasn't told me about you.' She raised quizzical brows in my direction.

'We haven't met for years,' I mumbled defiantly, avoiding her eyes.

'It seems only three days,' said Joe blandly, which in truth it was, though I had continued to go daily to the Green Lounge. 'You haven't changed, Mary. What goes on?'

'Nothing much. You tell me,' I rejoined tartly.

'Well, right now I'm waiting to meet a guy—say, you know him. Remember good old Steve? If this isn't a coincidence! You know what, Miss—' He turned to Fenella.

'Fenella King,' she supplied, with a bubbling laugh that contained all the scepticism in the world.

'Well, as I was saying, Fenella—the last time I saw Mary was with Steve.' He glanced up suddenly. 'And here's the boy himself! Right over here, Steve. Look what I found.'

I was no good at any of the games those two played, but I was even worse at this one. O'Mara came up unhurriedly, not a facial muscle out of control. 'Why, hullo there!' he said genially.

'Steve, meet Fenella. She's a friend of Mary's.'

She gave O'Mara a bright-eyed scrutiny. 'Do sit down and start picking up the threads. It's nice to see old friends reunited after such a long time.'

'Don't you two want dinner?' I cut in desperately. 'Look, there's a vacant table over there.'

'You're not trying to get rid of us, are you, Mary?' asked Joe reproachfully, beckoning the waiter.

Fenella leant her chin in her hand. 'You must excuse Mary if she doesn't seem sociable. She's been run ragged lately.'

'Oh? How is that?'

'She's been finding dead bodies. One murder—one suicide.'

'How very unpleasant,' remarked O'Mara, as though he were talking about the local drain. 'Do tell us about them.'

With an air of innocence, but with watchful eyes, Fenella recounted Kilcomoden's tale of woe. I did not know how accurate were her suspicions of the two men, but they were obviously not far off the mark. I listened in dumb endurance as they both made mildly appropriate noises.

'At the moment life is almost unbearable at our hostel—everyone is gloomy or snappish or secretive. If the police don't hurry up and solve their stupid murder, goodness knows what will happen. I can't understand what that detective man—what was his name again, Mary? You know—the one you said was a stuffed shirt.'

I felt O'Mara move slightly. 'I—I don't recall his name for the moment,' I managed to say.

'Well, it doesn't matter—he sounded a pill. But why doesn't he do something? Come around and question us and dig up some dirt.'

'Now, Fen!' I protested weakly. 'You know the murder has nothing to do with us.'

'Oh, of course not,' she returned airily. 'I dare say the charged atmosphere at Kilcomoden, the anonymous letters and Alison drowning herself are just a coincidence.' She glanced around, a half-smile on her lips and a lift to her eyebrow. 'A coincidence—like this delightful reunion of old friends.'

There was a moment's silence, then the American said sympathetically: 'You seem to be having a bad time. What you want is something to take your mind off things—a party, for instance. Give your girls something pleasant to talk about for a change.'

'Joe's idea seems an excellent remedy,' said O'Mara, and I gave him a swift, sidelong glance. They had another of their uncomfortable games in mind.

'No,' I said flatly. 'The nuns wouldn't like it, I'm sure.'

'Oh, don't you be a stuffed shirt too!' Fenella threw me a gay, challenging smile. 'You know you can talk Mother Paul into anything. Come on, Maria, play ball with the boys!'

I did not like the way she said that, but then I had not cared for anything Fenella had said over the last half-hour.

'I suppose you and Joe would like to come?' she said to the

detective, her eyes dancing mischievously.

He answered her coolly. 'That depends on whether we have a previous engagement.'

'I'll make sure you get plenty of notice,' she promised.

O'Mara glanced at her emerald. 'I hope it will give us an opportunity to meet the lucky man.'

Fenella jumped up. 'My Thomas! Thank goodness you reminded me. I promised to call him up. Please excuse me a moment—there's a call-box outside. Order me some coffee, Mary.'

'I'll come with you,' Joe offered, 'to keep off the wolves.'

Left alone with the detective, I said in a rush: 'I didn't come here on purpose. Fenella picked it by chance. And I didn't say that you were what Fenella—'

'We'll talk about that later,' he interrupted, with a twinkle. 'Listen—Joe wants to get right in amongst you this time. You got his idea, I suppose?'

'I did,' I replied resignedly, 'and so did Fenella.'

'Yes, she's a smart girl. How soon can you arrange this party business?'

'I'll have to talk to the rectress, and it will take some organizing. What exactly are you after?'

'We want to see all the hostel people along with their fiancés, boyfriends and various appendages. Make it a good show so that everyone will come.'

'You're asking quite a bit. I never felt less like a party.'

'Nor I,' he agreed, with a rueful smile.

'Is this an outcome of the other night? Did you know that Mother Paul was searching in the basement too? She thinks Braddock was after something—that he was the man who broke in a year ago.'

He nodded. 'We saw her—and the other woman as well. Don't worry about that now. Did you make more inquiries about the gardener fellow? Don't worry about your friend—Joe will keep her occupied.'

'If I know anything about Fenella, that phone call to Tommy was an excuse to give me the opportunity to speak to you,' I retorted. I just had time to report my visit to the salon of Stephanie et Cie, an abortive interrogation of Bartholomew and the final brush with

Lorraine, when Fenella and Joe arrived back. She had been working on the party, and had hit on the plan of a barbecue with square dancing on the floodlit tennis court.

Joe had undertaken to be chef. 'He says he knows a special way to do sausages and bacon,' Fenella declared, 'and, of course, it's an ideal position from which to give everyone the once-over.'

III

The drizzle of Friday evening, which had caused Fenella's hair to curl into crisp, shining ringlets and mine to lengthen dankly, developed into a steady Saturday pour. Everyone stayed indoors except Clare who went off, chest outflung, to play golf, and came back huddled and sneezing. Her pet theory that fresh air and exercise was a preventative of all ills became the subject of much semi-malicious banter, and was steadily plugged until Clare, who was feeling seedy, lost her temper. Another row flared up, everyone joining in to vent their feelings in an atmosphere of general bloody-mindedness.

The few optimists, who had been buoyed up by the hope of a clear Sunday, quickly fell into the slough when the rain still showed no signs of abating. The weather had become colder too, with several girls changing from their light spring frocks back into winter woollies. Clare, wandering about borrowing handkerchiefs and muffled up to her reddened nose in jumpers and scarves, decided that a fire in the common-room would be just the ticket to cheer everyone up. But there was a notable lack of enthusiasm when she called for volunteers to bring in the wood; most of the girls preferring to be miserable in peace.

'Come on, you lazy, liverish blighters!' she said, trying to whip up response.

'You had the bright idea,' someone growled. 'You go and get the wood.'

'I can't go out in the rain with this filthy cold,' she retorted, blowing her nose with a sound like a trumpeting elephant. 'Do you want me to catch pneumonia?'

'Yes!' There were a few laughs. We were at the stage when only the misfortunes of others could raise a laugh. Mabel Jones had raised a roar at dinner by tripping on the refectory stairs and bumping down in a sitting position, her hitched skirt showing pink, lock-knit bloomers. Even when Fenella and I offered our reluctant services, someone chimed in with, 'Aren't they martyrs!'

'Aren't we all sweet-tempered!' Fenella remarked, as I closed the common-room door. 'No wonder Verna looks so happy. Mary, have you asked Mother Paul about the barbecue? If the girls knew a party was in the wind, the atmosphere might lighten.'

'I mentioned the matter yesterday. She has to sound out the other nuns before giving permission, you know. Community life,' I explained, as Fenella made an exclamation of impatience. 'She recalled a story about St. Teresa of Avila playing the guitar for her nuns to dance to, and intends to use that as a basis of argument if Sister Em objects.'

'Then it's in the bag,' said Fenella, with a chortle. 'Look, we'd better get coats or something. I do wish Clare would stop making efforts.'

'We'll take Mother Paul's umbrella. She left it here the other day. And here's another one!'

'Oh—ah,' said Fenella portentously. 'I wonder how the big romance is going.'

I pulled out the rectress's gloves and tucked them in the hall-stand drawer. 'What romance is that?'

'My dear, didn't you know? Poor little Sparksie is courting our Mabel.'

'Don't be ridiculous!'

'No, really! Haven't you noticed? Bet you anything you like they're holding hands in the back parlour right now.'

'So that's why Jonesy has been dripping lace and beads lately. Well, good luck to them both!'

The wood shed was a hundred yards or so from the kitchen. We made the trip huddled together under Mother Paul's outsize umbrella, and ran into Bartholomew who was pottering about with a sack over his head. I had not seen him since questioning him as he cut the hedge. Fenella spoke a word or two in her usual cheerful way, but he merely grunted, throwing me an evil glance that made me glad I was not alone.

We carried the wood box through the kitchen to the service lift, pulled the rope, then made a dash up the stairs trying to beat it to the ground floor. But Mother Paul had already opened the doors and was inspecting the rising load with interest.

'An excellent idea! Nothing like a fire to make things cheerful. Mary dear, we have been very lax about our work. Do you think you could spare some time this afternoon?' She seemed to have thrown off her apathy of the past few days.

'I can come now, if you like.'

Fenella made a pantomime behind her back—eating an invisible hamburger with both hands and allemande-ing left and right silently—then lumped the wood box down the hall, humming a happy tune.

I nodded in direction of the common-room. 'They certainly need cheering up.'

'Why is that, dear?' the nun asked, opening the library door.

'Nerves are a little frayed, and this weather is just the finishing touch. If I could tell them about the party now . . .' I hinted delicately.

'Ah yes! The party. That's what I want to talk about. Light the gas fire, Mary. So chilly in here too.'

I found matches and crouched over the grate. Mother Paul drifted about, touching things aimlessly. She ran one finger over the keyboard of the typewriter and sighed. 'We don't seem to be making much progress, do we?'

I sat back on my heels, holding out my hands to the warmth. 'I intended to do some the other night—even went so far as to insert a new ribbon, but that is as far as I got.'

'I didn't mean that precisely. All this mysterious wickedness, and now the girls unhappy. I can understand some of it, but only in isolated pieces—so difficult to fit together.' She sighed again and jabbed at a key or two. 'You say you haven't used the typewriter, Mary?'

I glanced around. She was swivelling the ribbon discs. 'No, I haven't. Why?'

'Because somebody has. Several inches have been used.' She pulled out the ribbon and held it to the light. I remembered the message Joe had left just as she began to decipher it aloud. ' "Operation successful". How odd—sounds like a hospital report. I remember when poor Sister Felician—what's this? "One of the girls suspicious. Operations must cease until heat is off. Jess must hold supplies."' Mother Paul raised her head. 'Mary!'

I scrambled across the room and snatched the ribbon from her fingers without apology. 'Jess!' I breathed, examining the imprint of the type. 'Jess!'

'Perhaps we are making some progress,' Mother Paul remarked, in mild tones. 'But what does it mean? First of all the operation is successful and then it must stop. So contradictory and confusing.'

'Disregard the first part,' I said excitedly, discretion forgotten. 'Joe left that for me. Where it begins "one of the girls suspicious" is the important part. Mother Paul, I must get hold of Mr. O'Mara at once and tell him.'

I was half-way across the room when she called me back. 'Not like you to be impulsive, dear. Were you really going out with that spool in your hand to telephone from the hall where anyone might see and hear you?'

I smiled ruefully. 'Hearing that name made me lose my head. All right, what shall I do?'

'Put another ribbon into the typewriter first,' she rejoined serenely. 'If the writer of that message notices that the spool is missing, she will naturally suspect you.'

I set about inserting a fresh ribbon. 'Haven't I slipped already? ' "One of the girls suspicious"?'

'Perhaps she does not mean you, Mary. The contents of the message are not as important as the fact that someone here wrote it for a person obviously not at Kilcomoden. Including Jess, that makes three people involved.'

I stared. 'Three people!'

She nodded wisely. 'There are others outside in this conspiracy concerning Kilcomoden. Mr. O'Mara knows what it is all about, but evidently he can't prove anything yet. The reason for this tiresome party he wants you to arrange is to bring those three persons together.' She hesitated, then asked suddenly, 'Mary, who is Joe?'

'Some sort of associate of O'Mara's, though he insists he is not a policeman. He's an American.'

'And he was here the other night?'

'I'm afraid so,' I admitted meekly.

'I thought there must be a good reason for your staying up,' she said, taking the news with reasonable calmness. 'So bad of you, Mary. We can't have strange men wandering around. Sister Emerentiana wouldn't like it. Tell me, did they know what they were looking for and did they find it?'

I held up the ribbon. "Operation successful"—that is all I know. But,' I added slowly, 'they managed somehow to get out of the house through the cellars.'

'There is a trap-door opening into the fernery,' she announced imperturbably. 'I had a thorough search last night. There is an old cupboard with its top removed rammed against it.'

'Did you know about this trap-door before?'

'Indeed no! Sister would have had it closed up long ago. So unnerving to realize that it has been there all the time.'

'Mrs. Carron-Toyle probably knew of it,' I said thoughtfully. 'Wouldn't it have been used in the old days to deliver wine to the cellars?'

She nodded in agreement. 'But not now—it has some other purpose now.'

'I'm sure Mrs. Carron-Toyle knows something,' I said, suddenly. 'Why was she prowling around the other night?'

'I think she was curious because I had been asking her about the cellars. So dangerous when people haven't enough to occupy their minds. That Bassett child is another such person.'

'Don't you consider that the sooner we launch this party idea the better? We could get everyone's minds occupied then—from Mrs. Carron-Toyle down to Bartholomew.'

She gave me a sidelong glance. 'Ah yes, Bartholomew! Poor Sister Felician is finding him so difficult lately. Only in the nick of time did she stop him from cutting back the azaleas—and they are in full flower too! She was quite shaken and could only ascribe his behaviour to the devil's influence.'

'Sister Felician considers the devil is to blame for most of our worries,' I said, remembering the old nun's words. I told Mother Paul about the scene in the drive. 'You nearly scared me out of my wits when you grabbed me in the kitchen the other night.' The rectress turned her head slowly so as to look at me full face. But there was a faraway expression in her eyes, as though she were looking through me to something else. 'How very odd!' she said softly. 'But of course old holy people and young innocent children can always see things in simpler, clearer terms than the rest of us.' Presently she glanced at the ribbon spool which I still held. 'Look after it, Mary, and give it to the police as soon as you can. In the meantime you have my full permission to go ahead with the proposed party. Not only shall we be doing as the police request, but it will help lull a very uneasy conscience.'

IV

If crankiness and contrariness were outward manifestations of inward disquiet, then everyone in the common-room had an uneasy conscience. I went back to the girls intending to break the delightful news, but found the atmosphere so thick with gloom that party planning would be doomed at the outset. The proposed event would be merely seized upon as another subject for contentious debate. Knowing its ulterior importance I decided to await a more receptive mood. I set about trying to induce a lighter atmosphere, throwing an SOS glance to Fenella, who was engaging anyone who felt like a fight in cheerful acrimony. Fenella never lost her temper, but she took a mischievous delight in leading others on to do so, which caused just as much disturbance.

I moved across the room to Christine Farrow, who was sitting at the piano gazing through the streaming window, and playing the same few bars of a Chopin prelude over and over.

'For Pete's sake—can't you change the record?' someone asked peevishly.

'Play something we can sing,' I muttered. She glanced up quickly as though to refuse. She did not need a general malaise to make her contrary. 'Please, Christine!' I begged earnestly. Still scowling, she struck up 'Old MacDonald had a Farm'.

Clare, who had been poking at her fire and telling those nearby who complained either of the heat or the smoking that if they didn't like it to do the other thing, let out a jubilant shout. 'Good show! Bags I the pig,' and began conducting with the poker. Her vigorous contralto and my wobbly, but determined, soprano on opposite sides of the room gathered in a few more singers. Then Fenella's clear voice announced that she would be a kangaroo and immediately competition started for unheard-of animal noises.

Christine thumped away, an unwilling smile touching her wide, sulky mouth. I gave her a warm, grateful glance as she went from one song to another and the room was filled with cheerful, healthy noise. She made quite a hit and became almost gay as she obeyed the clamours to play this and that. Tea made an opportune appearance before the novelty wore off and everyone became exhausted. Then, just as I was about to broach the subject of the barbecue, someone croaked out, 'Let's have an auction!' There was a responsive roar and I sat down again.

Auctions were seasonal features at Kilcomoden, and an excellent and economical way in which to ring changes in your wardrobe. The procedure was to gather together the clothes you were either tired of or regretted buying and offer them for sale or barter. I explained all this to Christine when I brought her a well-earned cup of tea, and then went off upstairs to collect a pair of high-heeled white shoes that had nearly crippled me after one day's wear the previous summer. Lorraine eyed them thoughtfully as she came out of her room with several frocks slung over her arm. I marked a green linen sports dress amongst them that would suit me admirably for golf on warmer days.

Back in the common-room there was a groan as Clare produced a hat she had been vainly trying to get rid of for several auctions. 'What's the matter with it?' she demanded, planking the basin-shaped felt on her cropped head. 'This is a damn good lid—better than that bit of a thing of Jean's. Hers looks like a lump of mud that the daises grew through.'

'What am I bid?' Fenella cried. 'A beige gaberdine suit—worn well, but not well worn. If I have the blinking thing another season, I'll be a landmark.'

Under cover of the noise, a voice said in my ear: 'Isn't it nice to see everyone so jolly again! I was so afraid they would all start quarrelling in earnest. So clever of you, Mary!'

I turned to find Verna at my elbow, smiling in her inimitably unpleasant way. 'There's nothing particularly clever in starting a sing-song,' I replied. 'Hullo, have you got something for sale?'

She smoothed the nap of a short, powder-blue coat. 'You sound surprised—as though I should have something good enough. I know I haven't got the clothes sense you fashion-plates have, but it just so happens that this time I have got something worthwhile.'

'I haven't seen you wearing a coat like that before, Verna. When did you buy it?'

'Oh, I didn't buy it. How could I afford anything so expensive, and besides I know these pretty soft colours don't suit me.'

'Where did you get it then?' I asked, tantalized by a certain familiarity. 'Did someone give it to you?'

She gave a small titter. 'Well, it wasn't precisely given to me. But that doesn't mean I stole it, Mary. I suppose that is what you are thinking.'

'I'm not,' I replied. 'But if you like to imagine so, go right ahead.'

'Oh, I know what you all think about me, even though you don't say it in so many words. I don't know why it is, but . . .'

Bored, I transferred my attention to Lorraine, who had slipped on one of the dresses she intended selling and was parading it expertly. Her face was flushed and happy as the swirling yellow silk skirt was unstintingly admired. She did not look like a girl with guilty hidden corners in her life at that moment—but then none of the girls did. I gave a quick, searching glance around, but could not find one who seemed capable of writing that short, uneasy message which was recorded on the typewriter ribbon. Yet one of them must have written it—and the anonymous letters.

I brought my gaze back to Verna, studying her dispassionately as she kept on talking, but could find nothing that bespoke guilt and fear behind her slyly complacent face. 'What did you say?' I asked, for she had given me a fleeting glance as though to gauge my reaction to her remarks.

'Really, Mary! I wonder what makes you so absentminded lately. I do think it is rather rude only pretending to listen. I was saying that you could call this coat a sort of bequest—like that tennis racquet you got off with.'

'Racquet? What racquet?' Then I remembered where I had seen the coat before. It was Alison's. She used to fling it casually over a matching dress—her favourite dress with the full pleated skirt, which river slime had ruined past all recognition.

Verna's eyes were gleaming with malicious satisfaction. 'You seem quite upset, Mary. I wonder why?'

'You little beast!' I muttered thickly. 'What are you planning to do?'

Her smile grew. 'Surely I can sell it if I want to. Mother Paul said we were allowed to take anything of Alison's we cared to have. I don't think it quite suits me after all, although poor Alison did like it so. That hat of Clare's is more in my style, don't you think?'

'What are you trying to do? Stir up more trouble? Verna, don't be a fool!'

'You're very rude, you know,' she said gently. 'Just as well I don't take offence easily. Watch and see! You may find something interesting in this, Mary. After all, you are watching out for interesting things, aren't you?'

With this softly spoken taunt, she slid into the middle of the room where Lorraine, slim and laughing, was changing back into her skirt and jumper. Lorraine recognized the coat at once and the vivacity died out of her face.

'Now, here is my contribution,' Verna cried, turning around so that everyone could see it. 'A coat that has barely been worn. A lovely material and a lovely colour—whose favourite colour, I wonder? What am I bid?'

The stunned silence that fell on the room caused her to smirk happily. 'Come on, everyone! Just because it's mine doesn't mean that it's not a good bargain. Clare, what about your hat in exchange?'

Clare had turned an even more ghastly colour than was due to her cold. 'That's Alison's,' she managed to jerk out, after mouthing impotently for several seconds.

'It's mine,' Verna contradicted smoothly. 'Just as that handbag Betty took from Alison's room now belongs to her, and the stockings—'

'But I'm not trying to sell it,' Betty burst out. 'I'm not trying to exploit it and make everyone embarrassed and miserable.' Her voice shook and she moved away from the others into a corner. I went over to her.

'Steady on,' I whispered. 'Don't afford her any more satisfaction.'

'Ten bob!' I heard Fenella's voice and looked up sharply. 'Or this candlewick dressing-gown. The colour will suit you admirably, Verna dear—poison green!'

Bless you, I thought, as a general laugh went up and Verna lost her pleased smile.

Jean followed the lead. 'Fifteen shillings and a pair of crepe-soled sandals—just the thing for sneaking around.'

There was more outrageous bidding, but Verna had recovered her malicious composure and was pretending to regard the offers seriously. She kept running her hand over the coat as though testing its market value.

Then a clear, quiet voice spoke. 'I'll give you two pounds, Miss Bassett.' Eyes became riveted in amazement on Christine Farrow, but she ignored us all as she sat straight and still at the piano.

'You must want this coat very much. Miss Farrow,' Verna purred. 'Will the colour suit you, I wonder? You're very pale.'

'Two pounds,' Christine repeated. Then her restraint seemed to snap. 'It's worth two pounds of anyone's money to stop this vindictive nonsense you appear to be enjoying.' She got up from the piano stool, and instinctively a path was made for her. She drew the notes out of her handbag as she advanced towards Verna. 'Here is the money. Now give me that coat and get out!' The girl's quiet fury had us all agape, but Verna slid aside, still in command of the crisis she had precipitated. 'Not so fast! It's worth far more than two pounds. I know poor Alison paid—'

'Shut up!' Clare growled menacingly. 'You're not going to keep that coat now, Verna. Hand it over to Christine.'

'I'll close for three pounds,' Verna said, smoothing its soft folds meditatively.

'You'll take Christine's offer or nothing,' Clare said angrily. She pursed her thin mouth, running her hand down the lapels and patting the pockets. 'No, Clare—three pounds. It's worth . . .'

She broke off as she slid her fingers into one of the pockets, withdrawing a folded slip of paper. She glanced at it quickly and her expression seemed to alter.

I tried to push nearer. 'I'll give you the three pounds,' I said breathlessly.

She raised her eyes and looked straight into mine. 'Will you, Mary? Catch, then!' And she flung the coat over my head. By the time I had struggled free, she had left the room.

'What on earth . . .' someone began, but her voice trailed off into the uneasy silence.

It was then that I decided that the time was propitious to announce the party. The idea was seized upon with almost hysterical enthusiasm.

Eight

I

Both O'Mara and the American were waiting for me in the Green Lounge the following day.

I passed over the typewriter ribbon which had kept me awake half the night, so anxiously had I been guarding it. 'Next time you leave typed messages around, make sure the ribbon is a worn one,' I told Joe, as they studied the second message with gratifying interest. 'Mother Paul spotted it at once. Although she was quite nice about it, I didn't exactly enjoy having to explain about your midnight marauderings.'

'I'm looking forward to making the acquaintance of that nun of yours,' said Joe amusedly. 'Maybe we could learn a thing or two.'

'I'm sure you could. You'll have the opportunity on Wednesday, which is the date set for your wretched party.'

'How is everyone taking to the idea?' asked O'Mara.

'With fair enthusiasm. You have Verna to thank for that.' And I told them about the auction and its disastrous outcome.

'You'd better get hold of that paper she found in Alison's pocket,' he said, as though it were the easiest thing in the world to accomplish.

'If you can just tell me how,' I rejoined politely, 'I'll be only too eager to fall in with your wishes. Verna keeps to her room most of the time now, and makes sure of locking the door before she leaves. She won't give the paper up or even say what it concerns.'

'What about her window?'

I winced. 'Not even for you will I crawl round window-ledges with a drop of thirty feet! No, short of gagging the girl and tying her on her bed, I don't see—' I broke off as I caught O'Mara's suddenly thoughtful gaze. 'Ten to one the paper would be under the mattress if I did that,' I said lamely. 'All right, all right, I'll try something. Heaven protect me for the fool I am!'

Joe reached over and patted my hand. 'Ah, you've been a swell girl, Mary.'

'You are not really worried, are you?' asked O'Mara, agreeably concerned.

'Apart from a tendency to jump at sudden noises and a recently developed habit of glancing over my shoulder, I'm fine. I don't wish to appear impatient, but just when will you be through with my services? I would rather like to go out to pasture again.'

'Soon, we hope,' was the none too sanguine promise. 'A great deal depends on Wednesday night.'

Conversely, Wednesday night seemed to depend on a great deal — a spot on Betty's chin, a new peasant dress that was still at Fenella's dressmaker, someone's boy-friend who was requiring a lot of coaxing to don a plaid shirt, and above all the weather.

Sunday's rain had soaked into Monday with all the appearance of inexhaustibility. It was not until Mother Paul assured us of a fine evening that those with faith relaxed. Sister Emerentiana, on the other hand, was far from being assuring about anything. She scuttled round with sheaves of papers in her hand, working herself into a fret over crockery lists, seating accommodation and the advisability of informing the Fire Brigade in advance in case the barbecue fire got out of control. She did not like the routine of the hostel being broken at any time, but with a party there was a chance that all sorts of giddiness and unseemliness might break out.

'You must instruct your guests that no intoxicating liquor is to be brought into Kilcomoden,' she announced, and Fenella assured her that the only beverage other than coffee would be a special fruit punch that she intended making with her own innocent hands. The quartermaster seemed satisfied and went away, but, remembering the array of bottles under Fenella's bed, I voiced some suspicion.

'Just a little something to give the punch an extra flavour,' she replied airily.

There were other contretemps which marred the harmony of the preparations. Lorraine, who had been pointedly ignoring me since our last brush, suddenly attacked me in the bedroom passage throwing another storm of how-dare-you's and can't-you-leave-me-alone's into my genuinely bewildered face. It transpired that Stephanie had received an anonymous invitation to our party and intended coming. She had a yen to partake of our simple girlish pleasures. She thought nuns were quaint.

'Not guilty, Lorraine dear,' I got in, suspecting the rectress's hand. 'But why are you so sore about Mrs. Garland coming? No harm in her doing a bit of bucolic sightseeing if she wants to. Is it us or her you're ashamed of? I promise I'll behave myself broadmindedly—of course, I can't vouch for Bartholomew.' The shot reached its target and Lorraine's lovely face reddened unbecomingly. I watched her thoughtfully as she swished away.

A slap on the back brought me out of the reverie. 'Guess what, old girl!' said Clare's strident voice.

'What?' I asked, recovering my balance.

'I've got me a man for Wednesday's show.' Her strong, plain face was triumphant. 'Couldn't help overhearing what you and Lorraine were scrapping about. Frightful coincidence, actually. You'll scream when I tell you. He'll probably turn up in blue satin pants or something.'

'Not the woeful Rupert!' I exclaimed.

'Got it in one. He rang up and asked if he could come. Beastly cheek, of course—I barely know the guy. Says he adores my divine rudeness or some such rot. Can you beat it?'

It had never occurred to me before that Clare ever regretted her lack of feminine appeal. Hiding a sudden feeling of pity, I made a few appropriate comments and ended up by expressing honest relief when she promised to sit on the lout if he started showing-off. 'What about you, Maria? The faithful Cyril obliging?'

'Oh my goodness!' I said, aghast. 'Thanks for reminding me. I'll ring him tonight.'

'You mean you hadn't arranged for a partner?'

I thought I detected a look of fellow-feeling in her eye, and was nettled. 'Well, you know, I'll be pretty busy running things. It hardly seems fair to ask anyone. Although, as a matter of fact,' I added, trying to sound casual, 'Fen and I have a couple of friends who may show up. One is an American. He's promised to lend a hand with the barbecue.'

'Fine, fine!' she said, rather absently. Then she jerked her head at

Verna's door and lowered her voice. 'Miss Snooper trying to spoil the fun as per usual?'

'I haven't seen her today.'

Clare frowned. 'That rotten business yesterday, old thing—think there was anything in it?'

'What business?' I asked, carefully.

'The paper she fished out of Alison's pocket. Can't help wondering why she turned tail like that so quickly. Can't help wondering sometimes about Alison.'

'What do you mean?'

'Dunno quite. It's just—Maria, I would like to see what was on that paper, wouldn't you?'

I hesitated. 'What do you suggest? Verna won't tell anyone.'

Clare rubbed her chin. 'Must be some way we can search her room. Supposing we go over now and you make some excuse to call her away. I'll slip in and have a look-see.'

I eyed her doubtfully. 'All right! But I don't think we'll be successful.'

'Try anything once,' Clare said, squaring her shoulders like a Rugby player. 'Ready to move?'

As Fenella said once, Clare had about as much finesse as a knave-high suit. I did not rack my brains too hard for an excuse to call Verna away, because I knew she would never leave her room unlocked, and, furthermore, her suspicions would be instantly aroused as soon as she saw me.

Clare knocked smartly at the door. 'Yoo-hoo! Anyone at home?'

There was a soft movement the other side, then the scrape of a key. Verna's face appeared at the crack. When she saw who it was, she opened the door wide and her mouth spread into a long, toothless slit, which was for her a broad grin. 'Someone wanting me?'

'You're wanted on the phone,' I began. Then I caught a glimpse of the chaos that lay behind her.

'I say,' Clare observed. 'In a bit of a mess, aren't you? Been looking for groats or something?'

'You're so quick, Clare,' Verna remarked admiringly. 'Of course, I don't think the Scripture reference is quite in good taste, but—'

'Oh, can the piety! What's been going on in here?'

Verna surveyed the shambles of pulled-out drawers and stripped bed. 'It seems to me that someone has been searching my room. Now, I wonder why?'

'We haven't a clue,' I said dryly. 'It surely wouldn't have anything to do with that paper you found in Alison's pocket.'

'A dead cert it has,' snapped Clare. 'Sticks out a mile. Don't be so dim, Maria.'

'I rather think Mary was making a little joke,' Verna said in sweet tones. 'Now why should anyone want that poor little letter of Alison's?'

'A letter, was it?' I queried quickly. 'Has it been taken?'

'I wouldn't call it a letter exactly,' she said aggravatingly.

I controlled myself with an effort. 'Has it gone?'

'Oh dear me, no. I took the precaution of putting it in a very safe place that no one could possibly reach; but no one.'

'I don't know what you're after, Verna,' Clare said bluntly, 'but take my advice and give over this mysterious behaviour. You might land in a packet of trouble if you're not careful.'

'Oh, but I am careful, Clare. It is much safer to say nothing than to go round telling everyone my information. Don't you agree, Mary? That's your policy, isn't it?'

'My policy is to avoid trouble. Please give up that letter to Mother Paul.'

'You really think I should?'

'Definitely.'

She put her head on one side, and eyed us with a smirk. 'I'll think over your advice, Mary. Oh—and yours too, Clare. And now if you will excuse me, I must clear up the mess some very naughty person has made.'

'She hasn't the slightest intention of giving it to the rectress,' Clare muttered, as the door was locked again. 'Mary, have you any idea what all this is about?'

'Absolutely none,' I replied quickly. 'But I would like to know how anyone got into Verna's room.'

'Sister Em's master key, I suppose.'

Later that evening I made a few inquiries. Sister Em had not given up the key to anyone, nor could it possibly have been stolen from her.

It was amongst the bunch that dangled from her black leather girdle, continually becoming mixed up with her rosary beads.

II

Wednesday came without an appreciable flagging of general enthusiasm. There had been a few mutters of 'is it worth it', but fortunately the weather cleared mild and fine, cutting the moaners off in mid-moan.

It was with a sense of achievement that I went downstairs and out into the grounds to take a last look at the arrangements. For a while I almost forgot the original purpose of the party as the sweet, warm dusk settled over the garden and the coloured paper lanterns, which Mother Paul had miraculously persuaded Bartholomew to hang in the trees and shrubs, began to glow.

Our guests were due to arrive at eight, but already a few had collected near the gramophone in the tennis-court shelter to examine the records. There were occasional bursts of music as one of the girls' boy-friend, who was fortuitously an electrical engineer, did busy and important things to the public address system and the lights shining down on the extempore dance floor. A few more were gathered around the open fireplace, which had been built by our contributions when barbecues first became the rage. Bartholomew, looking more like a hill-billy, in his gardening clothes from which he obstinately refused to change, than the department store outfits of the other men, was building the fire up to a steady, red-hot glow.

Fenella danced up to link her arm in mine. She was wearing a gleaming jade-green skirt, which no peasant would ever possess, with a black velvet square-cut bodice and wisp of black chiffon knotted about her slim, white throat. I told her she looked enchanting and she duly admired my less dashing outfit of blue skirt and white organdie blouse. We checked over the arrangements together, panicking in the time-honoured fashion over whether there would be enough to eat.

'One sip of that concoction of yours and they won't care if they never eat,' I decided. 'Fruit punch, my eye!'

She giggled and then pointed across to the fire. 'I see your old friends have arrived in good time.'

'Who? Oh!' It was the American's costume that caught my eye first—tight Texan jeans, high-heeled boots and a shirt of unparalleled brilliance. It seemed to be Joe's deliberate intention to draw attention to himself. He quickly gathered an appreciative audience to listen to his wisecracks as he donned a ludicrous chef's cap. O'Mara was standing near the rectress, who was temporarily ensconced in a chair overlooking the court. I thought he looked rather nice, and marked his outfit of grey sports slacks and blue and yellow checked shirt as one that would blend favourably with my own, while dancing. Then remembrance of his primary purpose at Kilcomoden swept the aesthetic notion aside.

'Buck up, Maria,' Fenella said, eyeing me knowingly. 'You're allowed to enjoy yourself at the same time.' With a sudden yip she dashed off to greet her fiancé, whose expression showed that he thought her even more delicious-looking than I had. He was an engaging young man, with a tongue as quick and insouciant as Fenella's. He gave me a wave and a whistle, then pointed behind him. My own beau appeared out of the darkness and I suddenly wished that I was like Fenella and could dash up to him, thrilled that he was here to enjoy the fun together. Albeit, I was feeling rather cross with Cyril, as we advanced towards each other with unexcited tread. After my having stressed the nature of the party, he had come dressed in the most conservative of sports clothes.

'But I feel such a gig in a fancy shirt, Mary,' he protested, after I had expressed my displeasure. 'It's just not my style.'

'Nonsense,' I replied. 'Leave your coat somewhere and take off that discreet tie. I'm going to run upstairs for a moment. There's a gorgeous red scarf that will change your whole outlook.'

'What gets into people that makes them want to dress up?' he complained, obeying my commands.

'You're lucky we're not having a fancy-dress party,' I told him severely. 'There was some talk at first. You may have had to wear doublet and hose or come in your landlady's sheets.'

I ran indoors and took the stairs two at a time, almost crashing into Mabel Jones as we met on the landing. 'Sorry—I wasn't looking where I was going.' I pulled up, suddenly bemused by her appearance. She was wearing a skirt whose green and purple stripes were, unfortunately, horizontal, and a beige voile blouse festooned with pink lace frills. She had made some dreadful experiments with her face and hair. A sparse, frizzy fringe flapped over her forehead. Her mouth was a lop-sided grimace of lipstick, while two uneven blobs of rouge and a snowy-powdered nose completed the pantomime dame appearance.

'How do I look?' she asked, with a titter.

'Very festive.' I avoided a second glance at the bow of purple ribbon above the fringe. 'Uh—looking forward to the party?'

'It's going to be lovely!' she exclaimed, the coloured glass bangles on her scrawny arms clinking together as she clasped her hands ecstatically. 'I do so love seeing you young things enjoying yourselves.'

'No looking on tonight,' I said firmly. 'You hop right into the middle of things.' I had seen Mrs. Carron-Toyle's form on previous occasions when she either kept Jonesy at her side or sent her from the scene of the fun on numerous meaningless errands.

'Mrs. Carron-Toyle feels so well tonight too,' Mabel said ingenuously. 'She said I could join in if I liked to make a fool—I mean, if I wanted to. Isn't that nice of her? Of course, Dr. Yorke will be with her in case anything goes wrong.' She gave a long, quivering sigh. 'I feel so happy. Mary—'

'Yes?' I had turned to go past, but catching a glimpse of her thin, flat feet tilted agonizingly on spike-heeled silver sandals, I glanced hastily back at her face. She was smiling foolishly and a blush was rising to compete strongly with the rouge.

'Oh, nothing really,' she said, and gave another titter.

Mr. Sparks, I thought, watching her careful descent. Anyway, she doesn't look any worse than he probably will if he's come dressed for the occasion. Mr. Sparks in anything other than his neat blue pinstripe and little Homburg must look ludicrous.

Jean and Betty came giggling down the stairs. If the party had done nothing else, it had at least healed their late differences. They both looked devastatingly pretty.

'Oh, Mary, did you see Jonesy? Isn't she a scream? She came up to borrow some rouge. We thought we would die. We wanted to do her over like Verna, but she said no, she wanted to get used to the feel of make-up herself. Evidently we're at the beginning of a better and brighter Mabel. Methinks she's got herself a boy-friend.'

'She has—but don't you girls make fun about it.'

'Maria! Who?'

'Never mind. What have you been doing to Verna?'

'My dear! She was coming to the party in a ghastly woollen skirt and a jumper with meal spots all down the front.'

'To match the spots on her face,' Jean giggled. 'But we made her see the light, and she agreed to put herself unreservedly in our hands.'

'I bet she did,' I said dryly. 'What sort of guy have you made of her?'

Betty widened her eyes innocently. 'Mary, how can you! Verna is right up there, getting treatment that costs guineas at our salon—for absolutely nothing.'

'We've started her off on a mud-pack and those awful scaly, clammy hands of hers are in two basins of our special "He loves her lily hands" lotion. We're even giving her a home perm—that is, if that ghastly, stringy hair of hers will take it. So how can you think such mean thoughts!'

'You won't know her—when you see her.' Jean gave Betty a secret look and they giggled together again.

I suspected a catch. 'And when will that be?'

'Oh, a couple of hours at least,' Betty announced airily.

'Just enough to keep her from spoiling the party,' Jean added. 'She won't miss all of it, Mary, so don't look disapproving. You know you're glad really.'

I was. At least I didn't have to worry about Verna circulating through the happy, unsuspecting groups, spreading her peculiar type of poison. Joe and O'Mara would still be able to put her through their inspection hoops. Perhaps the girls' experiments would result in a better Verna too. It would augur well if their forcible beauty treatment made her attractive exteriorly. On this rather shaky philosophical conjecture, I collected the scarf and went back downstairs.

The party was in full swing and going well. It was developing into that sort of success that would be referred to for a long time as 'that super show we put on'. Even Cyril was doggedly enjoying himself; as though, having suffered the indignity of being draped about in my red silk scarf, he was determined to go the whole hog. Fenella had dragged him into her set where he was painstakingly applying his systematic mind to the caller's chant. I watched them for a while with the bright, determined smile of a wallflower. O'Mara had somehow got himself into the same square as Lorraine, who was looking stunning in a buttercup yellow frock with an enormous skirt and a tiny bodice. No doubt he was pursuing his line of duty, but I could not help wondering caustically what official question had brought the gay, vivid smile to Lorraine's lips and caused her to slap his hand playfully. His unusual bonhomie had successfully disguised him into just another of the genial, ineffectual young men on our guest list.

I wandered over to the barbecue fire where Joe was having a temporary respite from playing his extrovert role, his assistants having headed for the kitchen in search of further supplies of sausages and coffee. 'Hi, Mary! What swell parties you kids give!'

I perched myself on the brick wall and bit into a hamburger. 'I'm glad someone's enjoying it. Are you boys combining business with pleasure, or is it all pleasure?' I waved the hamburger round, indicating the groups on the court and on the bank above, where Mrs. Carron-Toyle, garish in purple velvet, sat with her dapper medical adviser, who was trying to look indulgently bored to cover up the fact that he felt out of place. The nuns had withdrawn to a discreet shadowy position on the terrace, where they would remain until it was time to retire to the cells. There was no one nearby, so I bent over to ask softly, 'Joe, who are you really?'

He glanced about swiftly, then grinned as he replied: 'Just a stooge, Mary. Just a cog in a wheel trying to do a job—a small job in a big operation.'

'A small job? Do you call two murders small?'

'I'm not interested in murders. That's Steve's department. It's the background to these murders—the underlying business—that I'm concerned with.' His smile had faded, and his expression had become grim.

'And even the underlying business is but a small section to your whole job—is that right?'

'Maybe,' he rejoined briefly. Some of the dancers were approaching, which prevented my pressing further questions. I slipped off the wall and wandered restlessly up to the terrace, where the nuns were twittering softly together. They loved looking on at our parties, and delighted with child-like admiration in our pretty frocks. The Garlands, mother and son, had just arrived and Stephanie's hair was under innocent discussion.

'Such an odd pair!' Mother Paul said in my ear. 'I wonder why they came.'

'Didn't you send them an invitation?'

She glanced up in surprise. 'Why no, dear. Nothing to do with me. Why do you look like that?'

I answered slowly. 'Because Lorraine didn't ask them either. She was quite upset when she learned Stephanie was coming.'

She was silent for a moment, surveying the scene below. Then she said in her irrelevant fashion: 'Mary dear, people keep wandering away. Sister Emerentiana doesn't like it. Do go and round them up. Chaperons are out of date, but not human nature. So horrid to ask you when you want to dance.'

'No, I don't. I'll be glad of something to do.'

She gave me a shrewd glance. 'Can't settle, dear? I know—very trying! I had a most interesting talk with Mr. O'Mara. Be patient and do as he says.'

'From which I gather everything is going to plan.'

Slightly comforted, I went off to play gooseberry. But Bartholomew had already been deriving grim enjoyment from the role. Whenever he saw a couple wandering off in a romantic mood, he would bee-line after them under the pretence of rearranging his lanterns. I met up with him in the lower garden and congratulated him on the effect of his lights without intending a double entendre.

'The party is certainly a great success.'

'Lot of nonsense,' he grunted. 'All this jigging about in velvet pants and the like.'

I pricked up my ears, for Rupert Garland had willowed in on the scene wearing maroon corduroy slacks with a white satin, Russian-style blouse. Clare was still rather dazed from her first glimpse of her self-bidden guest. 'Do you mean Mr. Garland? He and his mother run the shop where Lorraine works.'

'You needn't tell me,' he retorted, with a kind of suppressed anger. 'I know what kind they are. I've a good mind to go and put a stop to their flauntings.'

'Don't you dare make a scene,' I said sternly. 'You'd better go and see to the fire now. It needs building up.'

'Stop bossing me around,' he muttered, but he slouched off up the path.

After a backward glance or two, I followed the zig-zagging path which led to the river gate. I could hear voices nearby. Jonesy and Mr. Sparks, I thought, with a wry smile, recognizing the foolish titter and then Mr. Sparks's perfunctory little cough. It didn't seem fair to interrupt their tête-à-tête, so I tip-toed carefully past.

'But, Eric,' Mabel was saying, 'why can't we? Please let's tell them. We've waited so long.'

Farther down the path there were two more figures. One looked familiar, but before I could get near they broke apart and the girl came running up the path. It was Christine Farrow. She gave a stifled sob as she hurtled past where I stood in the shadow of the trees. Then a man came hurrying along and I waited until he was out of sight before I slowly made my way back.

'Where's Mary?' Fenella's voice came clearly over the noise. 'Has anyone seen Mary?'

'Here!' I called, coming out of the shadows.

She dashed up, pulling her fiancé along by the hand. 'Quick! Away from the mob.'

'What is it?' I asked anxiously.

'We've seen him!' She made the announcement dramatically. 'We both recognized him at once.'

'He wasn't wearing a hat, but I could swear he was the same chap,' Tommy endorsed.

I glanced from one to the other. 'Who? Oh, your mystery man who was hanging about on the night of the murder. Point him out to me quickly.'

Fenella shook her bright head regretfully. 'He's gone. He went sprinting up the drive just now.'

'Why didn't you tell me before? How long had he been here?'

'No time at all. I don't think he was gate-crashing. He came up the path not long after Christine.'

'Christine!' I exclaimed. 'Where is she?'

'She went into the house. Mary, what is it?'

'I saw her in the lower garden talking to some man—probably your friend the time-asker. I'm going to make her tell me who he is and what he's doing here. Look after Cyril, will you, Fen? I've been neglecting him badly.'

'The things you ask in the name of friendship! Okay—but what about Steve?'

'Who? Oh yes—er—Steve! He seems to be getting along all right.'

'I'll say!' Tommy interjected fervently. 'Every time I sight that chap he's got a different girl in hand. Right now he's going great guns with the red-hot momma.'

I took a glimpse of O'Mara being attentive to Stephanie Garland as they stood near the barbecue fire, then shot away towards the house.

III

The sound of the music and gay laughing voices faded away as I went into the quiet dimly lit house, and began to mount the stairs. I was filled with an unreasonable anger against Christine Farrow, unconsciously seeking in her a scapegoat for all my own misgivings and fears of the past week. If the connection between her and the mystery man had anything to do with the present state of affairs at Kilcomoden, now was the time to force her out of the silent unhappiness with which she perpetually frustrated all overtures.

'Mary!' The voice was a choking whisper.

I glanced up, then stood transfixed, my hand clutching the banister hard. Christine stood at the top of the stairs. Her face was ghastly and she kept coughing and trying to get her breath. The skirt of her cotton frock was daubed with blood which came from a slash on her hand.

'Come quickly,' she said, on a gasp.

I ran up the stairs. 'Your hand—what has happened?' I pulled out a handkerchief and wrapped it around. Then I raised my head and sniffed. 'What's that smell?'

She answered in little sobbing breaths. 'The room was full of it. I could smell it when I came up. I smashed the window to let air in. Mary—I think she's gone!'

'Gone?' I echoed stupidly. 'Who's gone?'

She dragged me along the bedroom passage. The sickening smell of gas was stronger now. 'Verna!' I exclaimed. 'Where is she?'

One of the bathroom doors stood ajar. There was a part vision of a chair, with someone sitting slumped forward as though asleep. I went in, my head reeling with the gas fumes which had come from the unlit bath-heater, and tried to rouse the pitiful, incongruous figure. There was nothing sly and complacent about Verna now.

'Verna! Wake up!' I tried to drag her from the chair, but her wrists were tied either side, with her hands drooping into twin basins of lotion placed on the floor. There was a cord about her body—a dressing-gown cord which held her securely to the chair. I recognized it as belonging to Betty's pink chenille robe.

'It's horrible—horrible!' Christine whispered from the doorway. 'What were they doing to her?'

I fumbled gingerly for a heartbeat, keeping my eyes away from the face smothered in a grey-coloured pack and the hair done up in a mass of curling-pins. There was no doubt at all that Verna was dead. Slowly I backed away from the grotesque figure, trying to control a feeling of sick revulsion.

'What do you know about this?' I asked Christine roughly, pushing her into the passage.

'Nothing—nothing. I told you—I smelled gas when I came up a few minutes ago.'

I avoided the undeniable expression of horror in her dark eyes. 'You were very anxious to buy that coat of Alison's that she had—the one with the note in it.'

'Only to stop that hateful scene.' She drew in her breath sharply. 'What are you trying to say?'

'Who was that man you were talking to tonight? He was seen at the gates on the night of the murder.'

'No one—I wasn't talking . . . He has nothing to do with this awful business. Have you gone mad?'

I passed a hand wearily over my face. 'Not yet, anyway. But there are things I don't understand about you, Christine.'

'They are none of your business,' she returned, with a flash of her old self. 'My private affairs have nothing to do with Kilcomoden.'

'The police might not agree with that.' I shut the bathroom door and locked it, removing the key.

'What are you going to do?'

'What do you think? Call the police.'

She placed herself in my path. 'Are you going to tell them about me and—'

'Of course,' I replied, watching her stricken face.

'No, you must not,' she burst out. 'I won't let you. I can't bear any more. Please, Mary—'

'Listen, Christine,' I interrupted, speaking in a steady voice. 'I think you have already guessed the truth about Alison's death. Now it's Verna. We can't go on like this. I must tell the police everything.'

She pressed her long, slender fingers against her temples. 'Alison. Verna. He didn't even know them by sight. Mary, I tell you—'

'Let me tell you instead,' I broke in. 'Whoever caused Verna's death knew that she was tied up in number three bathroom on the bedroom floor undergoing forced beauty treatment. Doesn't that rather cut out your—your . . . Oh, dash it, who is he anyway? You may as well tell me.'

'My husband,' was the muffled reply.

'Your what?'

She uncovered her face, and stared at me defiantly. 'Verna knew I was married.'

'Well, there's nothing to be frightened of about that,' I remarked, still rather staggered. 'No motive for murder that I can see—or is there? Why keep your perfectly respectable state a secret?'

'Verna knew that too. She remembered a photograph in the papers.'

'She would,' I agreed. 'But why have you left your husband?'

'I couldn't face him when I knew he was coming out.'

'Coming out?'

She nodded and said drearily: 'He has been in gaol. He was driving while drunk and ran over a child. It was my fault in a way—he always started drinking after a row. We'd just had a terrible quarrel—the same old theme, my music. He flung out of the flat and went off in the car. He was away all night. The next morning he was in police custody. They took me to see him.' She gave a long shudder. 'It was horrible—horrible. I never want to go through anything like it again. I thought when he came out we could make a fresh start, but when the time came nearer I panicked and left the flat. I wanted more time to think. But somehow he found out I was here and has been trying to see me.' She threw her hands out in a helpless gesture. 'And I still don't know what to do.'

'Well, don't ask me,' I said hastily. 'I know nothing about marital differences. And right now we've got more than enough to cope with. You stay here at the top of the stairs and don't let anyone come up. I'll only be gone a short while.'

I hurried out of the grim silent house, back to the music and light and laughter. Mother Paul called from the terrace as I passed, but I pretended not to hear. I wanted to find O'Mara.

He was standing in the group around the American, whose energetic party spirit was still unflagging. Under cover of a roar of laughter, I touched his arm. He looked round at once, amusement reflected in his eyes.

'Hullo!' he said warmly. Then the smile vanished as he saw my face. He took my arm as though to escort me over to the court, where new sets were being formed. 'What is it, Miss Allen?'

I found difficulty in speaking. All I could do was to press the key into his hand. 'What is this?' he asked.

'I locked the door,' I managed to say. 'We didn't touch her. It's Verna this time.'

He gripped my hand so that the key bit into my fingers. 'Verna? Come on—snap out of it. What's the trouble?'

'She's dead. Upstairs in the bathroom. Someone turned on the gas.'

For a moment he did not speak. The gramophone was screeching out some awful music. There were silly inane remarks around us, and empty laughter and the smell of sausages. I wanted to scream out to everyone to shut up and found myself saying politely instead, 'It's a good party, isn't it?'

'Yes, a very good party,' O'Mara replied evenly. 'And I want to keep it that way. If we skirt round the drive we should be able to get into the house unobserved.'

'Through the kitchen. It won't matter if you're seen there. Some of the men were helping to bring out the food earlier.'

'Yes, I noticed that.'

I knew what he meant. Anyone could have entered the house and stolen upstairs. 'But not everyone knew Verna was there,' I whispered. 'Jean and Betty were giving her a beauty treatment. They tied her in a chair—only for a joke, you know.'

'I heard about that. Someone was telling it, as a good story.'

'Then—'

'No, not everyone,' he interrupted quickly. 'Someone who knew it was possible to gas her.'

'One of us,' I said, but he did not reply. 'They had a chin-strap on her. She must have tried to call out. You can't make much noise when your jaw is tied up, can you? Then with the music going . . .' I had mental vision of Verna struggling against those silly, frightening bonds, trying to scream for help and turning her head away from the bath-heater which hissed out its inexorable flow of poisonous vapour. I could see her struggles becoming more feeble as she gave way to a merciful drowsiness.

We went through the kitchen, up the refectory stairs and along the hall. A light was switched on and I glanced up. Mother Paul was standing with Christine at the head of the bedroom stairs, her hands folded under her scapular as she regarded us gravely.

'Poor silly child! So foolish to play games with someone who is in deadly earnest, is it not, Mr. O'Mara?'

IV

The remainder of the party stays in my memory as a species of nightmare. In order to work quickly and anonymously, O'Mara had bidden Christine and me to keep the fun going until he and his men had finished their tasks. 'Tell Joe—he'll give you a hand,' was the curt order.

It was grim, but a good tumblerful of Fenella's punch helped. I pushed another down Christine and she played up amazingly, casually explaining to people how she had cut her hand opening a tomato sauce bottle. Joe was wonderful, though his voice was hoarse and his repertoire of wisecracks was wearing thin. We managed to keep it going for another hour, until I did not care if everyone was murdered. Never again, I thought, will I be an organizer of a Kilcomoden barbecue.

'I say, Mary!' Cyril came up, and I thought how silly he looked in my red scarf.

'What?' I asked, plucking it off him.

'Oh, don't do that. I was becoming quite attached to it. Who were all those grim-looking characters who turned up a while back. They seemed as though they'd come to the wrong place.'

'Have they gone?'

'That fellow in the check shirt—Fenella says you know him—pushed them out.'

'Thank heaven!' I said devoutly.

'Well, I must go too,' Cyril announced, as he settled back into his coat and tie with something akin to relief. 'It's been a great evening, Mary. Thanks for asking me along.'

'I'm afraid I didn't see much of you.'

'Why, that's so,' he agreed in surprise. 'Where were you all the time?'

'Oh—just organizing things.'

It was a word he respected. He nodded solemnly. 'Well, good night, old girl! I'll give you a ring sometime.'

The party dwindled away slowly. Fenella darted up, as full of vitality as though it were about to begin. 'Mary, someone says there was an ambulance outside. What has happened? You and Christine have been behaving like mad things the last hour. And where has your boy-friend Steve been?'

'Don't, Fen,' I said thickly, making a tired gesture with my hands. 'Verna . . .'

Jean caught the name as she passed. 'Verna! Good heavens! We forgot all about her. Hi, Bet! Did you do anything about Verna?'

'Is she still in the bathroom? And the party is all over! She'll be fit to chew nails.' They screamed with laughter.

'Be quiet!' I said roughly.

'Yes, dry up, you two,' said Clare. 'You'll be scandalizing the neighbours. What a night! It went well, don't you think, Mary? Hullo, is Mother Paul still about? That reminds me—I promised Sister Em to see that the fire was out. She imagines Kilcomoden will be burned down in the early hours.'

'Joe threw a bucket of water on it before he left,' I told her.

'Oh, good show! By the way, where did you pick up that character, old thing?'

'He's an old acquaintance,' Fenella chimed in. 'We happened to run into him the other day and suggested his coming along.'

'Well, he's certainly a good man on a party. So is his strong, silent pal. They absolutely made the show.'

'Yes, didn't they,' agreed Fenella suavely. 'I never thought Steve would be such a good mixer, did you, Maria? But he was in with everyone—even Lorraine.'

'What do you mean—even with me?' Lorraine drawled out of the darkness, as we strolled towards the house.

'You're so particular as a rule, ducky. No one less than scions of the upper crust seems to do for you.'

'She was showing her Mrs. Garland that she knew how to slum with the best. Tell us, Lorraine—did Stephanie find our simple pleasures amusing?'

'I'm sure I can't say, but it was easy to see poor Rupert was bored to tears.'

'Not half as bored as I was,' Clare retorted. 'Of all the fatuous fools, he takes the biscuit. Here's something he said! He wanted to know if he could borrow my handkerchief to sit on, as the grass might mark his trousers. And did you ever see such a getup?'

'What about Mabel Jones? I vote hers absolute tops. Those stripes! And did you see her being coy with poor little Sparks?'

'Mrs. Castor-Oil didn't last the distance. Bet she and that moronic doctor of hers went off for a quiet soak.'

'You're very quiet, Mary!' Fenella had slipped round to my side, threading her arm through mine. The touch of her soft, warm skin made me realize that I was cold. Somehow I was past all feelings and all thoughts. I knew something was about to happen soon which would cut short the usual party post-mortem, but my attitude was one of numb acceptance. I had formed no speculations.

'What are you thinking about?' she asked.

I raised my head as we approached the foot of the steps leading up to the front door. The rectress was standing there, a silent silhouette against the hall light. Christine Farrow was beside her. 'Like Clare, I was wondering why Mother Paul is still up,' I replied.

Then the rectress called down to us. Her voice seemed quite cheerful. 'Hurry up, girls! I want you all in the common-room. There is something I want to say.'

'What's up, do you know, Mary?' whispered Fenella.

I pretended not to hear and we all trooped inside, a little subdued now by the unaccustomed presence of the nun. I glanced at Christine as I passed. Her face was very pale, but she met my eyes squarely.

In the common-room Jean sank into an armchair and kicked off her sandals. 'After the ball is over! If it's a long session, someone will have to carry me to bed.'

Lorraine said petulantly: 'Really, you would think we were a pack of schoolgirls in for a lecture. I'm going up to my room.'

'Sit down and don't be silly,' said Clare. 'It isn't often Mother Paul asks to speak to us.'

'You know, it is like school,' someone confessed. 'I used to get a tingling feeling in my tummy. I've got it now. I remember all the girls with uneasy consciences would try and get out of these sessions.'

Lorraine gave a little laugh, which somehow did not ring true. 'I'm sure my conscience is perfectly easy.' But she sat down on a chair arm, assuming an air of nonchalance as she spread out her wide yellow skirt.

There was a moment of doubtful silence. Then someone giggled nervously and tried to lighten the tension. 'We're going to be torn off a strip over your punch, Fenella. What's the betting?'

'No takers,' Fenella answered promptly. 'No one passed out far enough for an ambulance to be called.' Under cover of the buzz of speculation that followed, she whispered again: 'What's keeping Mother Paul? It's not like her to build up an atmosphere.'

I shook my head and looked slowly around the room. Who? I thought, trying to choose one face. Some had that over-tired, wilted appearance which comes at the end of a party. One or two like Fenella, who had an inexhaustible supply of vitality, still seemed fresh and alert. Others had relaxed and were yawning without compunction.

'What's Christine been up to?' asked Fenella. 'She's in on this, even if you are not.'

Then Mother Paul came in and I thought she looked tired too. But some long practise of discipline was supporting her, not over-excitement. She stood aside and in bowled Mrs. Carron-Toyle, the expression of outrage on her face struggling with curiosity. Mabel Jones guided the wheel-chair to the centre of the room, and stood behind it, an even more ludicrous and pathetic sight under the strong centre light. Her make-up had worn off and the bow of ribbon had slipped over one ear, and she had changed out of the high-heeled shoes into a pair of brown-felt slippers.

The rectress moved gently around the room, gathering us all into her vision like one of those cameras used to take a wide group. 'And everyone so tired too,' she began, having said the first part of the sentence in her mind. 'Not a good time for bad news. I'll try not to keep you long, but I felt you should know.'

I gripped my hands together, my eyes fixed on her graceful black and white figure. I remember even now how she picked up a fold of Lorraine's skirt, let it slide through her fingers, then touched the wilting gardenia in Betty's hair for a brief moment before moving over to the fireplace. There for a short, barely perceptible second, her eyes met mine.

'Such a lot of unhappy events lately. First of all those anonymous letters, then that poor creature who was murdered at the gates and finally the tragedy of Alison Cunningham. No, not finally! But I did so hope and pray it would be. I thought you could all be happy again tonight for a short time—before the end.' Her voice rose slightly on the last phrase. By lightening her tone she deliberately made the words sound all the more ominous.

The silence in the room was heavy and mine were not the only wondering, fearful eyes that watched her.

Clare broke in harshly: 'Okay, Mother Paul! What is it this time? We can take it, can't we, girls?'

She put out her hands in a deprecatory gesture. 'I tell things so badly. Christine, my dear, will you come over here?' The girl crossed the room obediently and stood beside her. 'You tell them. After all, it was you who found poor Verna.'

'Verna!' repeated Betty sharply. 'What about Verna? We—Jean and I—'

'Hush!' Mother Paul raised one hand. 'Go on, Christine.'

The girl stood straight and tensed, her eyes fixed over our heads in a blank stare. She recited the facts baldly, as though she had been coached in her lines. 'Half-way through the party I entered the house and went upstairs. There was a strong smell of gas. I went to number three bathroom and found Verna tied to a chair. The gas tap was full on.'

Jean gave a short, sharp scream and broke into sobbing. 'I didn't do it! I didn't do it!'

Everybody's attention became riveted on her as she sat twisted in the armchair, with her face pressed against the back; all but Mother Paul who glanced intently around the horror-stricken faces.

Betty stood up. She was trembling slightly but she addressed the room with a desperate resolution. 'Jean and I tied Verna in a chair to make her up for the party. It was all in fun. She didn't seem to mind. She—well, you know how she is. She never allows anyone to make her lose her temper. But I swear we didn't—didn't do anything else.'

'Did you use the bath-heater at all?' the rectress asked.

The girl shook her head. 'We used the hot-water tap in the hand-basin to wash her hair. That comes from the electric tank. We weren't anywhere near the bath. Even if we had knocked against it acciden-tally, we would have smelled gas at once.'

'Were you two girls the last to see Verna? Or did anyone else go into the bathroom?' The nun glanced around the room encouragingly.

'What a question to ask!' Fenella muttered in my ear. 'As if any-one would answer that one.'

Jean raised her tear-stained face and gazed about her. She found my face. 'We met Mary as we were going down. She knew about Verna. So did Miss Jones. She was in the bathroom with us for a while.'

Mrs. Carron-Toyle turned her bulk and stared maliciously up at her companion, who was gaping like a terrified fish. 'Well, speak up, Jones! What do you know about all this?'

'Nothing, nothing,' Jonesy managed to gasp. 'I didn't touch the gas tap.'

'I was the last to go upstairs,' I said quietly. 'Miss Jones was leaving the house as I came in.' I tried to ignore the faces that jerked around in my direction and kept my eyes on the rectress. She regarded me in her usual serene manner, but I thought I detected an expression of strain; as though she was wondering if I would say the right thing. Christine, standing beside her, had become even more rigid. 'I went into my room to collect a scarf.' I continued. 'I neither heard any sound from the bathroom nor was there any smell of gas.'

'What time was that, Mary?'

'Going on for nine, I think. The party was well under way.'

Mother Paul turned to Christine. 'And what time did you go upstairs?'

The girl paused for a moment. Then she replied clearly and with a certain deliberation. 'About nine forty-five. I glanced at the hall clock as I came in.'

My eyes flew to her face, but fortunately like so many marionettes all heads had turned to the previous speaker. Christine was lying. It must have been after eleven when I followed her into the house. She was lying and Mother Paul knew it. She had certainly been missing from the party at that time, but she had been down near the river talking to her husband.

Clare moved restlessly. 'Where is all this talk leading us? We can guess what has happened. Between nine and nine forty-five someone slipped away from the party and went upstairs. Whoever it was knew that Verna was tied up and helpless—a sitting shot for murder.'

'Murder!' Lorraine cried out the word after her, and a few more girls began to weep hysterically with Jean. Fenella's fingers clenched slowly on my arm as I sat huddled on the couch next to her, listening dully to the commotion.

The rectress raised her hand again. 'Please be quiet for a moment!' The soft, clear tones brought us under control. 'You are not quite correct, Clare. It is true that Verna was, as you put it, a sitting shot for murder, but perhaps she is not yet dead. By good fortune she was found earlier than had been intended. They can do wonderful things in regard to resuscitation nowadays. Perhaps she may get better and then—who knows? She may be able to tell us just who it was turned on the gas tap.'

Nine

I

In the wretched days following the barbecue, the main theme plugged was that if Verna knew of the situation she had brought about at Kilcomoden she would be at the height of contentment.

'Such a pity she is not here to enjoy it!' remarked Fenella, looking at me under her lashes. She was given even more of late to those half-suspicious, half-teasing glances. 'Someone really ought to tell her. I'm sure a sudden cure would be effected. How is she getting on, do you know, Mary? All Mother Paul says—* and that vaguely—is that her condition is about the same.'

'I know no more than what Mother Paul reports,' I replied carefully; which in a way was true. My role as police informant was evidently finished. Though I continued to go each day to the Green Lounge, I had neither seen nor heard from O'Mara since the night of the party. But I knew Verna was dead and that the scene Christine and the rectress had played in the common-room must have been at his instigation.

The tension at Kilcomoden was reaching breaking point. It was not that murder was the topic of the common-room or the refectory—rather the reverse. The subject was painfully avoided. But you could read fear and uncertainty in the quick suspicious glances, the slightly hysterical laughter which greeted the smallest attempt at wit, and in the fact that everyone locked their doors at night.

There were times when I felt a surge of dispassionate curiosity and gazed searchingly at my companions. Who, I wondered again and again. Who was the Kilcomoden representative of that sinister trinity which Mother Paul maintained existed? What was the nature of their alliance that they did not stop at murder to pursue their illicit ends?

Fenella broke in on my musings once. 'You look as though you're wrestling with the devil, or at the very least suffering from indigestion.

I really think Sister Berthe's sausage mess tonight was over the fence. Evidently our Kilcomoden jitters have spread to the kitchen. And the porridge was burnt this morning too.'

I tried to smile. 'Fen, you're wonderful. What is the secret of your cheerfulness?'

'Low spirits are always a challenge to my sunny nature,' she returned smugly. 'Buck up, Maria, and stop brooding. Come out with Tommy and me. We're going to "Number Seven" to rub shoulders with the bloated rich.'

'A tempting invitation, but your beloved wouldn't thank me if I accepted.'

'If you're sensitive about butting in on romance, what about calling up Cyril?'

I shook my head. 'Not in Cyril's line.'

'Well, what about Steve?'

'Steve?' I repeated, bewildered. 'Oh, you mean—I haven't heard from him since the barbecue. Nor Joe,' I added flatly, and looked away so as not to see the swift, watchful glance Fenella was certain to give. For some unconscious reason I wanted to avoid intimate contact with her for a while. She went off with a swirl of her tulle ballerina and I slumped down to brood once more.

I had given up following O'Mara's instructions. Gone were the tactful interrogations, the spying on my companions' activities, and the mental assembling of events at the hostel which I would report the following day at the Green Lounge. The period of activity had ended, but in its place had come new worries. I had more time to think now, more time to interpret what I had once merely gathered and presented to O'Mara with a take-it-or-leave-it attitude.

On Saturday, Fenella asked me again to go out with them, and abused me roundly when I refused a second time. 'You're becoming introspective, Mary. Can't you snap out of it? Tommy and I are only going to look at a house, but the run will do you good. It's a dream of a place; fearfully expensive, but we'll make it if we want it badly enough. I loathe being frustrated because of money, don't you?'

I had heard Fenella talk like that before, but it had never worried me until now. When she went on to describe the new car Tommy had bought, I whistled and tried to say lightly, 'How do you manage it?'

'Oh, my clever man made something on the gees—or was it the Stock Exchange? I forget which. What does it matter when we've got what we wanted? Now why can't you come?'

I invented an excuse. I was playing golf with Clare. We had a tacit arrangement to play every Saturday, which Fenella knew I could have broken if I had wanted. This time she went off slowly, with a thoughtful expression on her face.

At first Clare was reluctant to give me the alibi. The hostel was split into two distinct groups. Some, like Fenella, were all for getting away and forgetting the conditions under which we were living. Clare and I belonged to the other group, which huddled about the house, stultified and solitary.

'I don't feel up to it, old girl,' she said.

'Oh, come on! It will do us both good. Besides, I told Fenella I was playing with you.'

'You two had a row?' Clare's gaze had become keen and watchful too.

'No, of course not. I just wanted to play golf.'

'Okay then!' She heaved herself out of the armchair where she had been sprawled on the last disc of her spine.

I gave her a playful slap on the back. 'Shoulders back!'

'Don't do that,' she said angrily. The light from the window was on her face. I wondered if mine had the same lined and worn look. 'Sorry, Mary. I'm a bit on edge. Maybe you're right. Let's get the hell out of this damned awful place.'

I waited in the hall while she went upstairs to change. Christine Farrow came down first, carrying her music satchel. I had barely spoken to her since the night of Verna's death. There seemed to be an unspoken agreement between us to avoid each other while the full story was in abeyance. 'Hullo!' I said awkwardly.

'Hullo,' she returned, her eyes on my clubs. 'Going out for a game?'

'Yes. Are you going to do a spot of practice?'

'Yes.' There was a pause. It was embarrassing knowing so much and not being able to talk about it. The same went for that mysterious husband of hers.

'Rather obvious remarks both,' I said brightly.

'Most remarks are. Have a good game.'

'Thanks. I hope the practice goes well.'

She nodded and went into the common-room. Presently I heard her warming up with a few arpeggios. Then suddenly the door flew open and Lorraine rushed out, the back of one hand across her mouth in a highly dramatic manner.

I made a grab. 'What's the matter, Lorraine?' She had rather been given to rushing from rooms lately.

'I can't stand much more!' she cried, with a touch of hysteria.

'Take it easy. We're all in the same boat.'

She looked at me as though I had said something terribly original. Then, disconcertingly, she burst into tears. 'Here, don't do that,' I said, patting one heaving shoulder. 'Things aren't as bad as all that.'

She raised her tear-stained face. 'They're worse,' she whispered. 'Worse! Oh, Mary, I'm so scared. I don't know what to do. If only I had someone to turn to.'

'What about your doting parents?' I asked unkindly. 'Send them a cable and Papa will charter a special plane back to Australia.'

Her face became distorted. 'I have no people,' she burst out. 'You know that.'

'What! No wealthy pastoralists touring Europe? Perhaps you made a slight mistake and they are just nice, ordinary folk getting along somewhere up country and terribly proud of their pretty, brilliant girl.'

She shook her head violently and came nearer. 'Mary, I must talk to you. You asked me before . . .' She broke off as we both heard a lolloping sound, and Clare came downstairs wheeling her golf-club carrier. 'Later,' she muttered, and fled upstairs.

'What's the matter with her?' Clare asked, with a backward jerk of her head.

'Conscience qualms. I think Lorraine has been playing with fire and the flames are starting to lick her pretty fingers.'

'That girl is fool enough for anything,' observed Clare trenchantly. 'Come on, old girl. Let's get Kilcomoden out of our hair.'

We went through the garden down to the river-path gate. Bartholomew was digging on one of the lower terraces, but he did not look up as we passed. 'Fire, fire,' I murmured reflectively.

'Come again?' said Clare, pulled up by the carrier as a wheel got caught in the lavender border.

'I was just wondering what Lorraine wants to tell me. She says she's scared.'

'Aren't we all?' she asked gruffly.

'Are you, Clare?' I hung back, surprised, and she passed through the gate with her head ducked.

'Well, browned off, anyway,' she shot over her shoulder, as we went single file along the narrow river path. 'Let's forget it for a while, Mary.'

II

The golf-links lay on the other side of the river just across the park. We crossed the footbridge in silence, Clare striding ahead and pulling her ridiculous little cart. She had dozens of clubs, some with silly woollen socks protecting them. She wore a leather mitten on her left hand and kept her tees in the band of her hat. I kept thinking what a good sort she was, and that I should not allow extraneous things like her jumbled service expressions and her two-toned brogues to irritate me.

Oddly enough, she must have been assessing my worth at the same time. Holding the first green pin while I puttered about an elusive hole, she said suddenly: 'You know, you're a good sort, Maria. One of the best. No wonder the kids, like Lorraine, go to you with their troubles.'

I scooped out my ball. 'That's very nice of you, Clare.' Privately I considered she had made me sound like a universal aunt.

We strolled across to the second tee. 'I mean it. You're the type who would never let a pal down—no matter what they did.'

'Your drive,' I said, standing aside. Clare had won the last hole, but she was off her game. She pulled her drive into the thickets bordering the fairway.

As I tee'd up, she asked, 'What's gone wrong between you and Fenella?'

'Nothing at all. Perhaps everyone is just a bit at loggerheads at the moment.' I swung uncaringly.

There was a sweet-sounding smack, then an echoing whistle from

Clare. 'One hell of a nudge! Good show, Maria!'

We called some following players through and went to hunt for her ball. Beating around the undergrowth, she said gruffly: 'Can't say I'm sorry. She's not up to your salt.'

'Who? What are you talking about?'

'Fenella King. Something not quite right there.'

I was trying to think of something to say when there, at my feet, lay her ball. 'Here it is! A good strong seven stroke should do the trick.'

She gave me a sidelong glance. 'You think Fenella is part of the Kilcomoden trouble? That is what's worrying you, isn't it?'

'I'm not—yes, I suppose I am worried, a little. Didn't you say we were all scared? Do let's go on with the game, Clare.'

I left her abruptly and went over to my ball, playing it so that I stayed away from her. We met perforce on the green where I paid exaggerated attention to putting in order to squash further remarks about Fenella. The unusual concentration paid off dividends as I holed from fifteen feet. 'I'll be giving you a stroke a hole yet,' I said.

She did not speak until the pin had been replaced. 'Have you heard how Verna is? There was some talk of her coming home in a day or so.'

I averted my head searching in my bag for an old ball. The next hole lay over a water-course, a veritable graveyard of balls. 'That should be—interesting!'

'Do you think it could have been an accident?'

I thought carefully for a moment. 'If it hadn't been for the scene Verna played with Alison's coat, I might have tried to believe it was.'

Clare also paused, before she said tentatively: 'Do you remember how Fenella put in the first bid at that bloody auction? Her dressing-gown or something.'

'Yes, I remember. My drive this time.'

Clare moved up behind me. 'You're certainly cracking 'em today, old thing. Maybe I'd better concentrate.'

We played the next three holes in fierce silent competition. A lost ball on the seventh fairway broke the spell.

'Who do you think did it?' asked Clare abruptly.

'Did what?'

'You know—Verna!'

'Perhaps I did,' I said lightly. 'My excuse of going upstairs for a scarf is considered pretty thin.'

Clare came alongside in one stride. 'Don't talk rot,' she said harshly. 'You would no more do a thing like that than—than write anonymous letters.'

I gave her earnest face a fleeting glance. 'Didn't the thought that I may have written the anonymous letters pass through your mind once? You looked at me strangely when I told you I hadn't received one. I can't think why I was passed over,' I added reflectively.

'Perhaps she likes you too well to do such a beastly thing.'

'Likes? Alison wrote those letters, didn't she?' I set another ball on the edge of the fairway. 'Two strokes penalty.'

'Fenella would never have sent you an anonymous letter.'

'No, I don't think she would,' I replied quietly. 'But there aren't many girls like Fenella.'

'I wonder if you know her as well as you think, Mary.'

I played my ball with immense care. It rose over the bunkers and trickled nearer to the flag than I would ever have dared to hope. 'There is always a limit to how well you know anyone,' I conceded. 'Perhaps, even then, what you think you know is partly illusion—because you've been looking at a person the wrong way round.'

Now, where have I heard that before, I thought, frowning at the ground as I strolled to the green. Oh yes, Mother Paul—something about turning the picture upside down. The picture of whom?

Clare's ball came out of a bunker in a shower of sand, and rolled madly to the far side of the green. She clambered up and saw the position of mine. 'Why so glum? You should be feeling bucked.'

'I wasn't brooding on golf but pictures—a portrait, to be precise. The face is shadowy and distorted, but it will be recognizable when I look at it the right way.'

'What on earth are you talking about? Shut up while I hole this beastly pill.'

I remained respectfully silent, but my mind was still on other matters. The picture was of someone I knew well—someone apparently harmless and above suspicion. Not Lorraine with her frightened outbursts or Christine with her obvious secretiveness—no one like that. They were too caught up with their own emotions.

'Who is it you are going to recognize?' asked Clare, after driving off from the next tee.

'Someone at Kilcomoden whom Alison was intending to blackmail. The person who knows the secret of our troubles.'

Clare handed me my bag. 'I say, old girl! You really are talking the most awful rot. Has the sun got you or something?'

I disregarded the well-meant platitude. 'Alison may have been a silly little feather-head, but she got to know about a mysterious plot which turned her into a menace to three persons and their criminal schemes,' I said slowly. Strange ideas were creeping up my mind, like clouds banking before a summer storm. I went on more quickly: 'An ingenious way of getting rid of her was devised. She was to be hounded into apparent suicide. The anonymous letter looked like Alison's work. They were the sort of thing she would do to make a sensation when life became dull at Kilcomoden. The notes were typed by various makes of machines, indicating someone who moves about a bit—which could have been Alison if you look at the picture the wrong way. Even the last letter—the one sent to Mrs. Carron-Toyle—pointed to her, because it was typed on the library machine presumably at a time when Alison was alone in the house.

'I think that note was specially timed. Knowing Mrs. Carron-Toyle's form, there was bound to be a fuss when she received it. The ensuing row was to be the climax to send Alison off her top. The real writer must have felt like shaking hands with you, Clare! You played right into the plot when you called that protest meeting in the refectory. Alison was in just the right shape.'

Clare said hoarsely, 'Don't, Mary—'

'Oh, I'm not blaming you. I also thought at the time that Alison was to blame for the letters. Don't you remember my being smarty-pants about it in the library? Come on, let's play golf for a change!'

We stroked side by side up to the green. I had had some more ideas by then. 'Alison had a secret appointment to meet someone that night,' I went on. 'Not only did I hear her go out, but I also heard someone else passing my room. For convenience we'll call that someone Miss X. Her job was to plant the suicide note. The only thing that puzzles me is how Alison was prevailed upon to write that note. What do you think, Clare?'

'I haven't the foggiest notion what you're talking about,' she said crossly. She was making quite a hash of putting, which suited both my score-card and my tenuous theorizing. I felt that if I let go now, something vital would be lost.

'I think I have it,' I announced presently. 'Alison frequently enjoyed suicide bouts. Suppose she wrote a farewell letter once just for the fun of it, and Miss X came across it and kept it for future use. By Jove, yes,' I went on excitedly. 'Here's another turn-up. What a blind fool I was! That farewell note was written on a sheet of exercise book. Alison did it at school ages ago—when she was aiming at suicide because of some girl's illness she was being teased about. That means—that means—oh, you've holed at last. Hold everything while I have a shot.'

I took a careful survey of the ground between my ball and the hole. Clare's shadow fell across the way. 'Mary, if Alison tried to kill herself once, then she must have committed suicide. You can't stop them once they get the notion into their minds.'

'What's the betting I sink this in one?' I asked, tracing an imaginary line with my eye. 'Yes, I thought like that at one stage. But I doubt if any of Alison's suicide intentions were genuine. On the school occasion she climbed on to the roof and had to be hauled down. You can bet your life she waited until everyone saw her. Remove your shadow like a good girl!'

Clare stepped back, and I sent my ball across. It ran round the lip of the hole before tumbling in. 'A possible conclusion is, therefore, that Miss X knew Alison at school. If that is so'—I stooped and picked out the two balls, tossing Clare's over—'all that remains is to get Mrs. Bert Baker to identify her.'

'Who on earth is Mrs. Bert Baker?'

'Alison's erstwhile crush. Golly, if Alison could see her now I bet she wouldn't bequeath her a ping-pong bat.'

Clare was becoming a bit tired of my enigmatic conjectures. She said forcibly: 'Now, look here, Maria! I don't know what the heck is the matter with you, but we came out to golf to forget everything. First you start on Verna and—'

'No, I didn't,' I interrupted. 'You did. You also got stuck into Fenella. But you're wrong there, Clare. Fenella's picture is hanging right way up.'

'I'm blowed if I know what you mean by that, but let's cut the nattering. Look, there's only one hole to go. I'll shout you a beer if we don't come even.'

We went across to the ninth tee, both staring at the ground. Clare's head hung from her hunched shoulders as she trundled her little cart behind her. I thought she looked depressed, but I had reached a stage when it was impossible not to go on. 'We'll go back to the subject of Verna.'

'I don't want to get back to Verna,' she snapped.

'Well, I do. I'm warming to my every subject. I have a hunch that if I mull over Verna, I'll recognize the portrait of Miss X.' I pulled out a number two wood. The fairway rose up from the ninth, with a narrow watercourse and thick undergrowth to hurdle. 'In fact, the drinks are on me if I don't. At the rate I'm going, I'll be calling her by her right name before you hole out.'

I was standing, feet apart, with the sharp angled club-head resting lightly behind the ball, when the enormity of my brash prediction suddenly hit me.

'Well, get on, get on?' said Clare testily. 'You seem to have the game sewn up.'

I raised my eyes from the bemused contemplation of an ant climbing over the club-head. 'I'm a fool, Clare,' I said unsteadily. 'Why didn't you stop me? I'm not sure I want to go on.' I wouldn't have tried if you hadn't started on Fenella.'

'Perhaps you'll get back to Fenella,' she growled.

I drove off after she said that. She was ready behind me as I brought my club down. Her own whistled viciously, sending the ball soaring away in a perfectly executed stroke.

'A lovely one, Clare!' I said, and her face lost its grim lines as she appreciated the tribute. We picked up our bags and strode up the rise. 'You know, I wouldn't be surprised if Verna was nothing to worry about.'

'Nothing?' she repeated incredulously. 'And she's coming back soon!'

For a brief period I toyed with the idea of telling her that Verna was dead, but decided against it. 'I don't mean that. I've been trying to fit Verna into the picture. My opinion is that she was not the menace to Miss X that she seemed to be. Verna, in her way, was—is—as foolish as Alison. You know how she is always pretending she knows more than the rest of us. That is her technique for finding out things. I think she deliberately planted a blank paper in that coat scene to try and trap Miss X.'

'You mean'—Clare's voice was hoarse again—'that note was a fake?'

I nodded. 'You remember when we went to her room and found it in a mess? Verna had that same smug look of triumph as she wears when she has wheedled an admission out of one of the girls by pretending she knows something. Her plan was to get Miss X in a panic and she certainly succeeded,' I finished dryly, pulling up and selecting an iron.

Clare walked on unheedingly to her own position. 'Out of the way. I might hit you,' I called, and she moved aside. I was just about to play the shot when I discovered a coincidence which added a few more lines to my portrait of Miss X.

'What is it?' called Clare, as I hesitated.

'I've just thought of something. I'll tell you when I catch up.'

She seemed as though to wait for me after I had sent my ball farther up towards the green. But as I drew near, she suddenly swung into her stroke and again her ball overtook mine. We played all the way up like that—Clare just a little ahead. There was great strength and co-ordination of muscle in her square frame. So long as she did not become careless, she could always beat me.

On the green, she was a stroke ahead and her ball lay within easy distance of the hole. Mine was right on the edge. 'Go on, hole out,' I told her. 'I shall advance by easy stages.'

She squatted down, her club in line with the hole. 'What were you going to tell me? You said you had thought of something.'

'I had a flash of clarity back there. My first summary of Miss X's portrait was that she was apparently simple and guileless. Even Alison thought she was easy money, while Verna considered her a likely person to tease.'

'Simple and guileless—sounds like Mabel Jones.'

'Yes, it does,' I admitted, startled. Then I remembered Jonesy's clumsiness. If she even fell downstairs, she could not have done the other. 'No, not Jonesy. She couldn't have accomplished such derring-do.'

Clare flicked away a blade of grass and stood up. 'Done what?'

'Do you remember we wondered how Verna's room was searched when she always kept the door locked? You suggested Sister Em's master key, but she had not given it to anyone. I asked her. No, there is only one way in which the room could have been searched. Someone got in through the window.'

Clare passed the blade of her club to and fro without touching the ball. 'Which means —?'

'Which means that Miss X must have risked a difficult and dangerous climb along that ledge which runs just below the windows. Do you see a connection there with something else I've told you? But I'm spoiling your putt. You've been testing for ages.'

'I'll play in a minute. Go on.'

'Surely you see the coincidence. When Alison tried to commit suicide at school, she climbed on the roof and some brave body had to go after her and haul her down. We have already established that Miss X knew Alison at school. I suggest that the person who pulled Alison to safety was the same person who climbed the ledge to Verna's room. That means Miss X is someone physically strong' — I paused as Clare jabbed at her ball and sent it careering wildly across the hole, to disappear into the rough grass bordering the green—'and athletic. Clare, you chump to miss such an easy one!'

She turned round and looked at me as I bent to pick out a putter. 'You've just about got it all taped, haven't you, Mary?' her voice was strangely quiet. Then she laughed. 'Go on—hole out. The drinks are definitely on me.'

Even then, I did not quite realize what I had done. The portrait was clear, but I had no instantaneous recognition. Realization came slowly and painfully. I was still thinking of the others back there at Kilcomoden, matching first this one and then that. I had them all in a sort of mental identification line-up. I had never thought to include Clare, who was beside me, or that dust had been thrown into my eyes when we found that Verna's room had been searched.

All through supper I sat in a huddle of misery and fear. I barely heard anyone who spoke to me and stared through them blankly without replying. My meal consisted of a cup of tea, which I half-spilled on the cloth when my hand shook with a sudden nervous spasm. If the police had asked anyone after my body had been recovered the following day, as was already planned, the consensus of opinion would have been that I had behaved strangely—that I had looked indeed as though I were at the end of my tether.

I was utterly alone in my unhappiness for I dared not voice my half-formed suspicions indiscriminately. Even Mother Paul had let me down. In a few hurried words I had asked her to be in the library after supper. She had been standing near the front stairs when the bell rang, seeing off the girls who were going out, and had answered my urgent undertone in a vague, rather loud voice. 'I don't think I can manage tonight, dear. Perhaps tomorrow.'

I thought she was being discreet and hurried to the library after supper expecting to find her waiting, serene and upright, ready to take over my terrible burden. The room was empty, but there was a sheet of paper in the typewriter. I hurried over to read it, thinking she had left a message. I could not imagine it not being from her. She must have known I had been out that afternoon with Clare. Without any hint of officiousness she always knew where we were. I even read the opening words thinking they were hers. *We can't talk in the house. It isn't safe. Please meet me at the gates at nine-thirty. L. L.*

Sick with disappointment, I puzzled over the initials before remembering Lorraine and the scene outside the common-room door that afternoon. More than ever I wanted Mother Paul. Why of all nights must she suddenly become obtuse? I was frightened and bewildered, and now there was this further complication of Lorraine. I had not remembered seeing her at supper, but in my dazed condition I could not have accurately named those who were. I had been so taken up with relief that Clare had not been present. I could not have stood that.

I paced about restlessly for a while, but still Mother Paul did not appear. To and fro—to and fro—until I could stand it no longer and went out into the passage. Sister Em was sitting on the hard little iron chair in the hall. Her hands were hidden under her scapular and her lips were moving slightly. I went up to her and asked if she had seen the rectress.

Her plain, severe face looked more careworn than usual. 'Mother Rectress left a message to say she would not be able to see you to-night,' she announced, in final tones.

'Oh—thank you.' I turned away, disconsolate, and wandered down the passage pulling at my underlip. The idea of ringing O'Mara had been in my mind for some time, but I had wanted Mother Paul's advice on what to do first. Had she not stopped me from acting impulsively once before? I eyed the telephone uncertainly, wondering how I could phrase my nebulous suspicion quickly and convincingly.

I went back to the quartermaster. 'Sister, will you do something for me? I want to make a phone call. It is very private and important and I don't want to be overheard. Would you stand in the middle of the hall and make a sign if anyone comes?' Greatly to my surprise, she agreed at once to do as I asked.

I got through quickly on the direct line O'Mara had given me, but he was not there and not expected back that night. Let down again, I thought, glancing along the passage towards the nun. 'It concerns the Kilcomoden case,' I whispered, and was told to wait a minute. Then another voice came on the wire and demanded my name.

'Oh yes, Miss Allen. I have a message for you if you rang. Mr. O'Mara said that you need not get in touch with him again as everything is under control.'

'But I have something terribly important . . .' I began. There was a click as the receiver was replaced, leaving me staring stupidly at the phone in my hand.

Sister Em's handkerchief fluttered as she took off her spectacles to wipe them. Then Mabel Jones came out of the common-room and paused to peer at the grandfather clock. We passed each other where the passage widened into the hall and she gave me a small, nervous smile.

'What was Miss Jones doing in our common-room?' I asked Sister Em petulantly, so disturbed by the second rebuff that even small incidents irritated me.

'She said she had left some knitting there,' the nun replied quietly, but she gave me an odd glance. 'Shall I leave the door now?'

'What? I mean—yes, I'll mind it now. Who has gone out?'

She handed over the list and went out of the front door. The clock struck nine and I was reminded of Lorraine's message. She had chosen a good time when the nuns would be out of the way and the Saturday nighters were far from being due to arrive home.

I went back to the library, brooding on O'Mara's curt message, and trying to subdue a feeling of angry disappointment. I had been finished with—tossed aside because I was no longer of any use. Even Mother Paul seemed to have lost interest. Admittedly my co-operation had been reluctant and I had shown very little initiative, but it was rather galling to realize that, when I really had something important, no one wanted to know about it. The police association against which I had been pulling all along had been severed abruptly, but instead of feeling relieved and ready to relax into my old peaceful existence, I was restless and nervous.

I watched the clock on the library mantelpiece, anxiously waiting for the time Lorraine had arranged. At nine twenty-five I slipped out through the windows and climbed down the terrace to the drive. The gravel crunched under my feet as I went swiftly along. It was a mild, starry night, with a sliver of moon showing up the ornate iron gates. I thought I saw a figure standing near one of the pillars, but decided it was a trick of the shadows. Lorraine was never on time for appointments. I was quite prepared to wait for several minutes.

The street outside was deserted, although car lights flashed by continuously at the top end where the bus route lay. We had often congratulated ourselves on our quiet backwater where there was no through traffic to render our nights hideous. Even if I had had time to scream at that moment no one would have heard me; while all I gave was a frightened, indrawn breath—thereby neatly inhaling the chloroform from the pad which was suddenly clapped over my nose and mouth.

Ten

I

I crept back into full consciousness, cold and nauseated and with the odour of chloroform still about me. The ground seemed to be lifting under my prostrate body, and there was a constant throbbing noise in my ears. I opened my eyes to a dim light just above my head with the discovery that my hands and feet were lashed together. It did not take me long to realize that the drumming noise was an engine and that the lifting ground was the motion of a boat at sea.

I felt very frightened and set my teeth against a rising surge of panic. The close confines of my prison did not help in this respect. I was lying on narrow slats in what seemed to be a kind of locker. My knees were slightly crooked and, when I tried to stretch my legs out, I jolted myself backwards against the bulkhead. There was another rack of slats above my head which held a lifebelt with the name of the vessel printed on it. I tried to read the letters, but the slats partly covered them and the light was poor. After making out an *S* with what seemed like another *S* alongside, I gave up and tried to think where I could be. What was going to happen to me I would not bring myself to consider, and concentrated on less important items to keep my imagination at bay.

I had just worked out that no big ship would roll so swiftly from side to side like this, when I heard the sound of voices and a narrow aperture was opened alongside. A stronger light was shone in and a man's head and shoulders appeared. I stared at him, terrified. It was Molloy, the boatman from near Kilcomoden. This was his launch I was on.

He inspected me with cold, evil eyes. 'She's awake,' he grunted over his shoulder.

Another man's voice, vaguely familiar, said: 'Move aside. I want to speak to her. You go up and keep watch.' Molloy vanished, and I found myself gazing incredulously at the small, rabbity face which had taken his place. It was Mr. Sparks!

'Ah—poor Alison's friend! Miss—er—Allen, if I recall rightly. This is an unfortunate business, Miss Allen!'

My mouth was dry, but I managed to say: 'What are you doing here? I don't understand—'

'I'm afraid you've been understanding only too well.'

I had never before noticed that Mr. Sparks's eyes behind the prim pince-nez were of a queer light blue. Their cold, merciless regard sent a tremble through me. I tried to recall the other Mr. Sparks—the perfunctory, insignificant little man for whom we had all felt a sort of amused pity. 'How dare you kidnap me like this! Untie these ropes at once.'

He shook his head. 'I regret this very much. Miss Allen, but I can't have you spoiling my plans.'

'What are you going to do with me?' I whispered, my burst of bravado short-lived.

He did not reply directly. 'Miss Parker tells me you have become acquainted with our little organization. We can't have that, you know. Braddock made that mistake and so did my late lamented stepdaughter.'

'Is Clare here? I want to speak to her. I know nothing of your schemes.'

'No, Miss Parker is not with us. In fact, I doubt whether we'll see her again for some time. That unfortunate incident which marred your delightful party the other night has quite unnerved the poor girl. However, she most obligingly warned us about you before she left town, and also undertook to get you out of the house in some way.'

That note from Lorraine, I thought. It was a fake. Clare knew she wanted to speak to me.

'I shall miss Miss Parker,' the little man went on, with a frightening loquacity. 'She has been most useful to me. At first I had considered using Alison, which was the reason for my placing her at Kilcomoden. Then I saw Miss Parker and recognized her from other days. She was far more suited to my purpose. After sounding her out, I found that she was only too eager to make a bit of money. She was also there at the hostel to keep an eye on Alison, who had quite a fear of her. You see, she once stopped the silly child from committing suicide. Whenever Alison got out of hand, she would threaten to expose the suicide note which she had kept. Alison seemed providentially ashamed of that little episode.

'All was going well, when what should happen but that stupid stepdaughter of mine somehow got wind of our organization. She actually took the extraordinary notion into her head that she could blackmail me. Silly, foolish child—it really quite upset me having to take drastic steps. But I could not afford to take chances with such an unstable person. Who knows what Alison might have done or said next—you know the sort of girl she was.'

I watched his terrible little face working as he talked of what he had done. It had been easy to entice Alison into meeting him near the river at midnight to discuss the terms of blackmail. She would have enjoyed the drama and secrecy, and would never have thought of any possible danger. She had been quite unsuspecting right up to the last moment, when he had pushed her into the river to drown.

'Of course, Miss Parker arranged about the anonymous letters and put the old suicide note in her room,' he added, as though reluctant to mitigate his triumph.

'And Braddock?' I asked, hiding my fear as I encouraged him to talk. 'What about Braddock?'

He gave his perfunctory little cough which had irritated me on so many occasions. 'Shall I show you something? I made it myself. I never thought it would come in so useful.' He bent out of sight for a moment, and then held up his umbrella. 'Look!' He gave the curved handle a turn or two and from the base of the shaft emerged a long, shining knife.

I swallowed on a dry throat, quivers of fear coursing through me. After regarding the knife with pride, he returned it to its sheath.

'I didn't know Braddock, so it really didn't upset me so much being a stranger. Of course, we had all been on the alert ever since Kilcomoden had been broken into a year ago. We thought someone must have heard of our little organization. But Molloy knew him. He has had some—ah—affiliations with the criminal classes. He guessed at once what Braddock was after when he saw him on his launch that afternoon. He demanded no less than to be taken into partnership!

I wanted to rebuke him for his presumption, but there wasn't time. Such a night it was—first, there was Alison to take out and then I had arranged to meet poor Mabel.'

'Miss Jones? Was she in on your schemes too?' I broke in, trying to prolong his story by digressions. I imagined I had caught a faint droning sound in the distance. There was a chance that other craft might be around—a chance that somehow I might be able to draw attention to my desperate situation.

'Mabel? Oh, dear me, no. I wouldn't trust her any more than I had trusted Alison. But I had to invent some excuse for keeping on calling at the hostel after Alison had gone. I've been working on Mabel for some weeks now. She is an incurably romantic creature. I told her Alison had some hold over me which necessitated keeping our mutual regard for each other a secret. I don't think I will have any difficulty continuing to string her along for quite an indefinite period. The dear woman is quite ready to swear black is white for my sake.

'Not that I expect any trouble over Braddock's death—there was far less risk killing him at once in your respectable garden, which was the meeting place Molloy arranged, than to be seen with him at some of his underworld haunts first. He was, I believe, the sort of man who wouldn't take no for an answer, and I certainly was not going to be coerced by such a person.

'Mabel was my reason for leaving my car at the hostel gates and walking Alison up the drive. She was in it when I got back, and we cruised round in circles—she was quite oblivious, bless her—until it was time for me to meet Braddock. I pretended that something had gone wrong with the car. I got out and lifted up the bonnet. That gave me the opportunity to slip through the gates and introduce myself briefly—and finally—to Braddock. It was all over and I was back in the car before Mabel realized I had gone.'

The drone seemed to be nearer. I said quickly: 'He didn't die at once. I found him. He spoke a woman's name—Jess. Who is she?'

'Jess?' Mr. Sparks appeared entertained by the information. He picked up the torch and shone it on the lifebelt above my head. It was easy to decipher the words now—*Jessie Belle*.

'Molloy discarded that name a long time ago. Braddock must have learned about it during his recent sojourn in prison. Some former—ah—associates of Molloy's are there. He may even have heard a rumour of what this particular lifebelt is used for and why it is kept in here. Actually, it is yet another of my little ingenious inventions which—' He broke off as a sudden shout came from above.

'There's a launch coming up on us, Boss. What do we do?'

The mad, retrospective expression was wiped from Mr. Sparks's face. He bent on me one long, terrible look. 'If you so much as open your mouth!'

As he spoke, a still brighter light filled the cracks and chinks of my prison. A faint hail reached my ears. Quickly Mr. Sparks shut the door of the locker. I heard his footsteps running along the deck.

A faraway voice spoke commandingly: 'Cut your engine, please. Police here!'

I threshed around, trying to work my bonds loose, fear and hope intermingled. Sparks and Molloy were exchanging rapid words, but presently the engine of the erstwhile *Jessie Belle* dropped to a feeble putter. Waves smacked and lapped against the bulkhead alongside me, and the movement of the launch increased as the police boat edged nearer.

'What do you want with us?' I heard Molloy snarl. 'Can't a man go night fishing without the cops interfering?'

'We'll talk about that presently. Here, catch this rope! We're coming on board.'

'Oh, are you!' Suddenly the engine of the *Jessie Belle* roared under an open throttle and I was thrown violently to one side, striking my head. Although dazed by the blow, I guessed that Molloy was attempting to make a run for it. The next moments were full of confusion and noise to which I listened with fluctuating emotions. There were gun-shots and shouts and thudding feet—with Mr. Sparks's voice raised to screaming pitch, like the squeals of a cornered rat.

With an abrupt clarity, a well-known voice sounded out of the mêlée, 'Where is she?'

I tried to give a feeble shout, but found I had no voice. Brisk steps approached and the aperture, which had revealed Molloy and then Mr. Sparks, was filled by another man—at whose appearance I burst into tears of exhaustion and relief.

'Mary! Are you all right?' O'Mara quickly untied the ropes and helped me out of the locker. His touch was so gentle that I clung to him, sobbing like a child. 'Don't cry. It's all over now, my dear.'

I was so astounded by his words, spoken in such a tender voice, that I stopped at once.

II

'Narcotics!' said Joe. 'It's the toughest racket in the world to crack. You push it down here and up it shoots some place else. That is why a special nation-wide organization was set up to deal with it.'

It was the following afternoon and we were in the library at Kilcomoden, where O'Mara had just introduced the American as an agent for the International Drug Organization to Mother Paul. I had been told of his identity when he had slashed through the lifebelt on the deck of the *Jessie Belle*, disclosing small packets tied up in hessian.

'I was sent over here from the States because your authorities were getting worried about the increase in local addicts. They had clamped down on imports of heroin for medical use, but still the stuff was creeping in. I had been in Sydney a few weeks, and got a few leads which led nowhere, when Melbourne C.I.B. contacted me. Their Homicide department was offering yet another possible line of research.'

'That was the hunch I mentioned to you, Mary,' said O'Mara ruefully, 'when I switched from thinking Braddock's murder was a gangster feud affair. The only information we managed to extort from his underworld associates was some casual reference Braddock had made to drug trafficking. When we linked him with the burglary you had a year ago, we decided that the locality of the murder was not accidental and that heroin might be the heart of the matter.'

'So your tasty dish was drug trafficking,' I said, returning his smile.

'It makes one quite sad to consider that Kilcomoden, however innocently, had a part in this infamous business,' remarked Mother Paul.

'Did you have some idea what was going on?' I asked her curiously.

'Not at first. I just could not work out what Braddock had wanted from here—even all those tedious newspapers I perused did not give me a clue. I stumbled on to the truth by merest chance. So annoying, for in detection one prefers to rely upon one's deductive powers, not good fortune. I knew when I picked up the wrong umbrella.'

I could not help laughing at the way she announced her defection. 'Yes, truly, Mary. Sounds so silly, doesn't it! I could not find my umbrella anywhere—or rather it was my gloves I had mislaid.'

'I knew you would forget where they were. You rolled them into a ball and put them into your umbrella which you left in the hall-stand.'

'Exactly, dear. But I picked up Mr. Sparks's umbrella instead. And it wasn't gloves I found, but heroin—though to be sure I didn't recognize it as such until I told Mr. O'Mara. I had often thought how odd it was of Mr. Sparks always to be carrying his umbrella.'

'Odd and unimportant,' I said, gazing at her affectionately.

'Molloy would bring the stuff up the river to Clare who would collect and store it in a disused cupboard in the cellars,' explained O'Mara. 'We found some that night we were here. Mr. Sparks's job was to sell it to his various clients. He would leave his umbrella in the stand for Miss Parker to slip in the packets at an opportune moment.'

'Or any messages she might have,' I added thoughtfully. 'Mr. Sparks was here that day I found my new type ribbon used.'

'A ring I broke up in San Francisco last year followed an almost identical routine,' said Joe. 'A pleasure boat cruising around the big ships in port—a lot of noise on board, necking kids and such. No one would notice if a ton of the stuff was passed.'

'I went on one of those cruises once,' I put in. 'Molloy would cut off his engine and let the launch drift about while he played his concertina. The girls heard Braddock make some reference about it to Molloy.'

Joe nodded. 'The concertina was probably a signal to the contact man on the overseas ship to watch out for a certain lifebelt floating in the water.'

There was a knock at the library door and Sister Emerentiana rustled in, wheeling a tea-wagon. We all stood up and allowed her to reorganize our seating arrangements. 'Someone is wanting Mr. O'Mara on the telephone,' she announced, whisking chairs into position around the table. Mother Paul took him out of the room, while I helped the quartermaster to spread the exquisitely embroidered cloth, which was usually kept for the Archbishop's annual visit. There were plates of a special Kilcomoden recipe fruit-cake and bread-and-butter, cut in such wafer-thin triangles that you always felt tempted to clamp four together.

They came back presently, looking grave. 'Miss Parker has been picked up,' said O'Mara, and I slopped some tea into a saucer as my hand, holding the tea-pot, shook. 'She was dressed as Mother Paul suggested she would be.'

I glanced from him to the nun, puzzled. 'I'm sure it was Clare who stole my visiting cloak last year,' Mother Paul explained. 'Such a good disguise; all she needed to add was some sort of veil. Even poor Sister Felician did not recognize her when she caught her once coming up from the river.'

'Have you suspected for some time that Clare might be involved?'

The rectress nodded. 'When I gave up wondering about Mrs. Carron-Toyle and that doctor of hers, I began to consider Clare. Do you remember the occasion when we decided the anonymous letters had been typed by various machines? She was in my mind then. Moving from school to school, it was probable that she would have access to many different makes. Then there was the strange fact of your not receiving one, and I remembered how well she liked you. But it wasn't until you told me of your visit to Mrs. Baker that I was quite sure, and was able to understand why the suicide note was so odd. All that pretty notepaper in her room, and Alison chose to write it on an old exercise book-sheet—just like the will.'

'But Clare dived in to try and find Alison. She was fearfully shocked by her death.'

O'Mara said dryly: 'You would have to be pretty hardened if your first murder did not upset you a trifle, even if you were only an accomplice before the fact. I have no doubt that Mrs. Baker will be able to identify Miss Parker as the P.T. instructress who rescued Alison from her suicide attempt at school.'

I looked back at the rectress. 'Then you must have guessed that Clare murdered Verna.'

She nodded again, and said dispassionately: 'She made a bad mistake over Verna. I would be very surprised if the latter knew anything incriminating. Perhaps Alison had confided to her over her former acquaintance with Clare. If she had any suspicions concerning the nature of Alison's death, her inquisitiveness would have then become centred on Clare. I am inclined to think that that note we found on the type-ribbon meant Verna, not you.'

'You knew all that, yet you would not let me talk to you last night when you must have been aware that I had been out with Clare.'

'Yes, so unkind of me, dear! And I could see how distressed you were,' she admitted, in tones of deep self-reproach. 'But I dared not even give you a hint. I told Mr. O'Mara after we found Verna that if we pretended she was still alive, Clare would probably lose her head completely. Tell me, dear, how did you make her?'

'She was trying to throw suspicion on Fenella. Quite unintentionally, I started looking at the picture the right way. But what is this hint you dared not give me?' I shot a calculating glance at the two men, but they appeared nonchalantly oblivious.

Mother Paul leaned over to pat my hand soothingly. 'Such an unpleasant time you had, but think how much worse if you had known.'

Light dawned gradually and appallingly. 'You mean you allowed me to get kidnapped by Molloy and Sparks—that I was used as a sort of bait?'

'Well, it was so difficult to prove anything, you see—even though Mr. O'Mara and this other gentleman had identified the three persons in the conspiracy. But if the wretches were discovered trying to murder you!' The rectress paused and beamed at me with innocent triumph.

After a moment or two of indignant silence, I said faintly: 'What an excellent plan! What would have happened if I had been murdered?'

'No fear of that, dear. Mr. O'Mara promised me most faithfully that you would have every protection, didn't you, Mr. O'Mara? So long as you did not do anything foolish—and you are such a sensible girl, Mary—there was no reason why the trap should not be successful.'

'Foolish!' I exploded. 'I've been a fool from start to finish; crazy to have allowed myself to become embroiled at all and finally to have aired my views to Clare.'

'Don't say that, Mary. When I heard that you had gone out with Clare, I hoped and prayed we might be nearing the end. You both came in looking so odd that I kept an eye on Clare. I overheard her ringing Mr. Sparks and then I saw that fake note from Lorraine. I got in touch with Mr. O'Mara at once and he agreed that we should act—though the action on my part was negative, I'm afraid. All I had to do was to keep out of your way in case you chose not to keep the pretended assignation with the Lawrence child. Do you know, Mary, he had the most elaborate network arranged—river police, motor patrols, even a funny little man perched up in the oak tree near the gates like Charles the Second; though of course walkie-talkies weren't invented in his day. I was so thankful that you did go through with it.' She seemed to imply that I did far better suffering agonies of fear than causing the police embarrassment. From the taxpayers' viewpoint, I supposed that she had something.

I turned to the two men and was slightly mollified to find them regarding me somewhat contritely.

'You've been wonderful, Mary,' Joe said quickly, with his disarming grin. 'I only hope they give me someone like you the next job I handle.'

'I'll write you out a testimonial,' I promised, 'and add a few details of what you expect of your unfortunate assistants—starting with aiding and abetting house-breaking.' I closed my eyes in painful reminiscence. 'The agonies I suffered that night too!'

The American seemed surprised. 'There was no need for the jitters. I practically went straight to the place where the stuff was stored. There is not much originality left anywhere in the world when it comes to dope-rings. Once you get a grip of your terrain,' he went on to explain, as though I were a promising cadet for the I.D.O., 'your next move is to collect all your suspects and give them the once-over. Again thanks to you for the party you put on, Steve and I were able to get right in amongst them.'

'I haven't worked as hard as that night since I gave up pounding the beat,' remarked O'Mara ruefully.

'You seemed to be thoroughly enjoying yourself,' I said, and received a grimace, intimate in its absurdity, for my hauteur.

'I was on the lookout first and foremost for Sparks. First impressions are sometimes amazingly accurate. You told me right at the beginning that you wondered if he had pushed Alison into the river.

Even before I met him and recognized the mannerism as part of his perfunctory little-man facade, there seemed to be no one else with whom she could have arranged to meet.'

'What mannerism?'

'Do you recall my asking you to go over and over that phone call you made to the hostel—the one that Alison answered confirming the river appointment, not, as you thought, a dressmaker's fitting? You employed a subterfuge to get her to speak first and—'

'But, of course,' I interrupted, setting my cup down with a clatter. 'I gave a cough and she thought I was Mr. Sparks. He had a habit of always clearing his throat before speaking.'

'Miss Lawrence also had a high priority on our inspection list. I got her talking about those parties Mrs. Garland gives in the city. Not only does the lady in question run a neat little gambling establishment, but she is not above providing other excitements for her guests. She is one of the ring's better customers, but the stuff hasn't been forthcoming lately and some of her friends are feeling the pinch. She and son Rupert got themselves asked to your party, the idea being to carry out a little transaction under cover of the innocent fun and games; which was precisely the sort of move Joe was hoping for.'

'You mean you actually saw Mr. Sparks pass over a supply of heroin to Mrs. Garland?' asked Mother Paul.

'Miss Parker did the passing to Rupert,' replied the American. 'Mrs. Garland handled the payment side. I saw her drop her open handbag at Sparks's feet—corniest gag in the world! He helped her to pick up her lipstick and things, but there was a wad of notes which he put into his own pocket. It all happened pretty fast, of course, but we were on the lookout.'

'Did Lorraine know about Mrs. Garland's passing round drugs?'

He shrugged. 'You can work that one out for yourself.'

I pleaded for her, knowing that she must have had some idea. 'I'm sure she didn't realize how serious matters were. She's only a silly child.'

'Oh, sure!' returned Joe, unconcerned. 'She only needs a spanking—she'll probably get it too. That old man of hers looks like one of the straight and narrow.'

'Who? What old man?'

'Your gardener guy—Bartholomew. Didn't you tell us that he once told you to leave her alone? Steve got quite a sob story out of him. Seems his wife ran off and left him stranded with the kid, and he's been scared ever since she'll follow in Mom's footsteps.'

'Incredible!' I exclaimed. 'But how stupid I was not to realize something like that before.' I thought of all the grand tales Lorraine had concocted concerning her parents. They were the natural imaginings of a young, lovely girl, encumbered with an unattractive, though no doubt worthy, parent.

'I believe the poor child's real name is Gladys Stubbs,' said Mother Paul regretfully. 'I can't say I blame her, do you?'

'Indeed I don't,' I agreed, and began to laugh.

III

We had come to the end, and the opportune entrance of Sister Em prevented the discussion from lapsing into reiteration. There was some latent theatre sense in the quartermaster; not only did she know how to set her stages, but she also knew when to wind up a scene. She started to clear away the tea-things quietly but purposefully.

'You must come and see us the next time you are in Australia,' Mother Paul said to the American. 'Very dreadful, but so interesting—your work, I mean.'

'That's a date,' he promised, as he shook our hands warmly.

She turned to O'Mara who was speaking another word of thanks for the help I had given. I shook my head. 'I would never have got in touch with you again, but for Mother Paul,' and thought momentarily—how dreadful that would have been after all!

'A mere jog of your elbow, dear,' she declared, regarding us benignly. 'Good-bye, Mr. O'Mara—I hope we'll see you soon and often.'

'I think it quite likely,' he agreed gravely, following her to the door.

I remained behind in the library and sat down at the typewriter, smirking foolishly at the Life of Mother Paul's holy Foundress. 'Well?' I asked, when she same gliding back again. 'Shall we continue with the saint?'

She stared at me thoughtfully for a moment. 'Mary dear, that nice,

steady young man—not the one who has just left, the other one—
Doctor of the Church!'

'Cyril?'

'Yes, Cyril. Don't you think you should tell him at once?' Then,
before I could answer, she added apologetically, 'I know I don't have
experience of such matters, but I could not help observing something
odd about you and Mr. O'Mara.'

THE END

MOTHER PAUL INVESTIGATES

Nihil Obstat:
 J. McGOVERN,
  Censor Deputatus.

Imprimatur:
 R. COLLENDER, V.G.
  Sydney, 5/3/'54.

CONTENTS

	Page
CONQUERESS OF EVIL—By Father Dominic	2
MOTHER PAUL INVESTIGATES—By June Wright	4
ST. JOHN OF GOD TRAINING CENTRE	10
THE SWAN RIVER SETTLEMENT—By Brother B. O'Grady	13
ST. BRIGID OF IRELAND—By Brother Flannan	17
CARITAS CORNER	21

CARITAS is the official organ of the Brothers of St. John of God in Australia and is published three times each year. Price, 3/- yearly. Address all correspondence to The Editor, St. John of God Brothers, 'Belmont Park,' Richmond, N.S.W.

PUBLISHED BY THE BROTHERS
OF ST JOHN OF GOD.

MOTHER PAUL INVESTIGATES

I first knew Mother Paul at school—a serene and scholarly nun gifted, as I realized later, with a unique ability in guiding rebellious young wills through the tiresome years of adolescence. We kept up a yearly correspondence when I left school to commence my nursing career. I came into more direct contact with her again when, with a severe bout of pneumonia, she was admitted to the private hospital where I was night sister.

Confounding her doctor by a miraculously fast recovery, Mother Paul began her convalescence by taking a lively interest in those about her. Within forty-eight hours she knew more about the staff than I had learned in two years. Being confined to her room her charitable curiosity was limited. But presently, when she was allowed to wander a little about the hospital passages, the other patients found in her a ready sympathetic listener to their maladies, both imaginary and real.

Coming on duty one evening, I found old Mrs Porter's smooth, handsome nephew chatting brightly to Stella while he waited for his aunt to finish her conversation with Mother Paul. Mrs Porter was an immensely rich and disagreeable widow. She was in the hospital undergoing treatment for diabetes.

Mother Paul talked about her new acquaintance as I was settling her for the night. "Such a sad life. She was one of three sisters and forced to marry a wealthy man very much her senior. No children— that is why she is so devoted to her nephew Clifford, even though he is not very kind to her. His mother was the second sister. Her death was a sad cross for poor Mrs Porter. The third sister is married, but Mrs Porter says the husband took a most unreasoning dislike to her and barely allows his wife to see her."

"You don't really believe all that, do you?" I asked.

Mother Paul's eyes twinkled. "I often find, dear, that even in the most biased of stories there are some glimmerings of accuracy. It is merely a matter of adjusting the facts." Then she added thoughtfully, "It must be dreadful to be rich—so bad for the character."

"The camel and the eye of a needle?"

"Not only that, dear. So bad for those about her. But I'm talking foolishly. I'm sure there is nothing to worry about."

Her words did not startle as much as the memory of them some time later.

I did not see either Mother Paul or Mrs Porter for two nights, for it was my mid-week off. On the third evening as I came on duty, Stella Bray was standing outside Mrs Porter's door ringing her little handbell. There was a faint look of impatience on her calm, lovely face, for it was well past visitors' time and Mrs Porter's three visitors showed no signs of leaving. I caught a glimpse of them through the open door—Clifford Hake, a fleshy-looking woman with a loud arrogant voice which marked her down as Mrs Porter's sister, and a faded meek little man whom I guessed as the husband with the unreasoning dislike.

From the bed Mrs Porter was shouting, "I know you are only waiting for me to die so as to get my money. But don't be so sure. You may receive a nasty surprise."

Stella rang her bell again and went in to break up the happy family. I dealt with a couple of my other patients and then returned to tackle Mrs Porter. Holding the door knob in her hand and looking as though she would like to slam it, Stella was saying soothingly, "Yes, very well, Mrs Porter. I'll tell her." She shut the door quietly and made a grimace.

"Did you get rid of them?" I whispered. "Why must visitors stay overtime? They forgot they keep the staff on duty. What was wrong with the old girl?"

Stella shrugged. "She likes wielding the big stick. I gave her a sedative. She doesn't want to be disturbed."

"I don't want to go near the old dear. Thanks, Stella. Did Clifford exude his charm all over you? Why the tuxedo?"

"He's going on to some dinner, I believe. Good-night. Will you be all right now? That nun of yours has been asking for you all day."

I went to see Mother Paul. She was sitting at the low window that opened onto the balcony, reading. She put down her book. "So glad to see you, dear. Did you enjoy your time off?"

"Yes, thank you. Has everything been all right? How is the friendship with Mrs Porter progressing?"

"I haven't seen her. A little dry man with a briefcase has been with her most of the time."

We talked for a while. Gradually the hospital settled into silence and darkness. I sat down at the dimly-lit desk at the end of the hall and began to enter charts. Paper work kept me awake and busy for an hour or two. Presently I got up and went along the hall intending to make some tea. Passing Mrs Porter's door, I noticed the light was still on. I opened the door quietly and put my hand in to the switch, which was operable also at the patient's bedside. Mrs Porter was asleep with the sheet pulled over her face as a protection from the light. A strong draught from the window almost pulled the door from my hand. The long balcony window was open wide. With the room in darkness I felt my way across quietly and pulled it down. The curtains ceased their long billowings, and the shut-out night breeze rendered the room strangely quiet.

It was the silence that caused me to check my step and to fumble automatically for my pocket torch.

I pulled the sheet down and shone my light full onto Mrs Porter's face. For a few seconds I stared aghast. I was as used to death as any hospital nurse, but not death like this — the swollen bloated face, the protruding tongue and the tortured eyes. I shut off the light, hoping to shut the sight out of my mind.

A bell rang from the board near the hall desk and I stumbled out of the room. An appendectomy was complaining of insomnia. I mixed a sleeping draught with shaking fingers, very glad of his company.

I stood in the hall wondering what to do — whether to summon Mrs Porter's doctor or the matron or the police or just to start screaming. Then I thought of Mother Paul, and the great load seemed to lift.

Mother Paul was fully awake in ten seconds and had a grip of the situation within another fifteen. "Strangled with her dressing-gown cord, did you say? Run outside, dear, and I will be with you in one minute."

How she kept her word I do not know, for it isn't as though nuns can cut corners over dressing. After a minimum of delay she joined me in the hall, not a fold of her habit out of place. She even wore a pair of black cotton gloves. "So confusing for the police. The fewer fingerprints about the better," she explained. I started guiltily, and she added, with her percipient shrewdness, "Well, it can't be helped, dear, but don't touch anything more."

I clasped my hands behind my back and followed her to Mrs Porter's room. "Now tell me exactly what you saw, dear. First impressions are so important."

"The light was on. I thought she'd fallen asleep forgetting to switch it off."

Mother Paul flicked it on with the tip of one black finger.

"And the window was wide open."

She moved across and pulled it up. I shivered and held the door wide open with my foot. "The sheet was right over her face. I—I just dropped it like that."

Mother Paul placed it carefully over the face and stood back to observe the effect. "Anything else, dear?"

"I don't think so," I replied, frowning at the bedside table. Mother Paul's eye was bright and alert. "Bedside lamp, a basket of fruit, two books, carafe and tumbler, clock. What is puzzling you?"

"I don't know."

"Well, never mind," she said comfortingly. "You'll remember when the time comes."

"Mother Paul, don't you think we ought to call the police?"

She was poking gingerly into the wardrobe. "Is this Mrs Porter's dressing gown? Yes, the cord is missing. Still knotted around the poor creature's throat. Now, isn't that odd! The dressing gown, I mean. The police presently, dear. First, old Father Smith. Only the good God knows what flash of His mercy may have pierced her poor soul in those last seconds."

I called the Priest and guided his footsteps to Mrs Porter's body. I left him with Mother Paul, warning him not to disturb the body more than necessary, and went to ring the police.

The next few hours were a maelstrom of detectives, doctors, photographers, finger-print experts and ambulance men until the time I was due to go off duty and the whole unpleasant affair resolved itself into Mother Paul and I facing a tough-looking detective in the hospital parlour.

"Mother Paul? Mother Mary St. Paul of the Cross?" he elaborated, and Mother Paul nodded meekly. "I've heard of you. What's it all about, Mother Paul?"

We told him everything we had seen and spoken of and what we knew concerning Mrs Porter.

Mrs Porter's sister, the husband, and Clifford had been summoned. They entered, aggressively, timidly, and suavely. The detective asked for their movements between the hour of eight, when Mrs Porter was last seen by Sister Bray and eleven, which the police doctor had given as the outside limit of her death.

"Outrageous!" boomed Mrs Wilson, "that anyone should insult the kinship of blood by inferring—"

"Please, my dear," interrupted her husband, dabbing at her hand like a mouse trying to soothe an angry lioness. "My wife and I, after visiting her unfortunate sister, went to the pictures. There is a theatre only a block away from here."

"You were together the whole time?"

"Of course."

The detective turned to Clifford Hake.

"Mr Hake?"

"Clifford went to a club dinner," snapped Mrs Wilson.

For a moment Hake seemed inclined to let his aunt's reply stand. Then he laughed and said in his most disarming manner, "I certainly intended to go, but at the last minute I felt I couldn't face it. These dinners are rather boring."

'Where did you go then, Mr Hake?"

"Back to my flat. I read for a while, had a drink and then went to bed."

"Can anyone vouch for that?"

"To be quite frank, no. Does it matter?"

"It may, Mr Hake." The detective addressed the three of them. "During your visit to the hospital last evening, I understand Mrs Porter became very upset. She was heard to say, 'I know you are only waiting for me to die so as to get my money. But don't be so sure. You may receive a nasty surprise'."

"My sister was always being vulgar about her wealth," Mrs Wilson said. "She often talked in that strain. But for Perce's persuasions, I would never have gone to see her."

"Then you did not know that Mrs Porter was seriously considering altering her will?"

"Most certainly not! Did you know, Cliff?"

"No," he answered slowly, "I didn't."

The detective got up and went to the door. A little man with a black satchel and an expression of distaste entered. I felt Mother Paul start a little.

"Mr Bone—Mrs Porter's solicitor," the detective introduced him.

"I thought he might be," Mother Paul murmured.

Mr Bone produced the new will that he had drawn up. "Not legal, you understand. Unsigned and unwitnessed. In the original will the main beneficiaries are Mrs Wilson and Mr Hake. Mrs Porter called me in for consultations extending over the last two days. She wished that her very considerable estate be spread instead over a number of charities. A small sum was to be divided between her first beneficiaries—that is Mrs Wilson and Mr Hake—and three other persons were to share in a similar amount. Mrs Porter wished to reward those who had been her faithful friends during her life."

Mrs Wilson stopped making noises of outraged indignation and gave a derisive snort. "She never kept one faithful friend, let alone three."

"The names of these three persons," Mr Bone went on severely, "are Mother Mary St Paul of the Cross—"

"Oh, dear!" Mother Paul said in an uncertain voice.

"Sister Estelle Bray and Sister Joan Brown."

"Oh, dear!" I repeated, stunned.

The detective's toughness seemed to soften. "Did you murder Mrs Porter so as not to inherit her money, Mother Paul?"

Mother Paul patted my hand. "Perhaps you'd better tell Sister Bray to come down, dear."

I fled upstairs and burst in on Stella counting a pulse. Her beautiful face lost its customary aloof calm when I told her what had been happening in the parlour. "I'm coming down with you," she declared.

The detective had become tough again, and was hammering Clifford Hake over his lack of alibi. He didn't look quite so handsome now, and his hands shook as he lighted a cigarette, playing for time before answering the detective's question whether he had ever used the balcony to enter his aunt's room.

"Cliff!" Stella said sharply, as we entered. He got up and went to her. "It's all right, Stella."

Mrs Wilson glanced from one to the other and said grudgingly, "You'll make a good looking couple. Why didn't you tell us before, Clifford?"

His laugh was shaky, too. "We didn't decide until just this moment."

"But, Cliff," Stella said insistently, "you said you were going to that dinner."

"Mr Hake," the detective began in an ominously official tone. He stopped as he caught Mother Paul's eye. "I'd like you all to wait outside for a few moments."

We trooped out in sombre file, and waited in the draughty hall under the chill impersonal eye of a police constable. My heart was thumping hard.

I knew that if Mother Paul was not satisfied with Clifford Hake's motive and lack of alibi, then she could be as dissatisfied with the Wilson's water-tight one.

After a long wait, we were called in. Mother Paul was standing at the window with her back to the room. I joined her and she gripped my arm hard. No, it wasn't so as to stop me from breaking away when the detective made his formal arrest. It was to give me support when Stella Bray started screaming and kicking, her loveliness now completely lost in the frenzy of her discovered guilt.

"Such a lovely looking girl!" Mother Paul said sadly, as, later that day, she sat at the low window opening onto the balcony. "They get so much from life and then expect more. Far better to be plain-pretty like you, dear. So often great beauty demands great material possessions. Stella Bray saw her chance with Clifford Hake, a beneficiary of an extremely wealthy woman. You know the way we patients tell you nurses everything. Probably Mrs Porter had let drop hints that there might be a little something in it for Stella. But Stella didn't want a little—she wanted a lot. Then there was Mr Bone. If I could guess from his appearance that he was a solicitor, so could she."

"But how did you know it was Stella?" I asked.

"There were several little odd matters; unimportant, but odd. The window was wide open so as to make it appear that someone entered from the balcony, but the dressing-gown, of which the cord was used to strangle Mrs Porter, was in the wardrobe. Now, if it had been hanging behind the door in view of the window, it would have been more reasonable. And then there was the sheet. Remember you told me, dear, it was right over the face. Who but a nurse would cover a dead face so instinctively."

"But I was sitting in the hall. She couldn't have entered Mrs Porter's room without my seeing her."

"And no one could have entered by the balcony," Mother Paul said, "because I was sitting at my window. That is why Mr Hake's not having an alibi did not seem as serious to me as it did to the detective. She was so cross with him not going to that dinner, wasn't she. The murder was committed after Mrs Porter's visitors left."

I goggled at her incredulously. "But I heard Stella speak to Mrs Porter."

"Quite, dear. But you didn't hear Mrs Porter speak to Stella. It was there she made her bad mistake. What were her words again?"

I answered slowly, "'Very well, Mrs Porter, I'll tell her.' Then she shut the door and told me she had given her a sedative and that Mrs Porter did not wish to be disturbed."

Mother Paul watched me closely. "Do you see the mistake now?"

I shook my head, feeling abominably dense.

"A basket of fruit, two books, a carafe and tumbler," she chanted softly.

"The medicine glass," I cried; "there was no medicine glass, and Stella wasn't carrying it, because she had her bell in one hand and she used the other to close the door."

"That's very good, dear. Stella was supposed to be off duty. If she stayed on, it must be with the appearance of giving you a hand—for example, soothing a restless patient with a sleeping draught. If she wasn't carrying out some nursing duty in Mrs Porter's room, what was she doing?"

I shuddered at the thought of what Stella was doing, and Mother Paul sighed without replying to her own question.

"Don't think me rude, dear," she said apologetically, "but I'll be glad when I can go back to my convent."

THE END

MORE BOOKS BY JUNE WRIGHT

MURDER IN THE TELEPHONE EXCHANGE

"A classic English-style mystery . . . packed with detail and menace."—*Kirkus Reviews*

June Wright made quite a splash in 1948 with her debut novel. It was the best-selling mystery in Australia that year, sales outstripping even those of the reigning queen of crime, Agatha Christie.

When an unpopular colleague at Melbourne Central is murdered – her head bashed in with a buttinsky, a piece of equipment used to listen in on phone calls – feisty young "hello girl" Maggie Byrnes resolves to turn sleuth. Some of her co-workers are acting strangely, and Maggie is convinced she has a better chance of figuring out the killer's identity than the stodgy police team assigned to the case, who seem to think she herself might have had something to do with it. But then one of her friends is murdered too, and it looks like Maggie is next in line.

Narrated with verve and wit, this is a mystery in the tradition of Dorothy L. Sayers, entertaining and suspenseful, and building to a gripping climax. It also offers an evocative account of Melbourne in the early postwar years, as young women flocked to the big city, leaving behind small-town family life for jobs, boarding houses and independence.

(336 pages, with an introduction by Derham Groves)

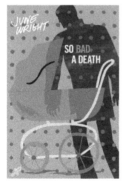

SO BAD A DEATH

When *Murder in the Telephone Exchange* was reissued in 2014, June Wright was hailed by the *Sydney Morning Herald* as "our very own Agatha Christie," and a new generation of readers fell in love with her inimitable blend of intrigue, wit, and psychological suspense – not to mention her winning sleuth, Maggie Byrnes.

Maggie makes a memorable return to the fray in *So Bad a Death*. She's married now, and living in a quiet Melbourne suburb. Yet violent death dogs her footsteps even in apparently tranquil Middleburn. It's no great surprise when a widely disliked local bigwig (who also happens to be her landlord) is shot dead, but Maggie suspects someone is also targeting the infant who is his heir. Her compulsion to investigate puts everyone she loves in danger. This reissue includes Lucy Sussex's fascinating 1996 interview with June Wright.

(288 pages, with an introduction by Lucy Sussex)

THE DEVIL'S CARESS

In her third published novel June Wright serves up a classic country-house mystery with a jagged emotional intensity that is reminiscent of Daphne du Maurier. Overworked young medic Marsh Mowbray has been invited to the weekend home of her revered mentor, Dr. Kate Waring, on the wild southern coast of the Mornington Peninsula outside Melbourne. Marsh is hoping to get some much-needed rest, but her stay turns out to be anything but relaxing. As storms rage outside, the house on the cliff's edge seethes with hatred and tension. Two suspicious deaths follow in quick succession, and there is no shortage of suspects. "Doubt is the devil's caress", one of the characters tells Marsh, as her resolute efforts to get to the bottom of the deaths force her to question everyone's motives, including those of Dr. Kate.

(224 pages, with an introduction by Wendy Lewis)

DUCK SEASON DEATH

June Wright wrote this lost gem in the mid-1950s, but consigned it to her bottom drawer after her publisher foolishly rejected it. Perhaps it was just a little ahead of its time, because while it delivers a bravura twist on the classic 'country house' murder mystery, it's also a sharp-eyed and sparkling send-up of the genre.

When someone takes advantage of a duck hunt to murder publisher Athol Sefton at a remote hunting inn, it soon turns out that almost everyone, guests and staff alike, had good reason to shoot him. Sefton's nephew Charles believes he can solve the crime by applying the traditional "rules of the game" he's absorbed over years as a reviewer of detective fiction. Much to his annoyance, however, the killer doesn't seem to be playing by those rules, and Charles finds that he is the one under suspicion. Duck Season Death is a both a devilishly clever whodunit and a delightful entertainment.

(192 pages, with an introduction by Derham Groves)